HEART
OF THE WOLF

Book Six in the Pantracia Chronicles

HEART
OF THE WOLF

Amanda Muratoff & Kayla Hansen

www.Pantracia.com

Cover design by Andrei Bat.

ISBN: 978-1-9995797-1-5

Third Edition: February 2024

Vivi

For the animals who changed our lives.

Penny

The Pantracia Chronicles:

Visit www.Pantracia.com for our pronunciation guide
and to discover more.

Chapter 1

Summer, 2610 R.T.

JARROD CAUGHT HIS HAWK ON his forearm while Damien and Rae approached in his peripheral vision. Dread filled his stomach.

Liala's leg bore no note, the metal cuff loose at her foot.

"What happened, girl?"

The hawk ruffled her umber wings.

Sun highlighted ominous red stains in her feathers, and Jarrod narrowed his eyes, touching the blood. "She's hurt."

Neco lifted his nose, sniffing the bird and whining his concern into Jarrod's head.

The thief flinched at the communication he still wasn't used to and stroked the wolf's head. *Be patient.*

"It's not Liala's." Damien stopped beside Jarrod and lifted

his hand to hover over the hawk's back. He flexed his fingers, and a pulse of light trickled from his palm, soaking into the dark smears.

Neco growled, feeding off Jarrod's anxiety.

If the blood isn't hers...

"It's Corin's." Damien's hazel eyes darkened, and his jaw tensed.

Jarrod sucked in a deep breath and shook his head. "I should never have left him. If I'd stayed—"

"You could be bleeding too." Rae put a hand on his arm. "Plus, we don't know the circumstances. Corin might be fine. Liala is trained to return to you, even if Corin has your whistle charm."

"She's right." Damien's tone wasn't convincing. "But Liala can tell me what happened." The muscles of his face slacked while he communicated with the animal. He'd explained the process of his soul temporarily merging with another multiple times but, even after linking Neco with his, Jarrod didn't fully understand.

Liala's feathers bristled, and she swung her head towards Damien.

Jarrod ground his jaw through the painfully long silence.

"She didn't see much. There's no way to tell exactly what happened since she doesn't understand it. An arrow almost struck her. That's the only thing she'll focus on." Damien took a step away, running a hand roughly through his hair. Touching Rae's arm, they traded a look.

Jarrod launched Liala back into the air with a flurry of her wings and glanced at his friends. "I need to send a letter to Sarth."

He jogged up the beach with Neco at his heels. He heard the sand shift as Damien and Rae hurried to follow.

The Rahn'ka caught up without apparent strain. "Because she proved to be so helpful last time."

Jarrod shot him a look. "Got a better idea?"

Rae threw something at Damien's back. "That wasn't her fault."

Damien rolled his eyes in a glower at Rae as he slowed his run. "I can still blame her."

They approached the pair of Art-grown homes at the edge of Maelei, gifted to them by the auer council for their stay on the island.

Jarrod flung his door open and found his pack. Rifling through it, he located parchment and graphite, quickly scrawling a message. The door opened again behind him as Rae entered.

"What are you thinking?" She scratched Neco's ears after he shoved through the doorway behind her.

"I'm thinking Corin's in trouble," Jarrod muttered, finishing the note. He addressed it to Sarth, requesting information about the capture of any high-ranking rebels by

Helgathian officials. "And I'm beyond useless stuck on an island."

Rae cringed when he looked at her, and he opened his mouth to rephrase. She held up a hand, dismissing his coming apology. "I understand. This isn't your fault though."

"Maybe, maybe not. But if I don't do something, whatever the result is, *will* be my fault. I need to get to Helgath." Jarrod folded the parchment.

"You can't go alone." Damien approached in the doorway behind Rae. He looked over her shoulder, his face grim. "I hope it's nothing, but I know my brother's ability to find trouble. You'll need backup."

"He's right." Rae nodded. "I'll be fine here until—"

Damien squeezed her shoulder. "No. The council will have to understand the circumstances and let you leave."

Rae shook her head. "Even if I arrange a meeting with the council, it won't be for days, plus travel. And I doubt they will put any importance on this."

"I'm not waiting to talk to them. I don't have time for their bullshit. Dame, if you want to stay with Rae, I won't blame you." Jarrod pulled his vest over his shoulders, wondering how difficult it would be to secure a ship to Helgath. Without more information, he needed to go to Mirage first.

It's not like I can just walk into Veralian demanding information. Not as who I am now.

Damien hesitated, looking at Rae and touching her cheek.

"What is it?" Rae covered his hand with hers. "You're thinking about something besides Corin."

Damien nodded, pursing his lips and leaning against the tree trunk forming the doorway. "If they arrested Corin..."

"That's a big *if*," Rae interjected.

"But *if* they have, there are other possible consequences..."

Jarrod lifted his gaze to Damien. "What are you talking about?"

"My parents." The Rahn'ka looked up. "The military doesn't hold the family responsible when one member turns traitor. But two..."

"You think they'll arrest your parents?" Rae straightened.

"I know they will. And it's not just an arrest I'm worried about. If they realize exactly how involved Corin is in the rebellion, they'll use whoever they can as leverage."

Jarrod clenched his jaw and motioned with his head to the side. "I need to send this. Then we should get a message to your folks."

Rae pulled Damien to the side to let Jarrod by, and he squinted in the sunlight. Searching the sky for his hawk, he whistled.

"You need to go." Rae lowered her voice, and the words barely reached Jarrod's ears. "I'm safe here, even if it isn't ideal."

"I don't want to leave you again. I swore I never would."

Liala landed on Jarrod's forearm, and he wrapped the message around the hawk's leg.

"Nothing will change between us. Not with time or distance. I know you want to stay, but if your family is in danger, you need to go. Don't stay here just because of some promise."

In Jarrod's peripheral vision, Damien leaned his forehead against Rae's. He kissed her, playing with the crystal dangling on a chain around her neck. "I'll be back as soon as I can. I love you."

"I love you too."

Jarrod secured the metal ring on Liala's leg. "Sarth. Go home." He sent the hawk back into the sky, and she screeched as she flew west.

Neco whined, pushing against the back of Jarrod's legs. His thoughts pressed against Jarrod's in a confused jumble and the thief closed his eyes.

His temples thrummed, and he stretched his neck. "Aye, Neco, you're coming. Calm down."

"Come on, Neco." Damien patted his thigh. "Give Jarrod a break. Hopefully, we can get a ship out today for the mainland."

"Durkinlanding is the closest port to Mirage."

"And you think we should go there first? Corin was in Lazuli last we knew."

"He could be anywhere. If we go to Mirage, we can prepare."

"All right." Putting a rough hand on Jarrod's shoulder, Damien gave him a hard, studying look. "Neco and I will go figure out a ship. A headache from a wolf constantly checking in on you is the last thing you need right now." He squeezed before walking west along the roadway, Neco trotting behind.

The wolf cast a worried glance back over his shoulder.

Jarrod nodded too late for the Rahn'ka to see, his gut hollow.

Rae touched his upper arm as she watched Damien go. "It might be Corin's blood, but that doesn't mean he's been arrested."

"Why do I feel like you're trying to convince yourself, too?"

Rae rolled her lips together. "I might be. I guess I'm just hoping. I haven't even met him yet."

Jarrod sighed and pulled her into a sideways hug. "I'm hoping, too. I think the two of you will really get along."

"He will be all right." She leaned on his arm. "I'm looking forward to having another brother."

Jarrod smirked. "Are you and Damien getting…"

"No. I meant through your relationship with him, not mine with Damien. Gods, how did we both choose Lanorets?"

"Because we clearly have the same taste."

Rae laughed. "I'll miss you. Again."

"Aye. But this time I won't worry about you, that'll be a change."

"You'll keep him safe, too, won't you?" Rae pulled far enough away to look at his face.

Jarrod looked at her softened eyes and furrowed his brow. "Of course. Though Damien's pretty good at handling himself."

"But this is Helgath." Rae's shoulders shuddered. "You'll have the better connections while everyone is trying to kill him for deserting." Her dark brows knitted. "What are you going to tell Sarth?"

"Damien will be fine. I'll tell Sarth only what I need to, and the guild knows he's off-limits."

"I'm not talking about that. I'm talking about getting the Hawks to help find Corin beyond basic information. If they *have* arrested him, you will need the resources, and Sarth won't lift a finger without someone stepping forward to lead the rebellion, you know that."

Jarrod nodded and sighed. "Aye. And I might have to tell her the truth. If I need to, I will."

"Now *that* I wish I could be there to see." She smirked.

Jarrod smiled. "Does this mean I'll finally outrank you?"

Rae laughed and slapped him in the stomach. "You'll never outrank me, even after you're on that throne of yours."

Chapter 2

RAE SQUEEZED DAMIEN TIGHTER. "AND I thought only seeing you a few times a week was cruel." His neck muffled her words. "I wish I knew when you'd be coming back." The thought of being without him, yet again, made her insides ache.

Kynis will be ecstatic.

"We'll send Din to you as soon as we reach Mirage and let you know what we find out." Damien kissed the side of her head, his lips lingering while he heaved in a deep breath. "I miss you already."

Her hands slid up his middle, and she deftly slid a folded piece of parchment into the inside pocket of his vest. "I miss you after we've spent the day together and I go home alone. This is entirely different. We need a new word." She looked up at him and kissed his chin. "Take care of yourself, all right? Be careful. And make sure Jarrod doesn't die again—"

"I've got it." Damien laughed, cutting her off. "Nothing crazy." He took her cheeks between his hands and lifted her mouth to his. With the exchange, a familiar warm sensation passed through her body. Damien had a habit of allowing his power, his ká, to swell just enough to tangle with hers even in the most innocent of moments, driving into a deep desire for more. But the act also left pieces of their souls knotted together long after they parted.

Rae closed her eyes to savor the feeling before meeting his gaze again. "Promise me I'll see you again."

"You will." He touched her chin as he smiled. "As long as you promise you'll remember me this time."

Rae grinned, holding back a retort. "Always. You'd better go before I completely lose all semblance of my former stoic self." Planting a hand on his chest, she applied minimal pressure.

He resisted the push long enough to give her another kiss. "See you soon, Dice," he whispered before taking a step back. He watched her through several backwards paces towards the gangplank, turning at the last instant to ascend the ramp.

Rae's eyes burned, and she swallowed. Fear of losing him swirled like a maelstrom in her chest.

Jarrod appeared next to Damien and lifted one hand to wave goodbye, the other scratching Neco's ruff.

Tears dampened her cheeks as she did the same. The two most important men in her life had become like brothers, and while they'd have each other's back, she wished she could go with them.

"Be safe, Lieutenant," she whispered as the gangplank parted from the dock.

Ropes creaked as the wind caught the sails, and the ship drifted away.

Rae remained, watching Damien as he leaned against the ship's banister.

The sand scraped across the dock behind her and she turned to see Maith approaching, his teal knee-length silk tunic catching in the ocean breeze. He stopped beside her and spoke in Auric. "I was wondering where you were. You're never late."

Rae nodded, looking back at Damien. She could barely make out his face, and he still leaned on the railing. "Just this once."

Maith looked out towards the boat, hesitating before he turned to Rae. Frowning, his angular features softened. "Did something happen?"

She sighed, stepping towards the end of the dock from where the ship had launched. "Jarrod's hawk returned. Bloodied. They're worried about Damien's brother and his family in Helgath."

Maith gave a grunt of understanding. "Rightfully so. Helgathians are barbarians." He placed a hand on Rae's shoulder, encouraging her to turn to him. "Is there anything I can do?"

Rae shook her head. "We have sent messages, including a warning to the Lanoret family. There's nothing more to do." She glanced at the ship again, no longer able to see Damien. Parts of his ká still warmed her heart.

"What of you, then? I find it hard to believe that it satisfies you merely staying here, uninvolved." He offered her a thin smile, a look of knowing in his deep-set purple eyes.

"I plan to speak to Kynis about that. I understand my term isn't over, but I'd like to meet with the council to discuss options. Circumstances are dire and sitting here, learning how to control the weather, feels beyond useless."

"The council will bend, unlike what Kynis wants you to believe."

Rae smiled half-heartedly. "Will you help me? Convince him, that is, to let me go?"

Maith heaved a sigh, taking her hand. "I'll see what I can do. Though I suspect some requirements will remain. I'll be going with you, should they let you leave the island early."

Rae nodded. "I assumed as much." Smirking, she pushed his shoulder. "It's too bad I can't stand you."

He laughed, following her as she made her way towards the beach and the compound. "This will be my first visit to the mainland."

Rae quirked her head. "Really? You've never left Eralas?"

He shrugged. "I've never had a reason to. Besides, I'm still young."

Laughing, Rae took his offered arm. "A youthful two-hundred. You're going to hate the mainland."

Chapter 3

WARM BLOOD TRICKLED DOWN CORIN'S chin, slowly drying and creating a persistent itch on his face. He swallowed, but his tongue stuck to the roof of his mouth and tasted like copper.

Something dripped in the distance, but it gave him no indication of which prison he currently occupied.

The facilities all smelled the same, drenched in musty blood and death. The soldiers who transferred him constantly changed, along with the method of transport. Days blended together beneath the blindfold during transport, leaving him oblivious to the sun's position in the sky.

Weeks must have passed. The only tell of time being the slow growth of his beard and the healing of each inflicted wound.

Grunting, he sat up and leaned against the cold stone wall. He hadn't envisioned his capture when he dreamt of the rebellion's progress. If he died, the rebellion would take a hit, but it could recover from that alone. When Jarrod learned of his death, he'd either damn the rebellion or take up the charge himself.

Jarrod. I'll get out of here, just to see your face again.

A male guard walked down the hallway of cells, baton at his side. He let it bang against each bar, creating a deafening reverberation.

Corin strained to cover his ears, his hands barely able to stretch the distance with the chain linking his wrists together. Sleep deprived, his head felt like someone had stuffed a hive of bees inside. He buried his head into his knees, but the incessant rapping of the baton intensified as the guard stopped at his cell.

"Rise and shine, traitor. We've got a special surprise for you today." The guard grinned beneath his salt and pepper beard.

"Oh goody," Corin grumbled.

The guard's keys jangled, and the process of moving to another room left Corin aching, especially with the rough jerks the guard provided to his shackles.

Corin landed hard on the wooden seat the guard shoved him into. Water dripped from several corners of the new room, stroking his nerves like a whetstone. He struggled as they secured his wrists and ankles to the chair. This time, they strapped his neck in place, learning their lesson after he'd broken the last interrogator's nose with his forehead.

"I hope you'll cooperate and answer my questions." A female soldier stood in front of him. She had shoulders like a man, and long black hair that matched her dark skin. "I understand no one has gotten you to speak so far, but that's all right. I enjoy a challenge."

"Lady, you don't know what a challenge is."

Might as well get comfortable. This will probably take awhile.

"Did Sergeant Rynalds know what a challenge was?"

The name spurred a twinge in Corin's chest that he fought to keep from his face. He hadn't expected to ever again hear the name of the officer he'd lured to an alley to be murdered. The bastard deserved it, but it'd still felt dishonorable.

"Who?"

The woman smiled. "That's all right. You don't need to use words to answer my questions each time. I know you're familiar with him. Were you the one who stabbed him?"

No, that was Jarrod.

"You know, I think we had a horse named Rynalds when I was a kid. He was a real pain in the ass, though. Liked biting the other horses and—"

Her steel-clad fist collided with the side of his jaw, his temple striking the back of the chair as the room spun.

Grimacing, he blinked away the white orbs in his vision.

"Being a smart ass won't get you anywhere." She inspected the armor at her knuckles.

"Actually, I've noticed it gets me a whole lot of places." Corin rolled a fresh pool of blood on his tongue.

She leaned over him, pulling his bottom lip down with her thumb to let the blood ooze out. "And how have these places fared for you? Are they getting better?"

"They each have their unique charm." Corin pulled his head away. "This one is particularly damp, which is good for the skin, you know."

A smile spread over her face. Squishing his blood between her finger and thumb, she wiped it on his cheek. "Do you prefer being able to see or hear?" She withdrew a needle-like blade from her waist.

Corin's heart thudded as he eyed it before he refused to give the threat any power over him. "Look, I know you're full of this sweet talk, but you're not really my type."

The woman walked around beside him and held the sharp point to his shoulder. She dragged the tip up his neck, towards his ear. "Who was the man you tricked authorities into arresting at the border crossing in Quar?" The needle tip touched his lobe before circling around the outer edge of his ear. "Do you really want my voice to be the last thing you ever hear?"

Gods, that'd be an awful reality.

Corin gritted his jaw, straining to keep his head as far from her as possible. "He looked a lot like a wanted criminal, honest mistake. Never saw him before."

The blade broke flesh in the concave spot in his ear. "I have a source who saw you with him later. Who is he?"

Corin hissed and clenched his teeth. "Sure they did. Bought the poor bastard a drink afterward as a way of apology."

"His *name*." She drew the device into the opening of his ear canal.

He squeezed his eyes shut. "I didn't ask."

To his surprise, the blade left his ear, and he exhaled a shaky breath.

"We'll see if your answers stay the same." Walking around to his other side, she leaned close to his ear. With a delicate touch, she turned his jaw to the neighboring cell.

Several guards blocked his view from the contents, but his stomach lurched.

"Here's some motivation for you."

The guards shuffled down the hall.

Tied to another chair sat a man in far better condition than a typical prisoner. He wore officer's regalia, the fine coat and vest of those high enough in rank to warrant comfortable postings where they commanded from a distance. Black paint marred the golden emblem on the left breast of his jacket, declaring him a traitor like Corin.

"Now, I know it's been awhile," the woman whispered in his ear. "So maybe you need a little help. You remember your brother Andros, don't you?"

Corin's gut lurched.

His brother glared at him from his cell, his green eyes like the fires of one of the deeper hells. Andros couldn't speak, a gag secured around his head, mussing the long locks of his blond hair that'd been in a neat ponytail at his neck. He didn't bother to struggle against his bonds, only stare.

Fuck.

Corin leaned his head back against the chair and stared up at the ceiling. "This is a waste of time. Andros knows nothing. He's not a part of this."

Andros grunted against his gag as if offering an agreement.

"Oh, but he is. Because he's *your* brother." Stepping around, the woman yanked the barred door of the cell open and flashed Corin a wicked grin. "And I don't need *him* to talk. Just you."

Corin grimaced, balling his fists because it was all he could do. "Andros and I hate each other. I don't know what you think you'll accomplish." It was a partial lie. He disapproved of Andros's blind loyalty, but he was still blood.

Entering Andros's cell, the woman kept her eyes locked on Corin. "How about we try a different topic?" She ran the thin blade over Andros's clean-shaven chin. He jerked his head away from her, but she gripped the hair on the top of his head, pulling it back. "Tell me about the Ashen Hawks. I know they're involved in your little uprising."

Corin's body tensed, his mind flooding him with a series of horrible realizations.

How does Helgath know about the Ashen Hawks being at all involved?

How do they know about Rynalds and to ask about Jarrod, even if they don't know his name?

Cruelly, his jumbled mind morphed what he saw before him. In the chair, in the other cell, he saw Jarrod, the torturer's tool piercing his flesh. Everything in him quaked, and he shut his eyes in a rush, trying to shake the images from his head.

When he opened his eyes again, the woman smiled at him over his brother's head. "Well, well." She hummed, drawing a tiny line of scarlet across Andros's cheek. "I think we finally found the right motivation. Shall we continue?"

Chapter 4

Autumn, 2610 R.T.

"GODS, BOY, WHY?" JARROD RAISED his arms to cover his face as Neco shook.

The wolf had leapt from the small boat early, eager to reach land, and soaked himself in seawater.

It took all the jewels that Damien had been hoarding to convince the captain of their transport to let them take a dinghy to shore before they reached Durkinlanding. Even with the capture of a high profile rebel, the searches of all ships would continue and they didn't have time for a complication.

Damien slogged through the shallow water, pushing the little lifeboat back into the tide, water gushing in through the hole he'd punctured in the bottom.

Neco grumbled, a low series of howls and barks that expressed his need to get his paws back on solid land. It continued into an explanation of why boats were the worst invention humans had ever made.

"A patrol is coming." Damien's senses buzzed. Letting his barriers down for the first time in months, he allowed the voices he used to loathe bring him some comfort.

None of them needed further encouragement to hustle across the rocky beach towards the brush on the rugged hillsides.

A rabbit fled the hiding place and Jarrod caught Neco by the scruff of his neck before the wolf's baser instincts led him into chase. The thief's eyes followed the furry creature as it bounded towards a bush, a glimmer in his dark irises.

After the patrol passed, they turned to ascend the craggy bank behind them, hoisting the wolf with them whenever his paws slipped.

Damien noticed Liala before she screeched to inform Jarrod of her approach.

They both heaved for breath when they reached the top, perspiration thick on their brows. Damien threw the packs he'd carried onto the ground and attempted to roll his sleeves up again. The ties on the wrists did little to keep the white material in place, and he'd already stripped off his leather vest and stuffed it into his bag.

Jarrod caught the hawk on his bracer and hurried to unwrap the note secured to her leg. Written in a code that looked different from the one Damien had seen Rae write,

Jarrod studied it after nudging Liala onto a nearby log. Only a few acacia trees dappled the rocky coast, providing shade for the wildlife.

Neco gave the hawk a dubious look.

"Don't even think about it," Damien scolded. "I know you're eager to hunt, but she'd rip your eyes out and you'd deserve it."

Neco whined, laying down and leaning against Damien's shins.

The Rahn'ka scratched behind the wolf's ears and looked up at Jarrod. "News?"

Jarrod growled. "Sarth isn't being very helpful. All she's said is that Helgath is bragging about a high-ranking rebel capture, but she doesn't know who or where they're being held, and she isn't keen to look into it further."

"Of course she won't... Our resources are limited without the Hawks, we'll need them. I could use the monoliths like I did to find Rae, but we can't rescue him by ourselves."

Jarrod retrieved his notebook and graphite. "Maybe I can convince Sarth in person to help."

Damien quirked a brow. "You know what that will take, right?"

Jarrod shook his head, writing. "It might not come to that."

"You telling her we're coming then?" Damien gestured towards the new note.

"No." Jarrod folded the note. "I'm sending Liala to Corin. If he isn't detained, then his reply can save us all a lot of time."

"What if he doesn't have your whistle charm anymore?" Damien looked at the hawk, who tilted her head.

Jarrod nodded. "I'll just have to hope he does." Wrapping the note around her leg, he lifted the bird from the log. "Corin. Go to Corin." Pushing her into the sky, he watched the hawk for a moment before turning back to Damien. "She will find the charm, even if he doesn't have it anymore. Might give us a starting point."

"I've always been curious about how the bond was formed. It sounds complicated."

"Not terribly." Jarrod shrugged. "Lucca makes it look simple. But she's always been a little batty."

"You mentioned that name before." Damien tried to remember when. It felt impossibly long ago, even though he'd known Jarrod for less than a year.

"Aye. She's Sarth's sister. A seer."

Neco gave a high-pitched whine, bored with the conversation and insisting again on chasing a rabbit.

"We should get moving. Maybe we'll get lucky and run into a herd of wild horses. Hope you're good with bareback."

Jarrod laughed. "I think I'd be all right. Might be easier just to stop at a town, though, and let me go *purchase* a couple."

"Always the practical one." Damien grinned, shouldering his pack again. "Though I know what both you and Rae think of *purchasing* anything."

"We're both quite good at it?" Jarrod motioned with his chin. "Don't lose your vest."

Damien looked down to see the leather hanging precariously out the side of his bag. He plucked it up, and something crinkled in the inside pocket. His heart leapt into his throat as he recognized the familiar confusion of finding something he hadn't put there.

Rae.

He reached into the pocket, silently cursing himself for not noticing it earlier. It'd been a week since they parted in Eralas and all that time he'd missed the obvious placement. She always played the games with him.

Taking out the note, he studied the exterior, turning it over. The pieces of Rae's ká that'd mingled with his had faded, but the piece of parchment resonated with a comforting sense of her presence.

"She got you again, huh?" Jarrod chuckled before he turned to walk towards Durkinlanding, Neco loping behind.

Damien didn't answer, unfolding the last note he'd receive for a long time.

Lieutenant,

An ocean in between, but never apart.

If something happens to you, I'm stuck with Maith. Keep that in mind if you get the inclination to do something stupid.

Love you, Dice

She'd drawn a sketch of a six-sided die in the corner, showing the numbers four, six, and two.

He smiled and lifted the paper to his lips, kissing where she'd signed. "Love you too."

Jarrod acquired two horses in town and found Damien on the outskirts far faster than the Rahn'ka expected.

Neco had vanished, finally able to hunt.

"Dare I ask?" Damien tied his pack to the saddle.

The thief shrugged. "Their owners were beating an elderly lady in the streets."

"Don't patronize me." Damien sighed, pulling himself onto the horse. "Already a traitor, I might as well be a horse thief, too."

"You say it like it's a bad thing. Besides, didn't you steal a horse with Rae in Jacoby?"

"In my defense, I had no idea at the time."

As Jarrod set off towards Mirage, he looked at Damien with a sobered expression. "This is too familiar."

"What is?"

"You and me. Off to find someone we care about imprisoned in Helgath."

Damien pursed his lips. The similarity was uncanny, only reversed. Rae was as good as a sister to Jarrod, and now they pursued the man the thief loved.

"At least this time around I don't feel like killing you the entire way?"

Jarrod smirked. "An ironic feeling after bringing me back from the dead. But, aye, I'm grateful for the change of heart."

"As am I, brother."

Mirage rested at the bottom of the valley of sand dunes, shimmering like its namesake. Long strips of fabric hung from the skeleton walls, designed to defend against sandstorms. They danced in the blistering winds blasting from the center of the Gilgas Desert. Despite the summer months ending, the sun's scorching heat required Damien and Jarrod to cover their heads and arms to protect from burns.

With the horses left on a post near the city well, Damien and Jarrod made their way through the narrow sandstone streets with Neco padding beside them.

As he had before, Damien accentuated the features Helgath wouldn't recognize. Abandoning his sweat-soaked shirt, he wore only his vest, leaving the tattoos of the Rahn'ka exposed. They ran in swirls and lines, covering his left arm to his wrist.

They continued onto his back and chest, peeking just beyond his collar onto his neck. He'd hidden them from the auer, determined to keep the secret of his power.

They approached a door different from the one they'd visited before, an unlit torch propped on the wall next to the door.

Jarrod rapped on the door, and the miniature, hinged peep-hole swung open a moment later.

"Can you bring in the torch?" A woman's voice carried through the opening.

Jarrod sighed. "Aye, but the night would snuff it out."

The door jerked open and the redheaded women stepped aside.

Damien glanced at the thief, following him into the compact room. "So when do I get to learn all the secret passwords?"

The woman closed the door behind them, eyeing Damien and Neco.

Jarrod looked at him sideways as he pulled a wall sconce to push open a section of brick. "After they have initiated you as a Hawk. Which will never happen."

Damien pouted while Jarrod stepped into the black maze beyond. "We have to do this again?"

Jarrod laughed. "Aye. But this time I'm following the rules."

Damien didn't bother attempting to access his power to see through the black. The memory of the ear-splitting sound the wards caused when an Art user attempted to access the latent world energies served as plenty of discouragement. It was pointless, anyway, and he clapped a hand on Jarrod's shoulder to follow him.

When they reached the end of the maze, Jarrod spoke. "Lykan, reporting home."

A torch next to the door lit and Braka lifted an eyebrow at them. The big man, built like a bear, lumbered towards Damien. "You again." He looked at Jarrod. "You're missing two this time, where's the others?"

Jarrod shook Braka's hand before walking past him. "Sika is safe in Eralas. And we're trying to find the other."

"The lippy one." Another thief chimed in from behind Braka. He looked familiar, and Damien felt fairly certain he'd been one of the thieves trying to restrain Corin.

"Nyphis." Jarrod led Damien inside. "Always a pleasure."

"It's Scellik now. I knew his big mouth would get him in trouble."

Damien's jaw tightened, and he looked at Jarrod.

"Sarth gave you the snake namesake with the promotion? I'm not surprised. And no one said he's in trouble." Jarrod frowned.

"Course not, not with his hero coming to his rescue, the honorable Lykan—"

Jarrod whirled around without warning, landing a punch squarely to the man's jaw.

Nyphis's head jerked back, and he stumbled before landing on his backside. He groaned, a hand on his face. "You hit like a girl."

Jarrod lunged for him, but Damien grabbed his friend's upper arm. It took more strength than he expected to stop the thief from leaping atop the other.

Neco bounded forward, teeth gnashing as he dodged low past Damien to go for Nyphis's throat.

"Neco!" Damien risked the piercing wail of the wards to add his power into the command. "Down!" The word went with a wave of his ká surging forward, forcefully gripping Neco's.

The wolf whined, his body hauled back by the tangle of Damien's Art. He snapped at the invisible tethers, turning to Damien with fire glowing in his amber eyes.

Damien stumbled to catch his balance behind Jarrod, seizing his other arm, and pulled him back. "Calm him down, Jarrod, before I have to do something else to stop him."

Jarrod ignored Damien, the muscles under the Rahn'ka's hold flexing.

Nyphis scrambled to his feet, eyes wide on the wolf. Metal glimmered as his hand shot to his boot. His gaze lingered on the growling beast before meeting Jarrod's. "I dare you. Tell your lover to let you go and we'll see what happens."

"Better back down, Nyphis... Scellik... whatever. Or I'll help them kill you." Damien cringed, forced to push more of his ká into Neco's bonds to be heard over whatever Jarrod was sending him.

"I'd listen to him, if I were you, Scellik." Braka crossed his arms.

Nyphis turned his head and spat out a mouthful of blood.

"Let me go," Jarrod muttered under his breath.

"Can't do that until you call Neco off." Damien squeezed him harder.

"That's enough!"

Everything froze, responding to the command from the leader of the Hawks with unwavering loyalty. Even Neco calmed.

Jarrod straightened, yanking his arm free from Damien's grip as he turned to face his superior.

Sarth stood clad in black leathers that fit her lithe body, tightly muscled despite the age apparent in her face. Grey streaked her auburn hair, gathered in a single braid and over her shoulder. She eyed Nyphis with her angry fern-colored eyes, knuckles white as she gripped her cane. "What was that about hitting like a girl? I really don't think you need any further demonstrations on how that's a compliment. Considering I heard what Eyenka did to you last week."

Nyphis cleared his throat. "Apologies, boss."

"You are dismissed." Sarth clenched her teeth, and the thief slunk away.

"We'll catch up later." Braka lowered his voice to Jarrod, patting him roughly on the back before departing.

The guild's leader approached Jarrod, eyeing Damien and Neco. "You've been gone for months without a word. Where have you been? Where is Sika?"

"Sika is in Eralas. She's safe, and she needs to remain there for some time, but she'll be back." Jarrod rubbed his upper arm where Damien had held him.

Sarth's mouth twitched in a genuine smile. "That's good to hear."

"I couldn't send word, as Liala was preoccupied, but we need to find Damien's brother. Have you learned anything new?"

Sarth shook her head. "I've sent hawks to Lazuli and Veralian, just this morning. They may have more information when they return, but Helgath is staying quiet about who it is they've captured. So it may take awhile."

Jarrod clenched his jaw, but nodded.

Damien glanced at him. "They'll announce it soon. They just wait until they can get all the leverage in place before making an arrest public."

Sarth looked at Damien again. "Lieutenant Lanoret. How good to see you again." Her dry tone suggested otherwise. "Do you plan to stay?"

"We don't really have any leads other than what your hawks might bring back."

"I'd hoped to get an answer from that brother of yours about who will lead this rebellion he's fighting so hard for." Sarth raised an eyebrow. "But if they've arrested him, the whole thing is destined to crumble. I made the right decision to stay out of it."

"This is a lot bigger than just a Lanoret and I think you know that." Damien straightened as he faced Sarth. "I don't get why you're hesitant to support something that you've been fighting for the entire time as the Ashen Hawks. Though, your methods of theft and assassination leave something to be desired."

Jarrod elbowed him in the ribs.

Sarth stared at him, her expression unreadable. "We'll talk later. I have questions for you, too, Lieutenant."

Damien's gut sank, a swirl of distant anxiety mounting. The affectionate nickname from Rae somehow sounded sinister from Sarth.

"In the meantime, get some rest. And a bath. The two of you look rather harrowed from your travels and you smell. You may use Sika's quarters, seeing as they are rather close to yours, Lykan. May I trust there will be no further bloodshed between you and Scellik?"

Jarrod took a deep breath and nodded. "Aye. I can't believe you promoted him and with a namesake, too."

"He's an idiot, but he listens to orders. I'll make sure he understands I will not tolerate his commentary. He's not immune to a demotion." She gave a small smile. "Perhaps I'll send Eyenka to encourage him to remember his manners."

Damien snorted. "He didn't hurt my feelings, any."

Jarrod rolled his eyes at Damien. "I'm quite happy with my choice of Lanoret, even if it means everyone knows. Feels silly to have hidden it, now."

Sarth shrugged with a knowing smile. "Being open about your preferences isn't the worst thing. No one tries to set me up with men anymore. Plus, the only reason I'm invested in discovering the truth about Captain Lanoret is because I know he is important to you."

Lifting his gaze, the thief sighed. "I appreciate your efforts. I'll be waiting for word. In the interim, assign me to a job if you need to."

"I have plenty of Hawks to call on. Take the break. This might be your last opportunity for a while." Sarth narrowed her eyes at Damien before turning around and walking away. "I meant what I said about those baths."

Chapter 5

JARROD SLAMMED HIS BARE FISTS into the sand-filled leather bag, one after the other, until his knuckles bled. Claws ticked against the wooden floor behind him, but he didn't turn around. Sweat beaded on his brow, but his breathing remained even.

"Neco told me one hawk returned?" Concern laced Damien's tone.

"Aye." Jarrod huffed between punches. "From Lazuli. Corin isn't being held there." He'd lost hope of his safety, since Liala had returned a few days prior. The note he'd written Corin still wrapped around her leg, she'd carried the whistle on Jarrod's gold necklace, both caked with mud.

Damien let out a long sigh, stepping behind the punching bag and supporting it to add extra tension beneath Jarrod's punches. "Anything from Veralian?"

"Not yet." Jarrod threw all his weight behind a right hook, causing Damien to rock back. He dropped his fists, inspecting his hands. Damien had already healed them on several occasions, but it required them to leave the guild to maintain his secrecy. Exercise proved the only thing capable of distracting the thief.

Neco pushed his nose into Jarrod's hand, licking it clean.

Damien looked down, taking his own half-hearted swing at the bag, letting it rock back and forth on the chain anchoring it to the ceiling. "We'll find him."

"Joining me?" Jarrod motioned to the training room. Countless pieces of equipment lay waiting, ready for another round of their abuse. Obstacles and climbing equipment decorated the walls.

Damien laughed and shrugged. "I was headed for the pools when Neco came charging down the hall and nearly barreled me over. But I could kick your ass first."

Jarrod smirked. "You haven't beaten me in days. Eager for a reminder of how that feels?"

"I've been going easy on you." Damien walked to the side of the room where a weapon rack sat. "Besides, that's been only grappling. I think it's time to bring in the weapons." He picked out a long shaft of wood and thunked it on the ground. He spun it, checking the weight and reach without looking at his opponent. Nodding, he stepped towards a small dirt arena lined with cobblestone.

Jarrod quirked an eyebrow, glancing at Neco as the wolf settled down to watch. Approaching the weapon selection, he chose two wooden short swords. "We don't have more practice knives. Haven't replaced them yet after we broke them last week."

"Is that you trying to get sympathy so I'll go easy on you? There aren't any practice Rahn'ka powers, either."

Jarrod rolled his eyes and approached the arena. "I don't need your sympathy, Lanoret, but I am a little honored that you compare my knife skills to your Art."

Damien shrugged, turning the action into a roll of his shoulders. He'd stripped his shirt, fully displaying the impressive pattern of dark blue tattoos on his left side. "I've seen how you use them. Might as well be the Art. Maybe Jalescé was wrong and you do have access."

Jarrod recalled the strange reptilian spirit that had taken a particular interest in him while they'd visited the Rahn'ka guardian's sanctum and smiled. "You done talking yet?" He spun the swords near his hips and spread his feet.

Damien grinned. "Not if you're going to—"

Jarrod lunged, striking low with his dominant hand.

Damien's quarterstaff interrupted the blow, catching the sword inches from his thigh.

The Rahn'ka countered, and they fell into a rhythm.

Jarrod's heart pounded in his ears, but his focus sharpened. He struck hard in succession, but neither of them landed any substantial blows. Stress leached from his veins, replaced by adrenaline rushing into his previously spent muscles.

By the time they stepped away from each other, both panted for breath.

"You still use a staff better than any of the Hawks."

"Will that gain me enough points to join up?" Damien grinned. He spun the staff in a series of whirls beside him.

Jarrod laughed. "Not even close, no matter how much you show off."

"Can't help it if I make it look easy."

Replacing his swords on the rack, Jarrod lifted the bottom of his shirt to wipe his brow. "You need to do more than spin a stick to join."

"Just imagine it's a spear glowing with the energy of ancient dead people." Damien walked towards the same weapon rack. "Makes it a little more impressive."

As Jarrod turned away, Damien jerked and the bottom of the staff knocked Jarrod's feet from underneath him. He stumbled, catching the staff. Chuckling, Damien let go of it and Jarrod landed on his back.

Growling, the thief whipped the quarterstaff at Damien's ankles, sending him sprawling with a grunt when he hit the ground.

Neco suddenly joined in the fray, leaping on top of Damien and causing another gasp for breath.

Standing, Jarrod smiled. "You ever notice how he listens to me better than you?"

Damien shoved Neco's chest, forcing the wolf off. He rolled before Neco could get back on top of him, pushing himself up. "Oh, I've noticed. Among other things."

"Other things?" Jarrod looked down at his dirty shirt with a scowl. He pulled it off, draping it over his shoulder.

Damien shook his head. "Doesn't matter. You want to go to the pools now, too? I think we both could use a good clean."

Nodding, Jarrod called Neco with a thought and the wolf loped towards him. "I could use a swim. But Neco wants to roam."

"Everyone seems used to him, should be all right. If he gets into any trouble, we'll hear about it pretty fast."

Jarrod patted the wolf's side and encouraged him off. Leading the way, he descended the levels of the guild's headquarters to the lowest one.

Natural rivers, heated by the channels of furnaces carved beneath, flooded the natural caverns. An inch of water covered the area, with deeper places dug out of the stone to create pools. Some were deep enough to dive into, others divided by constructed sandstone walls. Humidity thickened the air. Hooks adorned the near wall for clothing and weapon storage.

Damien stepped ahead of Jarrod, heading to a pool separate from the others. It had a half-wall surrounding it, giving it a modicum of privacy from the rest, but still open. Some members of the guild already occupied the other areas, indulging in what the hot springs offered, but the pool he and Damien preferred remained empty. Tossing his shirt over the low wall, Damien unfastened his breeches as he stepped out of his boots.

Jarrod followed suit, the gently bubbling water encouraging him not to delay. Naked, they both slipped into the pool, sinking to their necks before even speaking a word.

"I'm getting too used to this." Damien sighed, leaning his head against the stone wall behind him.

Jarrod rubbed the dried blood from his knuckles before dipping his head backwards into the water. "Are you actually considering starting the process to join the guild?"

"The perks are tempting. I see why the Ashen Hawks have never had a recruitment problem. Nothing but cold bucket showers in the military." He peeked with one eye to look at Jarrod. "Is there a policy for access for spouses of members? Because if so, I've got to decide which is easier. Joining or talking Rae into marrying me."

"Joining." Jarrod laughed. "Though I don't see an end to your visitation rights, so perhaps continuing to be a freeloader is your best bet."

"Freeloading it is." Damien paused as his smile faded. "What does Rae have against marriage, anyway? She won't talk to me about it."

"Have you ever *tried* to talk to her about it?"

"Well, sure... Kind of."

"Rae didn't exactly have the best role models to represent marriage. She wants to be her own person, not the wife of some man. I don't know if her views will ever change."

"But it's not like that. I don't want her to just be *Damien's wife*. I want to be Rae's *husband*. She's better than me and deserves to be mentioned first."

Jarrod smiled. "Give it time. If anyone can change her mind, it's you. But you won't succeed by pushing it on her."

"I know. But it's hard because I keep catching myself thinking about it." Damien laughed, running his hands through his hair. "Gods, I never thought I'd say that about a woman. I was convinced I'd die a virgin."

Jarrod coughed, clearing his throat. "A what? Was Rae your first?"

Damien's cheeks flushed. "What?"

"How has this not come up before?"

"Why is it important? It's private."

"It's *private*." Jarrod scoffed. "Not when I can hear you two next door, it's not." He bellowed out a laugh. "But it's cute."

"Don't say it's cute." Damien groaned. "We both know that's not true."

Jarrod smirked. "I've never seen a better match, and that *is* true."

Damien quieted for a moment. "Gods, I miss her." He glanced up at Jarrod with an unspoken apology in his eyes. "I know you miss him too."

Jarrod swallowed and averted his gaze to the steaming surface of the water. "I just hope the feeling is temporary." His imagination took him back to his last night with Corin at the inn before he'd left for Eralas. The way the captain had stepped up behind him and wrapped his arms around Jarrod's waist. The feel of his skin against his back.

I've never felt more at home in Lazuli, and I'm from there.

Uneven steps splashed on the wet stone floor, drawing his gaze upward.

Sarth walked to the edge of their pool, fully clothed and leaning heavier on her black cane. "Hate to interrupt, boys, but the second hawk has returned."

Jarrod rose onto a knee, his chest out of the water. "And?"

Sarth eyed Damien before focusing on the thief. "Your captain is being held in Veralian under substantial guard."

Jarrod closed his eyes, steadying his breathing as his throat tightened.

He's alive.

"Have they set the date for execution?" Damien kept himself submerged to his shoulders.

Sarth paused. "Six weeks."

Jarrod's stomach plummeted, and he sank back into the water. They could reach Veralian in less than that, but execution dates could change. Accidents could happen during interrogations, especially when the prisoner would die, anyway.

"It also seems that they've arrested another Lanoret, who is being held with the captain. But no one is talking about him. They only care about the captain, who is a hot topic in the streets because of his role in the rebellion."

"Probably Andros. He was stationed in Veralian and the easiest to get to. Nothing about my parents, though?"

"No."

"We need to leave for Veralian immediately." Jarrod pulled himself out of the water and crossed to retrieve his clothing while watching Sarth. "Will you let me take a crew?"

"Depends." Sarth turned back to Damien, who hadn't budged from the pool. "We need to have that chat, Lieutenant."

"Now?"

"Now. Let's go, soldier."

Damien's cheeks pinked, and he turned towards the wall where he'd draped his clothes. "I'm right behind you."

"He's a little shy," Jarrod whispered to Sarth.

The guild leader laughed and rolled her eyes. "I've seen plenty of naked men. You're nothing special, Lieutenant. And besides, you're not my type." She turned, humoring Damien by facing Jarrod while the thief used a towel to dry off before pulling his clothes on.

Damien moved quickly through the pool, pulling himself out and tugging on his clothing despite still dripping. He picked his boots up and carried them in his hand, shirt still untucked.

"Are you decent?" Sarth raised the pitch of her voice while smirking at Jarrod.

Damien grumbled something under his breath as he fiddled with the hem of his shirt. "Good enough. Ready when you are."

"Let's go, then." When Jarrod stepped to follow, Sarth held out a hand. "Sorry, Lykan, not this time."

Jarrod glanced at Damien, but nodded. After they disappeared up the narrow stairs rising from the pools, he followed, continuing to his dorm instead.

The entire time he waited for Damien to return, his nerves frayed. He busied himself with a trip to the falconry, checking on Din. He'd delayed in sending Rae her hawk, waiting for news of Corin. Now that he had it, he took the hawk back to his quarters.

When Damien finally returned, it was getting dark outside. He rapped once before opening the door for himself, as had become their custom. Neco came in with him, inviting himself onto Jarrod's bed.

Damien locked the door behind him and leaned on it, knocking the back of his head against it in a series of slow beats.

"Well?"

"She didn't like my answers." Damien shrugged. "But I didn't much like her questions, either."

"You gotta give me more than that."

"She's demanding that I declare myself the leader of the rebellion. Or she won't offer any help. Corin's the only thing holding it together, in her eyes, and she's not willing to bet on us making it in time. She wants assurances that the rebellion will continue without him if she invests anyone into his rescue, in case it fails."

"We can't save him without backup."

Damien's head thunked on the door again before stepping toward Jarrod. "You've got to talk to her. Maybe she'll keep it quiet for a bit longer and it doesn't have to be public, but she needs to know you will lead it."

"Damn it." Jarrod yanked his vest from where it draped over the back of a chair. He gripped the door handle and jerked, forgetting the lock. The wood splintered as he tore the door open. As he pulled his vest on mid-stride, Damien's footsteps echoed behind him.

Jarrod kept a fast pace as he made his way to the common rooms, figuring Sarth would join the crew for dinner.

The mess hall boasted high ceilings and extravagant chandeliers, aromas of food overtaking the air. Rows of banquet tables filled with most of the Hawks, ten chairs per table. At full capacity, the hall could seat five hundred members.

Jarrod's stomach growled, but he crossed the grand room towards the head table.

Sarth sat between two other Hawks, one Jarrod recognized as her brother. Silas, although a Hawk, didn't appear in places of authority often, his actual role within the guild secret even from high-ranking members. They whispered to each other while enjoying plates of venison, potatoes, and bread.

The chatter of diners reverberated through the room.

Her gaze lifted as Jarrod approached, and she shook her head. "Not right now. I'm eating. I know you're unhappy with my choice, but—"

"I need to talk to you."

"Nothing you can say will change my decision. I can't take these kinds of risks for a failed coup."

Jarrod ground his teeth as Damien and Neco trotted up on either side of him, a pace behind. "It hasn't failed, and it won't. Let me speak to you in private."

Sarth darted an annoyed glare at Damien, but refocused on Jarrod. Placing her napkin on the table beside her plate, her mouth tightened into a line. "Don't test my patience. My word is final. If the lieutenant does not wish to—"

"He doesn't need to. But I need to—"

Sarth slammed her fist onto the table, the surrounding plates clattering and wine sloshing from the rims of the cups. "Enough!"

The dining hall around them fell deathly quiet.

"Lykan, I've already accommodated and humored you well beyond what I should. Walk away."

Neco growled, a deep rumbling sound echoing through the quiet hall. The Hawks rarely saw subordinate behavior, and the tension thickened.

"Sarth," Jarrod whispered, his tone low. "I—"

"Get out—"

"I'll lead them!"

Sarth stood slowly. "Don't insult my—"

"I am a Martox." He swallowed back a rise of bile as eyes around him widened. Whispers murmured through the hall. "As a proxiet, I will assume command of the rebellion."

Sarth gaped at him, her brother squeezing her bicep. She pulled away and lowered her voice. "With me. Alone. Now." Turning, she limped away from the table towards a single door along the back wall.

Damien caught Jarrod's shoulder before he could walk away, turning him. *Be smart.* His voice rang in the thief's head. *Be sure. Everyone knows now.*

Little late, Dame. He nodded once before following Sarth.

When the door shut behind him and, even with a cane, Sarth reeled around faster than he expected. "How dare you blindside me. What were you thinking?"

Jarrod opened his mouth to answer, but she continued before he could.

"If you think I'll step down from my role here—"

"What? No. I have no intention of questioning your leadership here, regardless of the future, but I couldn't tell you before. It's complicated."

"Complicated," Sarth spat. "That's a bullshit excuse and you know it."

"Please." Jarrod took a step forward. "Will you let me take a crew to Veralian?"

Sarth pursed her lips, pausing. She leaned heavily on the cane at her side as she sighed. "I already have a crew in Veralian. Twelve Hawks. You can have them for this rescue mission. But Jarrod..."

"Aye, Sarth?"

"Swear to me you're committed beyond this one endeavor."

Jarrod swallowed, her green eyes boring into him. "I can't give you an exact timeline, but I *am* committed."

"Well, let's make it while I'm still alive, shall we?" Sarth shook her head. "Just to be clear, this doesn't mean the Ashen Hawks are joining the rebellion. Not yet. But I'd rather you not get yourself killed trying to save your captain. Would defeat the entire purpose of your confession."

Jarrod nodded. "I'll stay alive."

"You better. We're in real trouble if Damien ends up leading the rebels." Sarth rubbed her brow as she sat back into an overstuffed chair and stretched out her leg. "Nymaera's breath. If I'd have known who you were all those years ago..."

"You'd thank your lucky stars I wanted to become a Hawk?"

Sarth laughed. "I don't know, kid, but we'd be in a different place right now. I need time to think about this. Go get your man. We'll talk when you return. I want to see the smug look on that captain's face when you bring him back here, since I'm assuming he knows?"

Jarrod offered a sheepish smile. "Would it make you feel better if I told you he figured it out on his own?"

Sarth snorted. "After knowing you for how long?" When Jarrod didn't answer, she nodded. "That's what I thought. No, it doesn't make me feel better. You've been living under my roof for almost a decade. I should know these things."

"I *am* sorry about that."

Sarth sighed. "Make it mean something."

"I'll do my best. Will the crew be at the safe house?"

"I'll send orders for them to meet you there."

When Jarrod walked back into the mess hall, followed by Sarth, the noisy room quieted again as eyes turned to him. He rolled his shoulders as Neco trotted over. Stroking the wolf's head, he met Damien's gaze and nodded once. Walking between the tables seemed like a poor idea, so he motioned with his head for Damien to follow him back out the way Sarth had led him.

With a wary glance at Sarth, who took her seat at the head table once more, Damien walked to join Jarrod. He took his time, forcing Jarrod to endure the stares for longer than he wished.

As soon as the door shut behind Damien, voices erupted in the mess hall and Jarrod cringed. He scratched the back of his head, sighing.

"Well, that went smoothly." Damien raised an eyebrow.

Jarrod groaned. "I'll say. We're leaving tonight, so let's go get our shit together." He turned, walking down the hallway towards the dorms. "Sarth could've been a lot harder on me, all things considered."

"So what happened? With the look on her face, I half expected to need to bring you back from the dead again."

Jarrod huffed. "Me too, but she agreed to give us reinforcements. There are twelve Hawks in Veralian we can use."

Damien snorted. "Much better than I expected. She will help this time?"

"Aye. If you can find your way back to our rooms, I'll arrange for some horses."

"We've been here long enough, I've got this place figured out. Sarth should make me an honorary Ashen Hawk at the very least. Hey, you've probably got the pull to make that happen now, right?"

Jarrod rolled his eyes. "One thing at a time, all right? We'll talk about making you a pigeon later." He turned to leave and then paused. "Din is in my room. I've written a message to Rae, but I haven't sent him yet. Thought you might want to add your own with him, too."

A pensive tension passed into Damien's face, easing his smile. "I do, thank you. I'll take care of Din and meet you in the stables."

Chapter 6

Two weeks later...

RAE GASPED, SHAKING. HER BODY ached with the lingering nightmares and Maith's embrace tightened.

"You're safe," he whispered, stroking her forehead.

Damp strands of hair stuck to her skin, and she inhaled another unsteady breath.

The ship rocked, reminding her where she was.

On my way to Helgath.

She should have guessed that traveling back to the country of her torture would make her sleep even worse.

Maith laid next to her, and she turned, burying her face in his silk tunic, his arms encircling her in a comforting presence.

They remained like that until Rae could slow her breathing.

"More of the same?" He pulled away to look at her face before sitting up.

Rae nodded, swallowing as she pushed herself up to lean against the wall. Her instinct was always to apologize for waking him, for burdening him with the job of calming her down, but he'd told her enough times that he didn't mind.

"Do you want to go back to sleep?" Maith leaned against the wall next to her.

She shook her head. "Not tonight."

"Talk?"

Rae nodded. "I need some air. Maybe a walk, too?"

Maith gave a small nod and slipped off the bed to his feet.

Following, Rae stood and straightened her dress. Not bothering with her boots, she tugged their door open and led the way to the upper deck of the auer passenger ship.

As soon as the salty breeze brushed her face, whipping her loose hair back, she could breathe deeper. The star-riddled sky banished the horrors of her dreams, bringing her solace.

Her ever-present shadow, Maith approached silently behind her. The moonlight made his hair look silver, accented by his dark skin. "You must realize he'll notice."

Rae sighed. "I know. I was hoping they would subside before he had the chance to."

Maith frowned, watching Helgath on the horizon. "Something tells me that won't happen anytime soon. He'll understand, Raeynna."

Rae looked at her feet. "I'm not worried about whether he'll understand. I know he will. But he already feels guilty for giving me my memories back, and I don't want to make him feel worse."

"You still haven't explained how Damien accomplished that, either. To which I am immensely curious."

Rae gave him a tight smile, running her hands over her face. "You know I can't... He will already hate that you've been filling a role that should've been his."

"Ah. And yet, he fills a role I once pursued for myself. Our lives are not straight lines, you know that. Damien will understand that there is nothing more than friendship between us."

Rae laughed. "Will he? What if he doesn't believe me?"

"Then he doesn't love you."

Taking a deep breath, Rae considered the statement. "I don't think it's that simple. But I hope you're right. I hope he trusts me."

"If I may, I'd like to point out that you're hoping he trusts you, when you haven't yet trusted him with the truth of your nightmares."

Rae clenched her jaw. "You make a valid point."

They grew quiet and Maith turned to the dark horizon. The glow of sleepy fishing villages peppered the Helgathian coast, making it look far more innocent than it felt.

Rae had kept Damien in the dark about her nightmares from the beginning. They'd started immediately after he returned her memories. At first, she thought they would go away, and he'd never have to know. As they worsened, Maith learned how to calm her during the episodes, since he'd heard her screaming one night. Eventually, he started sleeping in her home with her.

If only I could somehow prove it was only sleeping to Damien.

She looked up at the sky and clutched the crystal pendant around her neck.

Damien loves me. He'll understand. He always has.

A low whistle sounded from one of the auer, vibrating through the cool night air. The small crew responded, lifting the sails. With nothing to catch the wind, the ship rolled over the waves, an anchor splashing into the sea.

Rae turned, studying the fishing village they'd make port at.

"Do you know where they live?" Maith nudged her shoulder. "I suspect we won't be able to disembark until morning."

Nodding, Rae looked at him. "It's an equestrian ranch just northwest of here. Should be a few days' ride."

Maith's lips tightened into a thin line.

"What?"

"Is it possible we'll be too late?"

Rae cringed. "I hope not. Damien said they'd come for his family. It's possible they won't even be there if they received the message he sent two months ago."

Din had provided Rae all the information she needed to push a meeting on the council and convince them to let her leave. Maith's accompaniment had been expected and not entirely unwanted. Her hawk circled above them, silent as the wind.

"You should put the cuff on me." Rae eyed the horizon. "Helgath can't know I'm here."

Maith frowned. "I still think blocking your access to the Art is a monumental overreaction. You really believe they would recognize your presence in this remote area?"

Rae swallowed, her throat tightening. "It's as much for me as for them. Please. I don't feel confident with my hiding aura yet, and I need the peace of mind if I want any hope of sleeping." Her hands shook, and she balled them into fists.

Instead of answering, Maith took her hands and encouraged her fingers to uncurl. "I understand." He slipped his hand into the little side pocket on his tunic, fishing out the piece of copper. "You won't be able to unlock it by yourself."

"I know. I understand. Just put it on." Rae turned to let him inspect the cartilage of her right ear. The long cut that'd been made the first time Helgath had put it on her still marked its old position, but a layer of skin had healed within. Unlike her hoops, which were small round piercings, this was a half-inch long metal blade inserted through her ear. The tiny 'keyhole' existed at the hinged back, a gear of sorts, only released by the mechanism Maith also held for her.

Maith's fingertips tickled near her temple, brushing her hair away as he positioned the tip of the sharp edge against the scarred flesh. "I'll need to pierce it again." When she nodded subtly, he ceased his hesitation and pushed the metal through.

Rae sucked in a breath and squeezed her eyes closed. She could handle the pain, but for an instant it brought her back to a darker place. The dirty stone walls of her cell closed in around her, the locks of her door grinding into place before she forced her eyes to open.

The gear clicked, the cuff's lock taking hold. The sound radiated through her entire body like an alarm bell, covering her power with an unmovable blanket. The void of nothing, the missing energies of her power, took more out of her than she expected. It hit her harder than last time, leaving the air in her lungs thin.

Holding out her palm, she looked at Maith as he placed the key there. "Thank you. I'll go get dressed so we can leave at first light."

"Are you sure you don't want to try sleeping some more?"

Rae paused, wondering when her next opportunity would be to rest. "Maybe a little. But only until dawn."

Chapter 7

Two weeks later...

THE GUARD'S BATON RANG AGAINST the bars of Corin's cell and he flinched as he always did. Groaning, he struggled to cover his ears, hands bruised and bloody. He gave up when he remembered they'd tightened his chains and his palms couldn't reach anymore without him standing. And that felt far too difficult.

"Today's the day. Time to meet Nymaera. If the rope's too short you'll end up strangling to death, but if it's too long... your head'll just..." The guard made a popping sound with his mouth, following it up with wicked laughter.

Corin thought of a million retorts, but nothing could vanquish the image of his brother's death days before. They'd unchained him that day, allowing him to watch through the narrow barred window of his cell that looked on the gallows.

They'd tied the rope too short, and Andros struggled for air as his feet flailed beneath him. The crowd had cheered, throwing rotten fruit at him until he hung limp.

No one saved him. No one came. He died and Corin wept.

The guards had thought the death would provoke Corin to speak, but it did the opposite. He hadn't said a word since it happened and to reward him, they'd moved up his execution date. Instead of two more weeks, he'd face Nymaera today.

In a strange way, it felt peaceful to know the torture would stop. Tired of the constant thirst and ache, he craved the slumber of death. He consoled himself to believe the rebellion would survive. That his death would be the catalyst to make it all possible. He'd be a martyr which perhaps was what it needed.

Yet, despite it all, he imagined Jarrod every time he closed his eyes. He saw him crouched at his cell door, picking the lock. He saw him in the crowds of the courtyard, shouting with the other people. He saw him hanging from the gibbet beside his brother.

A shudder ran down Corin's spine and his vision flashed as a baton struck the side of his head. He collapsed, hitting the ground. The chains attached to his cuffs clattered around him, no longer secured to the wall. Hauled to his feet, he struggled to keep standing as they shoved him from the prison. He glanced back at his cell, catching a view of the clear blue sky and the filling courtyard surrounding the gallows.

Sunlight blinded him, people chanting. He squinted, tripping on a stone, only to be jerked back to his feet. His hair hung around his face, sticking to his temples.

The air smelled fresh and, for the first time in months, he could breathe. Despite the taint of blood and dirt clinging to his skin and clothing, he sought to enjoy his last breaths. Looking at the end of the courtyard to the prison structure, he finally realized where he was.

Veralian.

He recognized the jagged black spires that served as the backdrop to all the executions held in Helgath's capital.

Six stairs took Corin to the top of the platform where the soldier guided him under the waiting noose, yanking his wrists behind him and securing them tighter with his chains.

Another pulled the rope wider before slipping it over Corin's head, cinching it around his neck. "Don't want no mistakes, now, do we?"

The only thing Corin could think about was how itchy the thing felt against his skin. He glanced behind him, making eye contact with the red-clad executioner who stood next to the lever that would end his life. The man stared, unfazed, his grey eyes like something already dead.

The prison warden sniffed as he leisurely made his way up the steps onto the platform, flipping through a fat book. He licked his thumb, using it to find the appropriate page before he thumped it onto the pedestal at the edge of the deck.

He glanced at Corin, a sinister smile on his lips. "Comfortable?" He spoke in a whisper, the crowd quieting to hear the list of his crimes.

"Just get on with it," Corin grumbled, turning to look at those who came for entertainment. He wouldn't give any of them the pleasure of a show.

"Corin Lanoret." The warden silenced the crowd. "You stand before your country and have been found guilty of murder, theft, and treason. Your sentence is death, to be carried out on this day. Do you have any last words?"

"I regret nothing."

The crowd erupted in shouts, mixed with cheers and anger. People calling for his death.

Corin's heart thundered in his ears. He watched the crowd as the warden slammed his book shut. While many cheered, some only watched. Their faces worn and tired, almost sympathetic. A raging hollowness filled Corin's chest. The pressure of the rope on his throat made his attempt to swallow difficult. He sucked in a breath, focusing on the blue sky behind the distant mountains.

A shout rocked Corin from the serenity he attempted, another following it. He looked towards the noise, a tussle of men, some in military uniform, trying to restrain members of the crowd.

The altercation escalated as a punch landed on a soldier's jaw and the warden stepped back in surprise, emitting a growl.

The guards beside Corin looked at each other in confusion as the crowd surged dangerously close to the rim of the gallows, shouting and standing on tip-toe to get a better look at the commotion.

"Hang him!" The warden slammed a fist onto his podium, staring at the executioner.

A loud grunt echoed, but it wasn't one of agreement. Corin dared a glance, and the executioner tumbled off the backside of the gallows.

What in Nymaera's dark name...

Hope rocketed through him. Corin could just make out the blood-red shape of the executioner as someone in a black hood pinned him to the ground.

Another tall figure, clad in black leathers, jumped onto the platform. He held no weapon, his face hidden in the depths of shadow under his hood.

Recognizing the square of the man's shoulders, Corin's heart leapt into his throat.

The guards on the ground scuffled forward, attempting to grab the man by the ankles, but he hopped to the side, stepping between the warden and the lever that would signal Corin's death. As he turned, his hood slipped off his head and Corin met Jarrod's gaze.

Corin's entire body wanted to sag in relief, but the noose kept his spine painfully straight.

The guard behind him shifted, lunging towards the lever and Jarrod.

In the flurry, Corin pushed his foot behind him and caught the guard's ankle. The man let out a surprised yelp as he fell to the ground. Before he could scramble forward, Neco plowed up the stairs and tackled him off the platform.

A guard stepped up behind Jarrod, grabbing his arm. The thief yanked it free and slammed his elbow back into the guard's face, pushing him off the platform with his boot.

The warden watched the ordeal with wide eyes, pointing his book at Jarrod. "You're a dead man." He took a step back as he spoke. The warden fished a chain from his neck, lifting a whistle to his lips.

Jarrod lunged, smacking the whistle out from between the warden's lips before he could blow. "In the name of House Martox, I command a stay of execution!"

It felt as if someone had pulled the lever and left Corin's stomach up above him. The lingering pain and the shock left his mind unprepared for what he heard. His eyes widened at Jarrod. "Jarrod, what—"

Before he could finish, the warden stepped up to Jarrod, tilting his head back to confront the taller man. "Who the hells do you think you are?" He jammed his finger at Jarrod's chest. "You must think I'm a complete idiot if you're going to cla—"

"Jarrod Martox. Son of Reznik and Sairin Martox. Under the authority of my House, I declare the Lanoret family under my protection. Any act of hostility against them will be considered a declaration of war against the Dannet families."

The warden gaped, mouth bobbing open like a fish.

Corin wished he had more energy to properly enjoy it. But he was still too distracted trying to comprehend what Jarrod was doing.

Dannet protection.

Damien pulled himself onto the platform from where the executioner had been secured. He pushed the black hood back, having trimmed his beard and hair short enough to look like his wanted posters again. His appearance somehow confirmed what Corin heard Jarrod say was real. Damien did not need to hide anymore.

Neco bounded up the stairs, making the warden jump as he took his position at Jarrod's side.

"You think you can halt proceedings with a wave of your hand and a beast at your side?" The warden turned towards Damien, his eyes widening. "And *that* traitor."

"I think he already did." Damien spoke quiet enough that only Corin heard. He loosened the noose and swooped it off of Corin's neck. Corin staggered back, but Damien caught him by the shoulder. "I gotcha."

Corin wanted to ask how they'd found him and why Jarrod was sacrificing so much, but he couldn't find the words. Instead, he focused on holding in the sobs that wanted to escape.

Guards still standing drew weapons, aimed at Damien and Jarrod. Reinforcements arrived despite the lack of whistle and scurried from the prison gates. They rushed into position around the walls of the courtyard.

The warden scowled. "You can't do this. This man is a traitor to our country, and we must deliver justice."

Corin eyed the guards outnumbering them, his pulse racing. Regardless of Jarrod's actual claim as a proxiet, the guards of the prison could kill them all and pretend it never happened. Proclaim profuse apologies to House Martox and say they had no idea that it was a legitimate claim. The Martox proxiet supposedly died long ago, after all.

"I think we have very different definitions of justice." Jarrod's jaw flexed.

Neco growled, and the warden took another step back. "Call your beast off or I'll order you all shot. You have no true authority here. This is my prison and we will execute this traitor as ordered by King Iedrus."

Movement shuffled within the crowds, drawing Corin's gaze. At least a dozen people appeared from the shadows, and the townsfolk shirked away as they raised weapons. Bows, swords, even a scimitar.

Corin's mind tried to keep up with the implications.

How did he get Hawks here?

Still supporting Corin with one arm, Damien withdrew a short sword to point it directly at the warden's back.

Jarrod glanced at the crowd, then at Corin, before looking at the warden. "My friends disagree. I have acted well within my rights as proxiet of House Martox, Warden. Continue to refuse my demands and you will become the traitor here."

"Nymaera's breath." The warden took a moment to look over the crowd. His grip tightened on the spine of his book as he looked at Corin and Damien, then back to Jarrod. "You openly defy our king?"

"My actions are not meant to defy, merely to seek real justice. I do not deny this man's actions against King Iedrus, but *my* investigation is ongoing. Until it's finished, no one will touch Corin Lanoret or his family." He enunciated each word pointedly, teeth clenched, and Neco snarled.

The warden stared at Jarrod. "This isn't over. I maintain my right of imprisonment under the orders of House Iedrus. Return the traitor to his cell." He gestured to his guards, who hesitated before they took a wary step forward. "With my word that he won't be harmed until we have observed all the formalities."

Jarrod turned and met Corin's gaze. Concern shone in the thief's dark eyes, his authority hiding the pain.

Corin leaned heavily against Damien but tried to find his footing. After all he'd suffered, he wanted to break down, fall to his knees and weep into Jarrod's lap while the thief comforted him. But he swallowed the suffering.

Just a little longer. He has a plan. He always does.

Corin supported himself after a deep breath and gave Jarrod a curt nod.

The proxiet lifted a hand and touched the scar on his chin, threatening all semblance of control Corin had established.

The twist of the chains behind his back brought him back as guards seized his bound wrists, wrenching him from his brother.

Damien took a step back, lowering his sword and lifting his unarmed palm up.

The warden stepped up into Jarrod's face as the guards pulled Corin towards the steps. "Don't think I don't have half a mind to throw all of you in a cell. You're playing a dangerous game here, boy. The Dannet families have no business with rebels."

"And wardens are disposable," Jarrod hissed. "Question my authority again, and it'll be you facing the noose next time."

Chapter 8

GODS, I HOPE HE HAS A PLAN.

Damien watched the guards lead Corin past Jarrod. His brother looked half dead, with an array of bruises and cuts on his body. He hardly recognized him beneath it all. Seeing Corin weak, leaning on him for support, made bile rise in Damien's throat.

The warden slapped a hand to Jarrod's chest as the guards led Corin away. "You may have staved off one execution, for now, but you're too late for the others." His taunt came in a low, breathy tone. When he removed his hand, he left a piece of parchment behind that floated towards the ground as he walked away.

Jarrod narrowed his gaze, stooping to pick it up. Unfolding it, he closed his eyes, head bowing.

Neco whimpered.

"What is it?" Damien stepped forward. He kept the sword loose in his hand, his senses aware enough to notice the executioner recovering from the ground behind the gallows.

Jarrod lifted a hand to his forehead, offering Damien the paper. "I'm sorry."

Afraid to open the familiar parchment, Damien glowered at the fine auer paper that he'd made fun of to make Rae laugh. He didn't need to read beyond the first word scrawled in his own handwriting.

"Shit." He sighed, heart dropping. "They must have intercepted the owl we sent from Eralas."

"We'll get Corin out tonight. And then go straight there. Maybe we can reach them in time."

"Tonight? But I thought—"

"Tonight," Jarrod growled. "He's not sitting in there another minute longer than necessary. You know Helgath will kill him before they bother scheduling another execution for him."

Damien swallowed. No matter how fast they freed Corin, the chances of them arriving in time to help his parents didn't exist.

They're already dead.

He looked out to the crowd dispersing at the insistence of the prison guards. The Hawks had all vanished.

"Well, everyone definitely knows now." Damien eyed the warden, stopped at the entrance of the prison, leaning close to talk with some guards and gesturing in their direction.

"Right now, that feels like the least of my worries. We need to rendezvous with the crew. Neco will have to go somewhere safe until after."

Neco whined, lowering his head.

After detouring to the northeast edge of the city to encourage Neco into the wilds, Jarrod led Damien to a bakery. They crossed into the alley beside it, entering the business through a service door.

As they passed the owner, she nodded once to Jarrod. "Flour is in the back."

Jarrod lifted a hand. "Eggs too, I hope."

As they descended the stairs, Damien quirked an eyebrow. "Is everything you say code?"

Jarrod laughed dryly, pushing a crate out of the way. "No, just conversation since she had customers." He flipped a rug aside and pulled open a hatch door, dropping inside.

Damien followed, still in awe of the tunnels spider-webbed beneath the city. The mystery of how the Ashen Hawks operated within the city limits plagued the local peace officers and military outposts. They were the best kept secret in Veralian, aided by the businesses that benefited from the Ashen Hawks' protection.

Stepping into the damp darkness, Damien allowed his senses to manipulate his field of vision. The voices proved a welcome distraction from the images of his brother. He didn't need to see, because Jarrod led the way, but he couldn't help his curiosity.

The damp stone belonged to ancient ruins, confirmed by the ká within them. They'd been forgotten for millennia, buried beneath the progress of human construction. Decorative carvings etched into the walls had faded over the years, but dim shapes of vines and flowers lingered beneath a film of lichen.

I wonder if the Ashen Hawks even realized the history down here when they claimed and hid these tunnels from Iedrus.

Damien hadn't started the rebellion, neither had Corin. Whether or not they realized it, the Ashen Hawks had. They'd stirred the pot of dissatisfaction with Helgath long before anyone else. They prepared the way for the perfect catalyst Damien unintentionally provided.

They rounded a corner to an area lit by oil sconces on the walls. The entire crew waited in a circular 'room', with a low brick ceiling and several tunnels leading off of it. The stone floor donned the image of a sun, with rays branching off each path.

"He shouldn't be here." A short woman in front stepped forward with her twin sister. They wore the same clothing, black leathers fitted to thin, curveless bodies. Straight muddy-brown hair framed their beady eyes.

"We can trust him." Jarrod walked past the twins to the rest of the group, leaving the Rahn'ka facing them alone.

Damien met the eyes of the one who'd spoken, remembering the vague warning Jarrod had given him on the way to Veralian about the twins being unpredictable. "You must be Meeka. Or is it Keema?"

"I'm Meeka." The other twin nodded.

"I thought I was Meeka today?"

They stared at each other for a moment.

"Fine, you can be Meeka. But tomorrow, we switch."

Seriously?

Damien pursed his lips instead of saying it aloud.

Meeka caught his wrist as he tried to walk past them, pulling him close. "I can see why Sika kept you alive. Maybe she'll share."

The other twin leaned towards Damien's ear. "Sisters share well and she's our sister, too."

His tongue tasted like acid as he confronted Keema, glowering. "I'll pass. Sika would agree that some spoils are best kept private."

The twins pouted in unison, Keema lifting a finger to trace the runes of the Rahn'ka visible on his neck.

Damien caught her hand by the wrist, squeezing it tight before he threw it away. The whisper of their ká in his open senses enabled him to snatch Meeka's hand as it crept towards his pocket. Twisting her wrist, he spun towards her, forcing her low to the ground. He ducked before Keema's arm could encircle his throat and stepped while yanking Meeka's arm behind her back. Drawing the blade secured against his forearm, he brought it up beneath Keema's chin and she froze, muddy eyes glaring.

"I said... I'll pass."

Meeka stuck her bottom lip out. "This one isn't very fun."

Her sister tilted her head around Damien's blade, her tongue snaking out to touch the steel. "I think he'd look better with a little less life—"

"Enough." Jarrod grabbed Keema by the collar and heaved her away from Damien. "I need you focused. Both of you. Cut it out or I'll cut you."

Damien threw Meeka to the ground, straightening and stepping over her while he stored his blade again. He walked to the edge of the room and leaned against the wall.

The twins exchanged a look and sighed. "Apologies, boss," they said in unison and rejoined the others without even looking at Damien again.

The rest of the Hawks fell silent as Jarrod gave them directions, each with their own job to accomplish. No one asked questions.

"Make this as bloodless as possible. More importantly, it needs to be silent. We can't risk witnesses."

"It's true then... Who you are."

Jarrod's shoulders relaxed. "Aye. Is that a problem?"

"No." The man's feet shifted.

"What is it, Ren?" Jarrod tilted his head.

Ren glanced at Damien. "Are we rebels, now?"

Jarrod smirked. "Haven't we always been?"

Smiling, Ren nodded. "I suppose."

"The guild hasn't joined the rebellion. Not officially. For now, we get this done."

The Hawks dispersed, disappearing into the blackened tunnels, snuffing the sconces. Shadows descended, and the proxiet approached him. The faint blue outline of his ká in the darkness vibrated in an agitated state.

"Ready, Dame?"

"As I'll ever be." Damien shrugged. "You weren't lying about the twins, though."

"Aye, but they were just trying to get a rise out of you."

"Almost worked." Damien eyed the tunnel the twins had vanished down. "I never saw Rae as the best with sharing."

Jarrod chuckled. "Pretty sure she'd skin any woman alive if they touched you."

"And that's why I'm a lucky man. Shall we?"

Nodding, the thief took off through the passageways until he reached a dead end and drew his hood over his head.

Damien caught Jarrod's shoulder. "You sure you don't want to sit this one out? If you're seen, Helgath will know you ordered the jailbreak."

"No one will see me." Jarrod pulled down a trap door from the ceiling.

Dim light flooded the tunnel.

"But if they do." Damien refused to let go of him. "It'll be the beginning of a war."

"They won't." Jarrod shrugged off Damien's hand. "I'm not leaving this in anyone else's hands, Dame. Not even yours."

"We both know I could handle this. Is it worth the risk? I'll have Corin back here before you know it."

Jarrod grabbed Damien by the upper arms. "Would you stay back if it were Rae? Would any risk not be worth it? I don't care if I start a war. I'm not waiting here."

Shutting his eyes briefly, Damien didn't need to think about his answer. He closed a hand on Jarrod's bicep. "All right."

Chapter 9

JARROD'S PULSE BEAT FURIOUSLY IN his ears as they maneuvered through the prison corridors. Occasionally, they'd approach a room and find guards already down inside. His crew moved efficiently, using concoctions to knock their enemies out.

As he descended to another section of cells, Damien at his heels, Jarrod slowed.

Torches provided enough light to see by, but most of the prisoners lay curled in corners or with their head between their knees. Luckily, Damien narrowed the search to this section, but kept his use of the Art minimal to avoid detection by prison wards.

Seeing Corin with the noose around his neck had rocked Jarrod. The thought of being only minutes later haunted him and his hands had shaken while he confronted the warden. It took every ounce of his self control not to run and embrace the captain, carry him off the gallows with the promise he'd never face them again.

The twins stepped around a corner, one dragging a guard by the foot to pile him on top of another already down. One sister met Jarrod's eyes and gave him a quick nod. She held up two fingers, then pointed them down the hall past Jarrod.

Jarrod nodded, crouching as he hurried around a corner. Putting a hand on Damien's chest, he encouraged the Rahn'ka to stay still in the shadows.

One twin picked up a fallen guard's helmet and tossed it down the hall they'd just walked through. It clanked against the floor, breaking the heavy silence.

Boots clambered from the opposite direction and two soldiers raced right past Jarrod and Damien. "Halt!" One rounded the corner, seeing the fleeing form of a twin. The other twin appeared out of the shadows, shoving the lead guard before kicking his feet from under him. The guards toppled on top of each other, cursing, and the twin snatched something from one of their belts, tossing it to Jarrod.

Jarrod caught the keys with his palm, suffocating the jangling noise with his glove.

Scrambling to their feet, the guards drew their swords and took chase after the fleeing twins.

Jarrod waited until they were out of sight. Still crouched, he crept from the shadows. He darted down the newly clear hallway, finding all the cells empty until he approached the last one.

Corin sat on the ground, his wrists chained to the wall above him. In the shadows of the cell, Jarrod couldn't make out more than the shape of his body and the ragged strands of his hair falling over his face. The captain lifted his head, eyes darting between Jarrod and Damien as he wobbled to his feet, using the wall for support.

Jarrod's hand shook as he inserted the key into the lock, twisting it until the mechanism clicked. He swung the door open, rising to his full height.

"Jarrod?" Corin's weak voice cracked.

"I'll watch the hall." Damien jogged down the corridor.

Jarrod yanked his hood down, crossing the cell to Corin.

The soldier's body relaxed, slouching against the wall, and Jarrod grabbed the cuffs binding his wrists. Unlocking them with another key on the ring, they swung to the captain's side, clattering.

Dropping the keys, Jarrod pulled Corin's shaking body into a tight embrace. He supported Corin as the captain's knees gave out, slowly lowering them both to the ground.

"I thought you were Helgathian assassins coming to kill me." Corin buried his face into Jarrod's neck. A sob escaped him, vibrating against his skin.

Jarrod squeezed his eyes shut as they burned. "You're safe." Tears ran down his cheeks. "Gods, I'm so sorry. I tried to find you sooner, but no one knew where you were."

Corin shook his head, pulling away enough to meet Jarrod's eyes. He lifted a battered hand to the thief's cheek, covering the cold wet of his tears. "This wasn't your fault. But you did cut it a little close, didn't you?" He smiled faintly.

Jarrod swallowed and forced a smile. "Better than being too late. I almost lost it, seeing you up there yesterday."

"I'm fairly certain you did." Corin leaned his head on Jarrod's shoulder. "I thought I was losing my mind when I heard it. But you told them all who you are."

Jarrod nodded, unable to let go of the man he loved. "And I'd do it again."

Corin quieted, his grip around Jarrod tightening. His hot tears touched Jarrod's neck, body shaking with another gentle sob.

"We need to get out of here." Damien's voice came from behind.

Jarrod inhaled an unsteady breath and loosened his hold enough to look at Corin. "Can you walk?" He helped him rise to his feet once more.

Corin struggled, but stubbornly attempted to support his own weight. He looked over at his brother and the two Lanorets stared at each other for a moment before Corin took a step forward and embraced Damien.

The Rahn'ka closed his eyes as his brother whispered to him.

"Andros."

"I know." Damien patted his brother's back. "Not your fault. But we can talk about it when we've got you out of here."

Jarrod ran his hands over his face, stealing his resolve. He entered the corridor and one twin appeared at the entrance with a wicked smile.

"All clear, boss."

Her sister appeared next to her, shirt coated in blood. "Had a minor complication, boss."

Jarrod frowned. "Just one?"

They both nodded.

"Clear the way to the exit." Jarrod pulled his hood back up. "Time for everyone to disappear."

The twins nodded in unison again. "Yes, boss." They turned, disappearing, but Jarrod could hear unconscious guards being dragged.

Damien shifted beneath Corin to drape the captain's arm around his shoulder. Corin batted at him, but Damien gave it right back. "It'll be faster, you dolt. Just let me help you."

Jarrod led the way out of the prison, back to the hatch within the sewers they'd entered from. He dropped into the tunnel first, then helped Corin, with Damien dropping in after and pulling the hatch shut.

Jarrod gripped Corin's hand, squeezing it, before Damien resumed helping support his brother as they made their way towards the passage marked with the sun.

Most of the Hawks were already there, whispering amongst themselves.

"Account." Jarrod eyed those around him.

Meeka lifted her chin. "All but Theisos. He got dumb."

"Where is he?"

"Wanted to check the coffers, boss."

Jarrod heaved a sigh. "I'll go get him."

Corin caught Jarrod's wrist before he could step away, surprising strength in his hand.

"My crew," Jarrod whispered. "My responsibility."

"I'll get him." Damien straightened.

"No." Jarrod looked at the Rahn'ka. Footsteps echoed behind them and he turned, Corin's hand dropping from his wrist.

Theisos approached, holding up two bulging pouches. "Fine dining tonight, my fellow feathered friends."

Jarrod glowered. "Follow the directions next time."

Theisos dipped his head. "Apologies, boss." He offered a pouch. "Peace offering?"

Jarrod smirked at Theisos and shoved the sack of coins away. "Good work tonight. Break off, resume posts. I'm sure Sarth sent instruction."

As the Ashen Hawks departed, Ren stepped aside to Damien and offered a piece of rolled up parchment with a grim expression. "My condolences."

Eyeing it, Damien took it with a weary nod of thanks and unrolled it. He skimmed the document, then folded it to stash it in his pocket.

Ren jogged to catch up to his fellow Hawks, and Jarrod approached Corin. He laced an arm under the captain's, helping him off the wall. "Bit of a walk from here. Let me know if you need a break."

Corin cast a baleful look at Damien, who just shook his head.

"Not until we're out of the city. I can't risk using the Art for something that would take that much energy."

Corin grumbled, but leaned on Jarrod. "What's the use of having a brother who can heal if he won't do it?"

Jarrod kissed Corin's forehead. "I don't know, but I won't complain about being close to you."

"Not exactly the type of close I want... But I suppose I shouldn't be too picky, all things considered."

Jarrod supported Corin as they followed the longest tunnel out from under the city. It took an excruciatingly long time to reach the final dead end with a wooden wall. Lifting his foot while still holding the captain, Jarrod kicked the wall, and it fell open outwards. Moonlight trickled in through a cave entrance twenty feet away.

As they stepped through, fresh air filled Jarrod's lungs. "How's freedom feel?" He glanced back as Damien shut the secret door behind them and it blended into the rock wall of the cave.

"Would feel a whole lot better if *someone*..." Corin glared at his brother's back. "Would get on with it and heal me."

Jarrod chuckled, carrying him a little further before helping him rest on a boulder at the mouth of the cave. He looked towards the dark shapes of the pine trees blocking out the stars on the horizon. "Neco's on his way, but I interrupted his chase."

"He'll get over it." Damien smirked.

Corin's eyes narrowed. Turning to his brother, he lifted a hand and pathetically waved it at him. "How's this work?"

"Gods, I forgot just how annoying you are." Damien sighed, kneeling next to him. He snatched Corin's hand out of the air, putting it down against his knee. "This will hurt."

Jarrod stepped back, taking in the sight of Corin with more clarity. The bruises, the cuts. The gauntness of his face from malnutrition. His ragged clothes hung on his broad frame, diminished of the muscle it'd had before. Anger rose in Jarrod's chest and his jaw worked. His hands balled into tight fists and he turned away.

Corin gasped as Damien's healing began.

Jarrod ran his hands over his hair, his pulse drowning out the rest of his senses. It thumped like a drum hammering within his head. He closed his eyes. As hard as he tried, he couldn't refocus for what felt like an eternity.

A distant hum of someone saying something he didn't understand came before a hand clapped down on his shoulder. He spun around, ready to swing, but stared into Corin's eyes.

"You all right?" Corin's voice sounded stronger, and he held his body straighter, despite still being covered in blood and dirt.

Jarrod swallowed. "Aye, I'm fine. Are you... Is Damien finished already?"

Neco panted from his spot near the boulder, tongue lolling to the side.

The thief furrowed his brow. "When did Neco get here?"

Corin narrowed his eyes. "You sure you're all right? I could have sworn I saw you scratch his head when he checked in with you right as he arrived. Admittedly, I was a little distracted by all the pain." He shot an irritated glance at his brother, who shrugged as he stood from his crouch.

The Rahn'ka looked at Jarrod, his brow knitted in a way similar to his brother.

Sucking in a deep breath, Jarrod nodded, waving off their concern. "Haven't exactly slept much."

"Now, that, I can understand." Corin squeezed his shoulder. "I feel like I could sleep for a week. But I think I need a change of clothes and a bath first."

"I have some clothes that'll fit you." Damien motioned towards the trees. "We'll just have to go get the horses we hid in the woods."

"Do we need to hurry?" Jarrod rubbed his jaw.

"What for?" Corin tilted his head. "Lanorets are protected by House Martox now. We can take some time to breathe."

Jarrod met Damien's eyes, trying to read the hardness in them, then cringed.

"Andros isn't the only one House Iedrus held accountable for our actions." Damien dropped his gaze. "They went after Ma and Da."

Corin's eyes widened, his face paling. "Why the hells did you waste time coming after me then? Fuck a bath, let's go."

Damien didn't move, watching as Corin walked away. "We're already too late." Keeping his voice low, he pulled the folded parchment from his pocket. He offered it to Corin. "Troops were sent out two weeks ago with a kill order."

Taking the paper, Corin's hands shook. He hurriedly unfolded it and lifted it into the moonlight to read. His knuckles tightened with each sweep of his eyes, the parchment wrinkling in his grip. Body tense, he crumpled the paper and threw it at the ground. He paced away, hobbling when his bare foot caught on a rock. "Where are the horses? We should still hurry. Might not be too late."

"Corin..." Jarrod kept his voice calm. "The chances—"

"There's still a chance. I planned for a problem back when Damien deserted a year ago. I built a bunker beneath the old barn for this kind of situation. They both knew this could happen."

Damien gaped. "They knew?"

"Helgath would burn every barn down to find them, even if they hid in time." Jarrod shook his head. "But I hope you're right. The horses aren't far from here."

Corin gestured for Jarrod to take the lead and they hurried into the woods.

They rode through the night, the Helgathian hillsides flooding with rays of sunlight as morning dawned over the eastern sea. The terrain grew treacherous as they entered a region rife with ruins, the stones themselves buried beneath the hills. The yellowing grass quivered in the chilled winds of winter's approach.

"Neco's hungry." Jarrod looked at Damien. "Is there a stream nearby for Corin to get cleaned up while he hunts?"

Corin drew up his horse's reins, steering closer to Jarrod. "Still crazy to consider you're bonded to Neco, now. That's the kind of shit I'm only used to from Damien."

Jarrod chuckled. "I'm still not used to it, but it's getting less... strange."

Damien glowered, ignoring them. "Better than a stream. There's a pond." He didn't offer any further clarification before he turned his horse and pushed him into a gallop west.

Jarrod followed, glancing back at Corin to make sure the captain kept up.

The hills dipped into a natural valley where grey rocks jutted out of the grass. A stream flowed over them, creating the roar of a ten foot fall into the pond below. The green grass around the stream grew tall, nestled in the cracks of what might have been ancient pillars that rimmed the edge of the water.

Damien dismounted first, urging his horse towards the water, and eyed the structure of rocks behind the falls.

You know you want to go check those out. Jarrod pushed the thought to Damien.

Damien laughed. *I know you want me to go check them out.*

Corin groaned as he dismounted, looking at his brother. "What's so funny?"

With an innocent look on his face, Damien shrugged. "Nothing."

"Uh huh." Corin pushed his horse to follow Damien's. He glanced at Jarrod. "Sure. Clothes?"

Damien nodded towards his horse. "Brown satchel. I'll go check out these ruins. Something is telling me I should."

Jarrod stifled a laugh, dismounting. "Good idea."

"Whatever." Corin waved a hand at his brother. "Don't get lost. We shouldn't stop for long." The captain pulled open the brown satchel and started rifling through it.

Jarrod crossed to the small body of water, kneeling beside it to splash some on his face. Stubble had grown over his usually clean-shaven jaw, and he made a mental note to shave later. When he looked at Corin, the man had already stripped off his shirt and was unfastening what remained of his pants as he stepped towards the water.

Dark brown marks stained his once-muscled torso and abdomen even though there were no wounds left.

Jarrod looked away, his stomach twisting.

"It's not that bad, is it?" Corin paused, standing with his toes in the pond. His pants unbuttoned, but still in place on his hips.

Jarrod shook his head, but his eyes burned. "No, not at all." He braced his hands on the ground before rising, making himself face Corin.

"Then what is it?"

Guilt washed over Jarrod and he turned away to drape his vest over his horse's saddle. "Nothing."

What I went through pales compared to what he did.

"I see." The water splashed, but the sound of Corin's steps faded into the roar of the waterfall.

Jarrod took a deep breath, failing to steady himself. His hands shook as he faced Corin again, hardly able to believe the captain was safe.

Corin stood in the center of the pond, the water reaching his hips. Locks of hair clung to his neck as he lifted another handful of water over his head. Thin drips down his back left trails clean of the prison muck. Cupping water over his arms, he waded towards the falls, his body sinking deeper.

Slowly approaching, Jarrod followed the water's edge until he stood as close to Corin as he could, his boots inches from the pond.

Corin glanced at him, but didn't fully turn. "Now you're looking? Just going to watch, then?"

Jarrod furrowed his brow, averting his gaze to his feet at Corin's sour tone.

"Sorry." Corin sighed. "You *can* talk to me, Jarrod. I won't break."

The thief lifted his gaze, his jaw working. He stepped into the water, not bothering to remove his boots. "Then you're stronger than I am."

Corin watched him, chewing on his bottom lip. "I don't know about that. Perhaps a little more sane, since I took my clothes *off* before getting in the water."

The water crept up Jarrod's body, weighing down the hem of his shirt as he approached Corin. "Shut up," he grumbled, tangling his hand back into Corin's hair and pulling his mouth against his.

Corin's lips responded to the heated kiss, and he stepped into Jarrod. Hand slipping around the thief's waist, their bodies met as the kiss deepened.

Jarrod ran a hand down Corin's back, holding him close as he pulled away, lips tingling. "If I *talk to you*, are you going to be a smart ass?"

With a low chuckle, Corin pushed his forehead against Jarrod's, flecking water on the thief's face. "I'll resist the temptation." His expression grew serious as he brushed his fingers over the proxiet's jaw. "As long as you talk to me."

"We were told you had two more weeks." Jarrod's grip tightened. "So we stopped to make sure we had supplies for after and then we heard about an execution. I assumed it was someone else, but I brought the team anyway to get an idea of their routine and so the crowds wouldn't think twice the next time we were there. Then I saw you... I thought I was too late. We hadn't even come up with a plan yet."

Corin ran his hand back over Jarrod's hair, holding his hips still close. "But you weren't too late. You saved me."

"Barely." Jarrod cupped both sides of Corin's face. He slid his hands to his neck, thumbs over his throat where the rope had rested. "I've never been so terrified. I would have done anything."

Taking Jarrod's hand, Corin lifted his knuckles to his lips and kissed them. "It's over now. Is that why you wouldn't look at me? Because it reminds you how you felt?"

Jarrod nodded, swallowing his emotion. "I keep telling myself it's over. But I can't seem to stop shaking. I didn't think

I could love someone like this." He laughed despite himself. "I think you broke me."

Corin kissed his hand a little harder and longer, then lowered it with a squeeze. "Now I feel pretty stupid for what I was thinking."

"What were you thinking?"

"I thought you blamed me." Corin touched his chin. "Hated me for pushing you until you had to use your proxiet status. That I was no longer attractive to you because of what Helgath did."

Jarrod's shoulders slumped, and he shook his head. "I could never think any of those things." He wet his hand before running it over Corin's chest, cleaning the filth away. "I love you no matter what and you didn't push me into anything. I already told Sarth the truth and using my name to free you was an option I'd already accepted."

"But if I hadn't been arrested in the first place—"

Jarrod pushed his thumb to Corin's lips to still them. "This would've happened, anyway. Things have changed over the last few months. I will lead this little rebellion of yours."

Corin's eyes widened, and he opened his mouth behind Jarrod's thumb, but then closed it before he grinned. "Am I allowed to be a smart ass yet?"

Jarrod's mouth twitched into a smirk. "That depends. Tread carefully or I might have to silence you."

A hum buzzed across Corin's lips, teasing Jarrod's fingertips. "I think I like the sound of that option better. It'll be scandalous, you know. A proxiet with a lowly, dishonorably discharged captain. People will talk."

Jarrod's gaze traveled over Corin's body before returning to his face. "I don't care. Let them talk. I'm never letting you go again. You know that, right?"

Corin smiled, playing with the collar of Jarrod's shirt between his fingers. "I do." He leaned in to give a slow, tender kiss. "Thank you."

A shiver ran down Jarrod's spine, and his chest rumbled. Placing a hand on Corin's chest, he encouraged him backward. "You're still covered in muck."

"And you're still covered in clothes. I propose we solve both problems."

Jarrod pulled his shirt over his head, dropping it in the water to let it drift back to shore. His skin heated as Corin's hands pressed to his chest, following the curve of his muscles. "I think this will do the trick." He guided Corin farther back, until the waterfall crashed onto his shoulders, separating them briefly as he kept walking.

Behind the fall, the sunlight turned into a pale blue, beams of bright light refracting up onto the rock wall behind Corin in flickering lines.

The soldier ran a hand through his hair, slicking it back in waves of curls Jarrod had never noticed before with how short he normally kept it. His eyes met Jarrod's, the dullness in them replaced by the usual spark he admired.

Jarrod leaned close, nuzzling near Corin's ear. "You're mine." He slipped his hand beneath the surface of the water. "And I will spend every moment I can making sure you know it."

Corin quivered, a small gasp escaping his lips. "Oh, and I am very willing." He grabbed the thief's belt, pulling him closer before he unbuckled it. "But I will make the same claim."

"Won't hear me complaining."

Chapter 10

RAE MANEUVERED HER HORSE OVER the uneven terrain, returning to the Lanoret ranch. Ducking under a branch of one of the few trees still standing, she tried to keep to the shaded areas and out of sight.

The open meadows offered little in the way of hiding places and with all the buildings burnt to rubble, it only made matters worse. The grass surrounding the property, dry from a hot summer, burned too, leaving the ground black and charred. The fire had spread over the weeks and continued to burn in the woods directly west, choking the air with smoke, and tainting the sun red.

She'd arrived barely ahead of the troops sent to kill Damien's family.

Rapping on the door weeks ago, she'd glanced around the property. Staff tended to horses, no one paying her any attention.

They never got Damien's warning.

Maith shook his head slowly, as if reading her thoughts.

The front door swung open, accompanied by the waft of meat cooking over the stove. A woman, tall and lean, used her apron to clean bits of flour from her fingertips. Her dirty blonde hair was tied half back on her head, streaks of grey stretching from her temples. "Can I help you?" Her gaze flickered to Maith. "Are you lost?"

Rae shook her head. "No, I'm sorry. Are you Lady Lanoret?"

She rubbed her hands a little more incessantly on her apron. "I am... And who are you?"

"My name is Rae. I'm... I'm a friend of Damien's. There's been some trouble, and—"

"My son is dead, miss, killed when he deserted his post. I'd appreciate you not dredging up those memories by going any further."

"Is that what they told you? Because I swear to you, he's not dead. I saw him only weeks ago, but that's not important."

"Then what is?" Damien's mother narrowed her eyes. She tugged the door shut a little more, as if shielding the rest of the house from Rae's eyes.

Rae sucked in a breath. "Helgath has captured Corin. You need to get somewhere safe."

A thud echoed from somewhere behind the door, vibrating the wooden porch under Rae's feet.

"Open the door, Viola." A man's gruff voice echoed from inside. "Let me see who's making wild claims."

Viola glanced behind her, letting the door swing open as a man with a crutch hobbled towards the doorway. Under the worn leather tunic, his body looked sturdy despite missing the part of his leg beneath his right knee. White peppered his red beard, framing the strong chin he'd given his son. "What is it you're claiming about my sons?"

Rae tried to muster patience. "Corin's been arrested by Helgath. And Damien said that if that happened, Helgath would send troops here with no pleasant intentions."

"You're implying not only that you've spoken to my son, the traitor, but also that his elder brother has made the same foolish mistake?"

Rae's stomach plummeted, not having considered that his parents would have disagreed with their sons' choices. "Yes. I don't know how to convince you..." She looked up, searching her memories. "He told me about Brynn, and he and Corin almost drowned in the river—"

"You can stop." Viola lifted a hand. She turned and looked at her husband, who narrowed his eyes. "Gage?"

Rae looked behind her at the road cresting the hill a quarter-mile away to make sure it remained empty. "Please, there isn't much time. What have you got to lose if I'm lying? I'm trying to help you."

Maith coughed. "I've only met your son, Damien, a handful of times, and he's rather unpleasant." He cleared his throat when Rae elbowed him. "She's telling the truth, though. As unfortunate as it is."

Gage snorted. "Unpleasant. Maybe you know him, after all."

"The boys got their smartass mouths from you." Viola folded her arms over her chest.

Damien's father thumped his crutch on the ground again, inching closer to the door. "You say we ain't got nothing to lose, but that ain't true. All we know, you're a spy come to check in on us again. But I'm sticking to what I always say. We ain't heard from our son and our other two boys are loyal soldiers of the king."

Rae bounced up and down on her toes, grinding her teeth. "That's fine. Stick with that. But can you do it from somewhere safe?"

Maith tapped her shoulder, and she brushed his hand off. He did it again, and she growled.

"What?"

He jerked his thumb behind him, and she looked. The sun glinted off the armor of soldiers marching over the hill, a crimson standard etched in gold raised in the air.

Rae's chest tightened. "Look. Do you believe me now? You need to get out right *now*."

Gage squinted at the distant hillside. He didn't bother excusing himself as he pushed her out of the way, hobbling down the set of stairs from the front porch. Viola vanished from the doorway without a word while Gage let out a sharp whistle.

A boy raking hay at the rim of a pasture looked up.

"Time's come, Hoit. Gather the staff and head for the west barn."

Hoit, no older than fifteen, nodded and dashed away, his rake tumbling to the ground.

Maith eyed Rae. "And my role?"

Rae glanced at Gage, then back to Maith. "Go with them, please. You can make sure they're safe."

Gage turned towards them, his hazel eyes darting back and forth between Rae and Maith. He lifted his crutch, pointing its end towards a distant structure. "I hope I don't come to regret trusting you're telling the truth. There's a bunker built beneath the barn there, prepared for such an occasion." He lowered his crutch and hobbled close to Rae. "When you're inside, knock twice on the rusted old plow and we'll open up."

Rae let out a sigh of relief. "I'll try to get you as much time as possible to gather your people. Please let Maith accompany you."

The auer bowed, gaining a skeptical look from Gage. "At your service, if I may help."

"Hope you ain't as frilly as you look," Gage muttered. "Viola!"

The woman appeared back on the porch, a pair of large bags slung over her shoulders. She labored forward with them before Gage took one up. Viola's brow knitted as she turned towards Rae. "You've really seen my Damien?"

Rae nodded. "I have. He's well." Her cheeks heated. "I love your son."

A sigh escaped Viola, making her look ten years younger. She smiled and reached to touch Rae's face. "Thank you."

Rae had stalled the soldiers once they arrived at the main house's front door by telling them stories and refusing them entry. By the time they shoved past her, the occupants of the ranch had long disappeared into the bunker, leaving the property empty.

While they ransacked the house, pulling apart furniture and cupboards, Rae elbowed the man holding her and rolled out the kitchen window. Her boots crunched in the glass as she landed on her feet and she sprinted for the sparse tree line, flinging the pasture gate open as she ran.

Men chased her, but she pulled herself up into one of the wide pine trees, climbing as high as she could.

They searched for her to no avail.

Holding her breath, she watched them light the homestead ablaze. Smoke blanketed the sky, and the fire spread over the grass, catching every outbuilding aflame as it went. The horses cried out as they fled from their stables, stampeding towards the gate Rae had opened.

Fortunately, her hiding place did not fall victim to the inferno, the grass as its base extinguishing before the flame spread further.

Night fell before the Helgathians departed.

She scaled down the tree, dreading what she might find in the bunker.

Stepping over the charred remains of the barn, she located the rusted steel plow beneath some ash and charred beams. The metal blade had melted into an asymmetrical shape. She hoped the bunker hadn't burned too, but the ground held firm beneath her boots. She banged her fist twice on the plow.

A loud clanking echoed up from below the ground, the wooden planks behind the plow bouncing up, then fell back down under the weight of the beams strewn across it.

Rae let out a breath, approaching the trap door. Hauling the beams aside, she pushed them one at a time out of the way.

Two still blocked the door when Maith grunted and heaved the door up, his auer strength shattering the burnt wood with the solid iron door.

Rae smiled at him and peered inside, finding many eyes looking up at her.

"Good, you're alive." Maith sighed. "I wouldn't have enjoyed explaining otherwise to Damien." He smiled at her, the black bags under his eyes proving that he'd been worried despite his cavalier attitude.

"I was worried about you, too." She nodded at him before finding Gage sitting among his staff. "Not too frilly, after all?"

Gage snorted. "Quite handy, actually. Don't think we'd have survived the heat without that Art of his."

Rae smiled warmly at Maith. "Thank you."

"Better come in before a patrol comes by." Maith leaned back, still holding the trapdoor over his head. He made enough space for Rae to wiggle down onto the ladder he stood on.

Maith shut the hatch behind her, sliding the massive lock into place.

"Once it's safe, I'll go back outside and find a horse. I can take you to town one at a time. Starting with you." She motioned to Damien's mother.

"I'm not going until you get our staff to safety." Viola looked at her husband, who nodded his agreement. "We'll go last."

"I see where Damien gets it." Maith gave them a bemused smile.

Forced to wait several days, the patrols around the property finally lessened enough for Rae to sneak the Lanoret staff past the property lines. Fortunately, the river which cut through the ranch had an underground tributary the family connected to a smaller room within the bunker, making their living in hiding more sustainable. She'd discovered from his parents that Corin had been the one to develop the idea and drill them on how they would empty the ranch with only a moment's notice.

Rae shook the memories from her head, guiding the bareback horse over the rubble towards the bunker. She'd gotten everyone else out, with only Damien's parents and Maith still inside the bunker.

I hope they got to Corin in time.

Movement in the blackened fields made her pause.

Dropping off the horse, she crouched behind charred rocks.

A man approached the skeletal remains of the western barn and she remained crouched as she hurried towards him from behind. He walked with purpose, his boots avoiding the fallen debris as he circled where the hatch to the bunker was, staring at the ground. He nudged one of the shattered beams with his foot and her heart skipped a beat.

Shit.

The man knelt, tracing a finger along the groove of the trapdoor.

Rae launched forward, boots sliding amid the ash, and tackled him.

Chapter 11

CORIN HIT THE GROUND, SENDING up a cloud of ash as all the air rushed out of him. Instinctively, he rolled onto his back, pushing down to crush his attacker. Legs wrapped around his waist like a vice, despite how hard he pressed against her.

She grunted, wrapping her arm around his neck with surprising strength.

They rolled over the trapdoor, further coating themselves in soot, while Corin fought to find a strong enough footing to wrestle her off him. He choked as her grip tightened while he grappled to pry her ankle from his stomach.

He threw his elbow back, connecting with her abdomen, and she yelped. Her hold loosened, and he grabbed her biceps to pry her free and throw her over his head. She tumbled, her body breaking through the fragments of the barn's wall, but landed on her feet.

Corin glared at the soot-faced creature who had attacked him, unable to make out anything but the odd green hue of her eyes. Before she could run, he lunged and tackled her to the ground. He fought to grab hold of her wrists, but she landed a punch to his ribs before he pinned her.

"Damn." Corin pushed her harder into the ground. He squeezed his knees tighter on her thighs, locking her legs in place. "You're a feisty one, aren't you?"

"And you're not very observant." She twisted to the side, her hands closing on a piece of charred wood before slamming it into the side of his head. It shattered, sending shards of charcoal flying. He closed his eyes, trying not to breathe, and she reversed the grapple, pushing him back.

Corin choked on the ash, unable to stop the cough that continued after she knocked the wind out of him again. He braced himself for the punch. When it didn't come, he peeked with one eye and saw the girl kicking as a pair of arms lifted her clean off of him.

"Whoa." Damien pulled her back and her eyes widened. "You said you would check the barn, Corin. Not start a fight with a—"

"Damien!" She breathed out the name, planting her feet and turning in his suddenly slack hold.

Corin coughed, sitting up and spitting ash out of his mouth. He glanced up to meet Jarrod's eyes. "Good timing." He brushed his blackened hands across his pants.

The proxiet grinned, motioning with his chin towards Damien.

Corin followed his gaze and choked again when he saw Damien kissing his attacker.

"I see you've met Rae."

"*Met* would be a loose definition." Corin reached up to Jarrod, and the thief gripped his hand, pulling him to his feet.

Rae parted from Damien and grinned at Jarrod, running into his arms.

Corin eyed his brother, who hadn't taken his eyes off of her yet. Black smeared the edges of his mouth. "You got a little something..." Corin lifted his hand to gesture at his own mouth.

"Could say the same about you, asshole." Damien glowered. "You're lucky you didn't hurt her."

Rae let go of Jarrod. "That's kind of my bad." She smiled sheepishly at Corin. "I saw him going for the bunker and I panicked."

"What are you even doing here?" Jarrod held her by her upper arms.

"I got your letter. So I convinced the council to let me go, and I got here in time to warn your family."

Corin gave a surprised grunt. "More than just feisty, then." He smiled, weight lifting off his shoulders. "So they're safe?"

Rae nodded, stepping towards him. "They're in the bunker. I've already moved the staff to the town... Sorry." She motioned to his appearance. "About all that."

Corin laughed and stepped into Rae, pulling her into a hug. "I think we've both suffered a lot worse."

Rae's arms tightened around him, and she whispered in his ear. "It's quite an honor to meet you, Captain."

"Honor's mine," he whispered back. "Been looking forward to meeting the woman that finally caught my brother's attention. Had wondered if he was like me and just not ready to admit it yet."

Rae laughed and let go, looking at his face. "Your hygiene could use some work, though."

"Jarrod's usually the one who takes me out back and washes me." He gestured his head at the thief.

"Oooh." Rae's eyebrows lifted, and she looked at Jarrod. "Sounds steamy."

"Are you two finished?" Jarrod rolled his eyes.

Rae let go of Corin, dusting off his shoulders as she did. "I think we're just getting started."

"Fantastic." Jarrod sighed.

Corin grinned, walking towards Jarrod. He teasingly placed his hand on his cheek, running his thumb over his jaw and leaving a charcoal stain in its wake. "You're cute when you're frustrated. I've mentioned that before, haven't I?"

Jarrod smiled, tugging Corin closer with a low rumble in his chest. "And you're cute all covered in soot."

Damien groaned. "They're like this all... the... time."

"And we're *so* much better at hiding our affection."

"Why can't I... Rae." Damien's tone darkened. "Why are you wearing that?"

Corin glanced at them as Damien touched a copper cuff on the top of Rae's right ear. He recognized it from the widespread use among the military.

"So Helgath can't sense me. I have the key."

Damien frowned, touching her jaw. "You don't have to be afraid of that anymore. None of us need to be afraid of Helgath anymore."

"What are you talking about?" Rae looked at Jarrod.

"It's true." Jarrod stiffened. "The Lanoret family is under the protection of House Martox now and, if the need arises, you will be too."

Rae smiled, her shoulders relaxing. "We should get your family out of there."

Damien nodded, kissing her forehead.

Stepping away from Jarrod, Corin started for the trapdoor of the bunker.

"Wait," Damien hissed.

Everyone froze, staring at him.

Corin opened his mouth to speak, but closed it to let his brother concentrate.

Damien's eyes unfocused, his head tilting slightly. It still felt strange to consider how much Damien had changed since Corin had last seen him. He felt more grounded than ever before, but he couldn't tell if it was Rae's doing, or the powers of the Rahn'ka.

Drawing in a sharp breath, Damien rocked from the trance he'd put himself in and blinked. He shook his head. "From the north, there's an entire battalion sneaking through the pines beyond the hill. But there's something else behind them. I just can't... quite place it."

"How fast? Can we run?" Rae turned to the north. "I thought you said we were safe."

"They must not care about the declaration Jarrod made as proxiet." Corin's hand closed around the short sword Damien had given him.

"Or they care quite a lot." Jarrod frowned. "They're probably ordered to kill me."

"Well, lets get my parents and get out of here."

Damien shook his head. "Not with Da's leg. There's no rushing anywhere. And I don't think we can outrun whatever is behind that battalion. It's definitely something Art related."

"I need this cuff off." Rae dug her hand into the pocket of her leather pants. "I'm useless with it on. I don't even have a bow."

"I can get you a bow." Damien nodded at his brother. "If someone else could use that tiny thing." He motioned to her open palm, holding the small gear-key that would unleash her Art.

Corin rolled his eyes. "Give it to me."

Damien plopped down onto the ground right where he stood. He crossed his legs and closed his eyes, entering a meditative state.

Rae held out the key and dropped it into Corin's hand. "Hurry."

Jarrod stepped around them to the north while Corin studied the tiny gear, poking it with a soot-covered finger before he turned to Rae.

"Pull your hair out of the way." The captain carefully took it between the pads of his fingers.

The half-inch copper cuff sliced through her cartilage, and the mere sight made Corin shudder. "How the hell do women pierce their ears willingly." The miniature key slipped between his fingers before he could get it in. He recoiled, trying to reposition it.

"It's not a female thing, trust me."

"Hurry," Jarrod warned, and Corin glanced to see soldiers emerging from the pines at the top of the hill to the north.

"This isn't really a thing you can hurry, my king," Corin growled. "Damn it, Rae, hold still."

Rae stopped bouncing, but her hands twitched. "Just get it off."

The gear slipped and fell to the ground with a little poof of ash.

"Fuck."

Rae knelt with him to help him search.

The ground vibrated with the pounding boots of the advancing battalion, grating Corin's nerves. He'd naively expected the king to play by the rules of honor if a Dannet family got involved with the rebellion. But now, it seemed Jarrod had finally gotten himself a poster, and the king had it out for him. Enough that he sent an entire squad of soldiers after just three men.

"Helgath has always been great at overkill," Corin grumbled, raking his nails through the dirt.

"Got it!" Rae deposited the key back in Corin's hand and stood.

Corin made the mistake of looking north. Running down the golden slope, he estimated a troop of the standard twenty-six soldiers. They'd forgone the standard approach, charging with swords already in hand, the sun shining on their silver battle armor.

"Hurry!"

"I'm trying!" Corin wedged the gear between his fingers again.

Damien sat there, eyes still closed, his hands resting with his palms up on his knees. An odd cloud of pale blue drifted in the air between them, pulsing in response to some invisible control he had over it.

The gear didn't fit, and he tried a slightly different angle, twisting his wrist awkwardly. Finally it slipped in, fitting snugly into the lock mechanism with a soft click.

Rae gasped, her right eye shifting to a topaz yellow.

The soldiers rushed towards them while Jarrod stood in the open between them.

And Damien's still just sitting there. How does he do it with all this noise?

Rae walked around Jarrod, and Corin stuffed the little device into his pocket. She outstretched her hands on either side of her, fingers spread wide.

Smoke billowed from the outskirts of the property and two cyclones of fire rose into the air from the burning brush. They climbed into the sky and surged towards Rae. The smoke thickened, blacking out the red sun.

She brought her hands closer together and the whirlwinds of flame tore through the ground, kicking up billows of soot.

Rae exhaled, clapping her outstretched hands in front of her.

The cyclones crashed together, engulfing the running soldiers in a flurry of screams. Heat rippled through the air, blowing Rae's hair straight back.

Corin squinted, protecting his face with his arm as ash and heat exploded through the air.

The fire calmed and Rae's hands lowered, her stature drooping.

None of the attacking soldiers attempted to rise, and she bowed her head.

"Nymaera's breath," Jarrod whispered in an exhale.

Corin leaned close to him. "Remind me never to piss her off."

Rae's chest heaved, and she turned from her destruction. Glancing at Damien, she gulped a mouthful of air. "Why do I get the impression that I don't have time for a nap?"

An unnatural howl rang up from the hills beyond, a leonine call that sounded like it came from the throat of something long dead.

Every bone in Corin's body quivered. "What in all the hells..."

Damien's eyes snapped open, his hand shooting out to the foggy air in front of him. It looked as if it would pass right through, but his grip closed around something solid. The mist flared into a hot beam of pale light, radiating down the elegant limbs of a recurve bow. He traced a finger through the air between tips, a weave of power following his gesture to form the string. Standing, he held the weapon out to Rae.

Damien blinked over her shoulder, looking at the fallen, burnt soldiers. "I think I missed something impressive."

"You did." Rae smiled as she took the weapon. "But this might make up for it."

Another howl rose, and Corin withdrew the sword at his side. He bounced the simple steel in his hand. "I want a fancy weapon."

Rae stuck her tongue out at him.

He returned it.

Damien rolled his eyes. "Can we discuss this later, maybe? When we're not facing imminent death?"

"One that could cut through anything. Like... *anything*."

Jarrod cleared his throat. "Uh, Dame? What are those?"

Corin turned to face the hillside, scattered with the charred corpses of Helgathian soldiers.

Past the dead humans, a flurry of creatures descended the hill at varied paces. Hulking bestial shapes ran amongst smaller forms, all sprinting towards them. Nothing moved as expected, using arms as legs, and some skittered sideways.

"Nymaera's name..." Corin whispered, taking a step back.

Jarrod exchanged a glance with Corin, moving to stand at his side.

With a hand outstretched in front of her, Rae walked towards the approaching beasts. As she stared, the fire rimming the dead soldiers rose, forming a wall a few feet tall.

A pulse of hot blue light emanated from Damien's shoulders, this tattoo glowing beneath his shirt as he thrust his hand out and the long shaft of his spear erupted from his fist.

His face hardened in focus. "Corrupted. Not enough time to explain, but they're..."

A beast burst through Rae's wall of fire, its chitinous beak snapping at the flames. Its bear body appeared unaffected by the heat and it barreled towards them on raptor clawed feet. It bellowed, tearing at the ash-covered ground.

Several more followed, each unfazed by Rae's fire. They shook embers from their patchwork fur hides, fangs gnashing.

The wall of fire collapsed as Rae brought her blue bow to her eye. As she pulled back on the Art-laden string, an arrow materialized in her sights. She let it loose, and it sank into the bear-creature's skull.

Its pace faltered, but only momentarily, still advancing with the arrow jutting out between its eyes.

"Shit." Rae lowered the weapon.

Damien charged in front of her, spinning his spear and plunging it into the creature's neck. It staggered, falling. Ichor spurted from where the spearhead pierced, pinning it to the ground. It cried out and lashed with its claws, forcing Damien to abandon his weapon and dive back. He took Rae with him, collapsing to the ground just as a smaller creature leapt onto them, digging its feline paws into his back as it continued its momentum forward.

Jarrod caught a beast by its reptilian neck before it could collide with Corin's chest and whipped it so hard to the side that its neck snapped. He dropped it, looking at the black muck left behind on his hands.

Its feeble body twitched, and Corin stomped the heel of his boot into its skull.

Damien scrambled to his feet with Rae, lifting his empty hand. Without needing his touch, the spear tore from the ground and flesh of the Corrupted, ricocheting back into his hand.

The Corrupted roared as Damien thrust his other hand forward. The air in front of him rippled, a shimmering wave of pale light cascading through the air. It tore apart the ground in its wake, sending hunks of burnt beams and rock spraying out of the way before striking the bear square in the snout.

The creature lifted its head, bulbous eyes glowing a sinister red, and stepped into the power.

Well, that's not good.

Damien grimaced. "They're resistant to the Art!"

Rae backed up, standing between the three men, and closed her eyes. "I hope you have good balance."

The ground beneath Corin's feet shook and Jarrod glanced down.

Burnt grass broke apart, falling in dusty chunks as the ground elevated. Stone erupted from beneath, rising all four of them higher.

Corin smirked at her ingenuity.

Higher ground should help.

The ground vibrated to a halt, six feet higher than it had been, and wide enough for the four of them to fight on if they were careful. The steep drop off prevented the Corrupted from overwhelming them.

"The summoners are up the hill." Damien looked over his shoulder at them. "You two distract them while Rae and I cut off the source."

"Sounds fun." Corin spun his sword in his hand with a glance at Jarrod. "I'm good at being distracting."

"Aye. Don't take too long."

Damien grasped Rae's hand, and they slid down the back of her embankment, breaking into a run to circle around the swarming Corrupted.

A dark shape leapt from where it'd crouched in the burnt grass, lunging for Damien's back.

Before Corin could yell to his brother, another furry form snarled and met the Corrupted midair. Neco landed on the feline beast, sinking his teeth into its neck and tearing the spinal column. The thing stilled, and the wolf bounded up the rocky hill to join Jarrod.

"Good dog." Corin gave Neco a quick scratch to the back of one of his ears. He crouched, picking up a rock in time to hurl it at the head of a Corrupted turning its attention around the back of the mound. It connected, and the creature howled, shaking its tangled mane.

Corin stood, but Jarrod pushed his shoulders back down. The hair on the back of his neck stood straight as something brushed past his face, a stinking hulk bounding clear over him.

It collided with the thief, sending him rolling off the other side of the miniature mountain.

Heart pounding, Corin withdrew the dagger secured at his arm and raced to the edge while Neco held off the other side.

Jarrod struggled on his back, the big beast slashing its teeth next to the proxiet's face.

Steadying his breath long enough to aim, Corin threw the dagger with all his might. The blade struck the giant rat-like creature between the shoulder blades and it hissed.

Jarrod gripped both sides of its head, as big as his own, and twisted.

A crack reverberated through the air. He yelled, dislodging the creature's head from its body and heaving it at an oncoming attacker.

Corin slid down to meet the distracted Corrupted before it could recover, slamming his sword through its ursine neck.

Jarrod closed a hand on Corin's arm, pulling him back up the rocky slope.

As they reached the top, the maned head of the creature he'd thrown the rock at peeked beyond the jagged ridge, launching at them.

Corin dove on top of Jarrod, landing them on the ground and narrowly missing its claws as Neco hurtled through the air after it.

Another came, only to be dissuaded by Jarrod's knife.

"Gods, will they hurry up?"

Barely able to hear him over the creatures' cries, Corin laughed. "What, you're not enjoying this?"

Chapter 12

THE TALL, UNBURNT GRASS ON the hill shielded Damien and Rae as they zig-zagged their way to the tree line. He focused on the dim shape tethered to the creatures below.

In the distance, Jarrod yelled, followed by Neco's vicious growls and the sounds of the Corrupted attacking.

They can hold their own.

Gripping the shaft of his spear, Damien glanced at Rae. Her right altered to the vibrant topaz hue he admired.

Having Rae at his side when stepping into danger had been normal, but now it felt foreign considering their time apart. The lingering surprise of her appearance on his family ranch had to be set aside for him to focus, but it crept forward as he met her eyes.

How did she convince them to let her leave Eralas?

Blinking through the grass, he shook the thoughts of Rae from his mind and focused on the steel armor ahead. Lifting a hand, he signaled to the side, and she nodded.

They separated, keeping low within the grass as they flanked a small clump of soldiers with a summoner in the middle.

Helgath's blatant use of practitioners in their military was a long-standing tradition, but to use Corrupted brought them to an unprecedented low. Summoning had always been a form of the Art forbidden by all the countries of Pantracia, one of the few things they agreed on. The only reason Damien even knew what they were was because of his training as a Rahn'ka. To exercise such exorbitant force against a deserter's family made no sense.

They've come for Jarrod, to eliminate the threat to the throne. We probably should have thought this through a little better.

He paused, stripping his boots from his feet before he continued. The dirt beneath his toes brought a surge of comfort, the ká of nature eager to assist as he tugged for power. The Corrupted resisted damage from the Art, but the same couldn't be said for the humans who controlled them.

Thin lines of power stretched through the air like a spiderweb, connecting to the one soldier responsible. They all dressed similarly, to shield the summoner from being easily identified, which would have worked against most. He looked like any other Helgathian, dressed in the dense armor, the maroon scarf secured about his neck with a golden pin.

Damien couldn't see Rae, but sensed her as she brushed against the ká of the grass. He closed his eyes, taking in the scene as his power saw it.

The faint outlines of the soldier's ká vibrated with anxiety. Some found the sight of the valley below exciting, others feared the Corrupted, subtly standing apart from the man controlling them.

The summoner's soul held darkness, seething against the purity it might have contained before Helgath forced him into service. Damien sought the solace of knowing the man couldn't be redeemed. His power had transformed him into something not unlike those he controlled. His shadowed ká served as the perfect point for Damien to take hold.

With a steadying breath, the Rahn'ka pulled the energy of his spear back into his soul and it vanished from his grip. With a flick of his fingers, the power re-emerged, thrusting forward like an invisible whip.

The summoner's eyes widened before Damien yanked. The faint blue shape of his soul ruptured from within, his body jerking back in a spasm before collapsing limply to the ground. The man's ká faded into the surrounding life as the other soldiers shouted in surprise.

Corrupted howled, their cries morphing to gleeful tones.

The soldiers' swords lifted, and they spun to find their attacker.

One focused in Rae's direction, and Damien's heart pounded as he stood to reveal himself. The soldiers leapt for him, but the closest tumbled with a spirited arrow protruding from his neck. One by one they fell, succumbing to the speed Rae gained by forgoing the need to draw.

Damien barely had time to shape his ká around the last soldier's neck, snapping it. Pausing, he examined the surrounding bodies, his muscles weary. He stared into the unfocused dead eyes of the man who'd stood apart from the summoner, and his chest tightened.

Approaching, Rae looked down at the valley, watching the beasts cease their attack and take off into the forest. She narrowed her eyes at the valley where Jarrod and Corin had been fighting. "Something's wrong. One of them is hurt."

"We should get down there then." Damien buried the aching lethargy in his muscles. He reached for Rae, turning from the destruction they'd wrought together. "Come on."

As they raced back down the hill, Rae squeezed his hand hard enough that it hurt.

Corin knelt over Jarrod, shirtless, a hand pressed to the thief's throat. The ash-stained cloth covered the proxiet's neck, turning what'd been still white, red.

Neco laid over Jarrod's legs, making Damien's heart thud.

Damien reached for the bow in Rae's hand. "Looks like I'll need that energy."

She shoved it into his hand before running to Jarrod's side.

A minute surge of energy pulsed into Damien's veins as he allowed the construct of the bow to collapse back into his ká.

Jarrod looked pallid, his breathing labored and wet. Watching the sky, he blinked, eyes wide. He tried to speak, but blood ran from his lips.

"Shut up, you idiot." Corin stroked his forehead. He looked up at Damien, his paled face clean where tears had already fallen.

Rae fell to the ground next to him. "You'll be all right," she whispered, touching his cheek as he closed his eyes.

Damien dropped to his knees near Jarrod's head, hands closing over Corin's to take their place. His body felt weak from all the power he'd used to defeat the summoner, but he argued against his protesting muscles.

Just a little more.

In his state, the chances of him successfully entering the Inbetween were slim, so he'd have to catch the man before his life faded. "Just relax, Jare. Stay focused on Corin and Rae. Stay awake."

Jarrod's eyes fluttered open, unfocused. More blood oozed from his mouth as his jaw opened and closed.

Rae took his hand, then looked at Damien. "He's so cold."

Neco whined, resting his head on Jarrod's abdomen.

Corin said something, but Damien didn't hear the words as he plunged into the meditative state necessary to work the power to keep Jarrod's ká in place. It already vibrated against the surrounding fabric, trying to join back with the power of Pantracia and venture into the Inbetween. He swallowed, compartmentalizing how much of his ká he could use to push into the thief.

Rae clamped a hand down on Damien's arm, silently giving him permission to use her energy, and he obliged. Her grip loosened as he borrowed from her, careful to do the same for her as he did for himself.

With the gravity of Jarrod's wound, it took all he could muster to hold the thief's ká in place and force the skin to seal. The state of Jarrod's soul felt odd, in deeper turmoil than when he'd interacted with it before. Looming death agitated the bonds and Damien realized just how much Jarrod had bonded not only to Corin, but to Rae and himself.

Those connections, however, paled compared to the one with Neco.

That's not how I constructed it.

Refusing to become distracted by following the lines connecting the wolf and thief, Damien pushed everything into the wound. He waited until he felt the skin starting to close beneath his fingertips and heard Jarrod draw in a dry breath, before he indulged in another peek.

Damien sought the tether between Jarrod and Neco's mind, which his power had made possible. The ends of it had frayed like a rope. New lines formed, linking them in unorthodox ways. The Rahn'ka had noticed in Mirage how Jarrod's strength had increased, surpassing what should have been physically possible.

This is why.

The connection to Neco had mutated. It pushed aspects of the wolf into the man, which Damien had read about but hadn't intended.

With the close inspection, the bond surged, pushing Damien out of Jarrod's ká. He recoiled, drawing his hand away with a gasp, as if the strike from the man's soul had been a serpent.

Jarrod wheezed a breath through clenched teeth, the veins in his neck bulging as Corin hurriedly pulled away his shirt, inspecting the healed skin.

When he didn't see the wound, the captain breathed a sigh and touched his forehead to Jarrod's before kissing it. "Thank the gods."

Rae bowed her head and then looked at Damien and nodded. Her demeanor slumped, her hand on his arm shaking.

Damien touched her wrist. "Sorry." His shoulders sagged as exhaustion overwhelmed every part of his body. "I needed a lot more energy than I thought."

Jarrod hardly moved, and Neco whined again. The thief's arm lifted, stroking the wolf's head before encircling Corin's shoulders.

Corin took his hand as he sat back on his heels. He looked over at Rae, then to Damien, furrowing his brows. "You guys look like shit."

Damien laughed, and even that took too much energy. "Just tired. We need to rest for a while."

Corin looked up the hill behind them, frowning. "We should get into the bunker in case more come. Do I need to carry all three of you?"

"I can help." A voice behind Damien made him jump, and he spun to look at Maith.

The tall auer stood perfectly clean, his hands folded in front of his hips. He glanced at the body of one of the Corrupted at his feet, nudging its serpentine tail with his fine leather boot.

"Great," Damien muttered, rolling his eyes. He looked at Rae, who leaned against his shoulder. "You didn't tell me Maith was with you."

Rae shrugged. "The price of my freedom. He's not so bad."

Corin jutted a finger at Maith. "But we trust him?"

"About as far as I can throw him," Damien grumbled and Rae half-heartedly smacked his chest.

Corin shrugged. "I'm betting you could throw him pretty far, so good enough for me." He stood, tugging Jarrod up with him. Wrapping Jarrod's arm around his neck, he gestured with his head towards Damien and Rae. "Can you get them?"

Maith stepped forward, and Damien growled. "I can get myself."

Rae reached for Maith's outstretched hand, scowling at Damien as the auer helped her to her feet. She leaned on him and Damien's stomach turned.

"There's no need for being stubborn." Maith eyed Damien, his stone-grey eyebrows knitting together. "Let me help you."

Damien glowered at his outstretched hand before he accepted it. Once on his feet, he tried to stabilize himself, but ended up needing to put a hand on Maith's shoulder, regardless.

The tedious walk to the bunker only exhausted Damien further. The trapdoor lay open and Corin stood at the edge, slowly lowering Jarrod inside.

Neco stood nervously near the ruined exterior wall of the barn, watching over Jarrod as he vanished from sight.

Damien stopped to touch his ruff when he whined. "Better get back into the wilds, bud. You won't like it much down there."

Neco perked his ears nervously after Jarrod, making Damien consider again the strength of their connection. Huffing, Neco turned away, licking Damien's fingers and bounding for the trees.

Corin lowered Rae into the bunker while she kept one hand on the ladder, disappearing inside.

"Praise the gods, you're all right."

It'd been so long since Damien had heard his mother's voice, he almost didn't recognize it. Heat burned his eyes, and he shook his head, finding the strength to enter next without Corin's help.

Turning from the ladder, Damien first saw his father, who supported his son after he stumbled on the uneven ground.

Gage looked older than Damien remembered, more lines at the corners of his eyes and around the frown of his mouth. But when their eyes met, a wave of relief passed through Damien. He'd been so afraid he'd never look at either of his parents again.

But the people closest to me made this possible.

He fell into an embrace with his father before he could fathom a more conservative reaction. The gasp from his mother threatened all remaining control of his emotions, and her arms encompassed him from behind. He turned to wrap his arm around her, burying himself between his parents with a sob of relief.

Another body joined the hug, and his mother's kisses turned to Corin's head.

"My boys." A cry of joy escaped Viola as she spoke. "I'm so glad to see you safe."

"Ma..." Corin cleared his throat. "Da, I'm so sorry."

"Hush."

"But..."

"Listen to your mother." Gage squeezed tighter on Damien's shoulder, roughly patting each brother.

The trapdoor clunked shut above them, plunging the bunker into shadows cast by little orbs of light flickering in the corners of the room.

Damien blinked, trying to take in the details despite still being entwined in his family's arms. Rectangular, the room had three doors that branched off the back end of it. The room they were in had long shelves and what probably meant to serve as a kitchen.

"You made some improvements, Da." Corin nodded. "I don't remember putting cots down here."

Damien lifted his head, turning to his mother, whose eyes were wet with tears.

She touched his face, seeming unwilling to let go. "Rae told us you were still alive and even then I was terrified it wasn't true."

Damien clutched her hand and smiled. "I'm here, Ma. I'm alive. Despite many people trying to change that."

She gave a little sob again and pulled him into her. His mother's arms wrapping around him brought peace, a comfort he'd forgotten. It made all the voices fade without him needing to keep the barrier in place.

"What was all that racquet up there?" Gage hobbled towards a cot with his crutch.

Rae leaned against a wall, sliding down to a cot next to Jarrod. The proxiet laid with his eyes closed and she pressed two fingers to his neck. Meeting Damien's gaze, she nodded once and stroked her friend's face.

Maith sat next to her, talking too quietly for Damien to hear.

"It's over." Damien sighed. "So it doesn't matter. But we need a little time to recover."

Gage narrowed his eyes as he sat but nodded, glancing behind Damien at Jarrod and Rae.

Corin stepped past his parents, kneeling beside the cot. He took Jarrod's limp hand, bringing it to his chest.

"Looks like that boy lost a lot of blood, but I don't see no wounds." Gage eyed his youngest son.

"It's..." Damien flinched. "Complicated." His parents turned their heads to each other, a multitude of questions on their faces.

"Everything's always complicated," Jarrod croaked and Rae smiled.

"Don't you even think about getting up." Corin put a hand on Jarrod's chest before he could try. "You need to rest."

Jarrod raised his hands in mock surrender. "Not moving. Am I allowed to speak?" His gruff voice made Damien wince.

Rae stood, silently offering to trade places with Corin next to Jarrod on the cot. As he settled down where she'd sat, she sauntered sleepily over to Damien.

Corin hesitated, a teasing smile on his lips as if he was considering denying Jarrod's request. His hand stroked over the proxiet's short hair as he lifted his head in his lap. "Well, I suppose I should probably introduce you to my parents."

Jarrod's brows raised, and his eyes darted to Gage and Viola. Breaking his promise, he tried to sit up, but Corin held him in place. He groaned. "Oh, come on, you're going to make me meet your folks while I'm on my back?"

Corin smirked and leaned closer to Jarrod, whispering something in his ear Damien was happy he couldn't overhear.

Jarrod laughed, then cleared his throat as Corin's mother approached him. "Sir. Lady Lanoret. I wish I could greet you properly, but it's a pleasure to meet you." His tone shook with remnants of laughter, and he offered a hand across the narrow walkway between cots to Gage.

Gage took Jarrod's outstretched hand without standing, giving it a rough shake. "Good to meet you, son. You a rebel like my boys?"

Jarrod coughed. "Uh..."

"Jarrod's the reason Corin and I are alive," Damien interrupted. "His connections allowed us to save Corin from the gallows and get out of Veralian."

"Jarrod..." Gage chewed on the name. "Why do I feel like I've heard that name recently?"

Viola batted her husband on the shoulder. "Because you have. Jarrod is the name of the—"

"Proxiet." Jarrod lowered his raspy voice. "My family name is Martox."

Gage's grip visibly tightened on Jarrod's hand, his eyes darting up to Corin, who lovingly traced circles around Jarrod's temple. "Martox... Well, it's certainly a pleasure meeting you then, my lord."

Viola leaned on her husband's shoulder. "Thank you for keeping my boys safe, Lord Martox."

Jarrod waved his free hand, cringing. "Please. Call me Jarrod. No need for formalities. And my reasons were entirely selfish, I assure you." He grinned at Corin, who touched the scar on his chin.

"You two are truly disgusting sometimes." Damien groaned as Rae leaned on him. He turned to his father, putting a hand on his shoulder. "Is it all right if we get some sleep, Da? I'm about to fall over."

"Of course." Gage gestured towards a doorway. "There's another pair of cots in there. I'm sure Maith wouldn't mind if you use his. Assuming he isn't using it himself."

Glancing around the small room, Damien realized Maith had vanished. He'd completely forgotten about the auer amid the greetings.

"We can share mine if he's asleep." Rae nuzzled against his ear.

Damien wanted to ask why Maith and Rae were sharing a room, but the invitation to her cot banished any such thoughts. He hadn't slept with Rae in his arms for far too long, and the idea made his heart thud.

With Rae close, Damien shuffled towards the room. Maith had left the door ajar, and it creaked as it opened.

The room was barely large enough for the two cots. Barrels and crates dominated the far wall, precariously stacked. The two cots ran parallel to each other, almost touching, and Maith already lay on his.

The auer opened his eyes, glancing at them before staring at the ceiling. "Good. You need rest."

Damien narrowed his eyes. "You think you could sleep in a different spot?"

Maith's gaze flickered to Rae, then back to Damien. He shook his head. "Not right now."

Rae's hand pressed to Damien's chest before he could voice a protest. "It doesn't bother me. Can we just sleep?"

Damien's body felt impossibly heavy, and it was the only thing that kept him from arguing the point further. He swallowed his bitter retort and walked with Rae to the cot, settling down with her onto it.

She curled up against his chest, her back to Maith, and Damien relaxed. Fitting as perfectly as he remembered, he nuzzled his face into her hair and took a slow, steady breath as their ankles tangled together.

He fell asleep before he could take another breath.

Rae flinched and whimpered, her grip on Damien's arm jarring him awake. Her nails bit into his skin and she let out a stifled cry, jerking away from him.

For an instant, the room spun, and he blinked to see through the darkness. The memory of where he was flooded into him, along with who he held.

Her feet shuffled, and she sobbed with a gasp of air.

He gripped her shoulder. "Dice, what's wrong?"

Rae curled in on herself, pulling her hands away from him. Her body shook, and she cried out again as if something was hurting her. Drawing a ragged breath, she choked out another sob.

She's still asleep.

He'd heard stories about soldiers with night terrors after surviving horrendous battles, even his father had suffered for years after his discharge from the military due to the loss of his leg.

Maith's hand closed on her upper arm, just above where Damien held her. "I can help."

Damien glared over Rae's convulsing shoulder, raising his voice. "I've got it."

Rae spun from him, flailing against the cot and rolling onto her other side, coming close to falling into the narrow space between the foot-high cots.

Damien caught her waist, tugging her in close to him. Ignoring her elbow striking his ribs, he buried his face close to her ear. "Wake up, Dice. It's just a dream."

Rae gasped, pushing him harder.

"Don't wake her." Maith sat up. He slid his cot back enough that he could sit on the floor next to Rae. "It will make it worse."

Rae yelled, and the auer didn't ask this time before pulling her out of Damien's grip. He held her back against his chest as she kicked out, nearly clipping Damien in the jaw. Stroking her hair, he whispered to her in Aueric.

Damien recognized some words, but the order he said them made no sense, which only infuriated him more. He sat up, reaching for her, but paused when she calmed against Maith's chest.

Her breathing slowed as she listened to his voice, the frantic movement beneath her eyelids ceasing.

The auer stilled his hands momentarily, lifting Rae from the floor. He gingerly placed her back on the cot next to Damien, who shifted to make space. Silently taking the Rahn'ka's hand, Maith guided it to replace his in the strokes through her hair.

Damien watched Rae's face as it returned to quiet sleep, caressing the length of her hair and along her temples. The anger in him faded, turning to astonishment and confusion.

Maith stopped speaking the words to Rae, cautiously waiting a moment before returning to sit on his cot.

"You've done this a lot before, haven't you?" Damien whispered, looking up at Maith.

The auer hesitated, but nodded. "It's why we share a room."

"How long?"

Maith sighed. "You know how long."

Damien flinched. "Why didn't she tell me?"

"You know that too."

He couldn't help the dry chuckle, almost turned sob. "Damn it, Dice. You should have told me."

Maith nodded. "I told her the same thing. She hoped they'd pass before you witnessed one of her..." He hesitated, trying to find the word. "Fits."

In her sleep, Rae nuzzled closer to Damien's lap, wrapping an arm around him.

"I was wondering if you could fix it." Maith motioned with his chin to her. "You gave her back her memories."

Damien looked up at Maith in surprise. He considered exploring Rae's ká to see if he could repair the damage, but working the Art in the auer's presence would be too risky. But now Maith implied something that made Damien's gut churn. "How..." He paused, but then shook his head. It was naïve to think someone wouldn't put it together. "Did you realize it on your own, or did Rae tell you?"

"She didn't tell me *how* you did it, just that you did." The longer sentences made the broken nature of his Common more evident. "She needed to explain why she didn't want to tell you about the nightmares."

"Because she knew I'd blame myself."

Maith nodded. "Raeynna never wished you'd acted differently and I'm relieved you could restore the lost memories. She would not be herself without them."

"Didn't I ruin everything for you when I did, though? Weren't you to be her husband?"

Maith chuckled. "I have plenty of time to find a wife. I'm not your enemy, as much as you wish it. I'm her friend and that's all. Yes, things changed between us, but she loves you. More than anything. I can't compete with that, even if I tried. We auer believe in a deeper love. You are her niané."

And she is mine.

Looking down at her peaceful slumber, Damien drew his fingertips across her jaw. He placed an extended kiss on her temple. "I don't know if I can fix it. I'm too weak to try right now. It will have to wait."

Maith nodded, taking a breath to speak, but hesitating.

Damien looked at him, studying the auer intently in the darkness. "What?"

Clearing his throat, Maith crossed his arms. "Do you understand the requirements of me to calm her each night?"

Damien furrowed his brow, chewing on his bottom lip. "I would assume it implies that sleeping arrangements like this are something longer standing." He considered for a moment if it meant the two had shared a bed. Jealousy bubbled in his gut as he realized Maith had likely slept beside Rae more than he ever had. But he swallowed to calm it before it took root.

I should be grateful for what he's done.

Maith nodded. "And sleeping arrangements is all they were. But she's afraid you'll be angry or question her loyalty."

She looked so peaceful now, curled up against his lap.

Damien twisted her hair between his fingers, trying to determine exactly what he was feeling. "I am angry. But not at her. Not at you. At myself. And of course I'm jealous, but only because I wish I could have been the one comforting her these last few months."

Maith fell silent for a few minutes, letting Damien swim in his own thoughts. His guilt. "Now that you can be the one, I'm sure you'll be better at it than I. I'll teach you the words, but I doubt you'll need them."

"I was wondering what the relevance of roses and rain were."

The auer smirked. "We used key phrases that she associated with calm while she was awake. They help during her fits. Should be easy for you, since apparently you speak Aueric?"

"Soon you'll know all my secrets."

Maith tilted his head and switched to speak Aueric. "Like how you restored her memories?"

"If we're stuck with you traveling with us, it's not like I'll be able to hide it from you. But I must ask you to keep it a secret. I can't pretend it's for Rae, it's only for me. The Council of Elders cannot know about what I am."

Maith quirked an eyebrow. "Now, I'm curious. Rest easy, the council is inconsequential for me. I'm a scholar, not a politician."

"In that case, I'd be curious to know what texts the auer might have in their libraries about the Rahn'ka."

Maith's eyes widened, and he sat up straight, speaking faster. "You're not implying that you *are* one. A manipulator of souls. Ancient Art-wielder haunted by voices. *Enemy* of the auer."

"Now you understand why the council can't know. And the voices have calmed down. I have them mostly under control now."

Maith exhaled a lengthy breath. "And you set foot on Eralas. I'm not sure whether to commend your bravery or damn your stupidity."

"How about foolishness?" Damien looked down at Rae, tracing her jaw. "I'd do it again if I had to."

The auer scoffed. "See? How could I compete with that?"

Chapter 13

JARROD PUSHED A STICKY PILE of black ooze with the toe of his boot, cringing. He lifted a hand, touching his throat where the beast's claws had torn his skin. Damien had healed him, but the thin scar left behind reminded him how close he'd come to death.

Again.

"What a disaster," he muttered, looking over the charred land. His voice still sounded gruffer, and he wondered if it would return to normal.

Some muck stuck to his boot, and he wiped it into the ash. With clearer eyes, he looked away from the carnage. His blood had boiled in the fight, reaching a peak when a Corrupted tackled Corin. He hadn't thought, still fighting his own attackers, before pulling the deranged creature off the man he loved.

Lowering his hand, he swallowed, swaying.

Corin's arms closed around him from behind, steadying the thief. "Maybe you should still rest? It's only been a few days, and you lost a lot of blood..."

Jarrod batted at his hands half-heartedly. "I'm fine." He leaned back against the soldier. The definition of Corin's muscles had returned and the strength of his body made Jarrod hesitant to pull away.

Corin must have sensed his uncertainty and wrapped his arms tighter, placing his chin against Jarrod's shoulder and kissing his neck. "It was crazy for you to pull that thing off of me the way you did. I almost lost you."

Jarrod turned his head into the touch, closing his eyes. "I'd do it again. With or without your brother here."

Corin shook his head, his freshly cut hair tickling Jarrod's earlobe. He didn't speak, holding tight to Jarrod from behind and leaning his head against his. His body stiffened, but he said nothing.

"What is it?" Jarrod placed his hand over Corin's.

Corin was quiet for another moment, squeezing tighter. "I'm not sure how to say it."

Jarrod turned within the captain's embrace, facing him. "Words usually help."

With his eyes shut, Corin chuckled and touched his forehead to Jarrod's. "Well, that requires finding the right ones first." He lifted his hand, touching the scar on Jarrod's chin with his thumb. "I know you are still Jarrod and still the man I love beyond all reason, but something has changed."

Jarrod moved his face away from Corin's, narrowing his eyes. "What are you talking about?"

Corin hesitated again, chewing his lip. "I didn't want to say anything, but after that battle... After what I saw you do..."

"What was I supposed to do? Let it rip your throat out?"

"You tore a head off with your bare hands. My sword could barely accomplish the same. Come on, Jarrod, you're not this naïve. Something's changed."

Stepping back, Jarrod ran his hands over his hair and turned away. His pulse hammered in his ears, but he tried to focus through it.

He's right. Something has changed.

Jarrod's gaze darted to the side as Neco's thoughts flashed into his mind. The wolf hunted and the thief's surroundings brightened. A haze hovered around some objects, but he ignored it and turned to Corin again. His breathing quickened. "Is that all you wanted to say?"

Corin looked something like the frightened rabbit Neco stalked in the bushes. "Yes."

Jarrod's shoulders slumped. "Why are you looking at me like that?"

"Because you look like you're ready to jump at me and I can't tell why."

Jarrod shook his head, reaching for Corin's arm. The soldier flinched, and he hesitated but stepped closer, touching Corin's wrist. "I'd never hurt you. Don't you know that?"

Corin glanced down to where Jarrod touched him, taking the thief's hand and entwining their fingers together. He lifted the back of Jarrod's hand to his lips. "Logically, yes, I know that. But that look in your eyes just now was the way you looked at the Corrupted before you ripped them apart."

Jarrod sucked in a deep breath. "Neco is hunting. Sometimes it's like I'm in his head. Or he's in mine."

Corin frowned. "And that's the only thing I can think of that might cause all this. Whatever Damien did to bond you and Neco together."

"I'll talk to Damien. I can't stand you looking at me like that."

Corin lowered his gaze to the ground, but took a step closer to Jarrod. "I'm sorry. You don't deserve it with everything you've done for me."

Jarrod pulled Corin into a tight embrace, revisiting the moments in battle where he'd felt the strongest. He hadn't considered it abnormal, but then he remembered how easy it'd become to best Damien in empty-handed sparring. The Rahn'ka had bested him half the time on previous occasions, but not once in Mirage.

What's wrong with me?

Sighing against his neck, Corin relaxed in Jarrod's arms. He pulled away just enough to look into his eyes. "Never doubt my love for you. Nor my determination to stay at your side. Not even this will scare me away, my future king."

Jarrod made a face. "Still going to love me when my days revolve around paperwork and politics? I imagine you destined for an adventurous life, not one sitting next to a throne. The ten years Eralas gave me have gone up in smoke and I can't do this without you."

"Ah, how quickly you forget my pension for forgery." Corin tapped Jarrod's nose. "While adventure may sound grand now, I don't fear the quiet days. In fact, they're sounding rather attractive after all of this." He gestured at the charred remains of his family farm with a frown. "I will be at your side, I promise. We'll worry about the details of how long I can remain there once you're crowned."

Jarrod scowled. "What does *that* mean?"

"I can't give you the things you'll need to be a proper king." Corin touched his cheeks. "I can't give you heirs to keep Helgath justly ruled, as much as I wish—"

"No." Jarrod shook his head. "There are other ways."

"Jarrod, you only just started admitting to those who have been your family for years that you prefer the company of men. I don't expect you to declare it to an entire kingdom."

Pulling him closer, Jarrod lowered his voice. "Then I suppose you'll be surprised, Captain. And it's not *men*. It's you. That's not changing. I'm not pretending again."

Corin finally grew quiet, meeting Jarrod's eyes. The soft brown in his looked doubtful, but he ran a hand back over the proxiet's hair.

Jarrod's heart twisted, and he leaned forward, claiming Corin's mouth. If he couldn't convince him with words, he'd have to do it with actions.

When he pulled away, he lifted a hand from his pocket, holding the gold chain still donning his whistle. He added his damaged signet ring to the chain and draped it over Corin's head.

Corin closed his hand around the ring, holding it tight as he looked at Jarrod. Releasing it, he brushed his thumb across Jarrod's scar. He remained quiet, studying Jarrod's face before his eyes darted over the thief's shoulder. He reached for the hilt of his sword as he took a step back.

Jarrod spun around, eyes landing on a single rider cantering towards them from the northern hill. He called to Neco through their bond and the wolf responded.

We have company. He sent the message mentally to Damien, moving to stand between Corin and the rider.

"Stay here." Jarrod walked towards the rider, glancing around, but nothing seemed amiss. Helgath wouldn't have sent a single person to kill him.

The rider slowed, stopping several yards away. "I bring a message for Jarrod Martox."

Corin stepped up beside him.

"You don't take orders well." Jarrod frowned.

"One of my flaws I suppose you will have to get used to, my king."

Jarrod rolled his eyes, looking back at the rider. "From who?"

"Lord Reznik Martox." The rider raised her fist to her chest.

"Shit."

Corin hummed. "Sounds like it's your turn to get some shit from your Da."

Neco bounded out of the southern trees, nearly knocking Damien over as he barreled past. The wolf stopped next to Jarrod, sitting on his haunches at the proxiet's request.

"What's going on?" Rae eyed the rider before looking at Jarrod.

"Message from my folks."

The rider dismounted, pulling off her helmet, and her curly blond hair caught in the wind. She tilted her chin down. "Are you him?"

Jarrod nodded, holding out a hand for the message.

She bowed at the waist, making Jarrod's stomach knot.

Need to get used to that.

Withdrawing a scroll from her maroon cloak, she placed it in his hand.

"Is it too much to hope for good news?" Corin glanced over Jarrod's shoulder at the scroll.

Jarrod eyed the wax seal belonging to his father. "Are there more of you?" He looked at the rider.

She nodded. "Aye, my lord, a half battalion waits east of Rylorn to escort you to a Martox galleon."

Jarrod clenched his jaw. "I see." Tearing the seal, he unrolled the parchment.

The woman scowled at Corin as he leaned further around Jarrod's shoulder to peek at the message.

> *Jarrod,*
> *It's time to return home. A ship is waiting for you in Rylorn to bring you to Lazuli. Don't delay. We've heard disturbing rumors of future attempts on your life. I promise things are different now, son. Come home.*
> *Your Father*

Jarrod rolled it back up, slapping it into Corin's hand, who passed it back to Damien and Rae. "Are you waiting for my response?"

The rider sidestepped, eyeing the two behind Jarrod. "Aye, my lord."

Jarrod looked at Corin, wishing he'd gotten those ten years. "I'll be there." He spoke without looking away from the captain. "Please alert the ship to prepare for five passengers."

Neco whined.

"And a wolf."

The messenger hesitated, but recovered quickly. "Aye, my lord." She mounted her horse, wheeling around and charging off to deliver his response.

Jarrod sucked in a deep breath and groaned with his exhale, turning to face Damien and Rae. "How's everyone feel about Lazuli?"

"Doesn't seem to be much of a choice." Damien frowned. "Will your parents support you and the rebellion?"

Jarrod hesitated. "It's been a long time, but people don't change. My father might, but my mother..." He shook his head. "Unlikely."

"We need to provide my parents somewhere to go." Corin motioned at the burnt ranch. "They can't stay here."

"Of course. We can take them to Rylorn with us, get them settled with a house there, and some new identities."

"Through the Hawks?"

Jarrod nodded to Damien. "We have a crew in Rylorn, unless your parents prefer Veralian. Either works. We can send Liala."

Corin's fingers brushed against Jarrod's palm. "I'll ask Da. Let them choose. It's the least we can do after getting the entire ranch destroyed. And forcing them to go into hiding."

Damien groaned, looking out over the blackened terrain. "It's strange seeing it like this. I knew everything was changing, but this just makes it more... real."

Jarrod sent a message to Veralian with Liala, containing instructions for Damien's parents. They opted for the capital, despite it being the site of their eldest son's death. They'd blend into the crowds there, and Jarrod felt more confident in the resources available to the Hawks.

In all the uses of Damien's power, the most convenient that morning was his ability to recall the horses let loose from the family paddocks during the fires. He even located the mounts they'd ridden from Veralian. Those with saddles went to the Lanorets first, leaving one tacked horse remaining.

The parting of the Lanorets came with extended hugs and kisses, with promises to stay safe.

Corin and Damien remained somber, even hours into the journey towards Rylorn.

"Dame." Jarrod drew the gaze of both Lanoret brothers.

Corin clicked his tongue, nudging his bareback horse with his heels to speed up, joining Rae in the front.

Damien eyed his brother's departure, but slowed to ride beside Jarrod. "Something wrong?"

Jarrod watched Corin's back, thinking through what he wanted to share with Damien. "I was hoping you could tell me." He looked at the Rahn'ka, his heart racing with Neco's as the wolf ran next to him.

His jaw flexed beneath his neatly trimmed beard. "Regarding?" His hazel eyes appeared dark, suspicious.

He already knows something's off.

"The bond. Is there something wrong with the bond?"

Damien looked away, staring ahead at the horizon, and Jarrod's stomach tightened. The Rahn'ka urged his horse a little closer to Jarrod's and sighed. "So you've noticed it."

Jarrod let out a breath. "Aye. What's happening to me?" The admission made his chest ache.

"I'm not sure, and I can't pretend to understand it." The look on Damien's face proved he disliked the thought as much as Jarrod. "But the bond is mutating in a way I hadn't expected. It's spreading to other parts of your ká, beyond those allowing you to communicate with Neco."

"So you knew about this already and you didn't think to say something to me?"

"I knew nothing concrete until I healed you. Felt foolish to bring it up when I might be imagining it."

Jarrod glowered. "That was days ago. You could have said something since then."

Damien sighed, rubbing the back of his head. "Didn't see a good time to bring it up. Besides, we're talking about it now, aren't we? I don't have a solution yet, so I was waiting."

Letting out a slow exhale, Jarrod cleared his throat, but the knot making his voice gruffer remained. "What *do* you know?"

"I know it's not just you being affected. I've noticed it in Neco too."

"His language usage. That's what you mean, isn't it?"

Damien nodded. "I tried to teach Neco words before, but they never seemed to stick. He always reverted to communicating through images and emotions. But lately, he's grasped Common, and started responding to me in it."

"Will the bond stop mutating?"

"I'm not sure. But I also don't know the extent of its effects on you, beyond the physical. I've noticed the change in your strength, but there must be more than that. Have you noticed any changes to your vision, or other senses?"

Jarrod looked at Corin, examining the haze surrounding him, drifting behind as he rode. He narrowed his gaze, wondering if his sense of smell could affect his vision. "I think I can see... scents," he muttered, changing his focus to the haze around Damien. Different and as distinct as everyone else. He shook his head. "I can hear better, too."

The hearing had been less of an advantage in recent days, after Rae's nightmares and Corin's painful conversation with his parents about Andros.

"What about emotionally? I hope Neco's anxiousness isn't rubbing off on you."

More than his anxiousness.

Jarrod clenched his teeth and shook his head. "What would it mean if it did?"

Damien heaved a sigh, glancing ahead at the others. "I should have done research and asked Sindré for help before I attempted to bond you two."

"Dame. Answer the question."

"I don't know for sure. But there are stories about the animals taking over the man, turning them into a mindless beast. But that's not what's happening. I won't let it happen."

Jarrod's insides knotted. "I... may have noticed some other things."

"Jare." Damien groaned. "If you've been noticing, you should have brought it up. I didn't think it was that serious yet."

"Just like you noticed something and brought it up without delay?" Jarrod sighed. "I was hoping I was imagining things. Plus, it kind of came in handy fighting those Corrupted."

"You mean when you got your throat ripped open?"

Jarrod frowned. "It was my throat or your brother's and I'd do it again."

"Well, next time, let him take the hit. Considering your bond and the fact that I've brought you back from death before, I'd rather not see if it'll work a second time the same way. The stories about men turning to beasts is nothing compared to those who return wrong from death." Damien ran a hand over the top of his hair, ending with a frustrated rub of his brow.

Jarrod looked sideways at him and tilted his head. "You know I can't do that."

"Gods, if I'd have known how stupid you'd get around Corin, I would have made sure the pair of you never met." Damien sighed, a distant smile teasing his lips. "I've never seen him like he is with you."

Jarrod's shoulders relaxed. "No? If it helps, I had no idea I'd get so stupid over him, either."

"Relationships were never a priority for him. No connection satisfied him, even those nurtured by the other person. We only served together for a brief period in Lazuli, and Corin had quite the reputation as a heart-breaker."

Jarrod smirked. "Sounds familiar. Hopefully, he'll spare mine."

"And you'll spare his." Damien gave Jarrod a suspicious look. "I don't know if I'd be able to put my brother back together again if he lost you, even with Rahn'ka powers."

The thief grinned. "That won't happen."

"You'll marry him then?"

Jarrod coughed, looking wide-eyed at Damien. "Am I supposed to ask your permission or something?"

"You better. It seems only appropriate. Unless you took the time to ask my parents."

Rolling his eyes, Jarrod scoffed, watching the captain's back. "I'd marry him."

"Your mother will *love* that. Not only have you started a war, but you're going to rule the kingdom with another man at your side."

Jarrod groaned. "My mother be damned. If I'm doing this, I'm doing it my way."

Chapter 14

RAE STRUGGLED AGAINST THE RESTRAINTS holding her wrists, and the rusted metal cut into her skin. She screamed as the whip lashed the bottom of her feet.

It's not real.

But the pain felt real.

Aueric words echoed in her mind, one at a time. Each calmed the fire in the room, diminishing the strikes against her. The rain misted her cheeks, the scent of roses drifting over the wind.

Damien's voice brought her home, where chrysanthemum tea brewed. She felt the warmth in her chest where his soul brushed against hers, their hands entwined instead of the cuffs on her wrists.

Her eyes opened, meeting the darkness of the room swaying with the rock of the ship. "Damien," she whispered, lifting her hand to find his face.

He caught her hand in his, bringing it to his cheek, and the stubble of his beard tickled her palm. "Shhh. I'm here." His arm around her waist tightened, encouraging her hips against his. His body felt warm, as it always did, a trickle of his power still seeping between them as his ká stroked hers to deepen their physical touch.

Rae kissed him, finding peace in his taste before pulling away enough to speak. "I'm sorry." Her lips still brushed his, banishing the nightmares.

"You don't need to apologize." He tucked her hair behind her ear, following the length back down over her shoulder. "I'll take waking up next to you in any form." He gave her a slow kiss.

Before their midnight affection could escalate as it often did, Rae pulled away, burying her face in his bare chest and breathing in his scent. "I missed this, Lieutenant." She kissed his skin, looking up at him.

His fingers playing along her back, he laughed. "What, no promotion yet?"

Rae grinned. "Is there a specific rank you'd prefer, my love?"

"It depends. What are my options?"

Rolling her eyes, Rae bit his chest. "You're fishing."

Damien twitched at the rough affection, but then he hummed. "Maybe. Can you blame me?"

Sliding to be eye-level, Rae touched her nose to his and ran a hand through his hair. "I suppose not. What's got you thinking about that again?"

Marriage, even if to Damien, still made her squirm. She cherished her freedom, her individuality, never wanting to become her mother. Though, she supposed it was unfair to assume the result would be the same. She loved Damien more than anything and wondered if her constant refusal would eventually deter him. The thought made her heart sink.

"I'm just thinking about it." His tone took on a defensive lilt. "But not with us, even though you know I..." He traced her collarbone. "Jarrod and Corin... I'm thinking about them."

Rae lifted her eyebrows. "Jarrod and Corin? You think they'll wed? Really? Jarrod?" She laughed, shaking her head. "You're kidding."

Damien wriggled in their bedsheets, shaking his head. "Jarrod told me he would. Despite everything, he wants to marry my brother."

Rae gaped at him. "Why?" She cleared her throat. "I mean..."

"It's bound to complicate things, but I suppose it's because he loves him. He wants Corin by his side in more than just appearance. It will flip Helgath on its head."

Rae furrowed her brow, contemplating the information.

She would never have guessed Jarrod to be the marrying kind.

If he can change his mind, maybe I can too.

"But what does Corin want?" She couldn't imagine marrying someone bound for the throne.

Damien shrugged. "I haven't talked to him about it. I've been trying to keep my mouth shut about this for the last week."

"You kept this from me for a *week*?" Rae smacked his chest.

"Hey, I thought you hated the conversation of marriage. I was being respectful." Damien rubbed the spot she'd hit.

Rae frowned. "I don't hate the conversation. I *dislike* the *idea* of being involved in one, is all. Other people are welcome to get married."

"Mhmm." Damien pursed his lips. "But you will forever be free of such frivolous bonds, I suppose? If I was a less secure man..."

Rae had thought about marriage more than she'd admitted, after spending extended time with Damien's parents in the bunker. With them for role models, she couldn't blame him for wanting it. Viola and Gage loved each other so deeply that it permeated every small interaction between them. Watching them as they embraced their two sons had made Rae's heart ache.

"You *were* a less secure man, if I might remind you." She kissed him. "Frivolous bonds have no place in my life. You are much more than that."

Damien ran his hands down her sides, playing along the bare skin past her cropped chemise. "I still believe my concerns are valid. Maith is such a... *pretty* man, after all."

"Maith? What does he have to do with anything?"

"Oh, come on." Damien frowned. "You know full well I've been horribly jealous of him for the past three months."

"Yes, but how is he relevant to this?"

"We were talking about my insecurities, weren't we?"

"And you still feel insecure about Maith?"

Damien sighed. "Not as much. But he's still pretty. And he's still *here*."

Rae grinned, kissing him again. "He's got nothing on you, Lieutenant." She pressed against him, rolling him onto his back. "I love you, you idiot. No matter who else is nearby."

Damien raised his eyebrows, lifting his head to the side of her neck and kissing her. "And I love you. Regardless of your distaste for marriage. And whatever chaos we're about to find ourselves in."

Rae smiled, weight lifting from her heart. "Thank you," she whispered, sliding her knees up to rest on either side of his hips. "Feel like sleeping?"

"You honestly ask that when you're in *that* position?" Damien's hands caressed up her thighs. "I hope you're not expecting me to say yes."

Rae laughed, pressing harder against him. "I'd prefer a no."

Chapter 15

"I ALWAYS HATED PUTTING THESE on," Jarrod grumbled. "The buttons are small and my thumbs don't work properly." The thief's hands shook, and he ran them over his hair.

Corin smoothed the wrinkles on Jarrod's shoulder, walking around him. "I'll get them." He started at the bottom of the delicate line of buttons on his vest. Working his way up, he tugged the material into place. The vest fit snugly, the muscles of his chest larger than they'd been before, but Corin wasn't complaining.

I'd much rather be taking his clothes off.

He forced himself to focus on the buttons instead of the way Jarrod's arms bulged against the thin white fabric of his shirt.

"Once we get you into this contraption, you'll look the part of a Martox." Corin turned to retrieve the long coat draped across the ship captain's chair. He walked behind Jarrod, holding it open as the thief slid his arms into the sleeves.

"Look the part... Add *act the part*, and we're back in the past, just eight years older."

"You're not that sixteen-year-old anymore." Corin bustled around to fidget with the jacket.

"No. Now I *definitely* know better."

"What do you think your parents will say?" Corin dared a look up at Jarrod's face. He was clean shaven, which Corin enjoyed because it allowed him to see the little scar he so loved. Jarrod had trimmed his black hair as well, cutting it close to his scalp.

"About what, precisely?" Jarrod fidgeted with his sleeves.

"I guess they have plenty to comment on, don't they?" Corin laughed, batting Jarrod's hands away to fix the sleeves and secure the silver buttons. "I guess what they'll say about the rebellion."

Jarrod's jaw flexed. "My mother will probably say that I'm being a child, supporting something so ridiculous. That I'm condemning our family with my actions and will start a civil war."

"Oh, she's just going to love me, aren't they?"

"Like her own." Jarrod's tone darkened.

Corin placed the decorative pauldron on Jarrod's left shoulder, latching the buckles across his chest, jostling the proxiet as he pulled them tight.

"I can't breathe."

Corin loosened the buckle a single notch. "How's that?"

Jarrod closed his eyes, shaking his head. "It's not that."

Pursing his lips, Corin raised his hands, pressing his palms to each side of Jarrod's jaw. He could feel his pulse hammering against his skin, even there. "Everything will be all right." He rubbed his thumb against his jaw and Jarrod met his gaze. "Just look at me and try to breathe slowly."

"I'm a thief, not a proxiet." Jarrod inhaled deeply.

"You're both, now." Corin focused on his eyes, pausing until Jarrod took another deep breath. "I'm sorry I've forced you into all this. I know you wish you could have waited the ten years the auer promised you."

Jarrod nodded but then shook his head. "This isn't your fault."

"It's a nice thought, but we both know that isn't true." Corin ran his hands down Jarrod's neck, tugging on the collar of the coat to position it.

"All right. It's partly your fault, but I made my choices and I stand by them, even if this thing itches." He pulled at the collar, scratching his neck.

Corin smirked and ran his fingers along the skin where Jarrod scratched. "If it helps, just imagine me taking all this off again at the end of the day. Assuming I survive it and your parents don't assassinate me on the spot for corrupting their little Martox."

Jarrod's chest rumbled. "I'd rather you take it all off right now."

Corin pouted. "After all that work?" He touched Jarrod's chin. "There isn't enough time for me to properly abuse such tempting thoughts."

Jarrod scowled and pulled Corin into him. "Later, then." He glanced down at the fine silver chains hanging from the pauldron. "What's the point of those, anyway?"

Corin sighed, trailing the silver across Jarrod's chest and latching them to little links on the right side of his chest. "It's a popular new style. All the rage amongst the uppity nobles, I hear. I'll have to get myself something similar."

"I like this better." Jarrod pressed a hand over Corin's shirt where the gold necklace hung with the whistle and ring.

"Well, yes. But who says I can't have both?"

Jarrod's eyes glittered with something Corin hadn't expected. "Oh, you'll have both. The country will expect nothing less."

An unusual buzz passed through Corin at the thought, making his stomach tighten. "Let's focus on me surviving meeting your parents first." He patted Jarrod on the chest. "We can talk about whatever that means later, Lord Martox."

Jarrod fell silent, looking away.

A stab of guilt joined the nervousness in Corin's stomach.

The ship's bell chimed, signaling they neared the Lazuli coastline.

Corin took a step back and eyed Jarrod up and down. The way he looked only threatened to make his heart beat even further out of his chest. Something about the way the clothing fit the proxiet's body and the deep maroon coat accented with fine silver stitching made Corin's mouth go dry.

"You look good." Corin cleared his throat and turned to tug on his own, less fancy, vest.

Jarrod eyed him, a strange softness in his eyes. "If it weren't for you, I'd have given up and gone in my plain shirt." The humor didn't reach the rest of his face.

"Good thing you have me then." Corin looked down, struggling to do his own buttons.

"Aye." Jarrod fastened Corin's vest for him. "Easier when it's not your own, I guess."

"Either that, or you're just too good at distracting me."

Jarrod paused, looking at the port window before back at Corin. "Do you mind giving me a minute? The distraction is mutual, and I need to think."

The request stung, but Corin locked the expression from his face. He nodded. "Of course." He patted the shoulder of Jarrod's coat, turning towards the exit. Determined not to look back, he closed the door behind him.

Damien stood against the banister of the ship, rubbing behind Neco's ears. His brother had put on far fancier attire than he'd seen him in for a long while, though nothing as regal as Jarrod's. It was a little reassuring to see that the tailor on the ship had also pestered Damien to appear more sophisticated for their presentation to House Martox. The fine black vest with pale blue accents matched Corin's.

"Where's Rae?"

"Getting dressed." Damien huffed. "The tailor kicked me out. And where is your other half?"

"Taking a moment on his own. Something about me being distracting." Corin leaned against the banister next to his brother, picking at the hem on his shoulder. "Did you get any kind of say in what you're wearing?"

"No." Damien tugged on the high collar around his throat, hiding his tattoos.

"Good, it wasn't just me then." Corin didn't much like the pants, in particular, which were tight in all the wrong places, loosening only just above his high boots.

The Martox galleon approached a pier separate from the trade and military docks of Lazuli. Corin knew about the private piers, having been able to see them from the city, but ships rarely stopped there. The Martox flag, usually only reserved for the battlements of their castle, had been placed on the edge of the dock, the silver filigree on the maroon cloth shining in the afternoon sun.

"If either of you laugh at me..." Rae's voice came behind them.

The brothers turned together towards her voice.

Damien choked out a gasp, and Corin chuckled.

Rae stood near the main mast, approaching slowly while holding the front of her skirts. They'd fitted her with a luscious green dress, cinched at her small waist. The square neckline accented her curves with a ruffle of white lace, which also decorated the ends of her long sleeves. Her silver ankle boots poked out as she walked, the narrow, short heel clicking on the wooden deck.

"My, my." Corin hummed. "Miss Raeynna. If I wasn't already in love with a man..."

Rae tilted her head at him, her wavy hair swaying with the motion. She stopped in front of them, looking at Damien, whose mouth hung open. "Do I look ridiculous? Tell me the truth."

Damien's mouth moved, but nothing came out.

Rolling his eyes, Corin elbowed his brother in the ribs. "You're supposed to say how beautiful she is. Not just gawk."

"Ow." Damien grunted, rubbing his side and batting at Corin. His eyes returned to Rae, focusing a little lower than her face.

Corin decided to give him the benefit of the doubt and believe he was looking at the crystal necklace resting against her tanned skin.

"Wow, Dice... Um... You look gorgeous."

Rae quirked a brow at Corin. "I might have to steal this dress."

"Can't let House Martox forget that you're a thief, first and foremost, of course." Corin grinned. "Besides, it shuts Damien up, so I will encourage such criminal behavior."

Rae laughed and stepped closer to Damien, kissing him, and the man looked like he might drop dead from sheer elation. "Thank you."

Maith emerged behind her, wearing nothing unusual for him.

"I see the tailor left you alone." Corin eyed the auer.

"Because I am far more prepared than the rest of you." Maith shrugged. "My attire is perfectly appropriate." He wore one of his long silken tunics, embroidered with fine stitching. Less layers than the rest of them, but fitting for the occasion.

More boots tapped on the stairs as Jarrod joined them. Neco trotted over to him, and the proxiet scratched the wolf's ruff as he approached. The only addition to his attire shone on his left hand. A new signet ring, in the same style as the one he'd given Corin, but unmarred across the crest.

"And I thought Corin cleaned up nice." Rae eyed Jarrod, who gaped back at her.

"I'm sorry, who are you?" Jarrod took her hand and pulled her from Damien to twirl her once.

The action made Corin's heart lighten.

"You're stunning." Jarrod kissed the back of her hand before letting it go.

"Better give her back before Damien starts to cry." Corin flinched when Damien punched him in the shoulder from behind.

The proxiet's gaze met his, and he smiled.

Corin stepped into him as Rae returned to Damien. He fussed with the already perfect edge of Jarrod's collar. "You look better," he whispered. "I worried you'd forgotten how to smile."

Jarrod cringed momentarily, but the smile returned. "I can't imagine what this is like for you. I'll do my best not to make it worse by letting my nerves get the best of me."

"Don't worry about me. You've got enough on your mind without that. But what's the worst that can happen? They're just your family, right?"

Jarrod stiffened. "Don't tempt fate. They've already dictated the approach order. And I'm supposed to walk with Rae, not you."

Ouch.

"Well, good luck wrestling her from Damien's arm."

"You misunderstand." Jarrod closed a hand around Corin's forearm. "I said I was supposed to, not that I would."

The captain's heart pounded, and he failed to lock the surprise from his face. He looked down to where Jarrod held his arm, then back up to his face. His stomach felt like it was back on the sea, being tossed around. "Do you think that's a good idea?"

"Aye. If I give them this, they'll know they can sway me. Walk beside me?" Jarrod offered his arm, vulnerability flickering over his face.

For what felt like the first time, Corin had no witty remark. His heart only hammered in his throat. Accepting Jarrod's arm, his body numbed.

Jarrod's stature relaxed, and he turned with Corin to disembark.

Neco loped on the proxiet's other side, surprisingly calm for finally being back on solid ground.

Two representatives of the House, who'd waited on the dock, followed behind them, with Damien and Rae after.

An entire battalion waited for them ashore, positioned in ranks that left a pathway between them. The walkway led directly to the raised portcullis of the castle's black stone exterior.

Being the center of attention was nothing new, having commanded, but this attention felt foreign.

Pretend it's like walking into the barracks, about to issue orders.

Yet, the feeling of Jarrod beside him threatened all sense of control. The proxiet's blatant disregard for what they had demanded left Corin disoriented. A strange combination of relief, pride, joy and fear creating a whirlpool in his mind.

The procession continued through the outer wall and into the expansive courtyard within. Black and white stone walls rose into towering stone spires, nestled behind a green lawn and brimming lake. The gravel road they walked on split before them, lazily circling around the pristine water, a fountain in the center. Offset from the two-tier decoration, a white bridge spanned the distance.

Their escort led them to the right, which seemed to be the more direct of the two paths.

Corin had held his tongue as long as he could. "How are you feeling?" He barely whispered, but knew Jarrod would hear.

"Like I can feel my mother's glare from here."

"Oh, is that what that feeling is? I thought perhaps I was just losing my ability to keep my heart in my chest," Corin grumbled and the thief smirked. "I've delivered orders in front of hundreds of men without so much as a blink..." He shook his head, squeezing Jarrod's arm tighter.

This is what I've wanted...

If he was to be at Jarrod's side, as he always dreamed, this was the life it meant.

They approached the intricately carved stairs leading to the front doorway, already held open by a pair of finely uniformed staff.

"And how does that compare to this?" Jarrod looked at Corin.

"Different. But the churning in my stomach isn't for me right now."

Everyone halted, turning to face the stairs. A man and woman descended, arm in arm. They dressed just as formally, Jarrod's mother in paler colors that complimented her olive skin, while his father wore maroon regalia with silver stitching similar to his son's. Their resemblance was uncanny, save for the grey peppering Reznik's black hair.

Sairin left her husband behind as she ran towards her son.

Jarrod's brow furrowed as his mother wrapped her arms around him, forcing Corin to step away.

"Oh, I only dreamt the rumors were true." She released him to look up at his face.

"Mother."

She swatted his shoulder. "Don't be so cold, we've been worried sick over you."

"Jarrod." Reznik's voice matched Jarrod's in tone as he eyed his son. The man's eyes misted with emotion and Jarrod offered him a half-hearted smile. "Thank you for humoring my summons. I'm glad it reached you. We have much to discuss."

"It can wait. I'd like to introduce you to—"

"Oh, you must be Corin!" Sairin reinstated the confusion on Jarrod's face, which matched Corin's. "Come, dear, it looks like Reznik will monopolize my son's time. Perhaps in the meantime, we can get to know each other?"

"Mother, we've had a long journey. I'm sure Corin would rather settle in, first."

"It's all right." Corin looked at Jarrod. He had to hope that Jarrod's mother's interest was a promising sign. "I'd enjoy that very much, Lady Martox."

"Call me Sairin. I'd like to meet your other friends, too. But something tells me I should get to know you first. Come. Do you drink tea?"

"It's been some time since I had the luxury." Corin steeled himself for the required formality, reminding himself this was not unlike talking to a superior officer. He glanced at Jarrod, who met his eyes.

Jarrod lifted his hand, touching his own chin, and Corin mirrored the gesture.

Sairin patted Corin on the arm, bringing his attention back to her before starting up the stairs.

Corin looked back to pass a silent exchange with his brother, who still stood with Rae's arm in his, forgotten by Sairin.

Damien looked about to speak when Reznik approached him, offering a hand in greeting.

Sairin paused near the door, asking one of her staff members to bring tea to the lower study.

When they entered the room, Corin tried to look bored instead of impressed. The study resembled a library, with tall shelves spanning two stories, a balcony rimming the second level. An enormous set of double windows stood with the curtains open, bright sun pouring through to fill the room with warm light. Beyond the window, Corin watched the red sails of the ship that brought them from Rylorn as they lowered to catch the wind.

So this is what it's like to be royal, I suppose.

"Come." Sairin gestured to a set of leather chairs beneath the window. "How were the accommodations for your journey? Comfortable, I hope?"

"Very comfortable, thank you." Corin approached the chair.

Damien and Rae hadn't complained about the luxury of their guest room, which had matched his. He never stayed in it, however, because Jarrod insisted Corin stay with him in the captain's quarters instead. But it'd be best not to mention that to Jarrod's mother, who Corin suspected would highly disapprove of their relationship. Sairin had condemned Jarrod's romantic preferences when he was sixteen, a catalyst for his decision to run away and join the Ashen Hawks.

But people can change. Losing Jarrod for eight years might have changed her.

Sairin settled into one chair, arranging the layers of her skirts around her small ankles. She looked so much younger than Corin's mother, but he supposed that had to do with the luxury she lived in. Her face didn't have the sunspots from working outside, and her hair was free of the grey that Corin had always known his mother to have.

He hesitated, but she gestured again to the chair opposite her.

"I don't bite." Sairin gave a girlish giggle and another wave of the hand. "Please, sit. I merely wish to talk. If Reznik insists on hogging Jarrod for now, I see nothing wrong in taking this opportunity to know you better. The message we received listed his companions, but not much more, sadly."

"If that were the case, Damien and Rae are far more interesting than myself. They might have proven better conversation." Corin sat. The stiff leather forced him to shift and try to find a more comfortable position.

Sairin shrugged with a tilt of her head. "Perhaps. But neither Damien nor Rae walked beside my son."

Corin pursed his lips, trying not to read into everything Lady Martox said.

Merely an observation.

"That's true. And I am proud to stand at your son's side."

Sairin lifted a hand to the serving girl who appeared in the doorway, and the girl brought over a tray. As she settled it onto the intricate table between him and Lady Martox, he eyed the two fine tea cups resting on fine porcelain saucers.

Sairin leaned back as the girl picked up an ornate teapot and filled the cups. The girl bowed her head before scurrying from the room.

"Am I to understand, then..." She picked up one of the tea settings, nestling the saucer in her palm. "That you are *involved* with my son?" Her tone was surprisingly gentle but Corin's chest tightened, regardless.

He eyed the tea meant for him, but left it, considering his options in answering Sairin and what he believed Jarrod would want him to say. When first learning about Jarrod's mother's opinions of her son's duty to carry on the family line, Corin had always prepared himself to lie to her. He'd suspected that the role for him to play would always be the lover who stood in the shadows. He wouldn't be a king. But when he'd mentioned such things to Jarrod, the proxiet had argued against it.

He wants me by his side. And there is no room for shame.

"I won't lie to you, Lady Martox—"

"Sairin, please."

"Sairin." The interruption disrupted his determined thought and filled it with uncertainty at saying her given name. "Jarrod and I are not ashamed of our love for each other, so I will not insult you by lying about it."

Sairin's shoulders slumped, and she lifted her tea to her lips. "I see... It is as I feared, then."

"With all due respect, I don't think there is anything to fear about it. I'd think you'd be happy that your son has found someone who would give anything for him. My intentions are genuine."

Sairin's lips formed a tight smile. "You misunderstand, young man. It is not you, yourself, who burdens my happiness. It's what you're seeking. My son was a kind boy, and I suspect he hasn't faltered from that trait. I don't doubt that he loves you, but as his mother, it terrifies me. You were nearly executed recently, saved at the last moment by a love-struck proxiet. If he will do that for you, I suspect his love has no limits. He'll die for your cause and then I'll truly have lost him." Her eyes glistened, and she looked out the window.

"You're speaking of the rebellion." Corin narrowed his eyes. "You think I am the one pushing him into joining it and that it will be his downfall?"

Sairin nodded. "You are welcome to correct me, if I am mistaken, but did you not talk Jarrod into being the rebellion's proxiet?"

Corin hesitated, unable to counter what she said. Jarrod had resisted joining the rebellion and had vehemently declined stepping into the role as proxiet. When he'd left for Eralas, Corin resigned himself that Jarrod wouldn't do it and began seeking alternatives. But then he'd been arrested and forced Jarrod's hand.

Staring at the intricate rug on the stone floor, Corin gritted his teeth. "I wish I could somehow express to you, ma'am, how important this rebellion is to the people of Helgath."

"And to you?"

"Of course. But it is so much larger than just one man."

Sairin nodded slowly. "I believe you, but the rest doesn't matter. As long as it's important to you, he will give you whatever you want."

Corin shook his head, swallowing. "No, you are giving your son too little credit."

Jarrod surely cares about the suffering of the people and not just me.

"Perhaps. But can you humor me and think of his happiness, for just this moment? He has a life here that he's returned to. A safe home and loving family. A bright future. He'll have none of those things with a rebel at his side. It's impossible."

Corin's back straightened, and he glared at the cooling tea he hadn't touched. "I do think of Jarrod's happiness in this. And I dare suggest that this *loving* home wouldn't be the place he'd return to should the rebellion fail today."

Lady Martox smiled. "Much has changed here since he left. I don't wish to argue with you, dear. I'm sure you can understand that as his mother, I only want the best for him. I'm sure you're a wonderful man, but Jarrod was fond of his betrothed, too. And her family has made it clear they'd be willing to keep the arrangement."

Eyes widening, Corin gaped at Sairin. "You seriously suggest that Jarrod follow through with a betrothal arranged eight years ago? I would've thought you'd realize it was a factor in his decision to run from this house."

"Dear, it's much older than eight years. It's been in the works since their infancy. And when Jarrod took a shining to her, everything became easier. While he may have told you it spurred his inclination to rebel, there are things you don't know." Sairin waved a hand. "But none of that matters. What matters is that my son survives the next month. The next year."

"I believe you don't—"

Sairin raised a hand, silencing him. "Please, Corin. Hear a mother's plea and promise me you'll think about it. It's all I ask. Think about what's best for the man you claim to love and will do anything for."

Corin bit down on his tongue, seeking the pain to center his thoughts. His mind whirled, prohibiting him from doing anything but what she asked. "Forgive my rudeness, Lady Martox, but I'm afraid my tea is not agreeing with me. I would like to take my leave, if I may."

Sairin rose from her seat. "Of course. I apologize if I've upset you. It wasn't my intention." She placed a hand on Corin's forearm and it took everything in him not to pull away. "And you have my deepest condolences for the loss of your brother. I can't imagine the pain your mother feels. Such a terrible way to lose a son."

Bile rose in Corin's throat, his mind tormenting him with the memory of Andros's death, his feet kicking at the air as he suffocated. No matter how he tried to banish the image, it wouldn't clear from his mind. Andros's purpling face transformed into Jarrod's, as it had in all of Corin's nightmares.

He emerged into the hallway outside the lower study, not remembering walking there. The door clicked shut behind him and the walls closed in around him. Staring at the polished floor tiles, he focused on the pale veins running through them to banish the images from his head.

Rae was not the only one who suffered from night terrors due to torture at the hands of Helgath. Corin usually woke up with cold sweat on his brow, but now it ran down his temples as he wandered down the hallway.

Impressive rib vaulting supported the ceiling, preventing the spires from collapsing into the living space. The stable architecture still felt like it was about to cave in on his head, and Corin turned down a hall he hoped would lead him outside.

Corin justified Jarrod's change of heart by believing the proxiet wanted to help the people of Helgath.

But can't he do that from his position in the Dannet family without joining the rebellion?

As the future patriarch of House Martox, he could influence politics and procedure, even if House Iedrus remained in power. All from the safety of his castle in Lazuli. He had no genuine need to be king. Jumping to those conclusions only proved how selfish Corin was.

Thankfully, even in the windowless hallways of the castle, Corin's sense of direction guided him through the castle kitchens to an unfamiliar courtyard. His gentlemanly appearance must have discouraged the staff from asking him where he was going as Corin pushed through the door and jogged down the steps. He could smell horses, signaling he'd accidentally found an exit near the stables, and tried to find comfort in the scents of his childhood.

Collapsing onto the step, Corin buried his face in his hands. He pressed his fingertips into his temples, pushing against the throb of his pulse.

"He sure is handsome. Even when he's frowning." A female voice echoed through the crack in the door behind him.

He tried to block it out, but something about the pitch in their voices permeated through his growing headache.

"Hush, you shouldn't be talking so blatantly. Besides, I heard he walked into the castle courtyard with a *man* on his arm."

"A man?" The other woman scoffed. "No way. Isn't he supposed to marry that noble girl? What was her name..."

"Evie."

"Right! Evie Olestin. I always liked the way she smiles and isn't afraid to say thank you."

"I hear her family might visit, since her *betrothed* has returned."

Corin growled, pushing his palms over his ears to block out the sound of their voices.

"Evie Martox has a nice ring to it."

"Give it a few months, at most. We'll be having a wedding here real soon."

Chapter 16

"I THINK THIS IS GOING pretty well, all things considered." Damien relaxed into the chair next to the ostentatious windows in Jarrod's private chamber. They had a remarkable view of the sloping valleys as they met the Helgath sea, and Damien considered how easily he could get used to it.

Neco thumped his tail on the floor beside Jarrod, watching birds flutter by the pristine panes of glass.

Jarrod quirked an eyebrow. "I think you're still drunk from Rae's dress."

Damien grinned. "She looked amazing." Leaning forward, he grabbed a decanter full of amber liquor. He popped the top, taking in the whisky's peaty aroma.

"And tell me again why you're here with me, instead of fawning over her?" Jarrod drummed his fingers on the wall next to the window he stood at.

"I'm playing the role of your best friend today to make sure you're doing all right with all this." Damien poured a finger width into two glasses. He lifted one to Jarrod's back, sloshing it around as if it would tempt him more.

The thief accepted it, downing the expensive liquor in one swig before handing it back for a refill. "Rae will love or hate my father. I can just imagine all the things he's showing her right now."

"I think you should be more concerned about all the dirt *Rae* has on *you*." Damien refilled his friend's glass.

Jarrod chuckled. "If my father finds out any of it, he'd probably just laugh. It's my mother's talk with Corin I'm worried about." His tone darkened, and he accepted the glass of whisky again.

Damien frowned and took a slow drink, enjoying the smooth flavor before he answered. "Corin will be fine. He can handle himself."

"You've never met my mother."

"True." Damien shrugged. "And from what you've told me, I should probably drink more of this before I do." He tossed back the rest of the drink and reached for the decanter.

Jarrod turned from the window, pacing towards his bed as he'd done several times already.

"Gods, man. Even with my barrier up, I can feel your ká bouncing all over the room."

"I'm a little agitated." Jarrod's empty hand twitched, and he rolled his neck. "Coming here was a terrible idea."

Damien laughed. "I fail to see the part where we had much of a choice."

"Ah, the power of the Dannet families."

"I hoped that my assault of questions in your mind during that unnecessarily long procession would help keep you distracted."

"It did. But did you have to mention proposing to Corin? I almost choked on the air itself." Jarrod drank his whisky, his pupils dilated, and he set the glass next to the decanter.

"I felt it was a topic worthy of my purpose." Damien took another drink while studying the small flex in Jarrod's ká. "Besides, the perfect occasion is coming in the next couple of weeks."

Jarrod met his gaze, pouring his own drink. "What do you mean?"

"Corin's birthday."

The proxiet stood straighter. "His birthday. Good to know, but don't count on living a marriage proposal vicariously through me."

Damien sighed, taking another slow drink. "Allow me some small joys, won't you?"

"Have you actually asked Rae?" Jarrod lifted the glass with a look.

"What's the point? She'll say no. Besides, I don't want to put her in that kind of situation when I'm aware of her feelings towards marriage."

"You're probably right."

"I thought you'd be eager to propose to Corin, considering the scandal it'll create in the eyes of your mother. Isn't that what you were trying to do by having Corin walk beside you?"

Jarrod furrowed his brow, studying Damien. "No. I did that because it's what I wanted, not to piss anyone off. I'm not trying to create a shit storm, I just want her to know she can't push me around anymore." His black pupils expanded to encompass nearly all his iris.

Damien nodded, lifting the decanter again. Without looking at the proxiet, he could sense the agitation growing. The invisible bond between him and Neco vibrated in unison with a low growl from the wolf.

Jarrod turned his attention to Neco, and the wolf calmed.

"That..." Damien gestured towards Jarrod with the decanter. "Would be the other reason I'm with you instead of Rae."

"What?"

"I'm sure it's the stress of the situation, but your—"

Someone rapped at Jarrod's door and they both stiffened.

Damien buried his senses beneath his barrier, locking them away.

The proxiet finished his third glass of whisky and set it down, stalking over to the door. He jerked it open and stilled.

A woman threw herself at him, wrapping her arms around his neck. Short blond hair swayed around her jaw, stick straight. Side swept bangs framed her gleeful, but otherwise plain face.

Jarrod awkwardly returned the embrace before pushing her back. "Evie. What are you doing here?"

The name sounded vaguely familiar, but Damien couldn't place it.

She grinned, her white teeth perfectly aligned. "We came straight away when we heard about your return. Ma and Pa are here, too. I could hardly believe the rumors. But you're here." She motioned to him excitedly. "You're really here."

Jarrod paused and then turned to Damien. "This is my friend, Damien. Damien, this is Evie."

My former betrothed. Jarrod's voice came through their bond.

Damien steeled the shock from his face, turning it into a smile as he stood. It explained the familiarity, because Jarrod had confessed the awkward situation to Damien during their months together in Eralas. But he hadn't mentioned the two of them were close enough to warrant a personal visit and a hug.

"It's a pleasure to meet you." Damien bent into a slight bow.

Evie curtsied and gave Damien a practiced smile. "A pleasure. Never thought I'd meet the infamous Lanoret deserter."

"Evie..."

Damien waved a hand, unfazed. Strangely, the words didn't sound so painful anymore. With Jarrod's recent decision to embrace his role, Damien had grown more accepting of his own. "Better to be a deserter than blindly follow what I no longer believe in."

Her eyes widened. "Bold words, considering where you stand."

"All the more reason to say them." Damien glanced at Jarrod. "But I am among friends."

"Friends, indeed." She looked at Jarrod.

The proxiet crossed his arms, and Damien helped himself to another glass of whisky.

Going to need this.

"I was hoping we could talk." Evie touched Jarrod's forearm. "Things have changed a lot since you left, but some things don't have to. My parents are thrilled that our arrangement is back on."

Jarrod's jaw flexed. "Evie, that's not happening. You know that." He walked away from her, copying Damien's desires and sipping another glass of whisky.

"Oh, I don't mean like *that*." She scoffed, stepping after him. "I know you'll never think of me that way..." Her gaze trailed to Damien. "Perhaps we should talk alone?"

"Oh no, I'm quite interested." Damien took a small sip. "Don't mind me."

Jarrod shook his head. "Ignore him, he knows everything, anyway."

Evie's eyes narrowed at Damien, but she quickly resumed her smile. "Less secretive these days?" She cleared her throat.

"Better company, perhaps," Damien muttered.

The woman's mouth twitched in the threat of a frown, but she exhaled slowly. "You will need a wife, despite your tastes. We both know it. And your mother would approve."

"My mother's approval means nothing to me."

"Regardless, if you honestly hope to challenge for the throne, you can hardly do so as a bachelor. What security is there for the country in a childless king?"

"You've thought this through." Jarrod downed his drink.

Evie averted her gaze to the ground for a moment with a firm nod. "I'm willing to bear your children even knowing that you won't love me like I do you. You can keep the company of men without my disapproval. I believe my offer is fair, and you'd be hard-pressed to find a better one."

Jarrod's jaw worked. "I appreciate the offer, Evie, but I'm not interested in a political marriage. I have never seen value in them, and you know that better than most. I have no reason to change, even now."

Neco, curled up on the rug, tensed as his head turned towards Evie. He barked, and she jumped.

"Hells, what is that?" Her voice rose several octaves as she backed up.

Neco stood, padding over to Jarrod's side, while Evie slinked a little farther away.

"My *dog*," Jarrod said dryly, then glanced at Damien. "Or maybe his dog. I don't know. Whose is he?"

Damien shrugged. "He started as Rae's, but I like to think of him as a free spirit."

"No one is a free spirit in this castle," Jarrod grumbled, scratching Neco behind the ears.

Evie sucked in a deep breath, holding her head higher. "I beg you not to dismiss me so readily. There's more I can offer."

Jarrod raised an eyebrow, but Damien could tell he wouldn't care even if she offered him all of Pantracia.

"I apologize, but I must tell you alone." Evie folded her arms over her layered red dress, waiting while Jarrod considered her request.

The proxiet looked at Damien and nodded. "Give us a few." *But don't go far.*

Damien eyed what remained in his glass and sighed dramatically as he downed the rest. "Very well." *I'll be right outside. Do you want me to listen in?*

Aye. I feel like I'll appreciate a witness.

Damien stifled his laugh as he crossed the room to the door. *So ominous.*

The door latched shut behind him and Damien settled himself against the wall beside it. Closing his eyes, he focused on Neco's familiar energy standing next to Jarrod.

Need to borrow your eyes and ears for a bit, bud.

The wolf responded with a pulse of agitated energy, passing across their mental bond in emotions greater than words. He replied after a mental huff, speaking in his newly acquired language skills. *Repay me in food. Pies. Liver pies.*

Ew. Damien smiled. *But you got it.* He knitted together the energies required. The first time he created such a bond with Neco, he'd needed to touch him, but months of practice had enabled Damien to link himself nearly flawlessly for a brief time from a distance.

The vision settled into Damien's head in a series of fuzzy images. They sharpened as the wolf's other senses compensated for the shades of blue and purple.

Neco padded away, but listened to Jarrod's rapid pulse. He curled up back on the rug, resting his chin on his front paws. His eyes darted up towards Evie's face, but didn't remain there. Instead, Neco focused on her hands, which she rubbed together nervously.

"Well?" Jarrod's tense voice sent a shiver through Neco. "What is it you think changes things so much? I don't need a wife anymore than I need a husband to accomplish anything."

Evie rolled her eyes. "But I have more power now."

"How so? It doesn't look like your family's station has changed."

"I'm not talking about my family. I mean me and just me. I have access to the Art, now."

Jarrod stood straighter and Neco's head lifted. "What did you do?"

Evie waved a hand. "It doesn't matter. We can use my power. Be unstoppable. Nothing would keep you from the throne with me by your side."

"Tell me the truth, Evie. You can't just *get* the Art. Where did it come from?"

"My... boss. He gave it to me. All I have to do is complete minor tasks for him..."

Damien's entire body tensed and it felt horribly distant with his consciousness inside the wolf. But Neco's body responded as well, rising to his paws.

Jarrod unfolded his arms, stepping back from her. "Did Trist get to you?"

Evie looked surprised. "How did you know it was her?"

"Because she offered me the same thing. But you took her up on it when I knew better. You fool! Why would you be—"

"Can you answer me? Is Jarrod in there?"

A different voice, apart from the others, interrupted Damien's thoughts. He felt something close tightly on his shoulder, ripping him out of Neco's mind. The whiplash made Damien's head suddenly pound as he blinked to recognize the face in front of him.

"Corin!" Damien's eyes widened. "Sorry, I didn't see you."

Corin scowled. "I've been trying to ask you if Jarrod is in his room and what in the hells you're doing out here."

"I, uh..." Damien sent a frantic message to Jarrod. *Corin's out here.*

Jarrod growled mentally at Damien. *Get him out of here.*

"Gods, little brother." Corin leaned in and sniffed. "Have you been drinking?"

Damien frowned, his mind whirling. "So what if I have? Come on, we should go find Rae."

Corin tore his arm away from his brother, frowning. "I came here to speak with Jarrod and I was told he'd last been seen going to his chamber. Then I find you out here in one of your stupid trances..."

Damien studied Corin, the tension in his brow and clenched fists hinted at the soldier's dangerous mood. He put his hand back on Corin's shoulder, tightening it when his brother tried to pull away again. "Corin, what's wrong?"

Corin grimaced. "I just want to talk to Jarrod."

"Now really isn't the greatest time. Please trust me. There are things you don't understand."

"Oh, I'm learning there is plenty I don't understand."

Jarrod's bedroom doors swung open and Evie stepped into the hallway, her cheeks flushed. She looked between the two of them and tilted her head, not bothering with her diplomatic smile. "Boys." She turned, walking down the hall.

Corin's frown deepened as he watched Evie walk away before turning back to his brother. "Who was that?"

Damien sighed and rubbed his forehead. "It doesn't matter, it—"

"Who... *was* that?" Corin's voice grew darker.

"Evie, she—"

Before Damien could explain any further, Corin threw his hands off his shoulders with an exasperated huff. He shoved past Damien and stormed down the hall opposite of the way Evie had gone.

Corin pushed past Maith as the auer rounded the corner. Approaching Damien, Maith eyed him. He opened his mouth to speak, but Jarrod exited his room at the same moment, slamming the doors behind him once Neco joined him.

"Where's Corin?" Jarrod looked at Damien

"I have a question." Maith lifted a finger.

Damien jutted a thumb in the direction Corin had gone.

"Did he see her?" Jarrod scanned for Evie.

Maith tilted his head. "Is this a bad time?"

"Yes. And I think he might know who she is. The betrothed part, not the..." Damien eyed Maith. "You-know, part."

Jarrod sighed. "Shit. I'd better go after him."

"Before you do..." Maith raised his voice and the proxiet finally looked at him. "Could you tell me your mother's maiden name?"

Jarrod's brow furrowed. "Leliset."

"Thank you." Maith continued down the hallway.

Jarrod shook his head and then jogged after Corin.

Damien caught Neco before he could bound after Jarrod, tugging on his ruff. "Better stay with me, bud."

Neco groaned, straining against the Rahn'ka before giving up.

Sighing, Damien shook his head and looked the way Evie had disappeared, then back at Neco. "Just what we needed to make everything more interesting... a Shade."

Chapter 17

JARROD'S PULSE HAMMERED IN HIS ears as he ran down the hallway after Corin. He'd half-expected to see Evie, but her news struck him like a brick to the gut. When the Shade prowling House Martox failed to recruit him, she'd evidently changed her sights to Evie. The tactic switch made sense purely because of Evie's inevitable joining by marriage to Jarrod. Trist, the Shade who'd tried to seduce Jarrod with power, clearly wasn't picky with which of them she corrupted.

Evie is a Shade.

His mind whirled with the implications. After learning much more about the wicked servants and their master from Damien, Jarrod had never been more grateful for his resistance as a teen.

Dealing with Evie would be unavoidable, but for now he needed to find Corin.

He turned a corner, descending a curved staircase, just in time to catch up to his captain on the other side of a spacious sitting room. "Corin." When Corin didn't stop, he caught him by the wrist. "Wait."

Corin spun, pulling his arm free from Jarrod. "For what, exactly?" His hard brown eyes glared.

"Whoa." Jarrod held his hands up. "What's wrong?"

"Don't treat me like I'm an idiot." Corin clenched his fists. "I know about you and Damien's little tricks. He was trying to get rid of me for a reason. And then I see your ex walking out of the room..."

Jarrod balked, shaking his head. "It's not like that. You know I have no interest in her."

"Well, maybe you should."

"What?" Jarrod gaped, scouring his mind for any hint to Corin's behavior. "What did my mother say to you?"

Corin's body sagged, his shoulders hunching. "Just things I should have already been thinking about. We both have plenty to consider, obviously."

Jarrod sighed, stepping closer. "I don't know what..." His voice trailed off as his mother exited a room down a nearby hall and started towards him at a brisk pace. "Look, let's talk about this later, all right?"

Corin took a step back from him. "Sure. Later."

"Please," Jarrod whispered through clenched teeth. "You'll join me later?" Despite the distance between them, he reached out and caught Corin's hand. He expected the soldier to pull away, but he didn't.

Corin looked down at their hands, chewing on his bottom lip. "I need a little time... But I'll come to your chambers later."

Jarrod squeezed his hand. "I—"

"My son! You've been home for hours and I've hardly seen you." His mother gently pried his hand from Corin's. "We've had no time to talk yet."

Stepping away, Corin tucked his hands behind his back and gave a curt bow. "Lady Martox." He pivoted, going back to the stairs leading to Jarrod's chambers.

Jarrod sighed, his body riddled with tension. "You haven't changed one bit, have you?"

"Now, now... It seems I'm not the only one. Come. I must talk to you now that your *father* is finished filling your head with nonsense."

Jarrod growled, but followed his mother to one of the castle's many studies. This one was small, with no windows. A skylight flooded the room with the sun's warmth, and Jarrod resisted the urge to unfasten one of his multiple layers of clothing.

"I'd hoped you'd grown up in all this time." His mother frowned. "And here you are, as selfish as ever. What are you thinking, coming home with a *rebel boy* on your arm?"

"You don't get to dictate my life." Jarrod slammed the door behind him.

"Maybe not, but I have more years than you. Do you know what you're doing? You're making foolish choices and for some trollop of a soldier, a *boy* of inferior blood. These rebellious beliefs are his, not yours. You will ruin yourself and this family if you don't start thinking like a proper man."

Jarrod could hear her voice, but had difficulty comprehending her words past the pounding in his head. His vision tainted, her form silhouetted by a haze of pink. Blood pulsed in his ears like a drum, demanding violence. Before his rage could manifest against his mother, Jarrod lifted a tea table adorned with books, a stack of papers, and an ornate lantern, and heaved it across the room. It crashed into a bookcase, splintering and sending parchment flying.

Sairin gasped, stepping back, wide-eyed.

"Do you ever shut up?" Jarrod shouted, breath coming fast. "I won't stand here and listen to you berate him, or me."

Sairin's mouth opened, and she took a step forward, but Jarrod's hand shot up and she froze.

"Think again before you try to talk to me or Corin. Or perhaps next time I'll *never* come back." He yanked the study door open, exiting the room and slamming it behind him.

Jarrod waited up for Corin in his chambers. The captain didn't show, and he paced for as long as he could, with Neco whining at him intermittently, until his body demanded sleep.

When he woke, Corin laid next to him, asleep. He laid on his stomach, arms tucked beneath the pillows. The thin pale scars Damien couldn't heal on his back stood out in the rays of morning sunshine

Jarrod's heart sank, wishing he could spend the day making things up to him. He had to get to meetings with his father. Rolling to face Corin, he touched the side of his face, tracing a fingertip down his jaw. Leaning forward, he kissed him, a missed calm washing through him.

Corin stirred, humming as his lips moved against Jarrod's to return the kiss before he even opened his eyes. It renewed gently, and the proxiet slid closer, running a hand over Corin's bare back. Rolling onto his side, Corin slid his rough hands over Jarrod's chest, daring him to forget all the trouble from the day before.

After far too short a kiss, their mouths parted and Corin's eyes blinked open. Touching Jarrod's jaw, his thumb ran over his scar.

"I'm sorry," Jarrod whispered, wrapping his arm around Corin's middle.

Corin's golden brows furrowed. "For what?"

"Everything. Everything that happened yesterday that upset you. I wish I could redo the day from the moment we reached the front doors."

Corin pursed his lips and glanced down at Jarrod's chest. His fingers idly played there, tracing small circles. "I'm sorry, too. But I don't blame you."

"Will you tell me what happened?" Jarrod guided Corin's chin up to encourage him to meet his gaze. "I can make some pretty educated guesses, but I'd rather you let me in."

Corin touched his wrist, turning it to his mouth, and kissed Jarrod's pulse. "Just a few surprises I wasn't ready for. Like seeing Evie walking out of your room."

Jarrod frowned. "I wasn't ready for that, either, if it helps. No matter what you hear, that's not happening."

Corin shook his head. "I don't even know why it got me so upset. I think it was more about Damien trying to keep me out. It felt like you were trying to keep something from me."

Only that Evie is a Shade now.

"This place can get under your skin, trust me, I know."

Corin gave a bitter laugh and nipped Jarrod's wrist. "I've noticed."

"Just talk to me, all right?"

Corin squeezed his hand and turned it in his to kiss Jarrod's knuckles. "All right. But only if you promise to do the same. No secrets between us, right?"

Jarrod nodded. "No secrets. I'll even share all the confidential things I'm sworn not to."

Corin smiled as their mouths met, shifting closer to Jarrod until their chests touched. The lack of hesitancy in Corin's lips helped the knot in Jarrod's stomach relax. He sank willingly into the affection, happy with each consecutive renewal.

A harsh knock on his door shattered his peace, jarring him from Corin's groaning lips. "I'm supposed to meet with my father this morning. Boring political stuff."

Corin traced Jarrod's jaw, pouting his lower lip. "Now?"

Jarrod nodded, kissing Corin's forehead.

"Do you want me to come?"

Jarrod reluctantly sat up, shoulders tense again.

Corin did the same, propping himself up with his elbows behind him, the sheets still draped across his waist.

"I haven't convinced my father to let any of you be privy to the discussions." Jarrod left the bed to retrieve a shirt. "He wants to talk about what my options are, considering what I've already done. I'll fill you in after, though, all right?"

Corin watched as he struggled with the small buttons, though his hands weren't shaking as hard as the day before. "All right." He frowned. "Perhaps it'd be best if I just hide out in here. I'd rather not run into your mother again."

The knocking sounded again, a little more insistent. "Lord Martox?"

Jarrod sighed. "Give me a minute!" He looked at Corin. "You can stay here all day if you want, but my mother will most likely be with me and Father, so you're probably safe. Plus, you can take Neco for the day."

Neco lifted his head off the floor and whined.

Corin eyed the wolf. "I don't think he likes that idea."

Jarrod smiled, pulling on a vest over his shirt. Unlike his usual attire, this one lacked the hidden knives within. "He just thinks you don't like him much."

"I like you fine... When you're not jumping on top of me in bed, stepping places you shouldn't."

"Neco would like to remind you that that only happened once." Jarrod grinned.

Corin rolled his eyes and stood from the bed, shuffling across the rug. He wore only loose burgundy pants that he must have found in one of Jarrod's drawers. The captain seized the front of Jarrod's vest and tugged him close. "Make sure you only agree to what you really want. Don't let anyone push you into anything you don't."

Jarrod narrowed his eyes, running a rough hand through Corin's hair. "That won't happen, you know that. *You* may sway my mind, but none of them hold any power over me. I promise."

Corin studied him, his eyes piercing deeper than Jarrod had felt before. He broke the stare, sending an unexpected shock through the proxiet.

"Are you all right?"

Corin half smiled. "I'm fine. You don't need to worry about me." He patted Jarrod's chest a little firmer. "Go do king stuff."

Uncertainty tugged at the side of Jarrod's mouth, but he nodded. His father would grow impatient if he delayed too long. "Make yourself at home, all right? What's mine is yours." He turned, heading towards the door.

"I know." Corin's tone lightened. "I already stole your pants."

Jarrod laughed. "They look good on you." He tugged the door open and a staff member waited in the hallway for him. Looking back at Corin, he smirked. "I'll take them back later."

Color rose in Corin's cheeks and he smiled more genuinely. "Something to look forward to then." He lifted his hand and touched his chin to mirror Jarrod's scar.

Jarrod mimicked the action, silently telling Neco to stay with Corin for the day.

When he entered the strategy room, his father already stood over the long table donning a map of Helgath. Maroon flags represented the five Dannet families. Gold accents for House Iedrus, silver for Martox. The other three's flags were rimmed with bronze, copper, and iron.

His mother stood by a window, looking over a parchment.

A man, occupying the space next to his father, looked up and smiled.

Frederix, his father's political strategist.

Makes sense.

"If you want to be taken seriously, work on your punctuality." Reznik smiled.

Jarrod smirked. "Are you kidding? This *is* punctual. I made it here before breakfast."

Sairin sighed. "This isn't a joking matter. We have an actual problem on our hands."

Resisting the urge to roll his eyes, Jarrod took a seat at the table and everyone else followed suit.

"Unfortunately, your mother is right." Frederix opened a folder. "Because of the declaration of protection for the Lanoret family, House Martox is already at odds with Iedrus. To properly gauge the support of the other families, we need time that we no longer have. The only option is to retract the protection order and proceed as if it never happened."

Jarrod stiffened. "Not a chance. That order is—"

"Son, they're traitors to our country." Reznik's tone was gentle. "Regardless of your friendship, Damien still deserted his sworn duty and Corin committed—"

"Aye, but they aren't traitors to our country. They're traitors to House Iedrus. The time has come for a change in power and I won't persecute the Lanorets for seeing it before I did. Iedrus is corrupt beyond reproach."

"You sound so certain of that, but how can you know?" Sairin motioned with a hand. "You've been off hiding from your duties, doing gods know what."

Jarrod laughed despite himself. "Hiding! No, mother. *You've* been hiding. Here in the safety of your beloved castle. I've been out there with the people. I've seen things you can't imagine. How can I know? I know because I've lived as one of the common people. I've witnessed injustice and corruption first hand, so don't you dare ask me how I know." His voice raised, and he exhaled slowly to bring it back down. "You wouldn't last a day out there without your name."

"Jarrod." Reznik kept his voice level. "I remind you to maintain your temper. These emotional decisions got our House into this predicament."

Jarrod closed his eyes, willing patience. "I won't retract the order."

"Only because he's sharing a bed with the harlot captain."

His temper flared, but he hardened his expression. "Perhaps removing your *emotion* on the matter would help, Mother."

Sairin's glare persisted, the muscles in her jaw twitching. She opened her mouth, but Reznik lifted a hand to stop her.

"Frederix, what are our options if the order remains in place?"

The advisor cleared his throat. "We would have a brief window to address the issue. The limitation period provides House Martox with three months to maintain the protection order in defiance of House Iedrus or dissolve it. From what I understand, Jarrod will maintain the order, officially signing it into law. The order will then proceed to House Iedrus, where the king will either accept your order or reject it."

"And if he rejects it, Jarrod must challenge the throne or be charged as a traitor if he still refuses to negate the order." Reznik sighed.

Jarrod nodded. "He'll reject it. And I will challenge for the throne."

Sairin choked on a laugh. "To what end? House Iedrus has been in power for hundreds of years. Besides, none of the Dannet families will support a man with no possibility of an heir. It will throw Helgath back into war the moment House Martox's reign ends with your death."

Jarrod clenched his teeth. "If those are your only concerns, Mother, I think we're doing all right. Perhaps, for a moment, you can put aside your personal feelings on the matter and consider there may be alternative solutions to the *problem* you keep bringing up."

"So you will wed, then?" Reznik tilted his head. "A union may be a potential catalyst for support."

"Aye. I will wed, but only if my *harlot* captain is willing."

"You dare..." Sairin hissed, murder in her eyes. "You will do no such thing."

Jarrod's hand balled into a fist, but he kept his tone even. "I will do as I please. I will do what's best for this country and if you don't like it, relocate."

Sairin opened her mouth, but Reznik lifted a hand again, rubbing his forehead with the other. "Matters of marriage aside, we don't have the forces to make a show to the other Houses to gain their support and avoid war. Even if we swayed one or two and civil war commenced, we don't have the troops required to defeat House Iedrus."

"This is also assuming we find proper grounds for making such a claim." Frederix tapped a finger on the table. "Proof of pure blood must be established."

Jarrod sighed, ignoring Frederix. "We have the support of Eralas's armies."

The room silenced, all three sets of eyes staring at him.

Taking a deep breath, Jarrod filled them in on the deal he made with the Council of Elders, leaving out the part that involved Rae.

"With the auer armies on our side... This might be possible." Reznik looked at Frederix, who nodded his agreement.

"Iedrus will try to kill you," Sairin whispered and Jarrod saw a hint of caring in her eyes. Concern about him or her only heir, he wasn't sure which.

"They already have. And you're right, they'll try again. I'm prepared for that."

"Aye, but are your friends?" Reznik leaned back in his chair.

Jarrod nodded. "Quite, I assure you."

"We heard a disturbing rumor prior to your arrival here." Reznik glanced at his wife. "Are you involved with the Ashen Hawks? They broke Corin out of prison in Veralian, but you know that."

Jarrod shifted in his seat for the first time, hating the memories of that day. "I am. And they will prove formidable allies when the time comes."

"An alliance with criminals?" Sairin's eyes widened. "Have you gone mad?"

"With our own armies, the Hawks, and Eralas, we'll be unstoppable." Jarrod glared at her. "The Hawks are more loyal than anyone here and already fight for the people every day. Iedrus propaganda would have you believe otherwise."

"And what of the rebels?" Frederix wrote something down. "This... captain you mention, he is the one who was charged with recruiting for such a cause, correct? His connections may prove fruitful in continuing to reap support. And a union with him would solidify their support. The name Lanoret is already known throughout the entire kingdom."

"Aye," Reznik agreed, to the obvious disdain of his wife. "But only if he can still contact those within Iedrus's military." He paused, drumming his fingers on the table. "We will draft the order of protection today for signing, but I want you to think about it before executing it. These things don't go by air messenger and will take time. Chances are, we won't hear Iedrus's official decision on the matter for several weeks."

Jarrod nodded. "I can do that."

"Despite the illusion of time, there is another matter we should discuss immediately." Frederix settled his quill onto the table. "We already know that this will escalate to the point in which we must make a show of strength to the other Houses. Prove that Martox is ready to rule. Part of that show requires you to establish your council."

Jarrod nodded again. "I will begin working on it and see you back here to sign the protection order this afternoon."

"Very well." Frederix nodded, then glanced at Reznik. "I will draft the order."

Over the rest of the day, Jarrod scrawled in a notebook, choosing advisors and masters for his council. He carried it with him to each meal and meeting, trying to come up with names in between discussions. Many of those who sat at his father's table when he ran away still did, but since he didn't know any of them beyond a name, he didn't have enough faith to put them in his most trusted positions.

The king's council needed a chief vizier to oversee the Art of the country. It was the easiest filled because the auer would make that decision for him.

Personal advisor, which Jarrod left blank.

Trade minister, also left blank.

Political strategist, where he jotted down Rae's name. She had a vast understanding of Helgathian politics, beyond what he'd expected.

Master of war. His graphite hovered over the parchment for an extended period before he wrote. *Corin Lanoret.*

He filled in Damien's name next to personal advisor.

Jarrod took a deep breath, then looked out the dark window. The sun had set some time ago, without him noticing. He'd signed the protection order hours ago, but it wouldn't depart for Veralian until morning.

Closing his notebook, Jarrod heaved a sigh. He needed to talk to his friends about their names being on the list before he could approach his family with his choices.

Which is bound to go well.

When he returned to his chambers, Corin slept already, and Neco was curled up near the window. His first inclination was to wake him, but he opted not to.

In the morning, Jarrod was summoned before Corin woke, so he left an apologetic note and departed for his early meetings.

The routine continued over the next weeks and Jarrod grew frustrated. He hardly saw anyone other than his parents and their advisors. He hadn't even kissed Corin in days, and it ate at him.

The only hope he'd hidden away laid in the surprise he planned for Corin that night for his birthday. Jarrod cleared his schedule for the evening and had arranged a private meal. The frigid weather leant little opportunity to eat outside and nothing could match the privacy of his chambers.

Jarrod set the table while Damien distracted his brother. He lit candles and, when the kitchen staff brought the platters, he arranged them on the white tablecloth. Steel domes covered their contents, and two porcelain plates set with silverware at their sides. A black, fist-sized box sat on Corin's plate, adorned with a solid silver bow.

His heart beat furiously in his ears, as he hoped the captain wouldn't think his efforts misplaced. He missed Corin's usual affinity for teasing, despite how it had irked him before. It'd been too long since they'd been able to relax enough to fall into their old ways.

Please make fun of me for being a sap.

He fiddled with one of the cloth napkins. The aroma of roasted venison filled his senses, and he poured two glasses of wine.

Hope you're ready. Damien's voice echoed in his mind. *He's on his way.*

As I'll ever be. Keep Neco with you and don't even think about trying to eavesdrop.

Oh, I don't want to, Damien sounded amused, even in thought. *Trust me.*

One of the doors to the chamber swung open and Jarrod turned from where he stood next to the table.

Corin looked up in surprise, hovering in the half-open doorway. The shock slowly faded into a soft smile as he closed the door slowly behind him. "What's this?"

Jarrod crossed towards him, taking Corin's hand. "I wanted to celebrate your birthday with you."

Shaking his head, Corin squeezed Jarrod's hand. "I should have suspected Damien told you, especially when he was very insistent that we spend time together today."

Jarrod smirked. "You could have told me yourself."

"I didn't feel it was important enough to outweigh everything else."

"Of course it is. I just wish it didn't take your birthday for us to find some time together. I promise it won't always be like this."

Corin looked down at their hands, swaying them slightly between them. "I hope not." His attention turned to the table under the windows. "You arranged all this for me?"

Jarrod smiled and nodded. "It's not that impressive, but that's what happens when a proxiet sets a table instead of the staff." He led Corin towards it while walking backward. "Are you hungry?" He chose a glass of wine and offered it.

"I'm always hungry." Corin smirked, taking the glass. "But you really didn't need to do this, Jarrod." His face looked oddly grim.

Jarrod shook his head. "I definitely did. I should have done more. Are you disappointed?" Shoulders slumping, he tried to decipher where he went wrong.

"No. Just surprised." Corin touched Jarrod's jaw. "Can't say I've ever had a proxiet set a dinner table for me."

"Is my political position the only unique distinction in that statement?"

It evoked a slight laugh from Corin, who took up the other glass of wine and put it in Jarrod's hand. "My, are we perhaps jealous, my Lord Martox?"

Jarrod's stomach rolled over. "Can you blame me?" He quirked an eyebrow. "You didn't answer the question."

Corin rolled his lips together as if contemplating answering. "Perhaps another has made the attempt. However." He gently clinked his glass against Jarrod's. "I've never accepted before." He lifted the glass to his lips, taking a slow sip. He somehow made the action look sensual and Jarrod's blood heated.

"I'm the lucky one, then. You should probably sit before you distract me from my purpose."

"Are you so easily distracted?" Corin played with the hem of Jarrod's collar. "I've had so few chances to explore the advantages of that lately."

Jarrod hummed. "It's a fault I blame you for." He eyed Corin's recently cut hair, unable to recall when that had happened. "I'm sorry I've been so absent."

"You have excellent reasons. Come, I'm actually hungry and those plates smell too tempting to ignore any longer." Leaning in, he kissed Jarrod on the cheek before he crossed around him towards the table.

He took a moment to admire the settings, tracing a finger

along the edge of the table. He caressed the smooth surface of the silver bow on the black box Jarrod had set on his plate. "Is this for me, too?"

Jarrod walked to his side of the table and nodded, anxiety building in his gut. "If you'll *accept* it. I'm sure you've turned down many gifts from others."

Corin smirked as he took his seat and set his wine aside. "Accepting gifts just complicates things." He touched the lump beneath the collar of his shirt, where the gold necklace and ruined proxiet ring hung. "Though, I think we've already well passed that point. Should I open it now, or later?"

A smile spread over Jarrod's face, and he sat. "Now?"

Corin nodded and lifted the black lid from the top of the box. Within it, on a satin pillow, sat a solid silver clasp meant to secure his cloak. The Martox jeweler had formed the silver into the Martox crest, with the initials 'CL' emboldened over top.

Corin's breath stopped as he lifted the gift from its box, nestling it in his palm. "Jarrod..." He opened his mouth again, but nothing came out. He clearly understood the significance.

Jarrod's heart raced. "Do you like it?"

He hesitated, twisting the clasp in his hand. "I thought only official members of House Martox are allowed to wear the crest with their initials?"

"Traditionally, that's true." Jarrod remembered the look on his father's face when he'd asked where to get one made. "But these are less than traditional times. And one day, perhaps you will be an *official* member of House Martox." His mouth dried as he watched Corin, suddenly very aware of his own tongue. He hadn't planned on being so forward, but somehow, his feelings ended up utterly exposed.

Corin ran his finger slowly over the edge of the pin, staring down at it. "Jarrod." His voice sounded hollow. "You shouldn't be making promises like this."

Jarrod's stomach sank. "I... I thought..." Breath hardened in his chest. "I don't understand. Has something changed between us?" He swallowed, but it did little to wet his throat.

Corin placed the pin back into the box. He kept his eyes averted, staring at the table. "This kind of change was inevitable, and we were just fooling ourselves into thinking it wouldn't happen." He gripped the edge of the table, his knuckles whitening. "I'm no good for you. Not with everything that's going on."

Jarrod's mind struggled to keep up. "But everything that's going on is *because* of you. I need you. Forget the pin. It doesn't have to be a promise of anything."

"That's my point." Corin finally looked up. "*Because* of me. Would you honestly be making these choices without me pressuring you into the rebellion?"

Shaking his head, Jarrod rapidly reflected on how the conversation took the turn it did. "Yes. Well, no. But that would be a bad thing, because this is what I *should* do, and you showed me how." He rose from his seat, kneeling in front of

Corin. "You only showed me it was possible, but no, I never wanted to do this without you. I *still* don't want to do this without you. That was the deal, that I'd have you by my side."

"But you don't *need* me. I only confuse the matter. If you really believe in the cause, I'll complicate the road to the throne. I threaten what you are capable of by being selfish in my feelings for you."

Jarrod reached for Corin's hand. "I don't care what the road there looks like, none of this is *worth* it without you," he pleaded, his pulse deafening his ears. "Don't do this, Corin."

Corin didn't pull away, but looked sadly down at their hands, shaking his head. "Please, don't make this harder than it already is. We can't keep fooling ourselves that this will work. You're going to be king and I'm just a soldier."

Jarrod shook his head, frantic for a way out. "Then forget it. Forget all of this and we'll leave and pretend it never happened." He stood, pulling Corin's hand. "Let's just go, we can—"

Corin tugged his hand back into his lap. "See, this is what I'm talking about. You're willing to throw everything away *for me.*"

"What better reason is there?" Jarrod's eyes burned.

The chair squealed across the floor as Corin pushed it back to stand, turning away. His shoulders hunched as he ran his hands over his face. "We can't do this, Jarrod. I can't allow you to keep putting me above your duties and our country. Above yourself. You don't need me mucking all this up, and I wish you could see that I'm trying to do this for you. No matter how much it hurts us both, this is for the best. We can't keep doing this."

Jarrod kept shaking his head, replaying where he should have made different choices.

We should never have come here.

Turning his back, he fought to understand what was happening. He walked away, hardly aware of the floor under his boots, and stopped in front of the window. Clenching his jaw, he hardened his resolve. No power in the world could make Corin do something he didn't want to.

And if he doesn't want to be with me...

His heart ached, and his hands shook.

Corin's boots shuffled on the floor closer, but the embrace Jarrod craved never came. "I'm sorry. I... we just can't... I'll go."

Blurry-eyed, Jarrod shook his head. "No, Corin. *We* can. *You* can't."

"You're right." Corin's voice was farther away. "I wish you could understand that I'm doing this because I love you. You'll be better off." The door clicked open.

Anger surfaced in Jarrod's chest. "You're just as bad as they are." His voice rose. "Dictating how my life should look. If you're leaving, gods, just *leave*." He closed his hand into a fist and leaned it against the wall, but it still shook.

Corin said nothing, slamming the door behind him.

Chapter 18

RAE STOPPED IN THE HALLWAY when one of the doors to Jarrod's chamber opened. She'd just exited her and Damien's room the next hall over, on her way to meet him in the dining hall.

That's odd. They should still be having dinner.

When Corin stepped into the hallway alone, her stomach sank. But when he slammed the door behind him, she frowned.

"Corin?" She slowed her pace to approach him. "What happened?"

The captain's body shook, leaning for a moment against the closed door before he pushed away from it. "Something that should have happened a long time ago." He stepped around her and started down the hallway.

Rae caught his forearm, her chest tightening. "What did you do?"

"Let me go, Rae."

Jarrod's angry yell accompanied a thunderous crash from inside the room and Corin flinched.

Her grip tightened, and she gritted her teeth. "What. Did. You. Do?"

Twisting his wrist, Corin tore his arm from her. "I ended it." Before she could react, he spun on his heels and continued down the hallway at a quickened pace.

Rae's heart squeezed, and she gaped at his back as he rounded the corner. "You're an idiot!" Looking down at the floor, she ran a hand over her braided hair. "Shit."

Turning, she walked to Jarrod's door and opened it without bothering to knock. Stepping inside, she gasped when a knife flew past her head and sank into the wall. She froze, meeting Jarrod's fiery gaze, but then kicked the door closed behind her.

Ignoring his closed fists, she stalked towards him and pulled him into a hug.

His body stiffened before his arms wrapped around her.

"Fuck. I'm sorry." She held him tighter as he slumped into her.

They stood together for several moments before he pulled away, his face hard.

Rae touched his cheek, never having seen him so distraught.

"What can I do?" She glanced sideways at the overturned table. Platters and food spread over the floor, broken shards of porcelain and glass reflecting the light of the candle still sputtering on the tiled floor. With a whisper of effort, she snuffed it out.

"Nothing." Jarrod's voice was gruff. He crossed to the wreckage on the floor and retrieved a silver object. Turning it over in his palm, he returned to her. "Take this. If I keep it, it'll end up at the bottom of the lake."

Rae looked down at the Martox crest and nodded, pocketing it.

Jarrod turned away, walking towards the window and kicking one of the steel domed covers out of his way.

"He'll come around. Do you want to talk about it?"

Jarrod shook his head. "No, he won't. He doesn't want this."

Rae sighed. "But I thought you two..."

"I did, too." Jarrod turned his head, his profile outlined by the moonlight. "He thinks I'll be better off without him."

Taking a deep breath, Rae tried to hold back her questions. "And what do you think?"

Jarrod paused, his jaw flexing. "I think I'd like to be alone, if that's all right."

Rae nodded even though he couldn't see her. "I'll come check on you later." She eyed the knife in the wall on her way to the door and glanced at Jarrod. Making a face, she yanked the blade from the wall and slipped it into the back of her pants before exiting, closing the door behind her.

Looking towards the dining hall, she grumbled under her breath and instead walked in the direction Corin had gone. After taking a few paces, Evie turned the corner ahead, approaching.

The blond woman made eye contact and gave a forced smile as she passed.

Rae held her breath as she kept going, glancing behind her as she reached the end of the hall to see Evie stop at Jarrod's chambers. Briefly, she debated going back, but decided Jarrod probably wouldn't even open the door.

While continuing down the wide halls, she hesitated at each room to peek inside, but didn't find the soldier. Rounding another corner, a draft brushed over her exposed skin and she shivered at the winter air. One of the castle's double oak doorways stood partially ajar, the culprit for the chill blowing in from the gardens. She hurried towards it, prepared to close it, but looked outside before she did.

Corin sat on a stone bench beyond a barren iron archway, the brown vines having shed their leaves for winter. He didn't seem to notice her, despite being turned sideways, his chin tucked into his chest. He shivered in the cold, hands locked behind his neck.

Sighing, she opened the trunk next to the exit, pulling out a clean woolen cloak left there by the staff for when they needed them outside. Stepping quietly into the garden, she closed the door most of the way behind her before approaching the captain. She draped the cloak over his shoulders and he lifted his head minutely.

His hands closed on the wool, tightening it around his shoulders. "Didn't think you'd be interested in checking on me." His voice quavered. She couldn't tell if it was the cold or the emotion, but his eyes shone.

Rae sighed out a breath of mist and motioned to the bench. "Can I join you?"

Corin shrugged, the motion exaggerated by the cloak. "Can't promise I'm pleasant company." He eyed her, frowning. "Aren't you cold?"

Sitting next to him, Rae touched his back. "It's not too bad out here. My auer blood helps me adapt. It's barely even winter."

With a nod of understanding, he tugged the cloak tighter.

"What's going on?"

"I thought I made it clear in the hall. I ended it." Corin looked away, gaze unfocused.

Rolling her eyes, Rae pulled the silver crest from her pocket, examining it in the pale light of the garden lanterns. "Was it this?"

Corin looked at her hand and sucked in a long breath. The slow exhale created a thick cloud of his breath in the air.

"Jarrod shouldn't be making promises like that. It just can't be. I won't ever be a Martox."

Rae stuffed it back in her pocket. "He loves you," she whispered, her eyes heating.

"And I love him. That's why I'm doing this." Corin's voice grew strained.

Shaking her head, she pulled his shoulders closer to wrap her arm around them. "I stand by my words that you're an idiot."

He laughed, but it was dry and short. "I won't deny that. But I can't keep pretending that all of this will work out. He'll be the king. He has no business with me for a multitude of reasons. It only begins with me being a man. He needs a wife... children."

Rae fell silent, thinking about his words. Leaning her head against his shoulder, she sighed. "Let me tell you something. He's been a Hawk almost as long as I have. Sometimes our jobs involve less than ideal means of getting what we need. And there have been circumstances requiring Jarrod to... use that pretty face of his. And he uses it well. On men, women... Gods, he's good at it. But it only ever went as far as flirting. Not just with the women, either. He wouldn't let it go any further and we have never questioned his loyalty to the Hawks." Taking a deep breath, she continued, keeping her head on Corin's shoulder. "I think he'll make a wonderful king, as he made a fantastic Hawk. He'll do what it takes to rule the country with honor. But if you think without you, he'll take a wife... Have children with someone else... You're fooling yourself."

Corin shifted under her, leaning his cheek against her head. "I think you're forgetting a vital part of how making children works. We wouldn't ever be able to have them, so that kind of overrules the whole idea altogether."

Rae shrugged against him. "I've seen that brother of yours do some miraculous things. He's bonded the minds of a wolf and man. He put Jarrod's soul back into his body. You don't think he might manage something to give you two a child?"

Chapter 19

CORIN STIFFENED AT RAE'S SUGGESTION.

Would that really be possible?

It was still strange to consider Damien's power and that it could affect such a personal matter. The thought sank into Corin's gut and left him oddly excited. But elation faded in light of his decision to end his relationship with Jarrod. It mutated into sickening jealousy at the possibility of Jarrod asking Damien to help him have a child with a different man.

How does that make sense... being jealous of a non-existent man, but encouraging Jarrod to pursue Evie? Rae's right, I'm an idiot.

"What are you two doing out here?" Damien slipped outside through the door. "I worried after you didn't come back for dinner, Dice."

Neco squeezed through the doorway behind him, trotting over to lick Rae's hands.

Rae's head tilted up. "Would it be possible, theoretically, for you to help Jarrod and Corin have a child?"

Corin's gut twisted so tight he thought he might vomit at the sheer uncertainty.

Damien paused for what felt like an eternity, his eyes widening. "That's a hell of a question to just throw out there. Why are we talking about this?"

Corin lifted his head off Rae's and looked at his brother. He choked out the question now eating at him. "Could you actually do something like that?"

Damien took a step forward, furrowing his brows. "I suppose it's theoretically possible. The process would be complicated, and I'd need to do a lot of research with Sindré. But a man can't carry a baby. There'd have to be a woman involved in at least that part."

Corin's shoulders slumped. "See." He bobbled Rae's head with his shoulder. "Can't do it without a woman."

"And what am I?" Rae scoffed.

Corin pursed his lips.

Is she offering to carry our child?

"Wait, why are we talking about babies?" Damien shuffled forward. "And you still didn't tell me why you're out here."

Rae sighed. "Because. Corin and Jarrod... have separated."

Neco whined, making Corin flinch.

Even the damn wolf is upset.

"What?" Shock returned to Damien's face. He crossed his arms, rubbing his hands against the thin white material of his shirt for warmth. "What's that supposed to mean?"

"That Jarrod and I are done. I ended it." Corin was growing tired of repeating the phrase, and the more he said it, the more it sank in.

It's over.

Damien groaned loudly. "You're an idiot."

Corin scowled. "Rae already told me that. Try something more original."

"How's Jarrod?" Damien lowered his voice, eyeing Rae.

She shook her head. "Not great."

"I should go check on him," Damien gestured to the door. He eyed Neco as he took a step backward. "Keep Neco here."

"He wanted to be alone." Rae sighed. "I told him I'd check on him later. It might be best to let him have some space."

"Is that how you tell yourselves you care?" A voice chimed from the doorway, the sharp tone grating Corin's ears. He recognized it immediately, having overheard Evie speaking to the staff in the halls.

Evie stood in a layered black gown, glaring at them. "What wonderful friends he has, sitting out here while he's a mess all alone."

Damien spun to face her, and his muscles tensed, hands balling into fists. He took a step inward, his feet spreading into the defensive stance hammered into them through years of training. The movement also put him directly in line between them and Evie.

That's an intense reaction for a spoiled rich girl...

Rae rose from the bench, the departure of her body heat making Corin shiver. "This is private. I don't think you understand the situation."

"Oh, I understand fully. The virtuous proxiet fell victim to the whims of a lowly rebel."

"Watch your tongue." Damien spoke before Corin could consider his own rebuttal. "This is no concern of yours and it'd be easier left before this grows any more complicated."

"Are you threatening me?" Evie gaped, lifting her hand to her chest in mock surprise.

Rae looked back and forth between them. "He's not threatening you—"

"Oh, yes, I am."

Neco growled.

Standing, Corin watched the tension in his brother's body, realizing the soldier in him prepared for something Evie couldn't be capable of.

What in the hells does he think she will do?

Corin couldn't decide if he needed to step in to protect his brother, or the other way around.

"Damien." Rae touched the Rahn'ka's shoulder, but Evie laughed.

"The delightful news is, I've finally got you all together." Evie smiled. "And when you're all *dead*, Jarrod will have no one left to fill the void except me." Her hand twitched and the shadows from the moon at her feet expanded. The darkness wrapped in on itself, bundling into a ropey tentacle slithering across the gravel walkway.

Corin didn't have time to consider what it was before the blackness lashed forward with obscene speed. He grabbed Rae's shoulder, pulling her behind him. The vine shot from the ground at him and he lifted his hand to protect his face. Pressure encircled his throat with bitter cold. The shadows constricted and he couldn't breathe.

Damien's power erupted from his fingertips in vibrant blue light, manifesting into his spear. It blurred into a strange glowing line as Corin struggled for breath.

Corin clawed at his neck, but his fingers couldn't find a grip. His legs buckled as the power tightened and yanked him to his knees on the ground.

Neco snarled, teeth gnashing, but Rae held him back.

The door blasted open behind Evie, ricocheting off the wall. A man shot from the dark hallway into the moonlight, rushing behind the Shade.

Evie jolted forward a few inches and her mouth fell agape as Jarrod straightened behind her. Her shadows disintegrated into flakes of ash, allowing Corin a deep, freezing breath.

He coughed, fighting to keep his eyes open to watch Evie look down, blood spewing from her mouth. Wheezing, her body jerked as Jarrod stepped back. She crumpled to the ground. Crimson oozed from a hole in her ribs, the back of her dress torn and bloody.

The stinging air forced another cough from Corin as he fell forward, gravel biting into his palms. His head spun, the stench of blood sticking at the back of his throat. He looked up as Neco lunged again at the dead woman.

Rae grabbed around the wolf's neck, kneeling next to him.

Jarrod stood, chest heaving, holding Evie's heart in his bare hand. Blood dripped between his fingers as he stared at it.

"Nymaera's breath." Damien turned his spear tip towards Jarrod, and Corin fought the inclination to tackle his brother. Before he could move, the spear vanished in a flash of pale light.

Neco spun, snapping at Rae's hold, and she hissed while recoiling. "Neco."

The wolf ignored her, turning to Jarrod. He slunk forward, head and tail low.

Jarrod looked up, his pupils dilated. His arm tensed before he dropped the heart. It squelched onto the ground.

Neco calmed, trotting forward to lick the dripping blood off Jarrod's fingers.

"She said she'd kill you all," Jarrod whispered, his eyes distant and impossible to read. He turned his gaze towards Evie's body and Corin followed it.

"She was a Shade?" Rae's tone vibrated with disbelief.

Looking at the woman's body and the now still shadows of the garden, Corin tried to comprehend what Rae was asking. "I was really hoping you guys were pulling my leg when you said Shades were real," he grumbled, rubbing his sore neck. "But how the fuck was Evie one?"

Damien didn't even look at his brother, taking a step towards Jarrod, who stood frighteningly still. "I could have knocked her out. You've seen me do it before. You didn't have to tear her heart out."

Jarrod looked at Damien, and his hands closed into fists. "I didn't have time to contemplate your *honorable* methods. I just needed to stop her."

Neco growled again, his aggression aimed at the Rahn'ka. Damien froze.

What's up with Neco?

Rae shook her head. "You *ripped* her heart out. How is that even possible?"

Jarrod looked at the wolf, and his hand turned slightly. Neco quieted and sat at the proxiet's side, tongue lolling out of his mouth as he received scratches. The eerie calm in Jarrod made Corin's head spin.

"Anyone going to explain what the hells is going on?" Corin looked from Rae to Damien

"The bond." Damien's arms flexed, his muscles still tense as if he expected a coming fight. "The one I created between Jarrod and Neco... it's been... changing Jarrod more than expected. We just didn't say anything before because—"

Jarrod's dark gaze found Damien. "If you're going to speak for me as if I'm not here, then I'll take my leave. I don't need this."

"Well, I didn't hear you offering to explain," Damien snapped.

"There's nothing to explain."

"You can't be serious." Damien gestured wildly at Evie's body. "You just put your bare hand through another human's rib cage and you think there's nothing to explain?"

Jarrod glared and Neco growled again, even though the proxiet still stroked his ruff.

"Don't you start." Damien waved a hand at Neco. "You're both smart enough to realize something is *wrong*."

"Good night." Jarrod's voice didn't waver. Turning, he stalked to the wide-open door and went back inside with Neco next to him.

Damien growled and took a step forward before Corin caught him.

He met his brother's eyes and squeezed his arm. "How bad is this?"

"Bad."

Rae stepped up next to them. "Should I go talk to him?"

Seeing the desperation in Damien's eyes, Corin shook his head. "No, I'll try." Before Damien or Rae could protest, he jogged to the door and slipped into the hallway. His heart pounded as he ran down the hall after Jarrod, stepping around the specks of blood he'd left in his wake.

"Jarrod." Corin reached out to touch the thief's shoulder before he opened his chamber door. "We need to talk about this."

Jarrod shirked away, but his calm demeanor remained as he grasped the knob. "No. We don't."

Neco stood next to him, watching Corin.

Corin didn't think before circling around to be opposite of Neco and grabbed Jarrod's hand away from the knob. "You killed Evie when you knew Damien could have stopped her differently. You didn't think. You just acted."

Jarrod's jaw clenched, and he pulled his hand away, stepping into Corin. "I didn't see you complaining about regaining your ability to *breathe*."

Every fiber of Corin's body wanted to back away from the viciousness in Jarrod's eyes, but he held his ground. "Why would you do that? Kill her? Even if she was a Shade, couldn't Damien have helped her?"

"I don't care," Jarrod whispered, his tone regaining emotion. "It doesn't matter who threatens you. I will always put your safety first, even if you're... not mine."

All the pain Corin had seen in Jarrod's face when he told him it was over came rushing back. It made his chest ache and his legs weaken. He couldn't maintain eye contact and stepped back. "Jarrod, I—"

"Take my room. I'll send someone to clean the mess. I won't be using it tonight." The proxiet's voice caught in his throat and he spun around, walking down the hallway.

Neco whimpered and ran to catch up.

"Where are you going?" Cori's voice wavered.

"To find my father." Jarrod didn't look back. "There's a dead Shade to deal with."

Corin watched as Jarrod turned the corner before falling back against the chamber door. Heat rose in his eyes as he slid to the ground. He tore the gold chain from beneath his shirt, clutching the ring and whistle. He pressed the cold metal to his lips, squeezing his eyes shut as tears welled.

Happy fucking birthday, idiot.

Chapter 20

Despite Damien's attempts to play peacemaker between his brother and Jarrod, the two avoided each other. He'd also failed to assuage Rae's anger, even days later.

She shut the door with extra force as she entered their room, interrupting his usual evening meditation. Her boots whispered on the rug as she crossed to her pack. Unfastening the drawstring, she dug through it with purposeful noise, encouraging him to open his eyes.

"Forget something?" Damien abandoned the rest of his nightly routine as he stood.

"Just getting my book," she muttered without looking at him. Pulling the loq'nali phén from her bag, she turned to leave with her Aueric ancestral text. "Sorry. I'll get out of your hair."

Each evening since the events of the garden, Rae had turned in early to avoid conversation. Damien hadn't pressured her. She had every right to be angry at him for keeping secrets about Jarrod.

He'd tip-toed around it long enough, and the interruption to his meditation encouraged his tongue. "I wish you wouldn't." He took a step towards her. "Can't you just yell at me so this can be over and everything between us can be normal again?"

Rae finally met his gaze, but her eyes lacked the fire he expected. "I don't want to yell."

"Then whatever will let you forgive me." He touched her arm. "I don't blame you if you're angry with me. But I did what I thought was best."

Rae took a deep breath, letting it out slowly as she watched his touch on her arm. "It's just not what I want." Knitting her brow, she looked at his face. "This isn't what I want."

"What *do* you want?" He grasped her other shoulder, facing her. "Let me fix this. All this silence is making me worry that I'm losing you."

Her shoulders slumped. "You're not losing me. And I feel like a hypocrite because I kept my nightmares from you, so I'm really no better. But I suppose that's beside the point. I don't want us to have secrets, no matter who they're about. I want you to be one person I can share everything with and for me to be that for you."

The decision to keep the truth about Jarrod's bond with Neco had eaten at Damien, but ultimately he justified it wasn't his secret to share. But looking at Rae, he knew he should have said it, anyway.

Rae sighed. "Asking you to betray Jarrod's trust feels wrong, but…"

"I should have told you. Looking back on it now, I see how foolish I was to keep it. What's happening to Jarrod is way bigger than him and me. I was stupid to think the problem wouldn't continue, that everything would settle and be all right. I was ashamed of myself for being the source of the problem. Not talking about it made it less real."

Rae rolled her lips together. "Is it going to get worse?" She rested a hand on Damien's chest.

He sighed, closing his hand on hers. "I don't know for sure, but I think it will. The changes seem to happen more rapidly now, for both Jarrod and Neco. Their ká are building natural walls against mine, too, because of my constant poking. The more I do it, the less likely I'll be able to help."

Leaning into him, Rae wrapped her arms around his middle, her book poking into his back. "I hate being mad at you." His chest muffled her words.

"Even when I deserve it?" He kissed the top of her hair as she nodded. Holding her made everything feel a little more bearable, considering the chaos of House Martox. Reznik had dealt with the body of the Shade discreetly, and Damien had heard nothing further on the matter. That the family could deal with such a thing so quietly almost made a shiver pass down his spine.

"I love you," Rae murmured, calming his paranoia.

"And I, you."

She pulled away and looked at his face. "They still haven't spoken. I've never seen Jarrod like this. He's such a shell of himself. I overheard his mother talking to his father, and she said Jarrod's considering an arranged marriage."

"That woman just doesn't give up." Damien frowned. "I still don't know what Corin is thinking. He's been avoiding me, too. He's buried himself in sending rebel correspondence out of the Lazuli barracks. Gods know how he gained access."

Rae studied Damien's face with more intensity and then looked at his chest.

"What?" Damien asked, catching her chin. "You're thinking about something."

She shrugged. "I don't understand either. They're perfect for each other."

"Too bad Corin doesn't see that." He sighed. "He's too bullheaded to let anything change his mind now. He just thinks he's ruining Jarrod's life by being with him." He touched her cheek, guiding her face back up to look at his. "But that's not everything on your mind."

Rae hesitated, shuffling her feet. "Your brother blindsided him. He didn't see it coming. Sometimes I can't help wondering…"

Damien furrowed his brow, trying to follow her train of thought.

The sadness in her eyes made his shoulders slump.

"Dice…" He traced her jaw. "I won't leave you. Ever."

A sheepish smile crossed her features. "Are you sure? What if I give you a pin with the Ashen Hawk's crest on it and it freaks you out?"

He laughed, poking her chin. "I've embraced my criminal habits now and am ready to be accepted as an Ashen Hawk, if they had such a pin. It's well worth the hot springs. Do they even have a crest?"

"No." Rae smirked. "Just for the hot springs, huh?"

"I don't want you getting the wrong idea or anything." He playfully thumbed her nose.

Rising to her toes, she kissed him. Her hand slid into his hair as his arms tightened around her waist, sending goosebumps down his back.

He sank into the kiss, pulling her tighter against him, grateful to further confirm for her he had no intentions of leaving.

I never could.

The very idea of no longer being able to hold her made him feel sick.

Breaking away from her mouth slowly, he trailed a line of kisses along her jaw, nuzzling near her ear. "I could never leave you. You are the only reason I still breathe."

Rae guided his chin back, kissing him hard. "Wouldn't kill you to say it now and then." Her eyes glittered with something unspoken.

"I'll try to remember that." He smiled, running his hand back over her braids. "In the meantime, is there any way I can make it up to you?"

Reaching to the side, Rae placed her book on a side table without letting go of Damien. "I can think of a few ways." She quirked an eyebrow. "And none require us to leave the room."

Damien hummed, running his hands down her sides to her hips. "I like these ways. Please continue to explain."

Laughing, Rae laced her arms around his shoulders, kissing him again. As she did, she pulled herself up and wrapped her legs around his waist, where he easily held her, his hands sliding around her backside.

The kiss deepened, their tongues meeting in hungry need of each other's affection. The feeling of Rae's hands running over his skin helped Damien finally relax and forgive himself. If Rae could, it made sense for him to do the same. Besides, he had no intention of abandoning Jarrod in his jeopardized state.

I need to talk to him.

The thought squeezed into his mind as Rae peeled off his shirt.

Tomorrow.

Damien woke before the sun, eyes lazily opening to the dull grey of dawn pushing through the curtains he and Rae had forgotten to close. Pressed against his chest, she slumbered peacefully. The thought made him smile as he brushed a strand of her chestnut hair from her cheek and tucked it behind her ear.

When he shifted to stretch his legs, her eyelids flickered, and she groaned. She pushed her face into his chest. "It's not morning yet."

Chuckling, he stroked his fingertips down her bare side beneath the sheets. "But it is. And it's come without a single nightmare."

Rae bit him, making him jump, before looking at him. "You calm me." Her gaze lingered on his mouth.

"Well, you won't hear me complain about this routine. If it helps with the nightmares, I'm willing to aid in whatever way possible."

Rolling her eyes, Rae kissed him. "And here I expected objections."

"I was once quite the shy soldier."

"I like this Damien better. And I'm taking *all* the credit."

"The credit is rightfully yours."

"Can we go back to sleep? It's early." She stuck out her bottom lip.

"You can. I need to catch Jarrod before he goes into his meetings all day." Damien gave her another quick kiss to satiate himself, but it made pulling away harder, especially when she whined against his lips.

He groaned, but slipped away beneath the covers to the edge of the bed before he lost all willpower. Standing, he lifted his arms to stretch, but also to tease Rae.

Laying her head on her pillow, she kept pouting. "But I'm not even wearing anything."

"And your cruel, seductress ways *almost* worked." Damien made his way to the wardrobe. The Martox family had been overly generous with their provisions of clothes, and he was growing used to having something fresh to wear every day.

Rae scoffed. "I could convince you if I wanted to. Lucky for you, I think you're leaving for a worthy cause."

Damien dared a peek over his shoulder at Rae. She lay on her side, hugging his pillow against her bare chest. Her back exposed, he could see the trails of her tattoos down her side.

"I feel incredibly fortunate then." Damien smirked, pulling on a pair of breeches. "Because we both know that you'd win." Retrieving a shirt, he crossed back to the bed and leaned to kiss her forehead. "Go back to sleep, Dice. I'll bring you breakfast."

"My hero," she swooned and closed her eyes.

Damien shut the curtains, receiving a hum of appreciation from her. He paused at the little table nestled near the window and poured cool water from a pitcher into a teapot. Adding the tea leaves Rae had taken to drinking each morning, he used a touch of power to heat the water and secured the lid again.

"For when you're ready to wake up." Damien settled the teapot back down, the ceramic clinking with another moan of gratitude from Rae. He admired the curve of her bare back before exiting their room.

Regardless of how light Rae made him feel, the looming reality of his coming conversation with Jarrod weighed heavily on his shoulders. He'd need the time with Rae after to help him recover from what he expected.

He hesitated at the door to Jarrod's chamber for a moment before he knocked. "Jare?" He leaned to listen for the proxiet's movements inside.

"Come in."

Damien did so, closing the door behind him. He eyed around the chamber quickly. "Where's Neco?"

"Hunting." Jarrod stood by his wardrobe. "He was desperate to go out running this morning."

Good. This will be easier without him here.

Jarrod secured bracers at his wrists. Already fully dressed, he looked up at Damien. "Everything all right?" His tone was even, but undercurrents of hostility still ran within it.

"Does something need to be wrong for me to come see you?"

"Of course not." Jarrod sighed. "Just a little on edge. You're up early."

"Usually am. Something about the way the ká of Pantracia changes when the sun rises. I just don't always stay awake." He offered a smile as he crossed towards Jarrod. He stopped to lean against one of the high-backed chairs, a breakfast setting on the little table beside them. The partially eaten contents of the single plate sat next to an untouched cup of coffee. "You want to talk about that edge you're on?"

"Getting a lot of pressure to formalize some things on the political side. King Iedrus will receive my formal protection order soon, and that's when things get real."

"You know, I wouldn't blame you if you pulled out of all this. The rebellion can find another way. And I'm already used to running."

Jarrod stopped moving and stared at him. "I thought about it." He shook his head. "But even if I'm doing this alone, it needs to be done."

"You're not alone." Damien took a step to him.

Jarrod smiled, but it didn't reach his eyes. "That's not what I meant. I wanted to talk to you, though."

Quirking his head, Damien paused. A strange nervous energy passed through his shoulders. "About what?"

"Sit." Jarrod motioned to the chair, rounding to take the other one himself.

"This is going to be one of *those* conversations?" Damien sat in the chair. He hoped whatever the proxiet wanted to discuss wouldn't make what he had to say harder.

"I don't think so." Jarrod ran a hand over his hair. "I need to choose my council to have a proper claim to the throne.

That means I need five people. A personal advisor, a master of war, a chief vizier, a political strategist, and a trade minister."

Damien gave a low whistle. "No pressure. Those are some big positions to fill."

Jarrod nodded. "And I've written your name next to one, in the hopes you might be agreeable."

"Me?" Damien tried not to look as surprised as he felt. Even if Jarrod had hinted at the possibility in the past, he'd always assumed his parents would correct the idea. "You think that's the best idea? Most of this country still sees me as a traitor."

"Dame, if I didn't, I wouldn't have proposed it. Those people are wrong and I think having you will go a long way to making a point. Even my father doesn't think it's a terrible idea."

"Your father agreed?" Damien couldn't control the crack of astonishment that time. "Jare, I'm not the best at politics, I think we've established that already."

"The political strategist spot is already taken."

"By who?"

"Rae."

Damien chuckled, settling back further into the chair. "That makes sense. So you're determined to make me a soldier again then? We both know I'm rubbish with finance."

"Actually..." Jarrod tapped his fingers together in front of him. "I'd like you as my personal advisor."

A ball of spit in Damien's mouth lodged in his throat, and

he choked. "You're joking, right? Personal advisor?"

Jarrod shook his head, maintaining eye contact. "Do you have reservations, then? I can't think of anyone else I'd want as my right hand."

"Oh, I have plenty of reservations. But you have plenty about being king, too, so I accept that as a necessity of the job." Damien rubbed his forehead, leaning against an armrest.

"You don't have to answer me right away." Jarrod rose from his seat. "Think about it?"

"I have to. But I want you to know that my immediate inclination is to accept. I want to, because I know how important it is to have someone you trust at your side and I'm honored that I can be that person. But stepping into such a public spotlight as a Rahn'ka..."

Jarrod lifted a hand and smirked. "There's no pressure. There are plenty of jobs in the kitchen should you request something lower profile."

Damien exploded with a laugh. "You're a bastard, you know that?"

The proxiet's smile quickly faded, but he turned away to hide it. "I don't want to get your woman in trouble, either. She hasn't accepted yet. Said she wanted to talk to you first."

"Sounds like we both have plenty to talk about then." Damien watched Jarrod's actions carefully. The sudden change in his mood seemed hardly like the thief he considered a brother. "But I'm not worried about me or Rae right now.

How are you holding up?"

Jarrod's vision met the floor and his body stilled as he stood behind the chair. "Better when I'm busy."

"Because then you don't notice whatever is happening to you?" Damien stood slowly.

Meeting his gaze, Jarrod cringed. "No. That, I notice regardless. But if I keep busy, sometimes I forget about him."

Damien pursed his lips, damning himself for inadvertently bringing up Corin. "We have to talk about what happened that night. I know you've been avoiding it, which is probably why you didn't ask me this sooner. Because you knew I'd bring it up."

Jarrod sucked in a deep breath. "Perhaps. But I think I have it back under control."

"Your father might be able to clean up a body for you, but this time around, we were lucky your anger targeted a Shade and not someone else. But when the next body drops, which we both know *will* happen, who's it going to be?"

"It won't." Jarrod's expression hardened.

"Jare." Damien sighed. "You can't keep lying to yourself about this."

"Are you proposing something? Because last I heard, you don't know how to fix it."

"Not here, I don't." Damien had thought hard about the situation and continually came to the same conclusion. "It's not the best timing, I know, but I think we need to go to

Jacoby. To the ruins where I received my power. Sindré—"

Jarrod shook his head. "Not right now. It will have to wait. I need to be here when we get Iedrus's written rejection. If I'm not, I'll be branded a traitor almost immediately. Being outside of the country makes it look even worse."

Damien cringed. "See, I told you I'm no good at politics." He collapsed back into the chair, rubbing his temples. "I can't continue to slow the bond anymore. Both your ká are growing agitated with my meddling. I'm afraid I'm making it worse."

"Give it a few weeks, at most. Once I have started the formal process, my family can take over for a while and we can talk about going to Jacoby."

"Your mother will love that." Damien watched the proxiet. "But you admit that something is seriously wrong?"

Frowning, Jarrod stiffened. "Aye," the proxiet whispered, turning away again. "Something is wrong."

"I'm sorry," Damien blurted, drawing his gaze back. "I became overconfident in my abilities. I shouldn't have attempted something so complex without studying more."

Jarrod's expression softened. "I don't hold it against you. I asked you to do it. Hopefully, we can fix it, but..."

"What?"

Sighing, Jarrod pulled at his half-secured bracer to finish buckling it. "If we leave here, where will he go?"

Damien's stomach twisted. He hadn't even considered his brother in the trek to Jacoby. "I suppose he'll stay in Lazuli. I hear he's been fairly involved in town, remounting his recruitment and correspondence for the rebellion."

Jarrod nodded once, stone faced. "I should get to my meetings."

"Right." Damien cleared his throat as he stood from the chair again. "I didn't mean to keep you. I'll speak with Rae and try to give you an answer to your question soon."

The thief's eyes glistened. "Thank you."

Someone rapped on his door, and Jarrod's gaze hardened. "What?"

The door opened and Maith stood with a book in his hands, hardly looking up. "Jarrod. Glad I caught you."

"You catch me every day," Jarrod muttered. "What's the question today?"

"What year was your father born? And I need the exact spelling of your great-grandfather's name."

Jarrod sighed. "My father was born in 2560 and my great-grandfather's name was Trennich." He spelled it out for the auer, who disappeared back into the hallway without another word.

"He's still here?" Damien frowned. "I'd hoped not seeing him meant he'd gone back to Eralas."

Jarrod scoffed. "I don't think he's ever leaving."

Chapter 21

JARROD SAT AT THE MEETING table, half-listening to his father's advisor drone on about strategy. His hand hung at his side, petting Neco.

It'd been two weeks since he'd asked Damien to be his personal advisor, and the Rahn'ka had taken his time accepting the role. Along with his acceptance came Rae's and, for the past several days, they'd both been involved in his meetings.

"I don't like the sound of that." Damien rubbed his eyebrows.

"It's a little archaic." Rae slid the document away from her towards the center of the table. "But it's been a long time since anyone has challenged the throne. They're hoping the reminder of tradition is enough to dissuade you from upholding your order."

And be prosecuted as a traitor. I'll take the gruesome bleeding.

"And how would you know?" Jarrod's mother challenged Rae for the millionth time that week, but the Mira'wyld didn't flinch.

"Because if someone threatened Jarrod's position, I'd advise him to do the same thing." Rae didn't miss a beat. "The old Dannet families would merely use it to gauge whether someone was worthy of the crown."

"But fighting a *bear*?" Damien threw his hands up. "They can't believe the old kings actually did that. It's clearly a metaphor for something else."

Jarrod lifted his hand, shaking his head. "Who cares? I'll fight the damn bear."

Sairin gaped. "You can't fight a bear!"

Reznik ran a hand down his face. "I know it doesn't happen often, but I agree with your mother."

"This isn't even important right now." Jarrod waved a hand in the air. "It wouldn't happen until I've already defeated Iedrus. I might die long before then. Plus, if we devolve into a civil war, the requirement nullifies."

"He's right." Damien nodded. "There are other things we should worry about. Like swaying the other Dannet families."

"And your missing name for master of war." Reznik tapped a parchment. "You filled the others, why is this one taking so long?"

Jarrod had chosen a longtime associate from the House of Martox to serve as his trade minister, leaving only one position vacant. "I need more time." He lowered his voice as he stroked Neco.

The wolf whined and Jarrod nodded.

"Why? We have plenty of suitable options for you to choose from. Auster..."

Damien leaned forward in his chair. "With all due respect, Lord Martox, this isn't something he can rush. Not with the pending war."

Jarrod stared at Neco's ears. "I'll give you a name within the week."

Satisfied, Reznik fell silent.

"When you're ready, we have names for your *consideration* for marriage." Sairin unfolded a piece of parchment.

Damien intercepted it before Jarrod could reach across the table and studied the names. He frowned as he folded the paper and held it up casually. "Can't this wait, too?"

"It would strengthen his appearance for the other Houses." Sairin shrugged. "Helgath has never had an unwed king."

"I'll look at it." Jarrod spoke in a monotone as he held his hand out for the paper. His insides numbed, and he nodded once at Damien to encourage him to hand it over.

The Rahn'ka's frown deepened, and he exchanged a glance with Rae as he dropped the paper into Jarrod's outstretched hand.

Looking at the list, Jarrod shook his head and whipped it across the table back towards his mother. "You know what? I don't care. Pick one."

"Jare." Damien stiffened. "You should keep control over this decision. Whoever your queen is will have substantial power."

Before Sairin could grab the list, Rae snatched it. "Could we have the room, please?" She looked at Jarrod's parents and Frederix.

After a brief pause, the three of them stood. "Breakfast will be served shortly, anyway. When you're finished, come eat with your family." Sairin had complained about his previous meals being taken in his room.

Jarrod said nothing as they departed, leaving him alone with Damien and Rae.

"Neco wants to go for a run." Jarrod stood.

"I'll take him." Rae patted her thigh.

The wolf loped over to her, leaning on her side as she scratched his ruff.

They left, too, and Jarrod endured Damien's stare. "What?"

"You're seriously considering letting your *mother* choose a wife for you? Gods, man, have a little respect for the thing I wish I could have with Rae."

Sighing, Jarrod walked behind a chair and leaned on it. "It's not a lack of respect, I swear. I just... don't care. I don't get the person I want and I see no point in trying to make something out of nothing."

"You seem like you haven't cared about a lot of things lately. I know you miss Corin, but—"

"Don't."

"You know he's not even sleeping in the castle anymore? He's gotten himself lodging in the Hedge."

A knife twisted in Jarrod's gut.

That explains why I haven't had to work as hard to avoid him.

Jarrod clenched his jaw. "And I hope he's finding suitable company for his nights, but I'm not interested in any of those women on my mother's list, so what difference does it make?"

"I get that you'll never have a genuine relationship with any of these women, so at least pretend to care about it politically." Damien picked up the parchment, studying it. "The roles they're in now and their personalities. All of this will affect the type of queen they will be. And whether or not you like them, their power will be real. And I don't particularly trust your mother with those decisions."

Jarrod gritted his teeth, but nodded. "You're right. I'll look at the list." He sighed, staring at the table, unable to shake his own insinuation of Corin sharing his bed with another.

"It's not happening," Damien whispered, responding without Jarrod needing to say anything aloud. "He's hurting, too."

Always in my head, even when not invited...

Exhaling slowly, Jarrod tried to push the pain back into the box he kept it in. "That's a shame. I'd like him to be happy."

"He isn't allowing himself time for anything but the rebellion now. It's remarkable he hasn't gotten the attention of the local peace officers, Martox protection or not. I heard the numbers of rebels hiding within the military is growing. He's still working to help you take the throne."

"It's what he wanted from the start." Jarrod stared out a window. "I don't think it matters who I am anymore, though. Can we stop talking about him?"

It's severely impeding my ability to pretend I don't miss him.

"I've noticed you're going running with Neco more." Damien obliged a shift of subject. "Is meditation helping?"

Jarrod shrugged. "Maybe. But if I don't run a few times a day, I get twitchy. Plus, I'm hungry all the time and my shirts are... tighter." He frowned, having ripped the sleeve of a thin shirt the day before.

"It's affecting you more physically, then. I hoped I was imagining the changes. We'll have to seriously discuss Jacoby soon."

"I don't know if I can go." Jarrod stared at the woodgrain on the table.

Damien sucked in a breath, but knocking on the chamber door stopped him from what surely would have been a disagreement.

A staff member appeared in the cracked doorway, looking apologetic. "I'm sorry for interrupting Lord Martox, but Master Lanoret's brother is here and asking to see him."

The proxiet swallowed and focused on keeping his breath even.

He's here. But not for me.

Damien eyed Jarrod as he pushed his chair out from the table. "Thank you, Keta."

The girl bowed and vanished from the doorway.

"I'll meet you at breakfast." Damien crossed to the door.

Jarrod nodded, holding the back of the chair. Waiting a few minutes after Damien left, he rolled his shoulders and stood straight. Although his appetite hadn't diminished, enduring a meal with his parents drove him to seek the solitude of his chambers.

The door to Damien's chambers stood ajar as Jarrod walked past it, Damien's voice catching his attention.

"You can't do that, it's suicide."

"I can't just sit and do nothing. These kids were arrested *because* of me, *with* me. I will not stand by and watch them die." Corin's voice made Jarrod stop.

"The warden must have realized you're in town and is using them to lure you out. If you do anything, he'll have an excuse to get you killed in the bloodthirsty mob at the gallows."

Closing his eyes, Jarrod tried to will his feet to continue to his own room.

Leave them be.

"Well, if you help like I'm asking, maybe that won't happen. I know you can watch my back." Corin's voice rose to match Damien's in volume.

"And how am I supposed to do that when the warden wants me just as dead? He'll get two Lanorets for the trouble of one."

Jarrod's pulse hammered in his ears, but he focused through the sound. Turning, he took the step needed to reach Damien's door, pushing it so it swung open.

Corin and Damien faced each other, mere inches apart despite their yelling. Corin stood taller than Damien, but the Rahn'ka didn't look the least bit threatened. The captain had returned to his old ways of dressing without his armor, comfortable looking breeches and a loose untucked shirt. He'd grown a beard, but it seemed out of neglect rather than choice, and his hair looked like it always did when he first woke up, sticking out at awkward angles. His eyes widened as they fell on Jarrod, but then hardened.

"Sorry, Jarrod, this is a personal matter with my brother." Corin turned back to Damien.

"Like hells it is," Damien growled. "And I've already said no."

"Are you joking? You're trying to *dismiss* me in my own home?" Jarrod stepped into the room and slammed the door with so much force the room vibrated.

Corin flinched and took a step away from Damien, further from Jarrod. He lowered his gaze to the floor and chewed on his lower lip. "I can't do this right now, I'm sorry. But I need to speak to my brother and I meant it's a matter you don't need to concern yourself with."

"Damien, will you give us a moment?" Jarrod couldn't look away from Corin.

"What?" Both the Lanoret men spoke in unison.

Jarrod stepped forward again, finally looking at the Rahn'ka. "A moment."

Damien narrowed his eyes. "You sure?"

Get out before I strangle you, Jarrod hissed at Damien through their bond.

Damien's eyes widened briefly, but then he nodded and started walking. *Fine. Try not to strangle him, either, even if he deserves it. It would upset my ma.*

A smile twitched at Jarrod's mouth despite the tension in his shoulders. *I'll keep him in one piece. I like your mother.*

The door clicked shut as Damien exited.

Corin turned away from Jarrod, facing the windows on the far wall.

"You can't go to the executions." Jarrod's tone softened. If he'd known of Corin's relationship with the recruits, he would have tried to lessen their sentences. It was too late for that now. Jarrod had heard about the executions in his morning meeting the day before, though hadn't known who it was. He hadn't bothered to ask.

Shaking his head, Corin crossed his arms. "I don't see it as an option. Those kids are there because of me. I'm responsible."

"They're there because they made a choice, knowing the consequences. If you go... your brother is right. They'll find an excuse to kill you and I won't be there to save you."

"That's not your job anymore. I wouldn't expect it of you again."

"And whose decision was that?" Jarrod's insides churned to walk closer, but lead filled his boots.

"I don't want your help. It's just... those kids are only sixteen. But I don't want you to get involved in stopping another execution. It's not fair of me to ask it of you. Not when things are so delicate right now. I'll figure this out on my own." Corin turned, still avoiding eye contact as he started towards the door.

Jarrod bowed his head, wishing he'd gone to breakfast. "You may not care, but I still do," he whispered and Corin stopped beside him. He closed his eyes, his muscles trembling. "I can't tell you what to do, but I can ask. I can beg. Are you going to make me beg?"

"Jarrod." Corin's body tightened. "I can't do this right now. You know I still care and that's the problem."

Taking an unsteady breath, Jarrod opened his eyes. "You

care for the rebellion more, I suspect."

Corin's head twitched in his direction, and Jarrod glimpsed his hollow brown eyes. "That's not fair."

Jarrod swallowed. "If you do this... Your rebellion will fail. Your proxiet will die in the street with you, and everything you did will be for nothing."

Corin shook his head, turning fully towards him. "No, you won't die. They wouldn't be stupid enough to do such a thing in public. But I might. And maybe that's what needs to happen. It's what I deserve."

Jarrod sighed. "Blood may course within my veins, but I promise you, I'll be dead in all other aspects. Can't say it's a far cry from where I am now."

Corin's eyes closed, head drooping forward. "Jarrod, don't make me promise this."

Jarrod took a backward step, distancing himself from Corin. "I'll never ask anything of you again. In any context, if you just... stay away from the gallows today."

Sighing, Corin looked up and met Jarrod's gaze. "Begging isn't very becoming of you." His lips twitched ever so slightly into a smile before it faded.

Jarrod looked down, fighting his instinct to enjoy their previous penchant for banter. "And you'll never have to see it again."

Corin hesitated, a slight quiver passing through his body. It felt like hours before he spoke. "I promise. I won't go."

Jarrod let out his breath, turning and walking towards the door. The air within the room thinned, leaving him light-headed as he yanked it open. His pulse deafened him to his surroundings as he passed Damien, headed for his chambers.

He heard a low buzz and suspected it to be Damien saying something, but he couldn't make out the words. He continued down the hallway and rounded the corner. Once he reached his room, he shoved the door open and slammed it behind him.

Jarrod's hands shook as he ran them over his hair, slowing his breathing and hoping his pulse would follow. Sitting in one of his chairs, he put his face in his hands, seeking his connection to Neco. In a breath, he was running through the woods with the wolf, even if only in his mind. The scents of nature relaxed him, his heart pounding from the run instead of emotion.

Time passed with uncertainty, but he stayed where he sat. People came, knocking on his door, but he turned each of them away.

"Jarrod?" His father's voice echoed behind his door. When he didn't answer, Reznik tried the locked knob. The man sighed and walked back down the hallway, murmured speech following as he found Damien.

Jarrod held his hands over his ears, not wanting to hear whatever they discussed. He tuned back into Neco, who now stood in the hallway next to Damien.

"He just needs time, today..."

Jarrod growled and broke the connection with the wolf, walking to his window. He watched clouds gather and block the sun's zenith, breaking out into flurries of snow. Numb to his own thoughts, he let himself wonder where Corin had gone.

What will happen if I leave?

Someone else banged their fist on his door and he hardly reacted.

"Go away."

"It's me." Damien called through the door. "It's important."

He'd either made the best or the worst decision when he appointed him as his advisor.

Jarrod sighed, finally unlocking his door and swinging it open. "It better be."

Damien stood in the hallway, Neco at his side.

The wolf whined, but he didn't understand Damien's haste and couldn't explain for the Rahn'ka as he often did. Instead, a flurry of concerned energy radiated from Neco, because he could smell the panic on Damien.

"Corin—"

"No." Jarrod shook his head. "I'm not talking about your brother right now."

"You think I want to? Just listen. He's going to that damned execution anyway, and he's recruited some backup. There's going to be a brawl."

Straightening, Jarrod frowned. "How do you know?"

"Rae's been following him all day. I didn't trust he'd do what he promised."

"He swore to me." Jarrod's chest tightened, and he ran a hand over his face.

Damien shook his head. "He's too messed up to be thinking straight."

"He doesn't want me involved."

"So you're just going to sit here, moping? While the man you're stupid enough to love gets himself killed?"

Jarrod threw his hands up and then dropped them. "He doesn't want my help, what am I supposed to do? Force it on him?"

"Yes! Fuck what he wants. I'm not losing another brother. If you don't get involved, then I will."

Jarrod glowered. "You realize you're supposed to follow *my* orders, right?"

"And as politely as I can say it, fuck you. I've already established I'm bad at following orders. But your flex of power to order a stay of execution will be a lot less surprising than mine."

If this will be my country, I'd better get used to taking charge. Plus, it won't look good if my advisor starts ripping souls out of people in broad daylight.

Rolling his shoulders, Jarrod nodded. "Just keep your Art in check. I'd hate to request your resignation so soon."

Chapter 22

RAE PEERED OUT FROM UNDER her hood at the gallows' stage, where two boys stood with nooses around their necks. Their gaunt faces screamed malnourishment and disparity. Death would be the solace they wanted, but Damien's brother had other plans.

Probably to join them.

Acquiring a bow had been easy, but she missed the blue spirit one Damien had crafted for her.

She slunk along the black lava stone walls of the prison courtyard. The overcast sky provided no shadows for her to hide in, and the snow gathered on her hood and shoulders. With her bow inside her cloak, she hid in plain sight in the crowds.

Months prior, this place had been the location of her torture for weeks, until her cousin Kynis rescued her and brought her to Eralas.

A shiver passed down her spine at the memory.

Crowds flocked to the courtyard, rarely opened to the public, making crossing the drawbridge easy while blending in. The ebony walls towered around them, but she did her best to ignore the uneasy feeling they created in her stomach.

The square courtyard felt suffocating with the tall spires on all sides, and the bottlenecked exit of the drawbridge created the perfect trap. The gallows' platform stood next to the back wall, a line of prison guards blocking the crowds from getting too close.

The reactions of the crowd ranged so greatly that Rae struggled to keep up with them. The bloodthirsty called for the nooses to be tighter while mothers quietly sobbed, clutching their children.

Rae stepped after Corin, who pushed his way through the throngs of onlookers. She kept her distance, observing others moving in sync with the soldier.

Where are you, Jarrod? I don't want to watch these boys die.

Corin reached the line of guards, who stood their ground, observing him as the rebels at his side encouraged the crowd back. The captain said something, but it was impossible to understand through the din of protests and excitement among the crowd. The white-haired warden paused halfway up the stairs, the prison log tucked beneath his arm.

People pushed back around Rae, but she held her position as they funneled past her.

The general discontent of the crowd changed to confusion and surprise as Corin drew his sword.

"Hurry, Damien," Rae whispered, subtly pulling an arrow from her quiver and adding it beneath her cloak.

The guardsman facing Corin took a step back, and he and his compatriots readied their swords as the warden finished his walk to the podium.

With a subtle gesture from the warden, the executioner stepped towards the lever and the warden addressed the crowd. "For acts of treason, the crown of Helgath sentences these rebels to death."

Corin rammed into the guard in front of him before the warden finished speaking, swords clashing as all the rebels joined the fray.

The executioner moved and Rae gasped, not having expected such a lack of ceremony. She lifted her bow from within her cloak before anyone pulled the lever and loosed her first arrow. It pierced the rope on the right as she nocked another, blocking out the surprised screams around her.

The executioner's hand reached for the lever, and he pulled as Rae exhaled. The rope extended, but her second arrow severed it and both boys fell to the cobblestoned ground in a heap.

Shouts erupted around her, people bumping into her as she readied another arrow. Taking aim for the executioner, reaching for a great axe, a beam blocked her trajectory. She lowered her bow to push through the crowds.

As she gained a new vantage, she lifted her bow again. But the executioner had jumped to the ground to complete his duty, only to be intercepted by Corin. They rolled, wrestling, and she didn't dare take the shot.

"Shit."

The captain, disarmed, slammed his fist into the executioner's jaw, but the big man turned his momentum against him, forcing him onto his back. Locking his axe over Corin's throat, he pressed his weight onto it.

Fur brushed past Rae's leg and Neco snarled. Screams erupted as the wolf launched himself at the executioner, tackling him off Corin with a flurry of teeth.

The man cried out as the wolf mauled him, and Corin dove for his sword before he stumbled to his feet. His shoulders rose with tension when he looked at Neco, blood oozing across the stone towards him. Turning, he looked at the crowd. Blood flowed down his lip into his rough beard, and his eyes met Rae's, the crowd around her dispersed after her shots.

A guard surged at Neco but Corin stepped in to counter, pushing the man back with a solid kick.

One of the sentenced boys tripped a guard that had rushed forward to finish the executioner's job. The guard fell into the other kid, who rolled to work in tandem with his fellow rebel. Even with his hands bound and in his weakened state, the dark-haired boy wrapped his legs around the fallen guard's neck, squeezing him until he dropped his sword.

Shouting near the drawbridge encouraged Rae to turn and observe a wave of new soldiers swarming the courtyard. Dressed in formal uniforms accented with black, maroon and silver, the Martox crest decorated the shoulders of those who entered. They pressed around the edges of the crowd, circling them in the center of the courtyard like sheepdogs containing the herd.

The rank of soldiers parted briefly at the sound of hooves approaching from behind, allowing the entrance of four riders. Rae's shoulders relaxed at seeing Jarrod leading them, Damien behind, followed by two decorated officers.

The Martox guards rushed forward and encircled all those who fought, restraining any who dared challenge their authority, whether rebel or prison guard.

Rae pulled off her hood and held up her bow in surrender, but someone yanked her wrists behind her back, anyway.

The crowd split as Jarrod and Damien rode forward, the Rahn'ka veering just enough to point at the guard behind Rae. "Release her, she's no threat to this."

The guard obliged, and Damien offered a hand to Rae.

When she took it, he pulled her up onto the horse behind him.

"Cutting it a little close, don't you think?" she whispered into Damien's ear.

"Apparently it takes time to put together an army." Damien urged his horse after Jarrod.

Standing beside the gallows, the Martox guard had secured everyone except for Corin, who'd confronted the warden atop the gallows platform, and Neco, who still mauled the executioner.

Neco's ears perked, his head rising, and he finally abandoned his target, running to join Jarrod.

As soon as the Martox guards encircled Corin, he froze mid swing and turned to face them. His eyes widened in recognition and he dropped his sword with a clang. The warden did the same, and they both lifted their empty hands.

Corin's eyes darted to Jarrod, who approached on horseback. His face contorted into a grimace as he lowered his chin to stare at the ground.

Perched atop his horse, Jarrod looked the part of a future king. He wore the same attire he'd complained about when disembarking the ship, little white flecks of snow speckling the fine maroon cape adorning his shoulders.

Jarrod halted next to the warden and Damien circled in front. The proxiet's expression looked deadly and silence descended. "By the power of my station, I demand that all executions of accused rebels cease."

The warden looked up at him, his face reddening with anger, but said nothing.

Jarrod continued, his voice carrying over the courtyard. "Anyone deemed a rebel is acting in the interests of House Martox and in accordance with the future king. Any act against them will be considered an act of treason."

Rae glanced to the side, taking in the wide eyes of the onlookers.

This will definitely change things.

"House Iedrus will deny such foolish claims." The warden scowled. "You may be able to cast your favor on the Lanorets." He darted a glare at Corin, who still stood beside him, eyes downcast. "But Helgath will not stand for your blatant disrespect for the throne and its law."

Jarrod shifted in his saddle, stepping onto the raised platform of the gallows and approaching the warden.

Neco leapt up next to him, snarling.

"And I will not stand for your blatant disrespect of my authority. Would you care to join your prisoners in a cell? Because I can arrange that. Unless you'd rather spend some quality time with my friend here." He motioned to Neco.

The warden looked down at Neco's bloodstained muzzle and took a step backward. His face contorted with disgust and looked across the yard at where all his men stood surrendered to the Martox guards. "You truly intend to challenge for the throne? With the rebels at your side?"

"Aye. And with more than just the rebels. Best choose the right side, Warden." Neco's jaws snapped and Jarrod stroked his head. "When I take the throne, I'll either take your standing or your head. Which will it be?"

The warden eyed Neco again, his lips pursed into a thin line.

A lone prison guard jumped onto the platform, inciting gasps from the onlooking crowd. He charged at the unarmed Jarrod with a raised blade.

Rae sucked in a breath, but Neco and Corin sprang into action in unison.

The captain spun on his heels and caught the soldier's wrist. With an expert twist and strike, the blade clattered to the gallows' deck.

The gigantic wolf rammed into the prison guard, knocking him from his feet. Before Neco could sink his teeth into the man's neck, Jarrod took one step towards him and the beast stilled. With his jaws still clamped around the man's upper arm, he growled and Jarrod nodded. Neco released him and the guard crawled away, whimpering.

Damien's spine straightened against Rae as the crowd murmured.

Neco trotted back to Jarrod, and the horses took an uneasy step away, but Damien calmed his mount with a touch.

The murmurs rose to a cacophonous roar as the excitement mounted among the people.

"Wolf king!" Someone yelled, and it caught like wildfire. Soon, the entire crowd was chanting.

Jarrod turned, facing outwards at the people, and Neco sat at his side. The proxiet lifted a hand.

It took several moments, but the crowd calmed, waiting.

"House Iedrus has wronged you." Jarrod lowered his hand. "Your children and your money taken to fuel a corrupt system. You deserve justice and not in the form of hanging children!" People started shouting again, cheering, but the proxiet continued. "I will bring you the justice you deserve! Mark my words, you will have a new king and a new Helgath."

Chapter 23

THE CHEERING EXPLODED, STRIKING LIKE a physical force, and made Corin's stomach twist into knots. He locked away the emotion attempting to surface, focusing on the lingering pain from the fight he'd endured. His swollen lower lip still bled, and he'd wrenched one of his knees in the tumble with the executioner. A bruised jaw. Minor injuries, considering the fate he'd expected upon approaching the gallows.

Jarrod turned from the crowd and the warden beside Corin dropped to a knee, bowing his head low.

Corin glowered at the man, and in his peripheral vision there was more movement. The surrounding soldiers copied the warden's gesture. He glanced up to meet Damien's eyes, hard with disappointment that reminded him of his father's.

Cringing, Corin lifted his fist to his chest and dropped to a knee before Jarrod, no matter how ridiculous it felt.

I didn't mean for this to happen. He wasn't supposed to come.

He couldn't look at Jarrod, able to feel his anger with each subtle movement. It made everything in Corin numb as he contemplated how the afternoon would have gone without the proxiet's involvement. He pressed the flat of his hand to the wood deck at his feet, wishing the cold snow would let him wake from the nightmare.

"Get up," Jarrod growled under his breath. "You're coming back to the castle. Do I need to have my men escort you?"

Corin grimaced and shook his head before he stood. "That's unnecessary. I'll obey."

Jarrod walked back to his horse, and Neco hopped to the ground. Mounting the grey stallion, the proxiet looked at Auster, the leader of the Martox guards, mounted next to him. "Stay here, see that this is dispersed peacefully. I'll need your horse."

Auster nodded, dismounting.

Jarrod looked at Corin and motioned his head to the waiting horse.

The captain didn't bother to retrieve the sword he left behind before he slid into the saddle.

People rose to their feet, parting to make a path for their exit, and Jarrod led the group out of the courtyard to more triumphant shouts. More chanting.

Wolf king.

Damien wouldn't even look at Corin as they made their way back to the castle. As soon as Corin had seen Rae's arrows rip through the nooses' ropes, he realized she'd been following him. He wondered if it was Damien or Jarrod's idea for her to do so. He hadn't even thought to keep an eye out for a shadow. Did both of them trust him so little? Of course, he deserved it. He'd broken his promise.

But Frez and Yeoman are safe.

Corin tried to find what comfort he could in it.

They're alive and so are you. Time to face the consequences.

He'd hoped the consequence might be his own death. It felt easier than continuing the way he was.

Neco took off into trees part way back to the Martox castle, disappearing into the brush.

Jarrod dismounted first on reaching the main entrance, and a stable hand took his horse. The proxiet climbed the stairs, not even looking back as he walked inside.

Rae slid to the ground, too, watching Corin.

Corin wobbled when he hit the ground, having forgotten about his sore knee while on the horse. Pain shot through his leg and he caught the saddle horn to stabilize himself. "Thank you," he whispered to Rae. "Those were some good shots."

Damien dropped off his horse, boots crunching on the gravel drive, despite the thin layer of snow. He took a moment to stroke his horse before passing the reins to the stable hand.

He lingered, listening, even if he wouldn't look at his brother.

Rae shook her head. "You're lucky. And my aim is only a small part of that."

Damien huffed a terse laugh. "I wouldn't count luck yet. Jarrod's not done with him."

Corin swallowed, looking up to the top of the stairs to see Jarrod had vanished.

"I think you're wrong, Lieutenant," Rae muttered, her tone disappointed. "I think Jarrod *is* done with him."

The finality of her words struck Corin hard in the chest. He clutched the saddle, trying to cope with the idea that it was finally over. This choice had dropped the final wedge into place. Jarrod would never forgive him, and perhaps that was how it needed to be.

Rae watched Corin. "You made the wrong decision. When you left him."

"How do you know?" Corin looked up from the ground at her. "I did what I had to."

"No." Rae shook her head. "You were selfish. He needed you. He still needs you." She put a hand on Damien's shoulder before starting up the stairs. Halfway, she turned to Corin again. "I know you think it's a bad thing that he would've done anything for you, but you two could've been unstoppable. You could've fixed this country together." She took the remaining stairs two at a time until she disappeared inside.

The pain doubled and Corin watched her go, unable to

think of a response. He'd tried to do all he could to help the rebellion after moving out of the castle, but there was only so much he could do from outside the military. His primary advantage has been working from the inside. And now, everything felt hopeless.

The stable hand took his horse away, removing Corin's source of stability, and he hobbled to the stairs. He collapsed, burying his face into his hands. He jumped when Damien sat down on the stairs next to him.

"Never in my life did I think I'd live to see the day my older brother would devolve into this," he grumbled darkly. "A coward."

Corin shook his head, shoulders trembling. "I can't do this anymore, Damien. I don't know what I'm supposed to do, and I feel lost."

"This isn't you, Corin. I've never seen you like this. What has made you so uncertain? Second-guessing absolutely everything? Breaking promises..."

"I couldn't let Frez and Yeoman die."

"Then why promise Jarrod?"

Corin sighed, tugging on his unkempt hair. "I didn't know what else to do. I couldn't let him keep looking at me like that."

"Like what?"

"Like he couldn't decide whether to punch me or kiss me. Hells, I wanted both, anything, but I can't let that happen. I can't let him make the wrong decisions because of me."

"Do you realize how insulting that is?" Damien knocked Corin's elbow out from under his head. "To Jarrod, I mean. Saying that he'll make the wrong decisions just because you're around?"

Corin hesitated, chewing on his lower lip. He opened his mouth, but Damien stopped him.

"If anything, his choices have been erratic and worse since you ended it all. He was willing to let his mother pick someone for him to marry, without even looking at the names. Rae's right, the two of you could have been unstoppable, but you messed it all up because you thought it was the right thing to do. Because you allowed yourself to believe you had all the information and were the only one who could *fix* something that wasn't even broken in the first place!"

"But I—"

"No, don't try to justify it to me." Damien stood, stepping to the ground and glaring at Corin. "We're all a mess. It's not just you! Rae's trying to figure out this whole Mira'wyld thing, I have the Rahn'ka, and now Jarrod is dealing with this entire thing with Neco. The last thing he needed was more instability by you not having the balls to stand next to him on the throne. That's what this is really all about, isn't it? You're afraid. You, the man who gave him a hard time for wanting to hide your relationship. Do you realize how hypocritical that is?"

Corin frowned. "What do you want me to do?"

"Apologize, for starters." Damien threw his hands up.

"Well, then I apologize."

"Not to me, you idiot! You know what I meant. You owe that man up there the biggest apology you can possibly muster. After everything he's done for you because he's stupid enough to love your sorry ass. He gave up everything he was for you, for this rebellion you claim to care so much about. Don't you care about anything anymore?"

"I don't know how to," Corin mumbled, rising to his feet. "There's no way Jarrod would even open the door for me right now."

"Then break it down. The Corin I grew up idolizing would do that. I don't know who the hell this man before me is, but he isn't my brother."

The words stung far deeper than Corin thought possible. He tightened his fist, considering punching his brother in the jaw. But the words echoed in his mind.

Before he lost the will to do so, Corin spun, marching up the stairs into the castle, turning towards Jarrod's room.

When he arrived at the door, the adrenaline from fighting with Damien still lingered and he knocked harder than he meant to. He didn't wait for a response before yelling through the door. "Look, I wouldn't want to talk to me either if I were you, but I need to say something."

"Go away, Corin." Jarrod's voice sounded surprisingly even.

"Damien said I should break down the door if you don't want to talk to me, so that's the next logical option for me if you don't open it."

A breath later, the door jerked open, but Jarrod blocked the way in. "What do you want? I figured you'd have left town by now."

"You told me to come back to the castle with you." Corin narrowed his eyes. "So why the hell would I leave?"

"Aye. And you did. Now that you're here, safe, you can go."

Corin huffed and shook his head. "Can I come in?"

"Why? So you can lie to me again?" Jarrod's jaw flexed.

"No, so I can apologize for lying. So I can apologize for all of it."

"Consider yourself forgiven," Jarrod muttered. "Have a nice life." He pushed the door to close it, but Corin stuck his foot in the doorframe.

"I need to explain." Corin pushed his hand against the door. "I haven't been fair and Damien's right, I've been a fucking hypocrite. Let me at least try to explain."

Jarrod met his gaze, pausing. "Fine, but when you're done, I want you out of Lazuli."

He cringed, struggling to nod in agreement, and lowered his voice. "Fine."

Jarrod stepped back from the door, letting it go, and walked towards his windows.

Corin tried to remember to breathe as he stepped through

the door. The room smelled of Jarrod and it made his knees weak. He missed the scent so desperately and caught himself glancing at the bed. Closing the door behind him, he slid the lock into place. He hovered at the door, unsure about taking a step into the room that already held such significance to him.

Watching Jarrod's back, Corin observed how regal he looked, still in his formal uniform. The winter sky broke into a billowing snowstorm, flakes circling on the windowsill. It made his mouth dry and threatened all reason. All purpose.

"I don't know how to express how sorry I am." Corin couldn't manage anything louder than a whisper. He shook his head as if it would sort the thoughts. "I didn't want to lie to you."

"And yet you did."

"I did." Corin dropped his gaze back to the ground. "I just didn't know what else to do. I couldn't let those kids die and I couldn't stand there with you begging me not to go. Every moment you were close threatened my resolve, my determination to stay away from you."

"Well, then I suppose you got what you wanted. They're alive."

"But I forced your hand *again*."

Jarrod huffed a laugh. "Don't flatter yourself. You can't force me to do anything. Damien would have gone if I hadn't and I didn't need my personal advisor using his Art in front of a crowd." He turned, looking at Corin. "Not good for politics."

Corin almost laughed, but the rising emotion stifled it. "I've been trying awful hard to make you hate me. Feels like I might be succeeding."

A knock came at the door and Jarrod rubbed his forehead. "What?"

Maith's voice came from the other side of the door, but Corin couldn't make out the words.

"Veralian." Jarrod rolled his eyes. "And my mother is from Ember."

How could he even hear that?

Corin ground his teeth. "Your mother must be thrilled."

Jarrod's expression deadpanned. "You want to talk about my mother?"

"Yes... No. I don't know. Damien said something that got me thinking, and I haven't sorted it all out yet—"

"Then come back when you have. Or better yet, don't." Jarrod took a step closer to Corin and stopped.

The room spun around Corin like someone had hit him with a club. "I tried to leave today, in a way. Every time I thought about getting out of town, I kept finding reasons not to. So when I heard about Frez and Yeoman, I wanted to save them, but I also saw the perfect opportunity. A way out."

Jarrod shook his head, walking forward. "You don't get to come here and make me care." His soft tone rose into a shout.

"And then yank the rug from under my feet! You already broke my heart once, and I'd prefer you not do it again. So don't humor me with talk of seeking your own death. Aye, I want you to leave. I want you as far from me as possible, because if I have to hear about each attempt you make, I will gather my entire army to stop you every time." The proxiet stopped a few feet in front of Corin, his chest heaving, and he looked like the king Corin had always imagined him to be.

Corin tried to maintain his anger, raising his voice to match Jarrod's. "You'll get yourself killed defending me. And then where will this country be without you to rule it? Where will Rae and Damien be without you by their sides? Where will I be?" He couldn't help the half-step he took, grasping Jarrod's vest with both hands. "You keep risking your life for me and I can't bear to be the reason you might die. I thought I saw you die when we were thirteen, before I even knew you, and knew I wouldn't love again. But now I *know* you and the thought of losing you..."

Jarrod's hand closed on Corin's wrist with an iron grip. "You already lost me."

"And I hate it." Corin's fists shook where they still held onto him. He stared at Jarrod's collar, trying to blink back the wetness in his eyes. "I can't stop thinking about you. Every time I turn around in the street I think I see you and I get excited. Every time I hear someone talking about Lord Martox, my stomach whirls around like it did when we first kissed. I want to leave Lazuli, to get away, but I can't." He shook his head, wanting so badly to bury it against Jarrod's shoulder, to weep into it like he had when Jarrod rescued him from Veralian, to crumble at his feet and beg forgiveness. "I'm just a soldier."

"Maybe." Jarrod's voice deepened. "But you were *my* soldier."

Corin closed his eyes, unable to stop the hot tears from falling down his cheeks. Swallowing, he tried to remember why he'd made the decisions he had. "I made a mistake."

"You'll have to be more specific."

Corin laughed roughly. "Ending it. I made a mistake. I listened when I shouldn't have and thought I was making the right decision. But I was wrong." He dared to look up, meeting Jarrod's glassy eyes for the first time. They bored into him, the darkness making every fiber of his body ache. "I am still yours, and these last few weeks have proven that to me. I could never stop loving you."

Jarrod stiffened, letting go of Corin's wrist, and the captain's heart sank. The proxiet touched Corin's chin with his thumb, mirroring the location of his scar.

The world around him moved in slow motion, his eyes defying his will and drifting to the proxiet's lips. The fresh scent of him and the way his uniform looked against the winter snowfall. Before his mind could question, his body demanded the close of the distance between them. Corin's hand slid down Jarrod's chest to encircle him as he kissed him.

Jarrod jerked away, wide-eyed, making Corin's stomach drop.

He took a careful step back as Jarrod studied his face. "I'm so—"

The proxiet followed with a step of his own, claiming Corin's mouth, forcing the apology to turn into a satisfied hum instead. Their kisses fell into the rhythm that Corin missed so much, Jarrod's tongue tracing the inside of his lower lip. The welcome feeling mingled with a surprising stab of pain where someone's fist had split his lip. He tried not to react, but a hiss escaped with a flinch and Jarrod pulled away.

The proxiet's thumb moved over Corin's lip, coming away with a dot of red.

"Well, that puts a damper on the moment." Corin sighed, but Jarrod smirked.

"I'll be gentle, then, Captain." He leaned forward and kissed the injured lip with breathtaking tenderness.

Every inch of Corin's body screamed, hungry for so much more. He pulled away painfully slowly and touched the scar on Jarrod's chin. "No need to be gentle on my account, my king. The pain is well worth what you offer."

Jarrod's jaw flexed, and he shook his head. "What took you so long?" He kissed him again before he could answer.

Corin drew Jarrod against his body with a firm grip around his shoulders. Losing himself in the escalating passion, he almost jumped when the back of his thighs hit the desk against the wall opposite Jarrod's bed.

Jarrod pushed him up onto the tabletop, forcing his feet from the ground. He yanked at the captain's shirt, tossing it to the floor. His eyes settled on the gold chain around Corin's neck, still adorned with the ring and whistle. Lifting it, he turned the makeshift pendants over, a thoughtful expression on his face. Lowering his mouth to Corin's neck, he left the captain heaving for breath and struggling with the buckles of Jarrod's pauldron.

Jarrod grabbed the pauldron, snapping the thin chains holding it in place to let it meet the floor. "Whoever designed this was obviously celibate."

Corin laughed, but Jarrod's mouth cut it off as he moved back to his neck, tongue teasing out a small gasp. He fumbled for more buttons on Jarrod's coat, but the proxiet batted his hands away.

Bursting buttons, Jarrod removed his coat and vest in one motion, letting them join the pauldron. His hands found Corin's sides, sliding up to his bare chest as Jarrod returned to his mouth. Nipping gently, he drew away to pull the thin white shirt over his head.

Before Jarrod could come back into him, Corin caught his shoulders and encouraged him to stand back so he could admire the subtle changes to the proxiet's physique. His muscles were more defined, harder than he remembered. Corin hummed in approval, tracing a finger down the lines of his abdomen towards the dark curling hairs peeking out of the waistband of his pants. "*Very* worth the pain." His fingers traced further, daring to tease the front of his pants. "I've been a complete fool."

Jarrod watched him with dilated pupils, hesitating before advancing and standing between Corin's knees. His mouth opened, but no words came and he kissed him instead. He savored Corin's lower lip before kissing his neck.

Hands ran over Jarrod's back, beckoning him closer as he tried to compose rational thoughts. Very few formed as Jarrod's fingers brushed over his hips, finding his belt.

Corin woke with his stomach growling and his body aching.

The sun glared through the window in a blinding white beam reflected off the snow-covered meadows.

He rubbed his eyes, trying to focus on where he was. The familiar canopy above the bed ran in a way he wasn't used to, and he realized he lay sideways on the massive bed. The pillows and blankets lay in different corners, only partially covering him and Jarrod.

The proxiet slept on his stomach lower on the bed, turned

at an angle that kept his legs from hanging off, his arm draped over Corin's abdomen. He looked perfect in the morning sunlight, his umber skin complimented by the deep maroon sheets. Just seeing him there made Corin's blood heat again, banishing any lingering winter cold in the chamber. He reached to retrieve a pillow, tucking it beneath his head so he could have an appropriate view of the peacefully sleeping man.

He touched Jarrod's hair, running his hand over the close cut and continuing down to trace his neck. As his fingertips passed over Jarrod's pulse, he hesitated.

That's faster than it should be...

Pressing his fingers, Corin tried to count the pounds of Jarrod's heart despite his slumber.

Jarrod's eyes opened, the dark brown momentarily replaced by bright amber before his gaze focused on Corin.

Whoa.

In the fervor of their night together, he'd almost forgotten about what was happening to Jarrod regarding his connection to the wolf.

The proxiet pulled his arm away, glancing at Corin's outstretched hand. "What are you doing?" He propped himself onto an elbow.

"Your heart is racing." Corin withdrew his hand, but promptly returned it to touch Jarrod's hair. "Dreams?"

Jarrod shook his head. "No..." He looked around his room, likely remembering the night before as Corin had.

"I'm surprised we didn't get people knocking on the door thinking you were being assassinated." Corin scooted lower on the bed. The action felt strained, and he groaned as he laid down onto his back. "Or that I was."

Jarrod's mouth twitched, but didn't break into the grin Corin had hoped for.

Corin frowned, reaching for Jarrod's hand. "What's wrong?" A sinking sensation filled him as he considered if Jarrod regretted the night. It'd been bliss for Corin, despite the plethora of bruises on his body from the rough nature of their love.

Jarrod sucked in a deep breath, gaze trailing to the necklace Corin still wore. "Where do you think you'll go?"

"Go?" Corin's tongue felt swollen as his mouth dried. "I'm not planning to go anywhere. It was you who I was kissing all night, wasn't it? Who I made love to? Why would I go anywhere?"

Jarrod met his gaze. "I didn't want to assume." He furrowed his brow and looked at the sheets between them. "Nothing's changed, and you left before, so..."

Corin grimaced, but resisted the inclination to look away. He encouraged Jarrod's chin up so he could look into his eyes. "I won't make that mistake again. It's clear that whether or not I'm here, you will still fight this battle. And I want to keep you safe. I don't see a better place than at your side."

Jarrod smiled, but it looked pained. "You said that before," he grumbled, touching the chain around Corin's neck. "I didn't expect to see this."

"You thought I'd take it off?"

"I figured it was at the bottom of the ocean."

Corin took his hand and lifted his knuckles to his lips, kissing them. "I never stopped loving you."

"Don't you understand that's what I'm afraid of?" Jarrod inched closer, wrapping his arm around him. "That despite it, you still ended things. Your love isn't enough to keep you with me."

Corin paused. He had a point, and he wasn't wrong.

With everything that was happening, it'd be easy for Corin to leave, but Jarrod would still be trapped in the same situation, still trying to become king and rule the country. Nothing really kept Corin there.

He looked down, trying to sort out an answer to how he could reassure Jarrod he'd be at his side through all of it and never leave again. The thought coalesced as he leaned closer to Jarrod, kissing his collarbone.

"I can't go through that again." Jarrod's voice lowered.

Corin nodded, his jaw brushing Jarrod's as he pulled back. He touched the scar on his chin, reaching with his other to lock his fingers with Jarrod's. "You won't. Marry me."

Jarrod's gaze narrowed. "What?"

"Marry me." Saying it aloud the second time, it sounded strange, but right. His heart beat wildly in his chest, knowing how absurd it must sound. "Let me tell all of Pantracia how much I love you, Jarrod. And promise to you in front of the entire kingdom that I will always be at your side."

Jarrod squeezed Corin's hand, but shook his head. "You don't have to do that."

"I want to." The idea excited him, even though Jarrod hadn't agreed yet. He sat up and the proxiet followed. "Jarrod Martox, I'd be honored if you'd agree to marry me."

"A lowly soldier?" Jarrod smirked. Light returned to his eyes, and he huffed. "I was going to ask you, you know. Not right now, but before. I've never wanted anyone like I want you. Of course I'll marry you, Captain."

Unable to form any semblance of words, Corin leaned forward and kissed Jarrod hard on the mouth, eagerly scooting closer until their chests touched. Their lips moved in tandem and Jarrod's chest rumbled, pushing Corin onto his back.

The proxiet pulled away enough to speak, leaving their lips touching. "But you have to shave first."

Chapter 24

NECO BOUNDED THROUGH THE CASTLE'S courtyard after the snowball Damien lobbed across the lake shore, using a bit of his power to make it sail further. He didn't have the heart to tell the wolf it would disappear into the snowbank and he'd never find the ball. The wolf sniffed and circled where it'd disappeared, spraying snow behind him as he dug.

"And you're sure they're both still alive?" Rae watched Neco.

"Positive. Both ká are still in this world. But I'd rather not keep checking in if you don't mind. I like not knowing what their ká are focused on."

Rae laughed. "So you think they made up?"

"If Neco getting locked out for the night is any indication, yes. I think it's a safe assumption." Damien couldn't help but smile at the thought as he picked up another handful of snow and threw it, clipping Neco in his haunches.

The wolf spun, snapping at the air and sending a cloud of frozen water vapor wisping around his head.

Rae wrapped her arms around Damien's waist, pressing her cold nose to his neck and making him jump. "Your brother better not mess it up again."

"I'm pretty sure it was Sairin who messed it up to begin with."

Rae bit his neck.

"Whoa, hey." Damien half-heartedly batted at her side. "Careful, or you might give me the wrong idea." He smiled, pleased for the time away from the meeting room. With Jarrod preoccupied, there was little purpose, and no one had been interested in disturbing him. Reznik had even kept Sairin away under Damien's advice.

Quirking an eyebrow, Rae tilted her head. "What, exactly, *is* the wrong idea? Then I can be more careful next time."

"Well, usually the wrong idea is the right idea, but only when we're inside in a warm bed." Damien nuzzled into her hair.

Rae pouted. "So restrictive. I think we should broaden your view of acceptable locations."

"I thought I was adventurous that time in Eralas."

Laughing, Rae leaned on him. "Yes. Probably the best moment of my life."

"Excuse me." A voice echoed behind them and Rae jumped, spinning them around.

A matronly woman in a simple layered skirt stood with a thick wool cloak around her shoulders and an olive green scarf that complimented her dark skin. "I'm sorry for the intrusion. My name is Julana. Are you Rae?"

Rae straightened, touching Damien's shoulder, and he relaxed his protective hold. She glanced at his face before looking back at the woman and nodding. "I am. Do I know you?"

"No. But Lord Martox told me who you are. You saved my son yesterday. You shot the rope."

"Oh." Rae exhaled and stepped forward. "How is he?"

"He's doing well, all thanks to you and Captain Lanoret. And Proxiet Martox, of course. Frez won't stop talking about the captain and the pretty archer who saved his life."

Rae laughed. "It was my honor." She accepted the woman's gloved hand and closed her other on top of it. "I'm so glad to meet you."

Julana beamed and lowered her hand. "I'd like to invite you to dinner tonight, if you'd be so kind as to oblige a modest family affair. You and your... husband?" She glanced at Damien and Rae's eyes followed.

Just hearing the term sent an odd shiver down Damien's spine.

Julana glanced at her feet. "Not that I would assume a proxiet or his advisors would visit such a humble home for a meal, I merely wish to convey gratitude in any way I can."

Damien smiled. "I'm sure Proxiet Martox would be honored to dine with your family, as are we, if his schedule wasn't so hectic. Though I'm not—"

"What my beloved *husband* is trying to say is that we'd love to attend." Rae quirked an eyebrow at him, reigniting the hum in him.

Julana beamed. "I am overjoyed. I had hoped you would be willing, but never..." She shook her head with a widening smile. "I left directions to my home with the staff." She gave a brief bow. "I don't wish to take up any more of your time."

Rae nodded. "Tonight, then."

Julana dipped her head in another bow before turning down the path.

Neco watched her from where he lay in the snow, burying his nose under its surface and flicking chunks into the air.

"Beloved husband, huh?" Damien stepped up behind her, wrapping his hands around her hips from behind.

"Are you objecting?" Rae tilted her head with a devilish smile.

"Certainly not." He nuzzled his face against her hair. A more serious conversation loomed.

But now isn't the time.

He buried his hands beneath her cloak, finding the small gap between layers to press his cold fingers to her bare skin.

Rae shrieked, leaping out of his arms and whirling around. She scooped up a handful of snow and pulled his shirt open with her other hand, stuffing the snow inside before running away.

The shock of cold running down his chest proved a worthy distraction and Damien cried out as he tugged at the fabric to free it from his pants and drop the unmelted snow back to the ground.

Neco yipped and chased after Rae, kicking up more snow as he passed by Damien.

Blinking through the flurry, Damien wiped the wetness from his beard, lunging to pursue.

Rae turned around, running backwards through the snow to taunt him.

Neco jumped at full speed, tackling her. She disappeared under the foot of white powder, the wolf assaulting her with kisses.

She squealed with laughter, shoving at Neco. "Damien! Not fair!"

"I didn't tell him to do that!" Damien sent a quick word to Neco, and the wolf calmed, backing away. He held out a hand to Rae, but when she took it, she pulled hard. The slick ground left Damien no traction, and he toppled into the snow beside her. Before he could react, she crawled over him, pinning his hips.

"If you didn't tell him to do it, then who did?"

Neco barked, bounding away.

Snow crunched beneath the boots of a visitor.

"I did." Jarrod approached from the direction of the castle with Corin beside him. He held out his hand to Rae, and she smiled as he helped her to her feet.

Her wet cloak and hair stuck to her, but she laughed as she offered Damien a hand.

He stared at her dubiously for a moment before he took it. With a surge of his power, he linked his ká to hers and encouraged them both to warm enough to banish the cold from their skin.

Rae smirked at him, eyeing Corin as she brushed the melting snow from her coat. "Is this a personal escort off the property, or...?"

Corin grinned and shook his head. "Gods, I hope not or I drastically misunderstood the entire evening."

Damien groaned, but with a wide smile. "Does this mean I have to put up with the two of you love birds again?"

Jarrod laughed, a sound the Rahn'ka hadn't heard in weeks. "It's only going to get worse, too."

"Worse? How could it get any worse?"

Jarrod glanced at Corin, tilting his head. "Gonna tell him?"

"I don't know, I kind of like seeing that dumb look on his face."

Rae bounced up and down. "Tell just me, then. I won't tell Damien."

"Gods, just say it." Damien rolled his eyes. "But if you say something crazy, like you're—"

"Getting married?" Corin smirked.

Damien's mouth fell open, along with Rae's. "You finally asked him?"

The proxiet shook his head, and Neco barked. "Wasn't me."

"*You* asked him?" Rae gaped at Corin, throwing her hands in the air. "How long have we been out here? When did this happen? It's been less than a day!"

"I think I need to sit down." Damien waved a hand at his scowling brother. "I can't keep up with this."

Rae squealed and leapt at Corin, wrapping her arms around his shoulders. "I hoped you'd revoke your idiot status."

"Gee, thanks." Corin hugged her back.

Pulling away, she kissed his cheek. "But you should shave first."

Corin gestured to his brother. "Why does he get to have a beard, but I don't? I thought it made me look older... wiser."

Releasing him, Rae rushed to embrace Jarrod.

"Rae doesn't like his either." Jarrod shrugged, receiving a nudge from her.

"What?" Damien frowned. "You've never said anything. I've had this for over a year now. I'm used to it."

Jarrod laughed and let go of Rae as she returned to Damien's side. "He's kidding." She cooed the words at him, running her hands into his short beard.

Neco barked and growled, drawing Damien's gaze first to the wolf and then to Jarrod.

The proxiet stood rigid, watching a trio of riders enter the property, heading for the front steps.

"Work never ends, huh?" Rae's tone tried but failed to diminish the abrupt tension.

"I'd better go." Jarrod pulled Corin into him for a kiss before heading back towards the castle. "I expect my advisors less disheveled for the afternoon meetings."

"Such a dictator," Rae grumbled with a smile, but concern lingered in her gaze.

"You're on his council too?" Corin stuffed his hands in his pockets. "I guess I shouldn't be surprised. Looks like it's just you and me this afternoon then, buddy." He leaned over to scratch Neco behind the ears.

The wolf licked his hand and then his ears pricked in the direction Jarrod had gone. He yipped and bounded off through the snow towards the proxiet.

"Oh, come on!" Corin threw his hands up in the air. "Don't tell me he's part of Jarrod's council, too."

Damien laughed, clapping a hand on his brother's shoulder. "You missed a lot, but we'll get you caught up. Don't worry, there's still a spot open. It'll be good to have you around again."

Corin gave a small smile. "I'm just lucky he forgave me."

Rae stepped closer to the men. "And if you break him again..." She poked Corin's chest. "This will be the spot my arrow hits."

Rubbing the spot, Corin laughed. "I don't plan on making the same mistake twice." His demeanor shifted as he turned to watch Jarrod and Neco disappear through the castle's front doors. "I'm worried about him, though."

"Worried?" Damien furrowed his brow. "This is the most stable and happy I've seen him in weeks."

"It's the changes. Because of the bond with Neco." Corin's face grew harder as he narrowed his eyes at Damien. "Because of whatever you did to him."

Damien flinched, rubbing the back of his head. "I think it's under control right now."

"But he's still been changing. While I'm not particularly complaining, four weeks is too short a time for the amount his body has changed. And his eyes..."

"His eyes?" Panic touched Damien's chest.

"They changed this morning. His pulse was racing even though he was asleep, and when he opened them, they were like Neco's."

"Shit." Rae looked at Damien. "That can't be good."

He shook his head, scouring his memory for every scrap of information he'd read about the Rahn'ka melding their souls with animals. His time with Yondé felt like decades ago instead of only a year. "I think it's another sign that the bond is getting stronger. That the wolf ká will take over more."

"That's what happened with Evie, isn't it?" Corin ran a hand through his hair. "When he gets emotional or stressed, you think the wolf's soul is overruling his human one? It was my fault."

Damien shrugged, his shoulders impossibly heavy. "You couldn't have known that would happen. But it's the most logical answer. I shouldn't have attempted the bond without researching more..."

"You're right, you shouldn't have." Corin advanced towards his brother. "What were you thinking?"

"And you've made all perfect decisions, right?" Rae stepped in front of Damien. "Give him a break."

Corin heaved a sigh and shook his head. "Sorry, Rae's right. But there's nothing you can do?"

"Not here." Damien put his hands on Rae's shoulders. "I need to return to the ruins near Jacoby to sort any of this out. I've been trying to convince Jarrod it can't wait, but he's resistant."

"There's a lot going on here." Corin nodded. "I can imagine it's nearly impossible to leave with where he's at in challenging for the throne. Maybe proposing marriage right now wasn't the best idea."

"No, that was probably the smartest idea you've had. It's giving him a foundation to stand on. He planned on asking you and I'm sure having you do it, especially considering everything, means a lot more than you think."

"I guess we can't all be as stable as you and Rae." Corin chuckled. "Some of us need the social and cultural significance of a ceremony to lock it in. Besides, I'm looking forward to seeing his mother's face."

Damien laughed, shaking his head. "Is that all? Not marrying the man you love?"

"Well, of course... that, too."

During the afternoon meetings, Damien kept a careful eye on Jarrod. Neco stayed at the man's side and, although life had returned to his eyes, a shadow loomed. Corin's return hadn't banished his snappy remarks or the moments when he seemed to tune the world out.

"Have you had time to consider the names I gave you yesterday?" Sairin focused on Jarrod as the meeting drew to a close. "They're all fine women."

Jarrod nodded, waiting as Frederix and Vinoria, his chosen trade minister, left the room.

Reznik remained, sitting in his usual high-backed chair, studying a list of representatives to send to the other Dannet families.

"Aye." Jarrod glanced at Damien. "Sorry, Mother, but I won't be marrying any of them." He stood, his chair screeching over the floor.

Sairin rose with him, frowning. "Those are the best candidates. There is no one better suited to be on your arm."

"I disagree with you." Jarrod patted Neco's head, the wolf's tongue lolling out of the side of his mouth. "As I already have a wedding to plan."

Reznik looked up abruptly, narrowing his eyes.

Tension flooded the air, and Damien felt almost giddy to see what was coming. He looked at Rae, but she stayed focused on Sairin. The Rahn'ka leaned forward in his chair without meaning to. Somewhere in the back of his mind, he prepared to intervene, but didn't know who would need the protection.

"What?" Sairin huffed. "You've chosen a wife without speaking to me about it first? I thought we agreed—"

"No." Jarrod held up one hand. "I haven't chosen a wife. I've chosen a husband, or rather, he chose me. Your meddling failed you, Mother, and I'd warn you against trying again. I *will* marry him."

Sairin opened her mouth, her chin bobbing like she was trying to find something to say. The only sound she could make was a disgusted grunt as she banged a fist on the table.

She glared at Jarrod, who calmly returned her stare, silently challenging her to say more with his stance.

Neco's hackles rose, but the wolf didn't make a sound.

Sairin spun from the table with another huff and stormed out of the chamber, slamming the door behind her.

Reznik rose from his chair. A smirk inched across his face. "Corin has returned, then?"

Jarrod's shoulders relaxed, and he nodded.

"Good." His father clapped Jarrod on the shoulder. "Arranged marriages aren't all they're cracked up to be. Proud of you."

Jarrod smiled and exchanged an embrace with his father before Reznik left the room, grinning.

"I like your da." Damien settled back in the chair and put his feet up on the edge of the elegant conference table.

Rae glowered at Damien. "I like him, too. He doesn't put his boots on the table."

Damien crossed his ankles and laced his hands behind his head.

Jarrod chuckled. "He liked Corin. I'm not surprised he's pleased."

"Foolish like his son, then." Damien grinned, rocking back onto two legs of the chair.

Rae lifted a boot and touched the top end of his chair with it, silently threatening to tip him backward with a mischievous smile.

He quirked his head, daring her to.

Raising an eyebrow at Damien, Jarrod tilted his head. "Got something to say, Lanoret?"

"We both know I always have something to say." Damien smiled back. "Part of why I'm a good personal advisor, right?"

"Don't you have a dinner invitation to get to?" Jarrod rounded the table towards the door.

"Right, the one you're *too busy* to attend? Let me guess, you'll be in your chambers for the rest of the evening?"

"Aye, quite busy. I have a wedding to plan and a man I miss. Enjoy your meal." Jarrod pulled the door open and exited into the hallway with Neco behind him.

Damien teetered back and forth playfully, looking at Rae. "I bet Jarrod never thought he'd be saying that out loud."

Rae extended her leg with a chuckle, pushing his leaning chair backward.

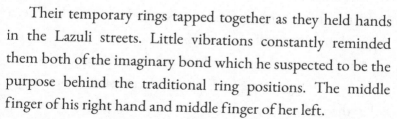

Their temporary rings tapped together as they held hands in the Lazuli streets. Little vibrations constantly reminded them both of the imaginary bond which he suspected to be the purpose behind the traditional ring positions. The middle finger of his right hand and middle finger of her left.

They'd agreed to play the part for the evening and Damien had constructed the rings with his Art and an old arrowhead of Rae's.

"You sure you're not going to get used to the ring?" Damien glanced sideways at Rae. "Maybe you won't want to take it off after?"

The sun was setting in the distance, leaving the streets shadowed by residential buildings. Pink and orange clouds brushed across the sky like a painting.

Rae's cheeks flushed. "Don't go getting any ideas, Lieutenant."

He squeezed her hand, the ring pinching his skin, but it was a welcome feeling. "I'll do my best to behave."

The door to the residence on the outskirts of the western Lazuli neighborhood opened before Rae could knock on it.

Julana ushered them inside and the aroma of hearty cooking filled Damien's nose. "You're timing is perfect! Please join us." She motioned them into a large sitting room, filled with comfortable looking furniture and a roaring fireplace.

Frez sat at the hearth tending to the fire. The young man looked healthier, even if only a day had passed. Someone had cared for the wounds on his cheeks, and his hair had been cropped short in small black curls.

An older man sat in one chair, bouncing a child on his lap before she wriggled free and chased after a sibling not much older than her. Two more children joined the fray, racing around the front room, the youngest barely able to walk in his efforts to keep up.

Toys clambered and crashed, creating a ruckus accompanying the squeals of the children, but Frez stepped around it all with practiced ease as he approached them.

"You must be Rae." A charming smile graced Frez's face, and he held out his hand. "I owe you my life."

Rae smiled, nodding, but ignored Frez's hand and pulled him into a hug. "I'm just glad you're all right." Releasing him, she stepped back as he stared at her.

His gaze lingered a little longer than it should have before flicking to Damien. His body straightened, adjusting to a salute. "Lieutenant Lanoret. You're a legend."

"Legend?" Damien steeled his face not to react. "Hardly. And not a lieutenant anymore, so you can relax, Frez. Call me Damien." He clapped a hand on the boy's shoulder, and he relaxed. "Whatever credit you give me for being the legend rightfully belongs to my brother."

"I was disappointed when my mother said the captain wouldn't be able to attend this evening." Frez's gaze returned to Rae. "But I suppose he's probably busy..."

Damien nodded. "He and Lord Martox have much to discuss and plan for. But I'm sure he'll come visit you. He was irate about the attempted execution. I'm glad we could intervene."

"Mhmm..." Frez stared at Rae, a smile lingering on his face.

Julana inserted herself into the conversation, tugging her son's head towards her to put a kiss on his temple. "I'm eternally grateful. I don't know what I'd do if I lost my oldest. I never liked him joining up in the first place."

Frez gracefully twisted from his mother's embrace, eyes still locked on the Hawk. "Where did you learn to shoot a bow like that?"

Rae shrugged, opening her mouth to answer.

A cry erupted from the front room as the youngest fell, knocked over by one of the others. Shuffling over to the baby, Julana picked him up, but he kept screaming. Bouncing him on one hip, she hurried towards the open kitchen area. Fussing over a pot on the stove, she tried to keep the baby boy far enough away to prevent him from reaching it.

The battle in the front room continued with the father mediating issues between the middle children.

Rae smiled at Frez. "If you'll excuse me. I'll tell you all about it later." She crossed the room, entering the kitchen.

Frez watched Rae from behind, and Damien studied the boy for a moment before he cleared his throat. Jumping, the teenager spun to Damien, who shook his head with an amused smile.

"May I?" Rae held her hands out to Julana for the baby as Damien joined them.

Julana hesitated before smiling and handing her son to Rae. "Thank you."

"And please, let me help here." Damien stepped towards the stove.

"Oh, that's not necessary. You're my guests."

"Perhaps, but I'd still like to if I may. It's been awhile since I've cooked on a proper stove." Damien also hoped that perhaps the distraction would help him avoid how Rae holding a child made his insides tingle.

Julana's face flushed, and she nodded. "All right, then. I'll fetch some wine from the cellar." Letting Damien take the stirring spoon, she disappeared around a corner of the house.

The baby stopped wailing, playing with one of Rae's braids. He tugged and put it in his mouth while she smiled. Giggles and shrieks erupted when she tickled his belly, and he pushed the end of her braid into her face.

Damien forgot to stir. He watched Rae, as entranced as the child by the little faces she made to make him smile. Adoring the sight, he imagined it becoming a normal evening for them.

Domestic life had never been something he'd put thought into, but suddenly it was all he wanted. His hand hovered over the spoon in the boiling pot until his palm brushed the hot metal, returning him to the present with a jerk. He stirred the pot, watching Rae in the corner of his eye.

Rae looked at him. "Are you all right?"

"I don't think so." He smiled. "I think you look perfect."

Her brows twitched, and she looked like she might tease him about it, but stopped herself when Julana returned in a hurry.

Holding two bottles of wine, the woman huffed out a relieved sigh when she saw her child happy in Rae's arms. "Oh, you're a natural. Del isn't usually so taken by someone new. Do you have children?"

"No. No children."

Not yet. If I even can...

Damien resisted asking Rae about it. But now he wanted to have the conversation. It was a complicated topic, considering the sacrifice he made when he received his power. When he'd drunk the potion to make himself sterile instead of allowing Sindré to force it on Rae.

Rae gave him a quizzical look, shaking her head. "We haven't talked about it."

"You have time." Julana offered the baby a stuffed toy from her apron. "You're young. Though your life seems to be far more adventurous than mine." She walked to Damien, encouraging him away from the stove so she could take over.

Examining the room, Rae hummed. "I don't know about that."

Julana laughed and nodded. "I suppose this is an adventure of a different kind."

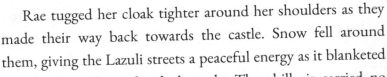

Rae tugged her cloak tighter around her shoulders as they made their way back towards the castle. Snow fell around them, giving the Lazuli streets a peaceful energy as it blanketed the remnants from the day's trade. The chill air carried no sound from the nearby residences, isolating them from the rest of the world.

Damien slipped his hand into her cloak, seeking her hand in the darkening night as they crossed beneath the orange glow of one of the street lanterns. "Are you cold?"

Rae squeezed his hand. "A little. But I'm fine."

The connection of their rings made Damien warmer without the aid of his power, especially when coupled with the images of her holding little Del. The child had refused to part from Rae for the rest of the evening, requiring her to eat their meal with one hand while she happily held him on her lap.

I know her thoughts about marriage... but children?

Children outside of marriage were common, so perhaps she still wanted them.

But can I give them to her? With how often we're together, wouldn't it have happened by now?

"What are you thinking about?" Rae looked up at him. "Are you not feeling well?"

Damien shook his head, trying to find the right way to say it. "Just seeing you with Del has me thinking. About children, which I know we've never discussed."

"Oh." Rae slowed their pace. "Is that something you want to talk about?"

"Yes," he blurted before he could consider a safer answer. "I think we should, shouldn't we? I'm honestly surprised it hasn't come up before, considering..."

"Considering?"

"If you became pregnant, you'd tell me, right?"

Rae stopped in the snow, looking at him with wide eyes. "As opposed to what?"

Damien shook his head, feeling silly. "Doing something about it without talking to me."

"No." Rae shook her head. "I mean, yes. Yes, I would talk to you. No, I'd never do something about it without telling you. Why are you asking me that?"

Relief passed over him, but it balled into his other anxiety. "I need to tell you something. Something I should have told you a long time ago. I've been afraid..."

Rae's eyebrows twitched together. "What is it?"

"Back near Jacoby, when all this Rahn'ka stuff started. Do you remember the ruins?"

"Of course. You got your first headache there."

Damien rubbed his jaw. "But you didn't see what caused it. What happened. What Sindré threatened against you. What I did that caused me to become a Rahn'ka."

Worry danced across her expression, and she squeezed his hand. "That was over a year ago. Why are you telling me now? What does it have to do with children?"

Damien took her hands, holding them against his chest. "You know how the guardians are with auer. They threatened to kill you for even setting foot in the sanctum, but then agreed to let you go, but only after removing your ability to have children."

Rae's jaw flexed, and she pulled her hands away from Damien. "What? You mean I can't... I can't have..."

Damien reached for her hands again, taking hold and squeezing them. "No. Not you." He lifted her knuckles to his lips, pressing her palm to his cheek. "I wouldn't make that decision for you. I drank from the vial instead of giving it to you. That's what held the power. I'm the one..." His face heated, tension building in his eyes. "I don't know if *I* can give you children."

Rae gaped at him, breath slowing. "You..." She shook her head and leaned into him, resting her head on his chest. "You should have told me."

"How?" Damien shook his head as he wrapped an arm around her waist. He kissed the top of her head. "I didn't know how. We barely knew each other when it happened. After I abandoned you for training with Yondé, I couldn't burden you with more."

Falling silent, Rae didn't move for several breaths before she tilted her chin up and met his gaze. "They also said I was your enemy and perhaps the goal was to trick you into drinking the vial all along. If I were a betting woman, I'd say you're perfectly fine, Lieutenant."

Damien paused. He didn't doubt the guardians' ability to be manipulative. Sindré had implied they'd lured him from Helgath all along.

Could it be possible? Was it all a lie?

He furrowed his brow, trying to stem the naïve hope budding. "But if that were true, then why haven't we conceived? We've certainly been..."

Rae chuckled under her breath and tugged his hand to resume their pace. "The tea I drink every morning isn't for taste, you know. In fact, it tastes terrible."

Understanding filled him as he remembered Rae's insistence on tea every morning. He never asked about the concoction of leaves she kept just for herself. "Oh. I hadn't thought about that, either."

Rae fell silent as they walked through the snow, it crunching under their boots.

"I don't know what's come over me, but having children is all I can think about after seeing how Del took to you. You'd be an amazing mother."

"I knew I should've dropped him or something."

Damien shook his head, smiling as he pulled her closer while they walked. "I meant it when I said you looked perfect. I know your mother and father's relationship has been part of the reason you don't like the sound of marriage. Reznik and Sairin aren't a glorious example either, but what about a child? Would you ever want one?"

Rae fell silent again, and for a moment he wondered if she'd answer him. "I'd consider it. With *you*, I'd consider it."

"Good, because now I'm imagining a house full of them. Like Julana's." Damien watched the expected cringe on her face, smirking.

"Whoa, whoa, whoa. How did we go from considering a child to a house full of them? Unless your Rahn'ka-ness grants you the ability to push them out of *your* body, I'd prefer we stick to one first."

"Well, I enjoy the process required for making more than one." He stepped into her and kissed the side of her head. "I'm teasing you, anyway. But now you sound like you're seriously considering at least one?"

Rae rolled her eyes. "Only because you tricked me into the lesser evil. I'll think about it, all right?"

"It seems pointless to talk seriously about it until we know, anyway. And like you said, now is not the time to be bringing a child into this mess." Damien sighed, the air clouding with his breath as he nodded. "I'll have to confront Sindré about it when we return to fix Jarrod and Neco."

"I think I'd like to have a few words with Sindré, myself." Rae looked up at the sky before eyeing him with a glimmer in her gaze.

Damien touched her jaw. "What is it? You're thinking about something else, too."

Rae hummed. "You'd be a great father."

The idea sent Damien's mind in a whirl. His stomach knotted pleasantly, and he stopped, pulling Rae towards him. "I hope so. But right now, I just want to make sure *you* are happy."

Rising on her toes, she kissed him.

Chapter 25

"MY HANDS WON'T STOP SHAKING." Jarrod tried and failed again to fasten the small chains attaching the useless pauldron to his shoulder.

"That's why I'm here." Rae took the chain and secured it.

He looked in the mirror, smoothing his hands over the formal maroon coat.

"You look great. And I'm sure Corin is just as nervous."

"That's not actually helpful." Jarrod frowned. "What if he changes his mind?"

"He's not going to. Besides, Damien's with him. I'm sure he'd gladly knock sense into his brother."

"Do you think I overstepped by bringing his parents here without asking him first?" Jarrod had welcomed Gage and

Viola that morning, sequestering them in the castle's sanctuary for the ceremony to maintain the surprise.

"Corin will be excited to see them. And you're overthinking things. Try to enjoy today. It's your *wedding* day." She grabbed the collar of his coat and shook him.

All Jarrod could think about was if everything had been properly planned. That the priest from Lazuli's temple would arrive on time and that his mother wouldn't find out. His father would officiate the ceremony and even he would keep the secret from Sairin. Once it was done, no amount of complaining from her could reverse the day.

"Can you go see if Corin is ready?"

Rae nodded, ducking out of the room in her layered black dress, similar to the one she'd worn during their arrival from the ship.

Neco nudged his nose into the door as it swung closed, whining.

Jarrod patted his thigh, and the wolf pushed his way in, letting the door shut behind him as he licked Jarrod's hand. "Are you nervous too?"

The wolf whined again and leaned against his leg, joining Jarrod's reflection in the mirror. His amber eyes shone in the dim candlelight of the little room off the sanctuary hallway.

Nerves built in his chest and the sound of his heart beating deafened him.

"Jarrod?" Rae's voice broke through the drumming and he snapped back to reality, facing her. "Are you all right?"

"Aye."

"He's ready."

Jarrod took a deep breath before walking into the hallway.

From the opposing room, Damien held the door open as Corin exited, meeting Jarrod's gaze. Jarrod hardly noticed what the Rahn'ka wore beyond that it was black and tailored, his eyes fixated on Corin.

The captain stepped into the hall, dressed in attire nearly the same as Jarrod's. Matte black boots met a pair of finely crafted maroon breeches with black stitching. The black shirt buttoned to his neck, but outside it hung the gold chain, still holding the damaged signet ring and whistle. The vest and coat boasted the formal style required of Helgath royalty, and Corin's broad shoulders bore it well. The accents of maroon complimented the collection of silver chains dangling from one side of the coat to the Martox crest pin high on the captain's left side, the one Jarrod had attempted to give him on his birthday.

Rae gave it to him.

Jarrod glanced at her before looking back at Corin.

The captain smiled, his warm brown eyes flickering over Jarrod. He'd finally shaven after teasing Jarrod that he wouldn't before the wedding, revealing his handsome, strong jaw and bowed lips.

Jarrod approached, touching his chin. "Not running for the hills, Captain?"

The smile broadened, and Corin shook his head. "I told you, I'm not making that mistake again. I'm ready if you are."

Nodding, Jarrod leaned forward and kissed him. "Good. I have a surprise for you."

Corin narrowed his eyes as he pulled back.

Damien cleared his throat. "Think we can save the kissing for the ceremony?"

"When you're king, you can make the rules." Jarrod took his time moving from Corin. He took the captain's hand, entwining their fingers as Rae stepped ahead and opened the doors to the sanctuary with Damien.

Despite the small dimension of the sanctuary, the high ceiling rimmed with decorative buttresses made the space feel grand. The four corners of the room housed multi-tiered shrines paying homage to the gods and their sources of power. Live and thriving trees represented the twin sisters of the wild and harvest despite the winter cold just beyond the windows.

Between each corner, carved into the stone walls, were the likenesses of the greater gods. The two sisters, Aedonai of spring and Nymaera of winter, faced each other, grasping a carved sword that dangled from the ceiling. At the center of the room sat a simple stone altar on an elaborate silver compass rose set into the ground, each direction pointing to a particular god. The sword of Nymaera and Aedonai pointed at the intricate obsidian bowl on the altar, the water within rippling with each slow, constant drip from the sword's end.

Reznik stood beside the altar, next to the priest, smiling.

Gage and Viola faced him, but turned around at Reznik's subtle indication of their arrival.

Jarrod lowered his mouth next to Corin's ear. "Surprise."

Corin's hand tightened on Jarrod's, squeezing hard enough to make his knuckles ache. "Ma? Da?" He let go, crossing to his parents.

They opened their arms together to embrace their son.

Jarrod looked at Damien, wondering if Rae had let the Rahn'ka in on the secret he'd only shared with her, but he looked just as surprised. He stepped forward to join the hug, unwilling to wait for Corin to finish first.

"I didn't think you'd be here." Corin grabbed his father's shoulders as the man struggled away from Damien. "What are you doing here?"

Rae came to stand next to Jarrod. "Told you."

Neco pushed his nose into Jarrod's other hand and he smirked.

Stay with Rae.

Gage gestured to Jarrod, turning Corin in his direction. "Jarrod sent word a few weeks ago and invited us. You didn't think we'd miss your wedding, did you?" The older man tugged on his son's coat to straighten it, one hand on his crutch.

Viola brushed Corin's hair back into place while he smiled at them.

"It means a lot that you are." Corin received a quick kiss on the cheek from his mother.

"Don't let us hold this up." Gage cleared his throat. "We're here for you and Jarrod."

Corin nodded and looked at Jarrod, his eyes glassy, and held out his hand.

The proxiet stepped closer and took it, his hand still shaking.

They stood before the altar while Reznik waited off to the side.

The priest began the ceremony, lifting an iron goblet between his palms. "If you would place the rings in the goblet."

Jarrod retrieved the silver ring he'd stored in his coat pocket and placed it in the goblet, watching Corin as he followed suit with a matching gold band. They jangled against each other as they hit the bottom of the cup, making Jarrod's belly do another flip.

Corin reached to reclaim Jarrod's hands, holding them tightly between them.

The priest lowered the goblet to the altar, setting its base into the thin layer of water so the drip from the sword above would land within the goblet.

The first drop pinged against the bottom of the cup and the priest spoke. "First, the blessing of Shen Tallas, whose water offers to cleanse these rings."

The next drop sounded, a little quieter than the first. "And Loman Ord, whose skies will always watch over you."

The rest of the gods' blessings blurred in Jarrod's mind as he stared at Corin. The captain's face looked calm, but Jarrod could see the little strain of tension in his jaw as he tried to look focused. Somewhere around Aedonai's blessing, Corin drew one hand from Jarrod's and touched his chin.

Jarrod's eyes heated, and he smiled, gritting his teeth to keep his emotions at bay.

The priest lifted the goblet, keeping it beneath the water as the last drop echoed through the room. He held it out across the altar and together they took it.

Corin's hands wrapped around Jarrod's, his warm touch combined with the cool surface of the goblet sending a flutter through him. The water had nearly filled the goblet which hardly seemed possible with how little time had passed. Its surface vibrated, and he tried to still the shaking of his hands. Corin's touch encouraged him to breathe as he remembered the next step of the ceremony.

"My beloved Corin. I pledge myself, Jarrod Martox, and the entirety of my soul and being to you and you alone. I stand here, before the gods and you, to declare my promise to always protect, love and cherish you in this world and the ones that follow."

Corin's eyes grew glassy, but he tightened his jaw and squeezed a little harder around Jarrod's hands before he spoke. "My beloved Jarrod. I pledge myself, Corin Lanoret, and the entirety of my soul and being to you and you alone. I stand here, before the gods and you, to declare my promise to always protect, love and cherish you in this world and the ones that follow."

Corin's words were the only thing able to penetrate the drumming in his ears and he swallowed, trying to listen to the priest's instructions.

"I drink of this chalice, blessed by the gods and our love. And with it, I am your husband." Jarrod spoke the last word slower, lifting the goblet to his lips and taking a sip of the cool water before lowering it again.

Corin extended his hands, his fingers brushing Jarrod's knuckles as he took the cup. "Will it still count if I spill some because I'm shaking so bad?" He smiled and Jarrod laughed, tension leaving his shoulders.

The priest smiled as well and nodded. "Though we would have to start the ceremony over."

Corin's eyes widened. "I don't think my legs will make it that long." He took a slow breath, and the cup stilled in his hands. "I drink of this chalice, blessed by the gods and our love. And with it, I am your husband." He held Jarrod's gaze until the chalice touched his lips and he drank.

Lowering the cup, Jarrod reached to hold it with him again and the priest guided their hands back to the altar. Working in tandem, they poured the contents of the goblet into their entwined fingers. The priest took the goblet, freeing them to pick up the rings from their palms.

"Treasure these rings, a symbol of your bond and promise."

Corin took Jarrod's hand first, sliding the cold gold over his wet skin on his right middle finger.

Jarrod repeated the action, slipping the silver band onto Corin's left.

The priest took a small step back. "Typically, this is when I would encourage a kiss, though I understand there is some formal paperwork—"

Jarrod stepped forward, ignoring the priest's instructions, and kissed Corin. The captain's lips were still wet and responded instantly to his. All the nerves in his muscles dissipated as he wrapped his arms around the man he loved. Pulling away after a breath, he stared at Corin's face. "I think I missed the last bit there, sorry. All I heard was *kiss*."

Corin laughed, but he didn't move away. He kept his arms wrapped around Jarrod's shoulders. "Paperwork, *husband*. There's paperwork."

Jarrod's stomach turned over. "Husband," he whispered, so only Corin could hear before raising his voice to a regular volume. "My entire life is paperwork."

"Appropriate then, that it continues on this most joyous day." Reznik stepped from behind a small table Jarrod hadn't noticed before. It sat in the corner next to Allara Saen's shrine, donning a large leather-bound book, spread open, and a quill with inkwell. Several scrolls curled next to the book.

Jarrod slid his hand into Corin's, feeling the pleasant connection of the two rings for the first time. "You should probably get used to this."

The doors to the sanctuary swung shut as the last of their friends departed and silence settled through the room, broken only by the constant drip from the sword.

Jarrod turned to Corin and heaved an exhale of relief at their solitude. "Please tell me you were nervous too." His pulse still echoed in his ears, making them ring.

Corin squeezed hard on his hand. "Of course I was. Apparently I'm just a little more steady handed than you, which isn't what I expected. You must be a lousy thief."

Jarrod smiled, but winced as a headache twinged. "The first time my hands ever shook was in Veralian, opening your damn cell door."

Corin's brow wrinkled as he ran his hand over Jarrod's hair and lowered his voice. "Do you have a headache?"

Resisting the inclination to brush it off, Jarrod nodded.

"I'm sorry. I want today to be perfect, but I can hardly focus beyond the pounding in my ears."

"It's probably the damn altar. The drip has been driving me crazy too. We can go somewhere quieter? And you know you don't need to apologize."

"It's also my heart." Jarrod looked at Corin and blinked. "And yours. This hearing isn't ideal. I just need to relax."

Corin pressed his hand to Jarrod's chest above his heart. "Then let's sit down. Fancy a particular god?"

Jarrod smirked. "Can't say I do. I think this is the first time I've been in this room since I was a child."

"I've seen full fledged temples with less elaborate shrines." Corin guided Jarrod to the north-west corner where Allara Saen's tree grew. "But considering your particular situation, I think the goddess of the wild is most appropriate."

Allara Saen's shrine rested on a raised stone level one foot above the ground of the sanctuary. The roots of the tree hung over the masonry, creating natural places for worshippers to sit underneath the budding tree. It grew wild with vines and ferns wrapping around its gnarled trunk, wildflowers sprouting from mounds of soil nestled into the planter rimming the stone step. It created a surreal image of the spring growth on the interior of the castle with the backdrop of falling snow outside the large paned window beside it.

Jarrod sat, watching Corin kneel before him. "We're married now. Do you realize that?"

"It is a little strange to consider." Corin took Jarrod's hand and traced the hammered-metal band on his middle finger. "I keep thinking things are the same until I feel this ring on my hand. And your father called me Lord Martox. That will take some getting used to."

Jarrod chuckled. "You could go by Lord Lanoret if you preferred, but I selfishly prefer Martox. Which is equally strange, considering I hadn't gone by that name for nearly a decade."

"I think you're a little biased, but I'll appreciate that we can be uncomfortable together." Corin grinned. "I still like the sound of Corin Lanoret Martox. Besides, I'm pretty sure I signed some paperwork making that official already." He lifted Jarrod's hand to his lips, then lowered it and rubbed his palm. "How's your headache?"

"Dull. It's not just the headache, though. I'm... twitchy. Like I need to go for a run or something."

"The snow has been keeping all of us a little cooped up. But it sounds like things are getting worse. Neco's been getting snippier, too. He almost took my hand off the other day when I tried to make him move off the bed."

Jarrod cringed, anxiety stirring in his gut. "Why didn't you tell me?"

"You have enough on your plate. I didn't think you needed more."

"Neco snapping at my husband is definitely something I should know." Jarrod couldn't prevent smiling at using the spousal term.

"When you smile like that, I can't tell if you think it's funny that he snapped at me, or if you're just being a sap."

"I'm being a sap." Jarrod touched Corin's chin. "And I'm allowed. It's my wedding day."

"Fair enough." Corin rose just enough to pull Jarrod's mouth to his. He kissed him slowly, banishing the pain in the proxiet's head and replacing it with a colorful haze. When Corin pulled away, Jarrod studied the aura-like shimmer surrounding him.

"You should see what you smell like, it's pretty."

He expected Corin to laugh, but his brow furrowed. Looking down at Jarrod's hand again, he ran his fingers along his knuckles. "Aren't you worried?"

Jarrod sobered, and his shoulders slumped. He wanted to say that he wasn't, but other words formed. "Aye. I'd say *worried* is an understatement to how I feel."

"Then we need to discuss going to Jacoby." Corin met his eyes.

"As soon as I've signed all I need to, we can go. I've already made arrangements for my absence."

"That sounds like the opposite of what Damien told me... He said you didn't want to go. But you've changed your mind?"

Jarrod shook his head. "I didn't want to go because I didn't want to leave you here."

Corin paused, squeezing Jarrod's hand. "I'm sorry. I'm glad now I can go with you as your husband. Damien sounds confident that he'll be able to figure out what's happening."

Looking at the floor, Jarrod took a deep breath.

What happens if he can't?

He imagined himself growing fangs and fur.

"What still needs to be done before we can go? Anything I can help with?"

Meeting his gaze again, Jarrod nodded. "Actually, there is. The only thing left is the formal challenge, but I can't do that without a master of war."

"You haven't picked one yet?"

"Aye, but he's given me no answer."

"Problematic already then. When did you ask?"

Jarrod quirked an eyebrow and tilted his head. "Right now?"

"Now? You mean me?" Corin gaped, his spine straightening. "Is that even allowed since we're married?"

"Aye. No rules against it. You're the most capable man for the job. I had your name written from the start, but things got a little delayed for a bit there..." Jarrod shrugged. "What do you think?"

"An intriguing offer. And, I have to admit, very appealing. I've been a soldier for so long I don't think I know how to stop.

Coping without my position in the military has been the hardest thing for me since Veralian."

Jarrod smiled even though his ears still rang. "Then I'll take great pleasure introducing my master of war at the meeting tonight."

"Then you won't be able to call me captain anymore."

"Mmm..." Jarrod kissed him again. "I'll always call you captain."

"It is less of a mouthful," Corin whispered between kisses.

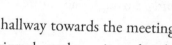

Jarrod strode down the hallway towards the meeting room, Corin next to him. He cringed at the voices already rising within the room and pushed the door open, letting Corin enter before allowing it to swing shut. "Are we late?" He looked at his mother, who glared at Damien.

Her fiery gaze locked on Corin. "What is *he* doing here?"

Watch out, she's in rare form already. Damien's warning surfaced in Jarrod's head. The addition to the already mind numbing din made Jarrod wince.

Another unusual member, Maith, sat next to Rae, with Neco chewing on an antler between her and Damien. A neat pile of scrolls and papers sat in front of him.

"What's going on?" Jarrod looked at his father, who appeared the calmest besides the auer.

"Maithalik has confirmed your true Martox blood, tracing

our lineage back further than even I knew. Your mother is unhappy with the positive development in your political career."

"I'm unhappy?" Sairin swung a hand around in front of her. "I'm furious. This whole thing is ridiculous, and it's all *your* fault." She pointed at Corin with a scowl.

Jarrod rolled his eyes, but his shoulders tensed. "Always the reasonable one, Mother."

"One would think you should be proud to be the mother of the future king." Damien leaned forward, his voice carrying confidently through the room. "Not behaving like a spoiled child."

"I'm the mother of a soon-to-be-dead proxiet. All for the greed of some rebels."

Jarrod rubbed his temples, and Neco rose to his feet.

"Now I see what you were trying to protect me from," Corin whispered to Jarrod.

"These meetings are closed door, Jarrod. Your harlot can't stay." Sairin held out a hand as her son approached the head of the table.

"Well, this *harlot* is going to sit right here." Corin walked towards the empty chair next to Maith.

"That's not your seat." Rae smiled and motioned to the empty chair at the head of the table opposite where Jarrod stood. "There."

Sairin stood. "Absolutely not!"

"Sairin." Reznik sighed. "You're making a spectacle of yourself."

"You're making a mockery of this House!" Sairin slammed her palms on the tabletop.

Neco growled, circling behind Damien to stand next to Jarrod.

"Mother." Jarrod ground his teeth. "You will show my husband respect or you will see yourself out."

Sairin choked, her wide eyes darting to find the ring on Jarrod's hand. Her face reddened, and she glared at Corin as he settled into the chair at the opposite head of the table. "How dare you think you deserve to be called a Martox... This House is..."

Her words kept going, but Jarrod couldn't hear them. He tried to focus on Corin, who sat calmly, despite whatever Sairin said, but Jarrod's heartbeat raged in his ears. Closing his eyes, he urged his breathing to slow, but his chest burned.

"You've killed my son!"

Jarrod's muscles flexed against his will, demanding action, and he squeezed the back of his chair. The wood cracked beneath his grip, Neco's teeth gnashing in the back of his mind amid an inferno. Snarls overwhelmed his thoughts, and he lost his mind within them.

Chapter 26

RAE GRIPPED DAMIEN'S ARM, WATCHING the wood splinter under Jarrod's hands. "Damien." She looked at Corin, who sat up straighter.

"You'll bring nothing but disgrace to this House." Sairin turned to Reznik. "And you. You knew about this?"

Damien reached across the corner of the table and closed a hand on Jarrod's wrist. "Block it out. Breathe, Jare. Remember what I taught you."

The proxiet opened his eyes, and they shone with amber as he looked at Corin.

Rae leapt to her feet, adrenaline rushing her veins with the scraping of chairs all moving back from the table.

The movement paired with the blur of dark fur lunging onto the table in a flurry of claws. Neco surged towards Sairin, teeth bared.

Damien reacted first, spinning away from Jarrod, and wrapped his arms around Neco's midsection. Yanking the wolf backward, claws scratched across the wooden surface as Reznik stood.

Sairin screamed as Damien tackled the struggling wolf to the floor, avoiding his snapping jaws and pinning him, his hands tight on the back of Neco's neck.

Reznik ushered Sairin towards the door, but she stopped next to Corin, who'd stood.

Sairin tore herself from her husband's hands.

Corin didn't look at her, watching Jarrod stalk forward. "Jarrod, stop." He attempted to step around Sairin, but she shoved his chest.

"Stay away from me."

"Jarrod!" Rae leapt and slid across the table. She landed between the proxiet and his mother and Jarrod turned his gaze on her. "You need to—"

Jarrod heaved her back across the table.

She let out a sharp breath with the contact of the wood, but turned her body into a roll, landing on her feet on the other side.

Neco snapped at her ankles and she yelped, jumping away.

"Neco's not listening!" Damien growled through gritted teeth as he pushed harder around the wolf's head. The faint blue glow of Damien's power glimmered at his fingertips, pressing into his fur.

Rae studied Jarrod. "He's not the only one."

Maith approached to help pin the massive wolf.

Reznik moved to approach his son, but Rae rushed around the table and grabbed his arm. "Wait."

Jarrod eased forward like a lion stalking prey.

Sairin blocked Corin's path to the proxiet once more. "You have ruined this family."

Corin's hard gaze dropped to her. "You're doing a good enough job of that all on your own. I'm the one here who actually loves and cares for your son."

Jarrod surged forward and gripped Sairin's shoulder, making her spin. His hand closed like a vice around her throat.

Shit.

Sairin gave a barely audible gasp, grasping her son's wrist.

Rae pulled Reznik back, her boots slipping on the floor as the man tried to intervene. "Let Corin handle this." Fear touched her stomach.

Corin attempted to wedge himself between Jarrod and his mother. "Whoa, Jarrod, stop!" He grabbed his wrist behind where Sairin clutched.

"I've had enough of listening to you." Jarrod's voice dropped eerily deep as he spoke to his mother.

Rae's heart raced, not daring to interrupt Corin's effort to restore Jarrod's awareness.

Corin repeated his name, running a hand over Jarrod's cheek and touching his chin. "Remember that match you lost in Degura?" His thumb traced over the proxiet's chin. "That ringing in your head is just from falling off your horse, Titian. You remember him, right? You hit your head on a rock and I came and pulled your helmet off. I was bawling because I thought you were dead."

What is he talking about?

Jarrod's head twitched, slowly turning towards him. Amber eyes locked on Corin's face, but his hand held firm at Sairin's neck.

Rae held her breath as Sairin choked, her feet kicking as she tried to back away and failed.

Corin ran his hand down Jarrod's loose arm, entwining their fingers. "What about that cold night in the desert outside of Mirage, when Damien disappeared to the ruins? We relaxed by the fire and forgot to eat dinner."

Jarrod's outstretched arm lowered, his grip relaxing as umber flickered back into his eyes, and Rae breathed a sigh of relief.

Corin ran his hand over Jarrod's hair, the hint of a smile coming to his lips. "You can relax now. Just let go."

The proxiet's gaze darted back to his mother, and he recoiled as though he'd been gripping hot coals.

Sairin wheezed a breath, leaning forward as she staggered back.

Rae let go of Reznik, and he stabilized his wife.

Corin stepped in front of Jarrod, taking his face in both hands. "Are you with me now, husband?"

Jarrod backed away from Corin, wide eyes lifting to meet Rae's. He scanned the room, breathing harder. Looking at his hands, he shook his head and pushed past Corin. The door ricocheted off the wall behind his exit.

"What have you done to him?" Sairin glared at Corin.

"I just saved your life, you crazy..." Corin shook his head. He turned to Damien, standing straighter than before.

Damien looked up from the now sleeping Neco, keeping a hand buried in the fur at his neck.

Rae rounded the table back to the wolf, kneeling next to him and stroking his face.

Corin straightened, his face growing stern. "We can't put off this trip anymore. Jarrod had made plans and I trust you can complete their arrangements."

Damien nodded.

"I'll see to caring for my husband. Bring any final paperwork regarding the Martox claim to the throne to me in our chambers. Jarrod will sign them as soon as he is well enough. I'll defer to Damien to explain the situation and trust his discretion on the matter." He turned to Sairin, and Rae stood. "I know you don't care for me, and truthfully, I don't much care for you, either. I'm sorry for the pain you've suffered, as well as that just endured. But I'm acting in your son's best interest. I love him more than you can possibly understand. I hope we both may use this time apart to find reason and understanding for each other." He walked past her, putting a hand on Reznik's shoulder before he left the room.

Maith eyed Rae, and she motioned with her chin to Sairin, who rubbed her throat, staring at the door.

Standing, the auer crossed the room and touched Sairin's arm. "May I have a look at that? Somewhere with better light, perhaps?" His smooth tone flushed Lady Martox's face as it usually did, and she nodded.

Reznik turned his hard gaze on Damien. "Explain. And do not insult my intelligence by lying."

Rae sat patiently while Damien filled Lord Martox in on the truth of Jarrod's condition.

At the end of the explanation, Reznik collapsed into his chair, rubbing his jaw as his son often did. "We cannot delay any longer on this. I have Jarrod's orders ready for when he departs. Once the last documents are signed, you best be on your way. Do you need a ship? An escort of Martox guards?"

"No." Damien's jaw flexed while he rubbed the back of his neck. "I don't want to risk anyone else witnessing Jarrod during the travels. We'll go by horse along the coast. A ship will be too claustrophobic and may make Jarrod's symptoms worse."

Reznik nodded, gathering up the remaining documents. "These circumstances are less than ideal, but it'll be far worse if Jarrod's condition cannot be corrected. I'd appreciate it if you provided me with updates on your progress." He held up the whistle charm for Liala Rae had forfeited to enable communication and looked at her. "I trust you'll teach me how to use this before you leave?"

Rae nodded as Reznik left the room. She sat on the floor with the slumbering Neco, petting his ears. "When I mentioned the possibility of us leaving to Maith a few days ago, he said he would stay here. What do you think about that?"

Damien smiled, and she rolled her eyes. "I think he's more useful here, anyway."

Rae drew in a deep breath, bracing herself. "I was thinking I might be more useful staying here, too."

"What? You want to stay here? I'd assumed..."

"I have a role to maintain now, with Jarrod's challenge. I don't want Maith thinking he can stay here and have all the control." Rae held Damien's gaze, but doubt surfaced. "You don't think I should."

Damien paused, leaning against the back of a chair. "No, that's not it. I should stay here, too, but that's not an option. And while I understand, I wanted you to come with us. I don't like the idea of being apart again."

Rae tilted her head. "I don't, either. I'd rather come with you, but... is it the best option?"

Shaking his head, Damien pursed his lips. "How much trouble could Maith really get into?"

Rae paused, considering. "He's never been to the mainland before, he doesn't know how things work here."

"Just stick him in the library and he'll be fine. He's hardly left it since we got here."

"Are you sure that's not your jealousy talking?" Rae looked at him again. "If Maith ventures into the city, he could get in real trouble."

He looked down, studying the floor. "But what about how I need you?" He looked at her and her heart swelled. "Leaving you in Eralas to go after Corin took all I had. I don't know if I can do it again. You keep me grounded, and I need that now more than ever."

Rae stood, her insides aching as she wrapped her arms around his neck. "You're right. I'll go with you, but I'll give Maith Din's last charm."

Damien smiled. "I have a feeling your hawks will be the best advantage we have in all this."

Two weeks later...

"Welcome home!" Maith's voice echoed through the great hall of the Ashen Hawk's hideout in Mirage, making Rae laugh.

"I can't believe you've been living here for a week already and haven't gotten kicked out." She glanced beside her at Damien and Jarrod, the three of them travel worn.

"I still can't believe he *beat* us here," Damien grumbled, low enough that only they could hear.

"He took a ship." Jarrod's tone lacked humor as he walked on Rae's other side, his hand entwined with Corin's. The captain had a strange ability to keep Jarrod more centered, even when Neco stood beside him.

Their journey towards Jacoby along the Helgathian coast had been tediously slow. They often stopped after only a few hours of riding to give Jarrod time to meditate.

Neco disappeared into the wilds for days at a time.

The hawk from Sarth came on the fifth day, demanding Sika and Lykan return home.

Sarth stepped past Maith, leaning on her cane as she grinned at Rae. "Welcome home, indeed." The sun shone in from the open ceiling hatches, making her hair fiery. "Good to see Lykan wasn't pulling my leg and you're alive, Sika."

Rae smirked as she crossed the hall to the leader of the Hawks. They embraced, making her grateful the hall empty and Sarth wouldn't hide behind the veil of authority she usually bore.

Sarth squeezed her shoulder as she looked at Jarrod next. "I believe you have some explaining to do. I'd like to know why in the hells I'm getting *owls* in my aviary. Why is Eralas demanding an audience with me and citing it pertains to you and your claim to the Helgathian throne?"

Jarrod cleared his throat. "Eralas will stand with House Martox for the throne."

"What business do the auer have in human affairs?" Sarth eyed Maith, who merely shrugged. She scowled, waving a hand. "This is all he gives me. Every day. But he's so pretty to look at, I let him stay."

Damien lifted an eyebrow. "Seriously?"

Rae laughed with Sarth and shook her head. "Thank you for taking such good care of him. I was hoping he might deliver whatever message you want to convey to Eralas for you."

Sarth tapped her cane on the floor and motioned for them all to walk. "That won't do, apparently. The Elder Council, or whatever, will be satisfied only by the visit of a *high-ranking Hawk*, should I be unable to make the journey."

"And I suppose the air in Eralas won't agree with you?" Corin stepped ahead to catch the door and held it for the group as they entered a small lounge off the back hallway.

Sarth quirked an eyebrow at Corin as she walked past him. "Captain Lanoret. So quiet, I nearly forgot you were here. Unlike you." She reached for his left hand, examining the ring on his finger. "I hear congratulations are in order." Looking at Jarrod, she smiled. "Glad your mission was a success."

They turned towards the collection of vacant stuffed chairs, each settling down. Damien remained standing, taking up position behind Rae, while Jarrod and Corin settled close to each other on a couch.

Neco sniffed the rug, huffing as he circled and laid in the center.

"Ah, my most troublesome group of people." Sarth smiled. "Where are we, in the political standings?"

Leaning forward, Jarrod filled Sarth in on the official challenge for the throne and the timeline for House Martox to sway the other houses for support. Along with his plans to use Eralas's armies as a show of strength. "The backing of the Hawks would be beneficial, but I can't pretend to know Eralas's agenda in seeking your audience."

Sarth stretched her injured leg out in front of her, wincing. "I know you must be tired of bouncing around this world..." She eyed Rae. "But I'd like you to be my delegate to go to Eralas. You're the only Hawk I trust who has the diplomatic mind to deal with it. Plus, as Lykan's political strategist, you're especially qualified."

Rae took in a deep breath and glanced at Damien before nodding. "I understand. I respect your decision."

"It's not *my* decision." Sarth paused, hiding her pain with her clenched jaw. "You aren't just my Hawk anymore, Sika. I'd like your agreement and that of your companions."

Jarrod nodded and looked at Damien.

Damien rubbed Rae's shoulder. "You know I'll support you. Sarth's right, you're the best choice to handle this situation."

"So the Hawks will join the fight?" Corin leaned forward. "They'll back Jarrod's claim to the throne?"

Sarth eyed him and exhaled a breath. "The Hawks will support Jarrod's claim. But I won't be agreeing to anything with Eralas unless it's in our best interests."

A slow smile spread over Jarrod's face. "Does that mean you'll alter policies to remain within the law once I'm king?"

The leader of the Hawks laughed. "Absolutely not. You'll just have to make sure I find no reason to steal from you."

Jarrod grinned. "I'd have it no other way."

"Though, without Iedrus on the throne, I'll find my hostility for the country lacking. Perhaps we'll stay on payroll as your secret assassins. Or I could retire."

Rae laughed. "You'll never retire."

Chapter 27

RAE GASPED, WAKING DAMIEN WITH a start. Her breath trembled as she reached for him.

Wrapping his arms around her, he encouraged her close as she pressed her face hard against his bare chest, a low sob tickling his skin.

The night terrors had lessened, but nightmares continued to plague her. While not as violent, he still loathed her suffering.

He pressed his lips into a firm kiss on her hair, stroking it back from her face. "I'm here."

The room remained perfectly still, the rest of the Ashen Hawks' dormitory beyond silent. Closed tight, the shutters on the window kept out the desert cold of pre-dawn.

Rae's body shook again with another steadying breath. "I hate this."

Falling silent, he ran his hand along the curve of her back, rubbing at the tension in her muscles.

"I know you said before that more meddling wouldn't be a good idea—"

"Dice..."

"I want you to try. Just look. Maybe there's something wrong. I've been through horrible things before without nightmares lasting so long. Please." Rae looked up at him. "I can't keep reliving this."

He tucked a strand of her hair back. Her two-tone eyes bore into him, making his stomach knot. "I don't want to mess something like this up again. Make it worse..."

Rae's brow upturned in the middle. "You've been neglecting your power for months. What if something happened when my memories returned to me? You're the only one who can help me. I trust you."

Damien watched her face, studying all the details he loved. The roundness of her cheek, the perfect curve of her nose. Her fearless spirit and strong-willed mind he remained in constant awe of. "I'm just afraid." He kissed her before drawing in a calming breath. "But I will look. Now is as good a time as any. The shift of dawn should help pull me out if something goes wrong."

Rae nodded, relaxing in his arms as she closed her eyes. "If you find something, fix it."

Linking into Rae's ká came easier than any other. Deeply familiar with the feel of her, he ushered his mind into the tangles of her soul.

His vision shifted, following the pale blue cords of thought and energy surging through her. He first felt the ripcords of her muscles in her back, where he held her. His fingers twitched as the Art obeyed his command to delve deeper.

Like a bird soaring up a stream, he followed the lines to the source, slipping into the web of her mind and memories. He'd been there before, in Eralas when he'd sought to undo what the auer had done to her. He did his best to remember where the dam had been, where Slumber had blocked everything she'd been before. It'd grown outward in a sprawl of ká-formed roots.

Thorny vines curled around her memories, agitated and unrelenting. It all stemmed from the single place he'd mended, his meddling having disrupted the balance. Where he'd sought to repair, a cluster of weeds had formed, sprouting from the divots he'd left behind when tearing down the auer's work. They grew wild, overtaking her memories in places that should have been able to wither and fade.

Gods, without me calming her ká for the past few months... Her body's response would've been so much worse.

Guilt rocked through him as he braced himself to untangle

the destructive knots. With each pluck at the strands of her ká, the thorns receded, her mind restoring to the paths originally intended. He'd studied the flow of human ká with Yondé as much as possible, though aspects still eluded him. But not with Rae. He'd known her before it all happened and had lovingly memorized every aspect.

He'd been callous before, distraught by her not remembering him. It'd made him sloppy, his Art responding to the emotion rather than to the logic a Rahn'ka needed to maintain. Everything around him warmed as he sucked in a deep breath and plummeted deeper into the sharp weeds.

Pain shot through him.

Damien almost recoiled before he reminded himself it was merely a memory. Not his, but his body felt it. The sting on the bottom of his feet mounted, starting with a low throb that built and tore up his leg, ripping his skin. He couldn't see the damage, but he felt it. He heard Rae's cries echoing off stone walls. His vision flooded with nothing but the pulse of her ká. They darkened, the vines turning crimson as he untangled them.

Another tug at a tangle of energy made his back arch. The strike of a boot against her back. He restrained a cry and gritted his teeth as he wrestled with the memory. Its webbed, bloody lashes ripping at his skin. His ká answered the call, surging through his hands to push the memory back into the depths.

The puzzle pieces of her ká fell back into place as he recoiled his power. His body ached, each inch of him remembering the pain she'd endured at Helgath's hand.

Damien blinked as dawn broke, suddenly aware of a draft in the room. A thin layer of sweat coated his body, and he wanted to curl against himself. But Rae was in his arms, running her hands over his temples to push back locks of his hair.

"You did it." Her tone sounded more at peace than it had in months. "I knew you could."

He tried to smile, but it came out as a huff. "I should have done that months ago." A chill passed down his spine. The tension led to a wave of pain through the muscles and he hissed.

Rae tilted his head towards her. "Are you all right?"

"No." Damien's stomach tightened, the remnants of the pain in his ká turning the ache into a ball of fury. "I don't want you to go to Eralas. I tried to be understanding of it, but the world is too dangerous for us to be apart right now." He pulled back from her, touching her cheek. "The auer can wait."

A frown twitched her lips. "You know it's better if they don't wait. They need time to assemble their armies, too. This isn't about you and me, and besides, I'll have Maith with me. Even if I didn't, I'd be fine. What's with the change of heart?"

Damien gritted his teeth and moved farther away. "I just can't. I don't know if I trust anyone right now. Even the Hawks. Iedrus's gold has swayed them before."

Propping herself up on one elbow, Rae scowled. "I trust the Hawks with my life. Just because Melnor proved unworthy doesn't mean the same for anyone else."

"But Melnor was trusted enough by Jarrod to come on his secret trip to find you... and he betrayed you both by trying to take me."

"And I'm sure Jarrod has damned himself enough for that choice, but is that what you're worried about? Someone getting to you here?"

"I'm not worried about me. I have the power of the Rahn'ka to help protect me." Damien sat up on the edge of the bed, looking back at her. "I'm worried about you. I'm worried about Jarrod and my brother. We're all targets. All thorns in Iedrus's side. And I'm worried about the consequences if I'm not there when something happens."

Rae sighed. "Look, Mister Rahn'ka, I appreciate your power and all, but I'm not a helpless damsel. I can fend for myself. I'm a Mira'wyld, remember?" The bed shifted as her weight moved.

Damien winced. "I know. But none of this makes us invincible. Even me. We're stronger together. And we can't be if you're in Eralas." He grumbled as he rubbed his hands over his face, tugging at the hairs of his trimmed beard. "Why can't Sarth go to the council herself?"

Rae stalked around the bed to stand a few feet in front of him, wearing Damien's tunic from the day before. "Sarth? Are you kidding? You want to send the leader of the Ashen Hawks to Eralas when she can't even walk without a cane? Do you have any idea the pain she's in daily? It is my *honor* to go in her place."

"I can heal her leg if that's the entire concern."

Rae threw her hands up in the air. "Damn it, Damien! I'm going to Eralas. I'm going today with Maith, and you're taking Jarrod to Jacoby with Corin."

"You mean I'm going to Jacoby with Jarrod *when* Sarth decides it's the right time. We're stuck here, remember? Because we can't tell Sarth why Jarrod *has* to go to Jacoby because she's too smart to get the Hawks involved if she knew about Jarrod's condition. I can't believe I'd agree with her on that. This whole situation is so fucked up."

"Semantics. So wait it out if you don't want to tell her. But that has nothing to do with me going to Eralas and you know it. Sarth is doing her best with the information we have given her."

"Sarth hates me enough as it is. Don't need to expand that by telling her what I did to one of her thieves." Damien rocked from the bed, standing and pacing towards the shuttered window. He leaned against the desk, the muscles in his back contracting. "I just... *don't* want you to go. I can't stand the uncertainty of it."

"Everything is uncertain." Rae's voice lowered as she walked past him to gather her clothing off a chair. "For all I know, you dumb boys will need me and I won't be there, but I need to do my part. And you need to do yours."

Damien glanced over his shoulder, narrowing his eyes. "What does that mean?"

Pulling on her leather breeches, she eyed him. "It means that this whole thing is shit and nobody's happy about it, but it will work out."

He heaved a loud sigh. "Sometimes I wonder how." He clenched his fists and turned to her, no longer bashful about his bare body. "How is this all supposed to work out? Right now I can barely guess at tomorrow."

Rae crossed towards him, shaking her head. "You just need something to look forward to."

Damien laughed despite himself. "Like the stress and duties of being personal advisor to the king? I assure you, I'm hardly looking forward to it. I'm terrified. This entire thing blew up in all of our faces—"

Rae pressed a finger to his lips. "That's not what I meant."

He forced himself to breathe instead of continuing his rant, closing his hand around her wrist. He turned her hand, kissing the back of it. "Then what?"

"A connection that neither distance nor time can change." Rae tilted her head. "Marry me."

A shock sparked in his stomach, but then resolved into a skeptical lift of his brow. "Pardon?"

Rae stepped closer, touching both sides of his face. "Damien Lanoret, will you *marry* me?"

His breath stopped as he met her eyes. "You're serious?"

She nodded, sliding her hands into his hair.

He froze, unable to comprehend what she was asking. Touching her cheek, he cupped it in his palm. With the contact, a slight surge of her ká passed into his and sent a chill down his body. "What's changed? I thought—"

"Well, that's not the answer I was expect—"

"Yes, Dice. The answer is yes." Damien shook his head as he leaned forward and kissed her hard. It renewed as he wrapped his arm around her waist and pulled her against his body, still leaning back on the desk.

Her arms wrapped around his shoulders and she sucked in a fast breath through her nose before parting from him. "I'm still going to Eralas."

Damien rolled his eyes with a chuckle. "I know." He ran a hand through her hair and kissed her forehead. "Just... be careful."

"You know I will." Rae touched her forehead to his. "And when I come back, I'll be your wife for real this time."

Chapter 28

THUMP-THUMP. THUMP-THUMP. THUMP-THUMP.

Jarrod stared at Corin's sleeping form, gaze trained on the artery pulsing at the side of his neck. The steady drum of the captain's heart contrasted with the escalating pace of his own.

Thump-thump.

He closed his eyes, trying to block out the sound. His heart wouldn't slow down, increasing in tempo until he thought it might burst from his chest. Sweat beaded on his forehead.

Red tinted his vision, daring him to slice the vein and free the blood. Cease the beating heart.

He eased himself away from the man he loved, fear knotting his stomach.

I'm losing control.

Rising, he yanked on a loose pair of breeches and snuck out of the room. Closing the door behind him, he looked down the black hallway, needing no light source to see. Scent trails drifted between rooms, but everyone nearby slept, their steady heartbeats reverberating in his head.

Jarrod covered his ears, growling under the weight of the drumming. Focusing, he tried to find the link to Neco, but it only made things worse.

He's hunting.

Bloodlust scorched his veins and, before he could consider an alternative, Jarrod sprinted down the hallway. He maneuvered through the guild's corridors until he reached the basement.

The four cells, with rough floors and exposed iron bars, were hardly ever used. Remnants of an old structure the Hawks had taken over and integrated into their base. So far below ground, the cool air echoed no sound, chilling his senses.

Grabbing a key off the wall, he entered a cell and slammed the barred door shut. Twisting the iron, he locked it and tossed the key across the room. It chimed against stone as it bounced against the bottom stair.

Backing up, his bare back hit the wall behind him and he drew his hands over his face. He sank to the floor, chest heaving.

Gods help me.

Chapter 29

"WHAT DO YOU MEAN HE'S GONE?"

"He's usually still in our room in the morning." Corin rubbed the remaining sleep from his eyes as he stood in Damien's doorway. His brother already hurried to put on his clothes. "I don't know where he is. I figured you could use your freaky Rahn'ka shit to find him."

Damien scowled as he pulled on his shirt and shoved past into the hallway. He paused, his shoulders tensing. "He's nearby. Still in the guild headquarters. But the wards are making it tricky for me to pinpoint..." He winced and rubbed his temple.

"Then we better get to Sarth and tell her to pull those things down. Something could be wrong."

"We're not going to Sarth. She can't know something is up."

Corin exhaled and threw his arms up. "Fine. Whatever. Just find him."

"I swear to the gods, if that man is just in the mess hall..."

Corin couldn't make out the rest of what Damien said as the Rahn'ka stomped down the hallway. He tucked his shirt in as he followed his brother.

When they found Jarrod, Corin's heart plummeted.

The proxiet sat in the corner of a cell, the room dark except for the pale blue light of Damien's Art pulsing from an orb hovering between them. Jarrod held his knees up to his chest, and his head rested against them, hiding his eyes. He wore only a thin pair of loose breeches, but the chill in the basement bit through Corin's thick tunic.

Corin rushed towards the iron, scrambling for the door, but found it locked. "Jarrod. Shit. What happened?"

Jarrod looked up and shook his head. His bleak gaze flitted between Corin and Damien. "It wasn't safe."

"What in the hells are you talking about? Who put you in here?" Corin tried the door again, shaking it. "Damien, find the key."

Jarrod lowered his voice. "I did."

A hollow knot took hold in Corin's gut. "*You* did? Baby, what happened?"

The proxiet's gaze dropped to his feet. "I thought I might hurt you."

Metal jangled as Damien found the set of keys and stepped forward. He eyed Corin and then Jarrod. "Do you feel in control now?"

"It doesn't matter. Open the damn door," Corin snapped, but Damien didn't move.

Jarrod kept his head down, only nodding his answer.

Corin snatched the keys from Damien, cursing as he struggled to find the right one. When the click of the lock finally came, he hurried to Jarrod, hardly able to breathe. Dropping to his knees, he resisted the temptation to pull his husband into him. He forced a calm touch to Jarrod's cheek. "Why didn't you just wake me up?"

"I couldn't think about anything other than your heart beat..." His eyes finally lifted, lingering at Corin's neck. "I didn't have time to explain. I just needed to get somewhere safe. Safe for you."

He lifted Jarrod's chin, encouraging his sight up. "You won't hurt me."

Damien's footsteps drew a glance from Corin, and the Rahn'ka knelt beside them. "I can try to see if I can put up some additional barriers, but I'm not sure how long they'll hold, or if they'll make it worse after."

Jarrod shook his head. "It's morning, isn't it?"

Corin nodded. "I was worried when I woke up and you

weren't there." He sat on the floor in front of Jarrod, resting his hands on his knees. "Why does it always seem worse at night? And when Neco is out?"

"I don't know. I can't sleep at night anymore..." Jarrod sighed. "I'm spending the rest of my nights in Mirage right here." He looked at Damien. "Keep the key, will you?"

"Don't be ridicu—"

"That's probably best." Damien returned the hard glare Corin gave. "We don't know how far this will continue progressing."

"Then you better bring a cot down here. I'm not leaving my husband here alone."

Jarrod shook his head, breathing faster. "You shouldn't stay down here. Hearing your pulse will make it worse, and I don't want you to see me like that."

Corin touched Jarrod's hair, running his hand over it.

"You need to listen to him." Damien put a hand on Corin's arm. "If he says you shouldn't, you can't. The bond is changing a lot more than just his ability to sleep, and you know that."

Corin breathed sharply through his nose, fighting the emotion stabbing at his eyes. "Then we're at least getting you some blankets. And I'm going to complain about it... all day."

A faint smile touched the proxiet's face. "Blankets sound nice. But do you know what sounds even better?"

Both Lanorets looked at him.

"Food."

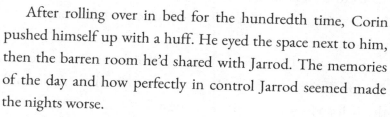

After rolling over in bed for the hundredth time, Corin pushed himself up with a huff. He eyed the space next to him, then the barren room he'd shared with Jarrod. The memories of the day and how perfectly in control Jarrod seemed made the nights worse.

I miss him.

Corin slid to the edge of the bed, pulling on his clothes. He hesitated when he instinctively went to grab his short sword. He always carried it, but putting it on his belt to visit Jarrod seemed silly.

It's not like I would use it on him. Even if...

Corin shook away the thought of his husband attacking him. His Jarrod. Despite all of Damien's warnings, he couldn't stay cooped up in the room while Jarrod was alone in the basement. In a cell. A nervous ball coiled in his stomach, but he yanked the bedroom door open.

Corin slowed when he reached the final stairway which led directly into the holding dungeon of the Hawks' headquarters. He and Damien had ensured that no one would realize what they were using the space for. Despite it originally being Corin's idea to keep the problems from Sarth's knowledge, he regretted it. They should have arrived in Jacoby already, but now they were held in place by responsibility.

Responsibilities Jarrod can't possibly deal with right now.

All correspondence with Reznik now came to Corin, and he handled all he could without Jarrod. Rumors had begun in Lazuli, with some asking why the proxiet hadn't been seen in public in weeks.

Corin lifted his lantern, casting its light across the room. Shadows of the bars stretched over the cell's dirty floor until they fell on Jarrod at the back of the cell.

The proxiet sat perfectly still on the cot, his legs crossed beneath him. The blankets and pillows lay strewn all over the floor. His eyes snapped open when Corin's boot hit the bottom step. The bright amber of his irises reflected the light he carried. "Corin." His calm voice did nothing to steady Corin's nerves.

"I couldn't sleep." He paused, studying Jarrod before he took a step forward. "Needed to check on you."

"It's not the most comfortable arrangement." Jarrod motioned to the cot. "But I suppose it's what I deserve."

"I wouldn't say that." Corin furrowed his brow. "You don't deserve any of this, my love."

"Will you let me out then?"

Corin stopped mid-step, lifting the lantern to get a better view of Jarrod's face. "You're not serious? You're the one who said you need to be in there every night." The nerves in his stomach doubled, reminding him of what a deer must feel when a lion crouched nearby.

Rising from the cot, Jarrod stepped to the middle of the cell and shrugged. "It's me. You can unlock the door. I can't sleep here, but maybe I could with the company of my husband in our bed."

"Are you sure that's a good idea?"

A smile spread over Jarrod's face, but it didn't reach his eyes. "Of course. Sleeping alone is killing my soul. Let me out?" He stepped closer to the bars, his boots silent on the floor.

Swallowing, Corin set the lantern on the ground. "I don't have the key. So even if I agreed, I can't."

The smile vanished from Jarrod's face and the proxiet stalked forward until he grasped the bars with both hands. His voice dropped an octave. "Then what good are you?"

"I came to check on you. To remind you I love you despite all this shit." Corin forced a slow breath, glad he hadn't stepped close enough to the bars to feel the need to move away. Even out of reach, he felt exposed in the middle of the room. He ached for his sword, but then remembered who he faced.

It's still Jarrod, somewhere in there.

Jarrod's arms flexed, and the muscles in his jaw twitched. "Let me out." His knuckles whitened on the bars and he growled, sneering as the iron bent apart under his strength.

Corin stepped back, eyes widening.

I knew he'd grown stronger, but... He's still Jarrod...

"I *am* sorry and I hope you can hear me through what the wolf is doing to you. *I love you, Jarrod.* My king, my love." Corin lifted his left hand and twisted the ring on his middle finger. "But I'm making this worse." He backed towards the stairs, unwilling to return for the lantern, or to look away from Jarrod as he strained against the bars.

The proxiet shook the cell door, the anger leaving his expression.

Corin hesitated at the bottom stair as he turned to go.

"Corin! Corin, come back! Don't leave me here."

He glanced over his shoulder, his eyes meeting those of the wolf in Jarrod. They bore into him and accelerated the panic beating in his chest.

Another eerie smile crept over Jarrod's face, and his voice lowered again. "Visit again soon, will you?"

Corin thundered up the stairs before he could linger any longer, Jarrod's laughter echoing behind him.

Fuck.

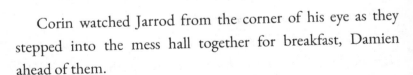

Corin watched Jarrod from the corner of his eye as they stepped into the mess hall together for breakfast, Damien ahead of them.

"You're quiet this morning." Jarrod kept his voice low, concern lacing his tone.

Corin ran a hand up through his uncombed hair. "Didn't sleep well. That's all."

"I missed you being there when Dame came to let me out this morning." Jarrod squeezed his wrist. "Is everything all right?"

Corin locked his jaw and nodded.

How does he not remember?

"I'm fine." He turned a little more and touched Jarrod's chin. "Everything is fine. I promise. I'm just hungry. I'm sure you are, too."

Jarrod let go of Corin's wrist and nodded.

Damien retrieved a plate of bread and cheese, bringing it to the table sequestered in the corner the three usually occupied. He narrowed his eyes at his brother as he settled down.

"I need to check in with Sarth." Jarrod didn't wait for a reply before walking away, straightening his posture as we went.

Damien picked up a loaf of bread, tearing off a chunk as he eyed his brother. "So what's wrong?"

Corin huffed. "Why does everyone keep asking me that?"

"Because you look like your dog just died." Damien took a bite. "Or that you saw a ghost."

"Ghosts aren't real..."

Damien lifted his eyebrow and opened his mouth before Corin cut him off.

"No, I don't want to hear it. Don't tell me they are. I have enough to be terrified of in this world without your creepy

Rahn'ka stuff." He turned, watching Jarrod as he approached Sarth's table.

The guild leader's face hardened at his approach, but it was impossible to hear what she might have said.

"I went to check on Jarrod last night."

Damien let out a loud groan. "You idiot."

"I know!" Corin put his elbows on the table, burying his head in his hands. "It was stupid. But I couldn't sleep and I just..." He met his brother's eyes, trying to read what they were telling him. All he could see was the concern and pity.

"It wasn't him." Damien settled his half-eaten piece of bread on the edge of the plate. "Whatever you saw."

"Logically, I understand that." Corin gripped his chest above his heart. "But here. I can't stand seeing what's happening to him. We can't stay here any longer if this is what he's becoming."

"This is the best place we could be. It's actually lucky we were here when this started happening. If we didn't have a place to lock him up, this could have been a lot worse."

Corin sighed, staring at the food and contemplating if he could stomach any of it.

"You going to see this through, big brother?"

He looked up and met Damien's hard eyes. "Seriously?"

"You don't have the most stable of records with this kind of thing. I know you love him, but when things get hot like this you usually—"

"Stop. I can't believe what you're implying." A wave of anger overthrew the despair and fear. "Jarrod is my *husband*, and I did not make that bond lightly. I won't leave him."

Damien chewed his lip. "You know it will keep getting worse, right?"

"Then fix him."

Damien started to speak, but stopped when Jarrod approached behind him.

"You know, when people shut up at your approach, that usually means they were talking about you." Jarrod sat next to Corin, but didn't look at him.

Corin placed his hand on Jarrod's, drawing his gaze. "Maybe. But you don't need to worry about it."

Damien nodded in agreement and picked up his half-eaten meal before shoving the plate towards Corin and Jarrod. "Eat up. Any progress from Sarth?"

Jarrod looked at Damien. "She's established a secure method of communication with Rae. We've discussed what is acceptable from the auer and she's fine taking it from here on her own as she knows I have business to see to. Means we can go."

"About damn time." Damien shoved the rest of the bread in his mouth.

Corin eyed his brother. "We need to prepare some things first, though."

A woman cleared her throat behind Corin, forcing him to turn towards the small figure he hadn't heard approach. She stood barely taller than him, even while he sat, her lithe frame hidden beneath layers of material forming her dress. A tan corset covered her torso, a splash of red fabric cinching her waist. "I understand you have a wolf problem."

Chapter 30

"WHO ARE YOU?" DAMIEN SCOWLED, examining the woman standing behind his brother and Jarrod.

"Lucca."

Why does that name sound familiar?

"Who?"

"She's the guild's seer. Sarth's sister." Jarrod looked at her. "Nice to see you, Lucca. What makes you think we have a problem? Has Neco done something?"

Damien's back straightened as he evaluated the seer's ká. The twists of the Art were vague and hard to place, but unmistakable.

Lucca quirked her head at Damien, a springy curl of her blond hair bobbing free of her ponytail. She broke the stare first, sucking in a little breath as she turned to Jarrod. "Come now, Lykan. You understand plenty well how I know."

Jarrod sighed. "Neco hasn't eaten a cat of yours, has he?"

"You don't look like you'd be related to Sarth..." Corin had turned to face the woman.

"I'm married to her brother." Lucca shrugged. "And typically Silas and I refrain from getting involved too deeply in Hawk business, but this one caught my eye. Especially when I examined the guild prison cells this morning..." Her gaze turned back to Jarrod.

The air between them filled with tension, silence hovering while Damien looked to Jarrod.

The proxiet cleared his throat. "Have you told anyone whatever you think you know?"

Lucca blew out a breath between her teeth. "I'm crazy, but not foolish. Of course not."

Damien crossed his arms. "And what exactly do you know?"

"Enough that you don't want me to talk about it out here in the open where interested ears might listen."

"Are you proposing something?" Jarrod ripped off a piece of bread.

Lucca paused before she lifted a hand and placed it on Jarrod's shoulder. Her eyes closed, and a shiver passed through her.

Damien loosened the barrier on his aura to gauge what Lucca performed. Her ká shone differently, prepared to accept anything from the energy around her. The connection, however, flowed so subtly that Damien would have missed it if he hadn't honed into it so carefully. It wasn't between her and Jarrod, but her and Jarrod's tunic.

What in the...

"Are you done?" Lucca stared at him, slipping her hand from Jarrod. "It's polite to ask before you investigate someone's Art."

Damien gut knotted. "How do you—"

"You three need to come with me. Somewhere private?"

Jarrod's chair ground over the floor as he stood.

Lucca led them down a stairwell Damien didn't even know about. He'd spent enough time in the Hawks' headquarters to memorize most of the passages, and the ones Lucca walked through weren't particularly hidden, but inconveniently placed.

"Why do I feel like she's leading us somewhere to murder us where no one will find the bodies?" Corin brought up the rear of the group as they walked down a spiral staircase carved into the stone.

Lucca laughed, and it echoed up the narrow passage. "I doubt I'd have much luck with that. And that's *without* considering the formidable Art Damien has access to."

Damien tensed, slowing before they crossed into the room at the base of the stairs. It was empty, and Lucca placed her lantern on a hook next to an open stone archway leading to more darkness.

"Who the hell is this woman?" Corin whispered in his brother's ear as he walked past towards Jarrod.

The proxiet stood stone still, studying the archway ahead.

"I think we're private enough now. And I, for one, would appreciate an explanation." Damien watched as Lucca bustled into the next room and emerged with a candle she held up to the lantern to light.

Jarrod frowned at the Rahn'ka. "You're with friends, brother, ease up. She sees things. Things that have already happened. I don't know how, but you're better off sticking to the truth, because she'll know if you don't."

Lucca smiled and beckoned them through the archway. She led the way with the little flame out in front of her. The light flickered off glass on the walls, but Damien couldn't make out the details. She went to the table at the center of the room, lighting a collection of candles.

"What is this?" Corin stood close to Jarrod without touching him.

"I forgot about this room..." Jarrod eyed the walls, walking into the darkness. "I never learned what all these are for."

How the hell can he see in this dark?

"You could speed lighting the candles, Damien, if you

assisted with that Art you keep so locked up. You can let it go. We're beneath the wards and they won't affect you here. No one above will sense it."

Damien hesitated, looking for Jarrod, but couldn't see him through the blackness of the basement room.

"Go ahead, Dame."

Among friends, huh?

He chewed his lip. "Won't be the way you're expecting..." He sucked in a breath and allowed the barrier on his power to slip. Speaking to the voices of stone around him, he gathered enough energy to flick it from his fingertips. He gestured to each corner of the room, where he suspected there may be sconces, and allowed the luminescent ká to find its way to each wick. The pale blue ebb of his energy amplified with an inhale of breath and surged to fill the room.

Shelves lined the walls, climbing from the ground all the way to the short ceiling. Jars of dirt filled them, all various sizes and shapes. Little bits of parchment with messy writing labeled each one. He squinted as he approached one wall, reading the names.

Waterfall behind the temple outside Ingston, Delkest.
Omensea, Isalica. Near the water.
Cave with the weird wall carvings in Dilae, Ziona.

Lucca eyed one of Damien's artificial flames and hummed. "Curious." She turned, walking towards the wall beside Jarrod. "Excuse me." She pushed him out of the way and plucked one jar up and popped its lid open. Tilting it, she poured some dirt into her palm as she crossed back to the table and put the jar down.

Damien squinted at the text on the jar.

Monolith ruins, south-west edge of Aidensar.

The Rahn'ka gulped.

Yondé's sanctum.

Lucca pressed her finger into the dirt in her palm, spreading it as she closed her eyes. Her body stiffened, the flows of the Art passing through her, focused on the dirt in her hand.

She pinched a bit, lifting it to her mouth where she placed it on her tongue. Another shudder passed through her body.

"What in the hells..." Corin looked at his brother, but Damien minutely shook his head, staring at the seer.

Jarrod approached them, lifting a hand towards Corin but lowering it without touching him. "Let her work." He crossed his arms.

Lucca's eyes snapped open. "Rahn'ka." She turned to Damien as he straightened. She had a smile on her lips, almost playful. "That explains a lot."

Damien didn't like how casual she was with the word. "How do you—"

"I know just as I know other things. The past." Lucca gestured around her. "My Art is limited, but vast at the same time. I only need a part of Pantracia to witness what happened in a particular place."

"But—"

"There isn't time to help you understand. After what I saw between you two last night..." She motioned to Corin and Jarrod. "Your time is running out."

Jarrod frowned. "What?" He glanced at Corin. "Last night? I didn't see him last night."

Corin shuffled his feet. "You did."

"Why don't I remember that? Was I asleep?"

"No. You weren't *you*."

"He's lucky he didn't get himself killed." Damien sighed, looking back to Lucca. "But you're telling us stuff we already know. We need to get to Jacoby and take care of it. We don't have much time... What good is hearing it again?"

"Ah, but now I understand and can inform you better." Lucca ignored Damien and went back to the wall near where the other jar had come from, muttering to herself. "Jacoby... Jacoby..." She ran her finger along the wall, tracking with her eyes. She finally crouched and filled her arms with a set of five jars, carrying them back to the table.

"Why didn't you tell me?" Jarrod lowered his voice to Corin.

"It didn't seem fair to. I know it wasn't you."

Lucca set the jars down with the clanking of glass and systematically unlatched their lids, tossing them to the tabletop.

"Is that why you've been off this morning?"

"Other Rahn'ka have attempted this bond?" Lucca paid no attention to the conversation, looking up at Damien for his confirmation. He managed a nod, but she continued before he could open his mouth. "And I suspect it has gone poorly before?"

"Yes. And I thought I built the proper—"

"The best of intentions, but you failed, Rahn'ka." Lucca stuck her hand into the first jar, pulling out a bit of dirt and rubbing it in her fingertips.

Damien growled. "Look—"

"Nope." She dropped the dirt back into the jar and moved to the next, repeating the process. "I need to narrow the timeline. What year would these mergings have taken place?"

Damien blinked. "Year? Gods, you expect me to know that?"

"True, I suppose the Rahn'ka were not the most dedicated to preserving their knowledge with a convenient dating system. Our libraries and academies are doing far better with that now, after the Sundering." Lucca dropped a speck of the dirt from the second jar on her tongue and shivered again.

Jarrod sighed and walked away with his hands on his head.

"What are you looking for?" Corin stepped towards the table. "You can help him?"

"I can guide our well-meaning Rahn'ka." Lucca didn't bother looking at any of them while she spoke. "Tell him what mistakes *not* to make."

Damien eyed Jarrod's back. "We need all the help we can get right now." He tried to ease his breath, calm his rapid heartbeat, knowing Jarrod could likely hear it.

"I need air." Jarrod bent his head forward, hands behind his neck.

"I'll come with you." Corin took the proxiet's hand, lowering it. He moved with him towards the exit. "Assuming you don't mind the company."

"I always want you with me." Jarrod led Corin from the room and they disappeared up the stairs.

Damien returned his attention to Lucca, waiting as she dipped her hand into the third jar. "What do you need from me?"

"A region where one of these bonds might have gone wrong. Somewhere for me to start."

Damien sighed as he wracked his mind for anything he remembered. So much had happened, that returning to his studies with Yondé felt impossibly long ago. "Everything was different before the Sundering. Do you have a map?"

Sorting through not only his memories, but those of Pantracia became a tedious one. He and Lucca worked into the night, forcing Damien to trust Corin to secure Jarrod himself. The scare from the night before would likely keep his brother away.

Corin returned to Lucca's jar room, settling onto the ground with a piece of wood he whittled.

Damien stared at the piece of parchment he'd scrawled notes on. So far, it was all things he felt he knew, and none answered the most important question.

"You cannot sever the bond." Lucca opened her eyes as she brushed the dirt back into a jar. They had filled the table, and several more containers occupied the floor. A map of Pantracia lay sprawled out in front of them, with 'X's drawn for the areas they searched for answers. Lucca leaned over and placed another near the mountains of Isalica. "Add that one to your list, it might be the most important. If you sever the bond, it will kill them both."

Don't sever the bond.

Damien underlined the words several times with a frustrated sigh. "Then hopefully Sindré can teach me how to build stronger barriers. We'll leave in the morning."

Chapter 31

Spring, 2611 R.T.

RAE WAVED HER HAND BEHIND her, urging the vines to cover her doorway once again.

Crossing her compact room, she heaved a sigh and sat at the desk near the window. It looked out on the Sanctum of Law, hidden behind a thin mist of drizzling rain. The impressive crystal roof stretched towards the sky, the glow within painting the canopy and raindrops.

Another tedious afternoon speaking with the council left her exhausted, but she needed to write all the information for Sarth in their coded language before she forgot anything.

Taking a sheet of parchment from the stack on her desk, she dipped her quill into the inkwell.

Sarth,

The meeting today went well. They've accepted that you have no plans to cease your usual business. In fact, I think a couple of the elders like the continued challenge to authority because it might keep the politicians in line. After Jarrod has acquired the throne, they'll cease correspondence if that is your wish. During the time of challenge, while Jarrod makes the show of power with Eralas's armies, they've agreed not to bring any Hawks to harm intentionally, but expect support and access to Hawk resources. This includes knowledge that may assist in guerrilla tactics. They've drafted a contract for you to sign, and I've included it with this letter. Hope all is well there.

Sika

Rae rolled the letter together with the folded contract and stood. As she entered the hallway, she turned away from the sanctum and headed for the gardens around the back of the dormitories.

A young woman, escorted by two guards and a scholar, approached and Rae sidestepped to let them pass.

A human on trial? That's rare.

Rae looked behind her at the group, narrowing her eyes before continuing on her way.

Once she sent Din with the message to Sarth, she waited in the warm spring air and watched the hawk soar west.

Another hawk screeched, and she jumped, looking up. "Liala?"

Digging her whistle charm out of a pocket, she blew it and caught the bird on her arm.

Pulling the note from her leg, she set the hawk onto a nearby log and unrolled the parchment.

Just as her eyes focused on the writing, a wave of power struck her senses hard enough that she staggered backward and dropped the note. It lit her body ablaze, veins searing in recognition of the Art.

What the hells is that?

Pure power spiked her adrenaline, and she spun towards the epicenter of the invisible explosion. The Sanctum of Law shone with motes of light in the crystal spires, the building itself glowing with fresh life with the Art flooding through it. Every auer in the gardens had turned to face it.

"The human?" Rae picked up the fallen parchment and looked around as guards raced in and out of doors, ushering bystanders towards the dormitories. Another pair went to close the tall vine-crafted gates that allowed the population to visit the complex.

A male guard, donning traditional light armor, approached her. "Under orders of the council, you are hereby quarantined in the east wing until further notice." He motioned to the building, the thin mesh chain mail at his joints silent with the movement.

Rae sighed, but knew better than to argue. She filed inside with everyone else, clutching the note in her palm.

Guards rushed back and forth in the banquet room of the east wing, looking far more concerned than Rae expected. The din of the room rose as they brought more auer inside, all speaking about the surreal power they'd sensed. No one knew what it was, but it'd come from the elder's sanctum.

The power vanished, and the room took a collective gasp.

Rae put a hand to her chest, willing her heart to return to a normal pace.

The concerned tones resumed, and the highest ranking official in the room, a silver circlet on her umber forehead, waved a guard towards the door.

Silence blanketed the room as Rae spotted the tops of two spears held by soldiers marching inside.

The Arch Judgment stepped onto the raised platform at the end of the banquet hall. Elder Erdeaseq's oak crown adorned his onyx hair, which fell against his neck. Folding his hands in front of him, his honey eyes looked almost bored as he addressed the crowded hall of at least one hundred auer.

"There is no need for the concern you are undoubtedly feeling. The entire council is well and the display you have all witnessed is under control. However..." He paused, casting his gaze across the entire room. "It is essential that what you may have felt remains only within your knowledge. I understand I am asking you to place a great deal of trust in us, your council, but I assure you the absolute necessity of this request."

A few whispers bubbled up around the crowd, but a raised hand from Erdeaseq silenced them.

"It is forbidden, and now punishable by the law of our council to speak with any not present about what you have witnessed today. Your confidentiality is your responsibility as an auer and we thank you for your adherence."

Rae furrowed her brow.

You just don't want all of Eralas to know that you let some kind of crazy power into your sanctum. However she got it past the draining chamber, she made fools of you.

"We cannot answer questions at this time. Instead, we request your patience and diligence regarding this matter." The Arch Judgment lowered his hands to his side.

Meaning I'm stuck here, I bet.

"The Sanctum of Law's gardens and dormitories will reopen shortly." Erdeaseq turned, walking past the guards back towards the entrance of the banquet hall, followed by his guards.

Yep. Stuck here.

Whispers began again, but remained controlled until the elder was fully from sight. Two guards took their position by the door, the vines growing into place to seal the room shut.

Sighing, Rae made her way towards one wall, slipping between auer who chatted with each other. Being surrounded by bodies made it difficult to breathe, and she let out a slow, relieved exhale when she pressed her back against the wall.

Pulling the parchment back out, she unrolled it and read.

Dice,

Not a lot to report, but I wanted to keep you updated. Sindré hasn't provided a lot of help and Jarrod continues to get worse. I can only risk making an attempt every few days before he and Neco block me out entirely. However, I've found a few new texts that might prove insightful. I miss you and hope you can join us soon. I'm not sure how much longer this will take. I'm still working on Sindré to let you stay in the sanctum with us. As always with these damn guardians, it's a slow process.

I love you.

Your Damien

Chapter 32

JARROD'S CHEST BURNED, AND HE coughed, bracing himself with a hand on the marble-tiled floor. He clutched his leather vest and wheezed.

Neco growled on the other side of the Martox grand ballroom, head lowered and eyes bright.

Flames licked up the pillars and walls, engulfing the ceiling in an inferno. The swooping banners of his family swayed, fire drifting down like falling leaves.

Sweat coated Jarrod's brow, a blast of suffocating heat lashing his face. Lifting his gaze from the snarling wolf, his stomach churned.

Behind Neco stood another version of himself.

Jarrod looked at his hands before returning his gaze to his amber-eyed twin. "Who are you?"

Neco snapped his jaws, and his body disintegrated into ash, floating away in the up-current of embers.

What is this place?

Jarrod's mirror image laughed. "The one in control. The stronger, superior king. You're too weak to rule."

He's the wolf part of me.

Swallowing, Jarrod rose to his feet, looking down at his thief attire that contrasted the wolf's royal regalia. "I will rid myself of you."

The wolf strode towards the tiered platform at the end of the ballroom, used for announcements. He sat on the throne wreathed with flames. Gripping the armrest, he gave a wicked smile. "You'll fail." He ran his hand lovingly over the throne's blazing wood. "I like it here."

"Where are we?" Jarrod watched the fire scorch the curtains, but the material wouldn't fall to ash.

The wolf rolled his eyes. He gestured towards his own head, leaning to one side on the throne. "You remember this place with so much fury. It's only appropriate for me to rule your mind from here. Besides, you've imagined this, haven't you? Your family home in flames? Especially after your mother's betrayal."

Jarrod's heart thudded harder. "I'd never wish this on my family."

"Lies. And weakness."

"No." Jarrod shook his head. "I may not agree with my mother, but that doesn't mean—"

"We were so close, too. To killing her." He twisted his hand to study his nails, frowning. "Then that stupid *captain* had to interfere."

Anger rose in his chest, and the flames around Jarrod roared higher. "You won't touch him."

The wolf grinned, standing. He hummed as he prowled down the stairs towards Jarrod. "Embrace that rage. That's all I need of you."

"I will destroy you, even if I destroy myself in the process if that's what it takes to keep Corin safe."

The wolf flinched, averting his amber stare. He shook his head, grunting in disgust. "Human attachments. Frivolous. Like these attempts they make at entrapping us."

"Corin is doing the right thing keeping me in the arena."

When the wolf twitched again, Jarrod narrowed his eyes.

He doesn't like it when I use Corin's name.

"I love Corin." Jarrod studied his twin as the wolf glared at him.

"Good. When he dies at your hands, I'll use every bit of your rage. Every bit of your grief will fuel me. Power me. And you'll be lost forever in the depths of your own inferiority."

Jarrod growled and lunged at the wolf, the blaze crackling in his ears.

The wolf's laughter echoed off the walls.

Chapter 33

"MORE BOOKS?"

Damien threw the stack he carried onto the low table beside the fireplace Corin stoked. Running his hands up through his thickening beard, he groaned.

"I need more than books." Jarrod stood, scratching his arm where claw marks scabbed over. "I can't..." He tilted his head, stretching his neck and sighing.

Damien glowered. "Well, since Sindré isn't helping, this is all I can do." He shot a look at the window of the ruined room, leading towards the outer courtyard with an altar Corin didn't know the purpose of.

"What use are those damned guardians then?" Corin shoved at the log in the fire, and the wood collapsed in a cloud of embers. He put the iron poker aside before he felt inclined to beat something with it.

The chill of spring still clung to the mountains of Olsa, but the fire warmed the small enclosed room. The sanctum boasted few areas actually amenable to living, and the three of them made frequent trips to Jacoby for supplies. The room with the fireplace had become the most frequented, even with its failing roof. Damien often settled himself on the rug and pillows to read the plethora of tomes he'd sorted through.

Jarrod stood, pacing. He rolled his shoulders, breathing faster than usual. When he stopped, his eyes glazed over.

He's communicating with Neco.

Dread knotted Corin's stomach.

"I told you to stop talking to him." Damien barely looked up as he flipped through musty pages, the writing blotchy and illegible.

The proxiet returned, glaring at the Rahn'ka. "It helps"

"That's because you're feeding the beast, so of course it's going to be quiet. But the more you use the bond, the stronger it will become until neither of us can do a damn thing about it."

Corin watched Jarrod, the constant anxiety in his stomach surging for a moment. The sun wouldn't set for at least another hour, but Jarrod was already showing too many signs that meant he'd need to be locked in the arena soon.

A howl rang out in the distance and Jarrod straightened, stretching his shoulders again.

The room froze for a moment, though Damien didn't lift his eyes from the pages. It felt as if none of them even breathed. Then the Rahn'ka slowly turned his page.

"Any word from Rae?" Corin sought any kind of distraction he could, sitting on the stone bench beside the fire.

"I'm going for a run." Jarrod didn't give anyone time to argue before he walked out of the room.

"Fuck."

"Go get him." Damien nodded his head towards the door. "He doesn't listen to me anymore. Maybe you can talk some sense into him. He won't get past the monoliths. Sindré has agreed to be *at least* that helpful. But better he not figure that out."

Corin pushed off the bench and hurried towards the door. If Jarrod intended to get away fast, the captain had no chance of catching up. But, stepping out into the front courtyard of the sanctum, his shoulders relaxed.

Jarrod sat on the ground with his back and head against the altar, eyes closed. "If I leave the sanctum and run, I don't think I'd come back."

Corin sighed, watching him for a moment before approaching. He crouched in front of him, touching his knee. "No, you probably wouldn't. So, I, for one, am glad you're still here."

The proxiet leaned forward, opening his eyes. The darkness housed flecks of amber, now a constant presence within his irises. "Aye. But the trees and the air... I feel so trapped in here. If I could just run... Maybe you could come with me?"

"You know I can't keep up with you." Corin touched his chin, rubbing the scar with his thumb. "We just have to find another way to let out your energy. Maybe sit-ups?"

Jarrod's chest rumbled.

"All right, a lot of sit-ups?"

"Sit-ups aren't enough. And you know that."

"I know." Corin settled onto the ground, crossing his legs and scooting close enough that he could lean forward onto Jarrod's knees. He rested his chin on his folded arms. "Perhaps we can talk about things that help calm you then? What brings you the most peace?"

Jarrod lowered his knees and lifted Corin's chin with one hand. "Definitely not you."

Corin smirked. "You know I'm rarely one to deny you, but it is getting a little late. Something else? Maybe the scent of lavender, or the sound of rain? Though those seem far too cliché for you, my king."

The amber in Jarrod's eyes shimmered. His gaze flickered to the side and back again, jaw twitching. "A little late, huh? You forget that to me, rain is like drums and lavender burns my lungs. It's not late, yet."

Corin raised an eyebrow. "The point is to calm you, not excite you more."

Jarrod frowned, leaning forward and giving Corin an oddly gentle kiss. "Fine. Calm. What calms me?" He pulled away, taking a deep breath. "Maybe your scent calms me, but it's more than that. It's your touch."

"I thought my touch elicited a different kind of emotion." Corin couldn't help himself in tracing a line down Jarrod's shoulder, following the bare curve of his muscles. His fingers played down the backside of his arm, following the shape of Jarrod's Ashen Hawk tattoo. He followed the line of each vertical blade without needing to see them.

A smile crept over Jarrod's face. "Well, it does, but they all stem from the same place. I want you because I love you, the same reason your touch calms me." He closed his eyes. "Especially when you do that. Tracing the ink. Though it would be better if my cuts weren't so damn itchy."

"I'll ask Damien to make some ointment for them tonight." Corin smiled as he began the pattern again, redrawing Jarrod's tattoo with his fingertip.

"Can't your brother just heal them? I don't know why the wolf version of me likes to fight with Neco so much."

"It's a way to get the aggression out, I bet. And no, he can't heal them. Any meddling with your ká makes yours—"

"Shhh..." Jarrod put a finger to Corin's lips and his voice dropped to a lower register. "What's not calming is when you sound like your brother."

A laugh passed through Corin as he shuffled closer to Jarrod. "Come here then, my wolf." He opened his arm, encouraging Jarrod to turn and lean against his chest while he moved to trace the familiar lines of his back tattoo through the proxiet's vest.

Jarrod sighed, touching Corin's leg. "I don't think I could do this without you. Keep my sanity, I mean. Even during the day, I can feel it under the surface... Struggling to take over." His breathing finally slowed almost to a normal rate, his hand coming to rest over Corin's heart.

Corin kissed Jarrod's hair, tightening his hold on him. "I love you. I always will."

After a pause, the proxiet hummed. "I should tell you something... I made your brother promise me and I don't want you to hate him for it."

"What are you talking about?"

"This might not work, whatever he's doing. There may be no—"

"It'll work."

"But if it *doesn't*, I don't want to live the rest of my life with the wolf in control. Do you understand? If I'm gone, I want you to let me go."

Corin's breath caught, but he needed to remain calm for Jarrod. With the proxiet so close, he was certain the man could hear every slight shift in his heartbeat. "I'm not going to think about that now." He retraced the outer edge of Jarrod's back tattoo.

"And you don't have to. But I do, because I don't know how long I'll be able to make these kinds of choices with a clear head."

"It won't come to that." Corin swallowed the tightness in his throat before it could affect his speech. "I refuse to lose you. Not when I finally have you as my husband. We have too much to do together."

Jarrod lifted his head from Corin's chest and looked at him, his irises holding onto only a tiny amount of their usual brown. "I won't give up, even during the night." He shut his eyes, cringing. "It's time for the arena."

Chapter 34

THE STREETS OF JACOBY ALMOST felt like home with the frequent visits for supplies. It seemed surreal to walk past the old prison house Rae had broken him out of and not fear being seen. Even if people recognized him, word of Helgath's political strife had reached Olsa. Jarrod's proclamation would protect Damien here, as well. The republic of Olsa would not put themselves in the middle of a pending civil war by meddling with a proxiet and his council.

Damien patted his pocket to ensure he had the paperwork, just in case he encountered trouble.

I wonder when Rae will arrive. She's overdue already.

The notes carried by Liala had confirmed her journey towards Jacoby from Eralas, but Rae never provided a specific day. They'd just agreed to meet in the city. It led to Damien inventing reasons to go to town, leaving Jarrod and Corin to their own devices in the ruins. He had to trust Sindré would intervene if it became necessary.

If that damn guardian ever does anything more than stand there and stare.

The guardian spirit had refused to answer Damien's questions and had barely spoken a word to the Rahn'ka since their arrival.

You created this problem, so you must solve it yourself. The stag had vanished into the ruins and refused to manifest in front of Jarrod or Corin. They kept themselves in vague gatherings of power invisible to everyone except Damien.

Damien's horse nudged him sideways on the street, frustrated by his daydreaming. He smiled, scratching his nose. "Sorry, bud."

He laced the horse's reins around the hitching post where he and Rae had stolen Zaili, his old mare. Glancing towards the tavern, he contemplated a drink.

I could definitely use one.

A small group of people inside cheered, throwing dice onto a table. Rae wasn't among them, so he moved on towards the town square, filled with open merchant carts.

He couldn't help looking at the rooftops. Rae had been there when they first met, watching his disagreement with a local merchant over the cost of his armor. He'd been forced after her by a local peace officer, and he smiled at the memory as he scanned the tiled slopes.

He paused when his eyes fell on a figure perched half-way up one of the slanted surfaces.

Of course.

Rae sat cross-legged, reading her Mira'wyld book. Her hair had grown longer since he last saw her, reaching her elbows as it had the day they met. In the same nostalgic fashion, she'd braided strands next to her face and one wide section down the top of her head.

A flurry of relief and joy washed through him at the sight of her. She was engrossed, not noticing as he leaned against the corner of the opposite building and watched her as she turned the pages. He rolled the sleeves of his cream shirt to his elbows, unfastening the buttons of his leather vest. Tensing his left hand, he gathered a part of his ká and pushed it towards her. The tangle of energy had no problem latching onto hers, eager to join in the same way it always did when they were intimate. He smiled as he watched her back straighten.

Rae looked up, gaze locking on him. A grin spread over her face and she snapped her book shut. She opened her mouth to say something, but a gruff voice yelled instead.

"Hey! Hey, you!" The same guard who'd given them trouble over a year ago huffed towards the building Rae sat on. He'd hardly changed, still rotund and red-faced. "Get down! Rooftops are non-walking areas!"

"Lloyd!" Rae held her hands up, still grinning. "It's so nice to see you again."

"You!" The guardsman's face purpled in recognition. "No! This is not happening again. Get down!"

Damien chuckled, crossing the road to approach Lloyd from behind. He leaned over his shoulder. "You going to ask me to go get her again? I'd be happy to volunteer this time."

Lloyd spun, forcing Damien to take a step back. The guard nearly lost his balance, but Damien caught his arm.

"Whoa, careful, big guy."

Lloyd gaped at Damien. "This can't be real. Impossible. You're that deserter! I had you!"

"And you lost me..." Damien looked up at the roof, where Rae had stepped to the edge and stared down at them with a playful smile.

"And me." She sat down, hanging her legs over the rim.

Damien reached into his pocket and produced the paperwork that Jarrod had signed and sealed with his family crest. "And before this misunderstanding progresses further, we are technically off-limits now."

Lloyd snatched the paper, burying his ruddy nose in it. His lips moved to form the words in silence as he read.

Rae laughed. "And, all thanks to you, we're getting married!"

The guard groaned as he thrust the paper back into Damien's chest. "That's it. I'm done. I'm retiring." He turned on his heels and marched up the street. "Vagabonds and criminals turned royal!" He waved his hands over his head. "Just don't burn the damn city down!"

Rae slid off the roof, landing on the street, and ran over.

Damien caught her as she jumped at him, spinning with the momentum before putting her down with a hard kiss. He couldn't bring himself to pull away, eagerly renewing it into another as he ran his hands over her hair. Slowly, they parted, and he smiled. "I missed you."

"And I missed you." She pulled him close, burying her face in his neck.

"So you still want to marry me? Enough to shout it from the rooftops... literally."

Rae laughed and pulled back to look at his face. "And I'll do it again. I actually want to marry you even more than when we parted."

"You never told me what changed your mind..." He played with one of her braids between his fingers.

"I'd been thinking about it long before I asked you. It all started with how your parents were together, and then with Jarrod and Corin's wedding, I kind of... changed my mind." She gave him a quick kiss. "You still sure you wanna belong to a thief for the rest of your life?"

"Whole-heartedly. You pocketed that part of me a long time ago." He grinned. "Besides, you're the political strategist to the future king of Helgath, and a Mira'wyld. I'd say I've done well for myself."

Rae's smile faltered. "How is our proxiet?"

Damien's shoulders tensed at the thought of Jarrod. "Worse. A lot worse. It's still progressing daily."

Sighing, she touched his face. "Then let's do it now."

"Do what? I've been working on it as quickly as I can."

"Get married." Rae's gaze danced between his eyes. "It might be awhile before we have another chance, and I know no one is here with us, but all I want is to—"

"Right now? You want to marry me *right now*?" Damien watched her two-tone eyes and felt lighter at the thought.

"Yes. I want to marry you *right now*."

"Then let's go." He didn't need to think about it. It didn't matter who was there, he just wanted to pledge himself to her just as Corin and Jarrod had done. "Right now."

"Lead the way, Lieutenant."

Rae followed Damien into the sanctum, their hands entwined and metal wedding bands touching. Before they could cross towards the east ruins where they'd arranged their living spaces, Sindré's form emerged from a swirl of blue clouds hovering on the ground.

They stood tall, a set of antlers wreathed like a crown. Nose upturned and shaped like a deer's, they glared with fathomless navy eyes at Rae.

Auer are not welcome here, Rahn'ka.

"I'm not having this conversation again, Sindré. Rae *will* stay in the sanctum with me. She is my wife, and you will not put that limitation on me or you risk losing your Rahn'ka. I've already put up with enough, considering you—"

"Human bonds of matrimony hardly matter to me." Sindré's voice echoed, a melding of voices creating the one ringing in Damien's ears.

Rae stared, wide-eyed at the guardian. "I'm only a quarter auer." She shrugged, grip tight on Damien's hand as she gave a wide smile. "And maybe I won't hold it against you that you tried to kill me before."

Sindré held perfectly still as they shifted their gaze from Damien to Rae.

"In fact..." Rae cleared her throat. "The auer aren't my friends, either. They imprisoned me for months, and I have no loyalty to them. You, on the other hand, have my utmost allegiance as I've pledged myself to your Rahn'ka."

They snorted, the deer-like action quivering through the human shape. Grabbing at the long skirt at their ankles, they lifted it and stepped closer to Rae.

Damien nearly intervened, but Sindré held out their hand.

The guardian spirit lowered their face to be even with Rae's, studying her. "If you speak true, then your allegiance should come with forgiveness for my previous actions. I cannot regret that which gifted us our Rahn'ka. He is not yet the oldest we have maintained, but he shows promise." They turned to Damien, somehow looking angry without their face changing in expression. "If he does not get himself killed."

"I'll try to keep him alive." Rae smirked at him before turning a serious expression to the guardian. "And I forgive your previous actions against me, but perhaps you will allow me to know the extent of those actions. Beyond obtaining the power of the Rahn'ka, were there any other side effects to the vial Damien drank?"

The spirit snorted again, rising back to their full height. "You mean besides inflating his arrogance even further?"

"Hey." Damien grumbled. "I am not—"

Rae chuckled. "Besides that, too."

Sindré eyed Damien before turning back to Rae. "No. Though, had it been you to drink, it would have reacted violently with your existing power. The results may have been more... catastrophic than mere infertility."

"So you lied." Damien glowered.

Rae elbowed him in the ribs. "Forgiven. May I enter?"

The spirit paused, then stepped to the side and dipped their antler crown in a slow nod. "With the understanding that you are loyal to the Rahn'ka, and as the mate of our single survivor, you may prove useful."

Damien scowled at Sindré, but ushered Rae forward. "You get used to how ominous they always are."

"Well, I think they're charming." Rae dipped her head at the guardian before walking past. Once they were alone, she took a deep breath. "Where's Jarrod?"

Damien took Rae into the east ruins, dug into the mountainside. He led her to stairs that descended deeper into the ground, a row of inset torches along one wall illuminating the metal door at the end. Its forged surface depicted vines, curled around each other, and a single indistinct orb at the center of the door. A rock, wedged into its frame, propped it ajar.

The Rahn'ka heaved his shoulder against the door, pushing it open for Rae to reveal the training arena beyond. Traditionally, the location had been meant for Rahn'ka to spar and hone their skills against each other, but time had weathered all. The oval space was empty, except for a bonfire at the center beneath a circular opening in the ceiling. At the far wall, a collection of stone appeared fused together like lava rock, blocking what might have once been another door. At the base stood a single cot with neat piles of folded blankets and pillows.

Corin's been tidying up again.

Breath huffed from the opposite side, and Neco's growl echoed off the walls.

"If you stopped wrestling, I could stop needing to bandage your arms over and over again!" Corin grumbled as he stepped back from a flurry of muscle and fangs rolling around in the dirt at the arena's right wall.

"Are they fighting?" Rae looked at Damien, concern etched on her face.

He touched her arm. "It's normal at this point. It's mostly play to get their energy out. But it gets a little rough. Best to wait until they're done."

"Rae?" Jarrod stood, shoving Neco off. He crossed into the beam of light coming in from the hole in the ceiling.

She smiled, crossing the arena towards him, leaving Damien by the door.

The proxiet grinned and started jogging towards her, but lurched to a stop halfway. His head turned, eyes darting to the side. His gaze focused, as if watching something along the arena's wall.

Neco lunged from behind Jarrod, teeth bared.

Rae stopped and backed up a step. "Hey, boy..."

"Neco, stop." Damien added authority to his voice as the wolf continued to growl in his approach. He couldn't speak directly to Neco's ká to push the order there. He'd ceased communicating with Neco and Jarrod in that way to help their ká to forget the manipulation of his.

The wolf charged, and Rae gasped as he launched off the ground. He tackled her, teeth gnashing as she cried out. She shrieked again, but Jarrod stood motionless.

Damien rushed forward, sliding across the dirt as he reached Neco and Rae. He locked his arms around the wolf's middle, yanking the beast off.

Corin came to Rae's side, helping her to her feet.

Her body shook, blood pouring down the arm she'd raised defensively over her face and neck.

Neco twisted his body, heaving his weight against Damien, throwing him back. The Rahn'ka shoved with all his strength, forcing the beast to the ground. Dropping him on his back, Damien held Neco's neck and jaw to keep him in place. The power of his ká shimmered in his tattoos, surging to further fuel his muscles.

Arms wrapped around his middle, yanking him off of the wolf with impossible force.

Damien rolled across the dirt a few feet with the throw, but Jarrod pinned him as soon as he came to a stop.

Amber eyes lit like fire and bored into him, the proxiet's hands at Damien's throat. "I won't let you hurt him."

The Rahn'ka wrapped his legs around Jarrod's hips and twisted to free himself of the man's grasp with the help of his power. He threw Jarrod to the dirt beside him, and the ground shook.

The proxiet rolled back to his feet, watching Damien do the same with an intense gaze.

"This isn't you, Jare." Damien rubbed his sore ribs, trying to catch his breath. "Get back in control." He refused to relax his power, watching the tension in Jarrod's body. In the corner of his eye, Neco struggled on the ground, roots entrapping him. Corin had drawn his sword and taken up a stance between the wolf and Rae, the blade ready in front of him.

Jarrod followed his gaze and yelled, turning to charge at Corin and Rae.

Damien coalesced energy into the palm of his hand and sent the lash of his ká at the proxiet. He seized Jarrod's soul, bringing him to a halt. The bond of the wolf roared, lashing out at Damien and making his entire being ache with fatigue far faster than it should. Panic forced the Rahn'ka into the crevices of Jarrod's consciousness, where he found the ebb of energy and tugged.

Jarrod collapsed as Damien stalked towards the snapping Neco. He wrestled free of the roots as the Rahn'ka balled his fist and repeated the action, pulling his physical hand back with it. Neco stilled, hitting the ground with a thump.

Corin's eyes widened. "What did you—"

"They're asleep." Damien winced as a headache mounted and the voices in his head burrowed through all his barriers. He met Rae's eyes, trying to shake the lingering adrenaline in his system.

Rae held her arm, blood covering her hand. "That's *way* worse than I thought it would be!" She gasped for breath, staring at Jarrod's limp form. "He could have killed you!"

Corin walked cautiously past Neco, his sword still drawn, before he crouched beside Jarrod. He placed his fingers to the vein in the proxiet's neck and looked up at his brother.

"Could have, but didn't." Damien rubbed his side where he was certain there were broken ribs. He looked at Rae's arm and walked towards her, examining the plethora of puncture wounds on her skin. "Let's get back upstairs and I can heal us both."

"What about them?" She motioned to Jarrod and Neco.

"I don't think we'll want to be here when they wake up." Damien turned towards his brother. "We've been putting it off, but it's time they don't leave the arena anymore."

Corin ran a hand over Jarrod's jaw. "When is this going to be over?"

Damien sighed, looking at Rae's blood on his fingers. "I don't know."

Chapter 35

Summer, 2611 R.T.

RAE PULLED HER DRIPPING BRAIDS up into a ponytail, securing them with a strand of leather. She squeezed the ends as she walked, leaving a trail of water on the sanctum's mossy ground.

The short monoliths surrounding the altar in the front courtyard had grown thick with summer vines, flower buds blossoming in the shadows of the canopy above.

Ignoring the ruins to the right, which they'd made their home for months, she walked towards the distant crumbled structure on the far side.

The stone walls had collapsed, but wooden beams with a roughly hewn roof dominated one side of it. Corin had helped Damien in rebuilding a place to better keep the valuable tomes of the Rahn'ka protected from the elements. The rest of the old library remained in ruins.

When she rounded the open archway at the front of the structure, her gaze fell on Damien sitting inside near a glassless rose window.

He didn't look up, brow furrowed as he read.

She entered the room, pulling her shirt to fan air beneath it. When Damien still didn't look up, she frowned. "You have that look on your face like you've discovered something important." Sitting next to him, she poked his ribs when he ignored her. "Hello? Damien?"

Damien's eyes shot back and forth across the page and he frantically flipped back one, then two, to reread. "This." He breathed, tapping his finger on the Rahn'ka text. "Is important."

"Something to help Jarrod?" Rae leaned over his shoulder and a drip landed on the page.

Damien swiped the droplet off, pushing the book away from his chest to protect it from her wet hair. "No. Much more important. Now, if you wouldn't mind avoiding destroying irreplaceable knowledge, I'd appreciate it if you took your sopping wet hair over there..." He smiled, gesturing with his chin.

Sighing, Rae sat down and stuck out her bottom lip. "You used to like my sopping wet hair."

He sighed and scooted to make space for her on the bench beside him. "I'm sorry. Perhaps when I'm not learning something that could change the fate of the entire world?"

"That's rather dramatic." Rae leaned on his shoulder, smiling as she felt his tunic dampen. "Are you going to share this irreplaceable knowledge or just boast about finding it?"

Damien scowled at her but brought the book back into his lap as he crossed his legs beneath him. He pointed at an elaborate symbol in the top corner of the page. "Rahn'ka isn't too far off from Aueric. Do you know this character?"

Rae's eyes landed on the pages, but the words made little sense. She shook her head, skimming the rest of the pages until her eyes found something familiar. She pointed. "Does that say Mira'wyld?" Sitting up, she pointed at the word next to it. "Rahn'ka? What is this?"

"It's... a recipe?" Damien shook his head. "Or... instructions. It's a binding spell."

"To bind what?" A knot formed in her stomach.

"Something unfathomably powerful." He scanned through the page again, tracing the text with his finger. He flipped a few pages and pointed at another symbol. "The Rahn'ka get a little flowery with describing things, but I'm fairly certain it has something to do with Shades. And whoever... whatever their master is."

"Uriel," Rae whispered.

Not supposed to say his name out loud. Oops.

Bellamy had been afraid to say it, as if it'd summon his master just to speak his name.

Damien's body tensed against her as he turned his head. "You know its *name*?"

She nodded, squeezing his arm. "Bellamy told me. I didn't even think about it until now. What do you mean, *whatever*? Bell said that he's a powerful practitioner. How old is this tome? Uriel couldn't have been alive so long ago..."

Damien's brow furrowed. "I'm not sure. But this text describes that power like a parasite. It describes a creature that infects the consciousness of a person and creates servants to further its reach."

"Sure sounds like Shades to me." Rae rolled her lips together. "But Damien, that's impossible. That would mean... he's... *it's* been around since..."

"Since before the Sundering. Way before it, actually." Damien flipped back again to the first page he'd shown her. "The Rahn'ka are awful with dates, but this says it was bound beneath the ground somewhere in the north-west. And it happened a short time after the first Rahn'ka. In fact, it claims the Rahn'ka were created to battle this thing."

"And what does a Mira'wyld have to do with it?"

"One was part of the first binding." He gave a little grin. "So much for Sindré's hate of auer. Looks like the first Rahn'ka was friends with one."

Rae chuckled without mirth. "That's all it took to bind Uriel? A Rahn'ka and a Mira'wyld?"

"No." He touched the ink on the page. "But some of it is confusing. This says the binding also needed *a Shade redeemed*, and an *abandoned host*, whatever that means." He touched the next spot. "And *the Berylian Key, divided*."

Rae blew out a slow whistle. "That's a tall order. But, hey, we already have two parts?" She shook her head. "What's an abandoned host?"

He let out a breath. "I have no idea. But at least I know what tomes I'm going to be focusing on while we wait for Jarrod's ká to allow me to affect it again." He snapped the book shut and set it aside. "Who knows, maybe Sindré will be helpful with this subject. Though they seem insistent that I have to do all the reading myself." He rubbed his eyes, shutting them as he rested his head back on one of the mullions of the window.

Rae closed her eyes, putting the bits of information together. "A host. You said that Uriel is like a parasite, right?"

"That's what the book describes it like. An infection. Who takes over bodies."

"Making them his hosts." Rae slapped Damien's chest and his eyes popped back open. "He's been alive for so long because his face isn't *his*. He takes bodies! That means whoever he is, was someone before. Had a *life* before. We need to find out who he is."

"If Shades are any sign of what its power is capable of, I'm afraid what might happen if it continues to amass more. The text described it as being fascinated by politics and meddling."

"Well, that explains Evie."

Better her than Jarrod.

Damien hummed. "You're right. It'd probably be trying to use Jarrod to take the throne if he hadn't said no. But how do we figure out who it is right now?"

Rae groaned. "I don't know. And we can't right now. I know you need to wait before you try to fix Jarrod, but we can't start something else until that's done."

Damien sighed. "I've done all I can with the information from Lucca's visions to guide what techniques I could use. I've read and reread the tome about bonding a ká to an animal at least fifteen times, so I know exactly all the places I went wrong. I *think* I know how to fix it, but I can't risk trying to manipulate his ká for another month at least. There is nothing else I can do. And maybe something in all this might give me some perspective with Jarrod. I just have to keep reading everything I can." He stifled a yawn as he leaned over to pick up another book.

Rae kissed his cheek and pushed the book back down. "Tomorrow, husband."

Three weeks later...
Autumn, 2611 R.T.

Rae looked up from her book at the sound of heavy feet.

He's never in a rush...

The Rahn'ka skidded to a stop under the stone archway, wild eyes locking on hers in the dim light of her candle. "We have a visitor."

Shutting the book, Rae stood and furrowed her brow. "Who?"

"A Shade wandered into the arena with Jarrod." Damien grabbed her hand. "And I've seen him before. The one from Lazuli."

Hope erupted within her. "Bell?"

Damien's face turned sour, and he squeezed her hand. "No. The one who was after Bellamy."

Rae's heart plummeted, her veins heating. "Where is he?"

I'll kill him.

"Whoa, hold on." Damien took both Rae's shoulders, turning her to face him. "We shouldn't jump to violence. He didn't use his power... even when Jarrod just about cut his throat open. Something's going on with him. He knows what I am."

Pausing, Rae tried to hear his words. "Why would I care about that? He's the reason Bell is dead. And... wait. Jarrod almost cut his throat? With what?"

"A knife."

"Where did Jarrod get a knife?"

"My dumbass brother."

Rae sighed and lowered her voice. "Show me the Shade."

Damien nodded, turning with her back down the half-ruined hallway. One side had completely crumbled, exposing the walkway to the elements. Roots and ferns grew between the stones, swaying in the autumn breeze. The other side housed the spaces Damien and Corin had converted into bedrooms.

Corin emerged from one, brushing his hands together as he closed the door. "Bastard's heavy." He eyed Rae, then back at the door. "Good thing it's my turn to stay up watching Jarrod tonight, won't need my room. Do I get an explanation yet?" He crossed his arms and leaned on the doorframe as he looked at his brother.

Rae put a hand on the captain's shoulder. "Maybe don't give him another knife."

Corin winced. "I didn't like watching him tear up the deer carcasses we throw into the arena with his bare hands. He usually ignores the plated meals."

Damien frowned. "I had to knock him out."

"And that'll delay fixing him for how long?" Rae huffed. "To save a Shade."

"A Shade?" Corin stood up straight, glowering at Damien. "I helped carry a fucking *Shade*? What the hells—"

"Can you both stop with the Shade thing?" Damien's jaw flexed, and he looked at Corin. "It's getting late. You need to get to the roof to watch him. Gods know the mood he's going to be in when he wakes up."

Corin grumbled, looking towards the shadows beyond the crumbled hallway wall. "Fine." He poked his brother in the chest. "But you better come explain this all to me when you can." The captain spun and stomped towards the ladder they'd crafted to gain a vantage on Jarrod's imprisonment inside the arena. The only way to see the proxiet was through the opening in the ceiling.

Damien stepped between Rae and the door. "Before we go in there, I need you to promise you won't do anything rash. Put everything aside and look at him as a man. Trust me."

Rae stared at him, her desire to trust him warring against the pain of losing Bellamy. "Fine. Is he unconscious?"

"Yes. Blood loss. Neco bit him, bad, and I still need to heal him."

Resisting the urge to roll her eyes, she stepped around Damien and pushed open the door to Corin's room.

Laying flat on his back, the Shade's bloodied appearance and closed eyes softened Rae quicker than she'd hoped. Thick stubble covered his jaw, his dark brown hair cropped short on the sides, a longer lock falling over his tanned forehead. A thin white scar ran down the side of his face.

Gods, he just looks like a man.

She approached the cot, eyeing the oozing wounds and the tiny slit at his throat where Jarrod must have threatened him. "You took someone important from me," she whispered, crouching next to the cot. She studied his face, her resolve to kill him waning. "That book said we'd need a Shade redeemed to defeat Uriel."

Damien shuffled up beside her. "We do. And I already know I can separate him from his power. I've read about it, and the man seems to be trying to do it on his own anyway, like Bellamy was. His ká is a mess."

Rae cringed, emotion tightening her throat. "Why now? Why not before he..." She bowed her head and took a breath.

"You know that if it hadn't been him, it would have been another. Uriel is the one who went after Bellamy. The creature is to blame."

Standing, Rae motioned to the damage Neco did. "You should heal him then, but I don't want anything to do with him." She turned, stalking towards the exit.

"I probably won't make it to bed tonight. I shouldn't leave the Shade to roam, all things considered."

Rae nodded and paused in the doorway. "I'll bring you some water and linens, and if my hunch is correct, you haven't eaten." She tilted her head. "I'll bring you food, too."

Damien's eyes swept from her, back to the Shade. "Thank you." He settled down onto the stool beside the cot, pushing down the hilt of a sword she hadn't noticed was in his belt until then. It'd been so long since she'd seen him hold any kind of weapon. He looked up at her and smiled. "I love you."

Chapter 36

THE SKY FADED TO DEEP purples, forcing Corin to abandon his reply to Reznik until he had more than moonlight to write by. Settling the stack of parchment and quill on the flat part of the roof beside him, he placed his hands on his lower back to stretch.

He sat cross-legged on the thick lip around the circular opening in the arena's ceiling, positioned so he could see Jarrod's unconscious body on the dirt floor far below. He looked dead, causing Corin's stomach to flip uncomfortably before resettling into its constant state of tension.

Reaching to his belt, Corin withdrew the knife and picked up the scrap of wood he'd brought up with him. Squinting through the dimming light, he put his knife to work on the half-carved cup. He started digging at the interior as he looked back into the arena.

He's gone.

The knife slipped and Corin cursed as it caught his thumb. He put the knife and cup beside him, scrambling towards the opening as he sucked on the wound.

Neco no longer lay in place either and, for a moment, everything in the arena hung eerily silent.

Movement flurried and Jarrod sprinted towards the door, making Corin's heart jump at the possibility Damien had left it open.

Jarrod slammed into the steel door with his shoulder, grunting as it didn't budge.

Neco barked, growling as he dug beneath the exit.

Panting, the proxiet kicked the door, and Corin could feel the vibrations all the way onto the roof.

Corin bit his tongue. Every time he had yelled at Jarrod in the past, it'd infuriated him more. His knuckles whitened as he gripped the edge of the roof to restrain himself.

Jarrod punched the door, leaving a slight dent that he stared at before hitting it again. "Let me out!" He hit it again, leaving behind blood splatter on the metal as his knuckles split. Jogging backwards, he ran at it again.

Neco dodged out of the way of the impact, snarling before resuming his digging. A pulse of power flashed light blue at

Neco's paws, and the dirt remained in place despite his attempts.

"He was mine to kill!" Jarrod's arm hung limp, and the proxiet walked calmer towards the wall. Without hesitation, he jerked his shoulder into the wall and the joint popped back into place. Growling, he stormed away from the door before charging at it again.

He's going to break bones.

Panic coursed through Corin as his eyes darted around the rooftop. He couldn't allow Jarrod to continue. Damien wouldn't be able to heal the man if he injured himself, all part of the time required to build barriers around the wolven ká.

Time that was reset again by that damn Shade showing up.

When his next body slam failed to open the door, Jarrod yelled and resumed punching it with both fists. "Open the damn door!"

"Jarrod!" Corin had limited options to gain his husband's attention. "Please, stop!"

Amber eyes locked on him, both Jarrod and Neco's. "I'm sick of being caged like an animal! I *will* kill him."

Well, you kind of are an animal right now...

Corin chose a lie to calm the proxiet. "He's already dead. Lost too much blood from Neco. You can stop."

Jarrod stalked back to the door and kicked it. "I won't stop. I'm tired... of being... a prisoner!" His voice bellowed through the arena, words enunciated between kicks.

Corin scanned the roof, spying the worst idea he could come up with. To deliver meals for both Neco and Jarrod, they'd rigged a hook on wooden scaffolding beside the opening. Corin gathered up the rope coiled beneath it, wrapping it around the hook in a slip hitch, pulling tension onto the length. He looked down, his heart pounding as Jarrod slammed into the door with his shoulder again.

Neco left Jarrod's side, prowling circles beneath the ceiling opening.

Corin kicked the rope around his leg, pinching tight against his worn breeches. But Neco gave him pause, and the captain waited, wincing with each slam of Jarrod's body against the door.

The wolf snarled up at him, teeth gnashing.

Jarrod yelled and stumbled, holding his shoulder as he leaned against the steel. Blood caked his hands and the door, smearing over his dirty vest.

"Come on, baby, Damien can't knock you out again..." Corin whispered to himself as he contemplated the length of the rope. "It'll just set us back even further."

Jarrod switched shoulders, turning to his left side to slam it against the door while his other hung limp, dislocated for the second time.

"Fuck."

He'll kill himself.

Sucking in a breath, Corin debated his options, but his

heart only gave him one. He double checked his knot, kicked the back end of the rope down into the arena, and pushed himself into the open air.

The rope around his thigh pinched tighter with the tension as he controlled his descent, hesitating when Neco prowled under the rope. It dangled ten feet from the ground, but the massive valley wolf leapt and snapped at its frayed end.

This is crazy.

Corin stopped just out of the wolf's reach and looked at Jarrod. Their eyes met and Jarrod's amber irises sent a chill through him. They suited him, and the captain had grown accustomed to looking into them before they'd locked him in the arena permanently. But Corin hadn't touched Jarrod in months and everything in him ached to do so again, regardless of the danger.

The proxiet ceased his assault on the door. "Shhh..."

Neco stopped jumping, backing up and looking at his companion.

"Let's not scare off our guest." Jarrod approached the wolf, still eyeing Corin. "Having second thoughts? It's safer on that roof."

"Maybe." Corin heaved a breath before he slipped further down the rope. Before he could question his own resolve, he yanked himself back up, loosening the tension just enough for the knot to fail. The rope slacked, and he dropped with it the short distance to the ground. He landed in a partial crouch, watching Neco as he stood up. "But I trust you, Jarrod. Whatever part of you is still in there."

Neco growled, and Jarrod stroked his head, dampening his fur with crimson. "Easy, boy. This one's mine." The proxiet charged, grappling onto Corin with his good arm and tackling him.

Corin demanded his muscles relax and take the hit without causing damage. He collided with the ground, knocking all the air out of him. He lifted his arms defensively towards his head, trying to make eye contact with Jarrod. "I'm not your enemy. I won't fight you."

Jarrod's left hand clamped around his throat, but recoiled a moment later. He lifted the gold chain, adorned with the whistle, signet ring, and Jarrod's wedding band. The proxiet had given it to him to keep safe months ago. He studied it, turning the ring over in his fingers.

Cautiously, Corin moved his open hand towards Jarrod's chin, running his thumb over the light scar left behind from his failed tournament in Degura.

Jarrod flinched and slapped the captain's hand away, returning to grab the necklace. He yanked it, snapping the clasp, and threw it across the floor. "Your tricks won't work."

"It's not a trick, baby." Corin relaxed his arms to either side of him, calming every instinct to defend himself with a slow breath. "I know you're still in there and I'm still in love with you, despite all of this. You're still my husband, even if you throw those rings away."

The proxiet's hand returned to his throat, but didn't squeeze. He breathed hard, fingers twitching. "If you don't fight me, you'll die."

Corin straightened, swallowing against Jarrod's grip. "You won't kill me. I trust you."

Jarrod squeezed. "Fight."

"No." It came out gruff against the pressure.

Neco snarled somewhere above Corin's head, but Jarrod's gaze shot up, silencing the wolf.

Frustration built in Jarrod's expression and he growled, squeezing harder. "Fight me, damn it."

Corin reached to Jarrod's right arm and shook his head as much as he could. He tried to swallow, but couldn't as he touched Jarrod's skin. It was sticky with blood, but he ignored it as he ran a fingertip down where the tattoo marked the proxiet's dark skin. He watched the amber in Jarrod's eyes, determined not to look away despite the white spots appearing in his vision.

Jarrod's grasp loosened, and he looked at where Corin touched the back of his bicep. He shirked away, letting go, and stood.

Corin sucked in a cool breath, coughing as he rolled onto his side. He looked at the embers of the firepit, little bits of flame still illuminating the arena. Jarrod's gold wedding band glittered with the chain where it'd landed near the stone rimming the pit. Corin crawled towards it, gathering it back up as he stood.

The proxiet had moved to the wall, using it once more to put his shoulder back in its socket with a grunt. "You shouldn't be in here." He didn't turn around, voice low.

Corin eyed the collapsed rope, squinting at the night sky through the opening. "Little late now."

Neco padded over to the far side of the arena, reclaiming a bone to chew on.

"I can't protect you." Jarrod pressed his hand against the wall.

Is Jarrod back in control?

Pocketing the necklace, Corin took a slow step forward. His face heated with the emotion of seeing Jarrod so close and in so much pain. He shook his head, even though Jarrod couldn't see it as he walked towards him. "You don't need to." He hesitated before he touched Jarrod's back, one hand over the worn leather of the proxiet's vest, above his back tattoo.

Jarrod spun around, taking Corin by the wrist and pushing his back into the wall. He leveled their faces, gripping him by the arms. "The wolf wants to kill you."

A chill rushed through Corin, wholly inappropriate for the setting or time. He froze, his body tensing. "But you don't. And you won't let it, will you?" His voice barely rose above a whisper as he watched his husband's dangerous gaze.

Jarrod studied the captain's face, but shook his head. Tilting his head, he kissed Corin, pressing him harder against the wall.

The rest of the world vanished as Corin returned the rough kiss, running his hand up Jarrod's cheek, the cold metal of his wedding band against his jaw. He felt so helpless against him, and the passion made his knees weak. Eyes fluttered shut as Jarrod pressed harder and Corin responded.

Pulling away, Jarrod met his eyes, the amber tones dominating the brown. "I want you."

Corin's heart sped, and Jarrod's eyes flickered to his chest in recognition. Placing his hand beneath Jarrod's chin, he lifted his gaze back up. "You will always have me. I've missed this." He ran a hand down Jarrod's front, playing along his exposed muscles and the hem of his vest. "I want you, too."

Chapter 37

STARING AT THE STAR-RIDDLED SKY through the hole in the ceiling, Jarrod stroked Corin's bare back. The captain laid with his head on Jarrod's chest, tracing patterns on his skin, their naked bodies entwined.

Conflicting desires still warred in the back of the proxiet's mind, even during the moment of peace. He felt satiated, but the wolf within still hungered for freedom.

This is the most I've felt in control in...

Jarrod frowned, his hand pausing at Corin's shoulder. "How long have I been in here?"

Corin remained quiet as he kissed Jarrod's chest, then looked up at him. "A few months." He kissed him again near the nape of his neck, then returned his head to his chest and heaved a sigh. "I've missed you. I needed this as much as you did, probably."

Wrapping both arms around Corin, Jarrod closed his eyes and breathed his scent. "It was a stupid, dangerous thing to do." He kept his voice low. "I can't suggest you do it again, but I'm glad you did this time. You have no idea how difficult it is to overpower the wolf, and I'd never forgive myself if I hurt you."

Corin smiled against his skin, tracing along his abdomen. "Is that an order, my king?" He heaved a sigh and shook his head. "I know you're right, all teasing aside. But Damien should have this figured out soon. Assuming knocking you out last night didn't set us back too far."

Jarrod rolled onto his side, facing Corin. "I will never order you." He touched his husband's face, focusing to keep his vision clear as his hand trailed down to the captain's neck where bruises already formed. He swallowed, closing his eyes. Corin's touch on his chin encouraged him to open them again, and he studied his somber face. "Will you forgive me for all this?"

"I already have." Corin brushed his fingers over his jaw and kissed him.

Taking a deep breath, Jarrod clung to the affection before pulling away. "You're about to be in trouble."

Corin groaned and buried his head in Jarrod's chest.

"Corin!" Rae leaned over the opening in the ceiling. "Are you *insane*?"

"Yes! Only us insane people here! Better go away before you go crazy, too!" Corin nibbled at Jarrod's collar before he sighed and whispered. "I just wanted the rest of the night."

Jarrod smirked and met Rae's gaze as she stiffened. He nodded. "It's me right now."

I'm so sorry for what happened, Rae.

She smiled. "It's good to see you. But Corin can't stay in there."

"I know." The proxiet kissed Corin's forehead. "Time to go."

"I'll come open the door." Rae disappeared from above them.

Corin whined, but slowly pulled away. Propping himself up beside Jarrod, he ran his hand over the proxiet's thickening hair and down his jaw. "I love you."

"And I, you." Jarrod took a steady breath, trying to calm the instincts that weren't his. "Go. It's getting more difficult. But promise me you won't come back in here until Damien has fixed this."

Corin frowned, but nodded. "I promise." He leaned over to kiss Jarrod again, more deeply, before standing to retrieve his clothing.

The wide latch in the door boomed in Jarrod's ears and he focused on the dying embers of the fire to keep his body still.

Run for it. His wolf twin stood beside the door with a smirk. *Now's your chance.*

He clenched his jaw as his ears rang, muscles quivering.

Not real.

The wolf hallucination stalked after Corin, glancing back at Jarrod. *Are you ready to watch him die?*

Jarrod bit his tongue to keep from answering the invader in his mind as rage sparked imaginary flames around him.

The captain paused in the doorway, his shirt still in his hands. He looked back at Jarrod, his eyes distant before the door slammed shut and he was gone.

Chapter 38

One month later...

DAMIEN SLIPPED OUT OF THE room they'd transferred Kin to, accidentally closing the door with more force than he meant to. He winced on the Shade's behalf, able to sense the copious amounts of pain he endured through separating him from his corrupted power.

He'd learned the man's name in their first conversation and, after three weeks of delicately parting the pieces of the Shade's ká from the weavings of Uriel, he felt the man might finally recover from the withdrawals. The Art his servitude gave him proved far more addictive than Damien could have predicted.

Moving Kin to a darker space became necessary because light made his nausea and headaches worse. He hardly slept, complaining of nightmares and visions of his master coming to murder him. He confided in Damien far more than the Rahn'ka expected, even explaining the events responsible for the spider web of scars on his back. Punishment his master had inflicted with shadow whips across his flesh when he'd lied after killing a fellow Shade.

Rae could probably understand his pain better than I ever could.

Neco's howl reverberated through the halls, and he met Rae's concerned eyes.

Damien "What's wrong?"

Her shoulders slumped. "Jarrod's spiraling again and Corin keeps saying he wants to go in there, but that's a terrible idea."

Damien rubbed the bridge of his nose. "I can't do anything for Jarrod, not yet. But I'll talk to Corin. I'll tie him down if I have to." A distant headache lurched, the voices breaking through the cracks in his barrier because of all the work he'd been performing.

Rae touched the side of his face. "Are you all right?"

"I will be. It's just difficult trying to open up enough to sense what Kin is thinking. It's allowing some of his symptoms to slip through to me. But at least I can shut them down. Poor bastard can't."

She stroked her thumb over his bottom lip, sighing. "You're spending a lot of time with him."

"He's just a man who made a poor decision. Well, a string of poor decisions, but I feel sorry for him. Once you get past the Shade thing, he's a decent person. He feels remorse like any of us."

"It's still odd you're friends with him, but I understand. Did you get anything else out of him about that woman, Amarie? If she really has the Berylian Key, we can't waste any time finding her."

It seems rather convenient that another part of the binding spell is connected to a fourth piece. Even if the Berylian Key, divided, makes no sense.

He smiled and turned her hand with his to kiss her palm. "Always thinking about business. I don't think he has any clue where she is, even though he loves her. I'm still working my way back to the Berylian Key topic. But I found out something interesting... She died."

Rae gaped. "She's dead?"

"No, that'd be the interesting part. She came back. There's a lot of emotion bottled up around it in him and trying to read his ká is like sticking my hand into a fire. But I suspect it has to do with her access to the Art. Have you had any luck checking the library for anything about the Berylian Key?"

Rae nodded. "I found a text that says some interesting things. I'll go get it while you talk some sense into your brother?"

Damien kissed her hand again. "I don't deserve you."

She smiled and lifted onto her toes to kiss him. "And don't you forget it."

Corin crouched near the edge of the roof's opening, peering down at Jarrod while he and Neco tumbled together in a cloud of dust. The wolf broke off from the man, howling before diving back in and Jarrod wrestled Neco to the ground in a flash of teeth and claws.

His brother barely glanced at Damien, his jaw hardening. "Rae sic you on me?"

Damien sighed. "You know, I have enough on my plate with this Shade *and* Jarrod. I don't need a stupid brother too."

"Just look at him." Corin motioned to the tussle as Neco let out a whimper and Jarrod immediately released him. The amber in Jarrod's eyes blazed, his teeth flashing in the bonfire light. "He's not even there anymore. It's all the wolf."

"Not for much longer. I'll—"

"It's been months, Damien." Corin's voice rose as he wheeled around on the Rahn'ka. "And you've done absolutely nothing. And now that you've got a new project to worry about, you've completely abandoned Jarrod."

Damien glowered. "Feel better now? Accusing me of that?"

"Fuck you."

"You know why I can't do anything for him right now. But soon. I'll check again this afternoon..."

"You said *soon* a month ago. And he was at least partly himself then."

Damien ran his hand up through his short hair, rubbing the back of his head. "We're all doing what we can. I might only have one shot at this and I don't want to try too early and ruin it."

Corin turned back to the hole in the roof, watching as Jarrod and Neco separated, each going to nurse the wounds they'd inflicted on each other. "I hope whatever the hells you're doing with that Shade is worth it."

"I hope so, too." Damien chewed his lip, crossing to Corin. He put his hand on his brother's shoulder. "All this has gotten so fucking complicated. I'm sorry."

Corin shrugged off his touch. "Don't apologize, it makes it harder to be mad at you."

Damien snorted. "I swear I'm doing all I can. And I *am* sorry. I can't imagine—"

"Just shut up about it and fix him. That's all I want right now." Corin crossed his arms, grabbing his own biceps. "I won't go down there again. Go deal with your stupid Shade thing so you can see if Jarrod is ready yet. I want my husband back."

"You sure it's not that you're tired of taking care of all his proxiet paperwork for him?" Damien gave a half smile.

"Paperwork is easy. It's listening to your voice that's hard." A lopsided smile twitched his lips.

Damien shook his head and slapped Corin hard on the shoulder. He didn't say a goodbye, making his way back down the ladder.

The auer is back in the—

"Please, Sindré, I've said it enough times. She's my wife, not some auer. And I asked her to do so."

The muddled shape of a stag manifested in the corner of the ruined hall, the spirit's eyes piercing into him. A wave of irritated voices pulsed against his barrier and he hardened it.

"And will you stop trying to punish me with more headaches? It's getting exhausting blocking them out."

I am displeased with the continued presence of you and your friends *in my sanctum.*

"I would love to get out of your hair and it would happen a lot faster if you *helped me.*"

The stag huffed, shaking their antlers dangerously close to his chest as they walked past him. The form disintegrated into a cloud of pale blue motes, vanishing into the foliage of the crumbled hallway.

"Great talk!" Damien yelled into the air as he rolled his eyes.

Rae rounded the corner, holding a tome to her chest. She tilted her head at him. "Sindré again?"

"Nothing makes them happy." He took the book from her, peering at the cracked leather spine. He wasn't able to translate the symbols before Rae frowned and took the book back.

"You mind?" She leaned against a crumbling wall, flipping the book open near the middle. "Look here. It has the symbol for the Berylian Key several times on these pages. This one..."

She pointed to a symbol. "Appears next to it several times. What does it mean?"

"May I?" Damien asked with a smile, holding out his hands.

Sighing, she handed him the book and leaned on his shoulder. "I'm wondering if I should have taken Andi's advice and ran away with you, found a quiet spot, and lived a peaceful life with lots of babies." She quirked an eyebrow. "Though I'm still not sure on the *lots* part."

Damien laughed and eyed her. "We still have time to discuss that. Though, with the way things are..." He shook his head and tried to focus on the text in front of him. "It seems so impossible with everything going on. But it also feels like there will never be a right time, you know?"

Rae nodded against his shoulder. "I miss the good ol' days when we were just stealing horses and killing Reapers." She looked up at him, the play in her voice not reaching her eyes.

"And running instead of trying to fix the mess others have made?" He heaved a sigh. "Though at least one of these messes is definitely *mine*."

"I just miss you."

He met her eyes and his resolve weakened at the split topaz and green hue of her eyes. "I'm sorry." He leaned his head against hers. "I feel like that's all I'm saying nowadays, but that I'm still not saying it enough."

Rae sighed. "I wish—"

"Wait." Damien's awareness tingled with a wave of pressure against his barrier. He almost dismissed it, thinking it was Sindré again, but sought the source of the disruption.

Kin.

Damien squeezed Rae's shoulder as he stepped away and closed the book, tucking it beneath his arm. "Kin's heart just stopped."

Hurrying down the halls and into the narrow passages that led deeper into the ruins, Damien slid to a stop in front of the Shade's door before he flung it open. Tossing the tome onto the table in the room, he crouched beside the cot.

Kin lay perfectly still, his face sunken and contorted as if in pain even without breath. It hadn't been long enough for his ká to separate from the body, a journey to the Inbetween unnecessary.

Damien shoved his palm against Kin's chest, channeling his power through his arm towards the man's heart. The Shade's ká thundered to life, squeezing the muscles around the life-giving organ, and Kin's eyes shot open.

With a sigh, Damien rocked back onto his heels. "Interesting. I didn't expect that to be a symptom."

The Shade flinched, then rolled onto his side to face the wall, tugging on his dirty tunic. His once-finely crafted clothing stuck to his back with sweat, frayed at the edges from travel. In the weeks within the sanctum, his beard had grown thick, making him look older.

"I'm not an experiment. The nightmares are nothing new." Kin's pillow muffled his words.

"I didn't mean the nightmares, those are definitely normal. I was referring to your heart. It stopped."

"Told you I was dying."

Damien chuckled and stood to retrieve the book. "Guess I have to stay and babysit now." He eyed the narrow space at the end of the cot, and batted at Kin's feet out of the way before he sat, pulling his legs to cross in front of him. He checked the spine of the book again, holding it into the dim candlelight.

At least he left one lit instead of burying himself completely in darkness.

The yellowed pages crackled as he opened the tome to the page Rae had shown him.

"A little light reading?" Kin peeked over his shoulder, squinting.

"We can call it that. You might make all this research easier on me if you'd tell me more about the Berylian Key and how it relates to your friend."

Why is that the only topic he won't talk to me about?

Kin huffed. "I'll pass."

"Then I'll talk." Damien turned another page, watching Kin from the corner of his eyes. "If you witnessed Amarie return from death, and she is also linked to the Key, then I must assume the events are related. So, either the Key brought her back, or..." He tilted his head and read over some text in front of him.

The tome talked about the power of the Berylian Key in a way he hadn't expected, and he quickly reread it, trying to understand why it referred to the Key as a 'she.'

She?

Damien's chest tightened with the realization. He turned his ká's attention back to Kin as he considered aloud. "Unless she doesn't have the Key at all—"

"Just stop. She *doesn't* have the Key."

It's something far more complicated.

The Shade's ká explained everything in its tumultuous state, despite trying to hide the truth.

"Of course she doesn't. I've been daft. She doesn't *have* it. She *is* it, isn't she?" Damien gaped at Kin. "That's why she couldn't die. That's why Uriel wants her. Gods, does Uriel know the Key is a person?" He slammed the book shut and stood up.

Kin groaned, rolling onto his stomach to bury his face in his pillow. "I never said that."

"But it's true. You're far worse at hiding your thoughts in your current state. Amarie *is* the Berylian Key. Kin, this is remarkably important. Where is she?" Damien dropped the book onto the table.

"Like I'd tell you if I knew."

Damien sighed. "Would you be more cooperative if I told

you there might be a way to sever her from the power?"

It has to be possible, because of the requirement to imprison Uriel. The Berylian Key, divided.

Kin stiffened, facing Damien without sitting up. "How?"

Damien smirked. "Just have to provide a different vessel for the power. It used to be in an object, so there's no reason it couldn't be again. Time it right... and it should be simple enough."

"You make it sound like you're just planning a trip to the tavern down the street."

"For me, that's all it is. If the steps were followed in the right order, it would work. Her soul would need to leave her body, and while it's gone, I entrap the power. Then, bring her back." After saying it, he considered how crazy it all sounded, even if it was possible.

"Wait..." Kin lowered his voice. "You're talking about killing her."

"Only temporarily."

Kin let out a long exhale. "And that's a trip to the tavern for you? I don't think I want to know what you'd consider complicated."

A fist thundered on the door, and Kin jumped.

"Damien!" Corin sounded panicked.

Looking at Kin, Damien sighed, hardening his barrier against the coming headache once more. "This. *This* is complicated."

Damien didn't wait for Kin to respond before he hurried to the door. He slipped through it without allowing Kin and Corin to see each other. "What?"

Corin huffed for breath. "Jarrod's gone."

Damien's stomach flipped. "He's what?" He didn't wait for Corin before he dashed down the hallway, his brother thundering behind him. "Where's Rae?"

"Where do you think? She's chasing him."

"Fuck." Damien loosened the barrier again, and the headache rolled into his senses along with all the voices of the sanctum. He inquired as quickly as he could, trying to find the familiar bonds of Jarrod and Neco.

The brothers raced up the stairs, breaking into the late afternoon sunlight near the front of the sanctum. The place looked almost serene, the mid-autumn breeze spreading the blanket of yellow and orange leaves strewn about the courtyard.

Neco sniffed the ground, whining as he paced beside Jarrod.

The proxiet stood near the monoliths at the entrance, a hand on the faint barrier blocking him from total freedom. The air shimmered with the power of the ká Damien had harnessed from the plants growing on the stone. It wove together like an impenetrable curtain of glimmering runes and motes of power.

Jarrod paused with their approach and looked to his right where Rae stood with her bow nocked and drawn. "You won't kill me."

She aimed at the proxiet. "I don't need to kill you."

Damien caught his brother as Corin shouted and tried to lunge forward. "Wait."

She loosed her arrow. It cut through the air and grazed Jarrod's arm.

Neco snarled, surging towards her as she nocked another arrow. The second shot whizzed past the wolf, clipping his haunches. He leapt at her and she rolled out of the way, leaving him to skid into the crumbled wall behind her.

The proxiet looked down at the superficial wound and chuckled. "Your aim used to be better." He stalked towards her, but she stood her ground while watching him.

Neco collapsed before he could take another step towards her.

"My aim is perfect." She looked sideways at Damien and nodded.

Jarrod frowned, staggering. He stopped, narrowing his eyes at her. "You used the... You poisoned me..." His eyes rolled back, and he dropped in a heap.

Corin's grip tightened on Damien's arm before the Rahn'ka took a step forward, looking at Rae. "How'd he get out?" His eyes passed over Neco and then to Jarrod, while Corin hurried towards him.

The Mira'wyld glowered. "The door was open, and I didn't open it. So what do you think?"

Corin knelt, glaring at his brother before Damien could accuse him. "Wasn't me."

Damien growled under his breath, rubbing at the pulsing pain at the back of his head. "Sindré?"

The guardian's ká resisted Damien's summons and left him with a feeling of annoyance and a refusal to apologize.

Rae crossed the courtyard towards Damien. "I know you said you needed another week, but it seems we're out of time. You need to try now. The toxin will only last a few hours."

Damien pushed up his sleeves. "Seeing as I have no choice, I guess it's time to try." A nervous energy he'd been denying twisted in his gut. "Help me carry them to the altar."

Corin and Damien worked together to move Jarrod, positioning him at the base of the short pillar at the center of a swirl of stones on the ground. Gathering his power, he stomped his foot once onto the ground and cleared it of debris. The leaves exploded in a foray of colors, brushing past Rae and Corin as they brought Neco to lie on the opposite side from Jarrod.

"Do you need anything from me?" Rae straightened, gaze lingering on her unconscious friend.

Damien stretched as he looked at the altar and shook his head. "Just time and quiet. If you two could stay outside the stone circle." He lifted the bowl that rested upon the altar towards the waiting vines dangling from the tree above. They stretched to entwine the bowl so Damien could pull himself onto the stone. He tucked his ankles beneath him, centering himself to find the balance he'd struggled with when first granted the power.

Closing his eyes, a steady breath worked in tandem with his ká to give him the clarity he needed.

"That can't be comfortable," Rae whispered to Corin, sitting with him near the far wall.

Damien hadn't even needed to open his eyes to see where they sat, the entire sanctum visible without it. Each ká's presence painted a perfect image of what it belonged to in his mind.

"Shhhh." Damien brought a finger to his lips, prohibiting the rest of his body from moving. When he lowered his hand again, resting it on his knee, he tuned his awareness to focus only on the power ebbing from the altar and within the two laying at its base.

The lines connecting Jarrod and Neco spanned every inch of space between them, entwining every part. It'd gone well beyond the simple tether Damien had crafted between their minds and grown at a rate far worse than he could have imagined. It'd been months since he'd sought to work on the bond, and like an untended garden, the growth had festered.

Gods, please let this be possible.

The peace the drug brought to Jarrod's ká allowed Damien the opportunity to slip into his spirit as if he were a dream. The usual resistance the Rahn'ka had grown accustomed to wasn't there, like guards fast asleep at a city gate.

Relief washed through him and he took from the power of the sanctum to delve deeper into Jarrod's soul. He didn't know how many times he'd read the tome about connecting ká and the weaves he passed seemed perfectly predictable now, when they'd felt like handling lightning only months before.

He wracked his memory for all the failed attempts Lucca had explained. They let him focus on finding his way to the right streams of Jarrod's ká. Too many Rahn'ka before him had become distracted, trying to fix too much.

Focus on what's important. The emotions. The control. Then build an impenetrable wall.

Damien took a step, watching his bare foot touch the marble tiles. Heat blasted against his chest, whipping his shirt against his skin. The stone burned the soles of his feet, but he forced his ká down to ignore the pain. Around him, the ornate arches and pillars burned. He recognized the architecture of the massive ballroom he'd seen in passing during his initial tour of the Martox castle. The banners wavered in the updrafts from the raging fires, the chandeliers balls of white-hot flames. Embers dripped to the floor like snowflakes.

Damien lifted his hand in front of him, his ká vibrating beneath the vision of his physical body.

"Welcome, my friend." Jarrod's smooth voice came behind him, and Damien spun around. The proxiet sat on a throne on a raised platform. Six tiered stairs surrounded it, layered with a maroon rug.

The Rahn'ka pursed his lips, holding the power ready as he studied the figure. Not a single burn marred Jarrod's formal attire, his black boots reflecting the inferno. Amber eyes glittered, a smile on the proxiet's face.

"I'm not your friend. And you're not Jarrod."

"Ah, perhaps you don't see me as your ally, but I owe you my existence. So kind of you to come in person to allow me to thank you." The wolf version of Jarrod rose from his seat. "Though, I'm afraid your journey has been in vain. Soon, the weak man you seek will be gone forever, and I'll be the one left to rule. We both know you don't have the guts to kill your friend as you promised."

Damien grimaced. "It won't come to that." With a thought, the Rahn'ka pushed power down his arm, and his tattoos erupted with light, penetrating through the white fabric of his shirt. His fist closed around the shaft of his spear, the runes around its blade humming. "This ends here. Now."

"You wish to fight me?" The wolf laughed, clapping his hands in slow applause. "How valiant... and foolish. I own this space. You cannot win."

"Maybe not." Damien spun his spear, approaching the center of the ballroom. "But I will fight you."

I have to imprison the wolf.

The wolf held his empty hands out at his sides. "I'll let you have the first hit."

Seeking the energies of Jarrod's ká that composed the room, Damien exerted his own force upon it. With a flex of his fingers, the stone at the wolf's feet ruptured, exploding upward in jagged spikes of marble and wood.

The wolf disappeared into flecks of ash, reappearing at Damien's side. "You missed, but I'll let you try again."

Damien whirled, the base of his spear aimed for the wolf's gut. The wolf's forearm blocked the attack, and the Rahn'ka redirected his swing to bring the spearhead down.

The metal tore through a cloud of ash, and Damien spun around as the wolf's fist slammed into his jaw from the other side. Before he could recover, a vice grip closed around his neck, forcing him upright.

Choking, Damien lashed his weapon at the wolf's ribcage, feeling the impact as amber eyes bored into him.

Teeth flashing in a growl, and the wolf flung Damien backward.

Damien's ká and body ricocheted off one pillar, soaring into a mass of flames. He gritted his jaw at the searing pain, trying to remember none of it was real. Using his tattoo to channel the power, he pounded his fist onto the marble floor. Cracks of pale blue light spider webbed from the impact, misting up to squelch the surrounding flames.

As he recovered to his feet, the wolf brushed his hand over the bleeding wound in his side, and the injury vanished. The perfectly clean formal wear showed no sign of the successful blow. His eyes flashed as he stalked forward, the previous humor gone from his face. "I'm losing my patience. Come over here and let's end this."

Put out the fire. Jarrod's voice reverberated into Damien's head as barely a whisper.

Jarrod?

Damien hid his surprise from his face. He eyed the chandelier hanging above and slid his foot behind him. His toes brushed over the cracks of the marble, cooled by the sensation of his own ká still trickling from the breaks. Coiling the power up through his muscles, he launched his spear towards the ceiling.

Metal twanged as the chain supporting the chandelier broke, the orb of raging fire crashing to the ground like a meteor above the wolf's head.

The wolf snarled and vanished again, reappearing several feet away. At his sides, two valley wolves manifested, teeth bared. "You cannot win!"

Damien sprinted ahead, his eyes locked on the faint flicker of blue runes buried at the center of the chandelier. The spear exploded with vibrant lights, a wave of ká passing over the flames like a breeze. When it sucked back into the spear with a hum, it extinguished the fire.

The wolf yelled, gasping as he glared at Damien. "Kill him."

The beasts lunged, racing across the tiles without touching them as they barreled towards Damien.

The gnarled iron of the chandelier misted with Damien's ká as he leapt over it. He grasped the shaft of his spear, tearing it free as he ran for the other side of the ballroom. With a sweep of his power, a force field tore across the marble. Each reverberating crack consumed the flames, leaving behind pale blue motes.

Another figure materialized between Damien and the advancing beasts. Jarrod met the Rahn'ka's gaze. "Keep putting the fire out. I'll distract the wolf."

Shoulders sagging in relief, Damien nodded. "You have to imprison him, this is your ká. You have the most control here." He eyed the advancing wolves, but Jarrod caught the first one by the ruff and heaved it across the room. It disintegrated into embers before meeting the floor.

The second wolf lunged for his throat, but Jarrod caught it and squeezed, making it vanish as the first.

Turning away as Jarrod approached his wolf twin, Damien focused on the wall ahead, coated in flames. He centered his breath, forcing the ká still trapped in the ground to slide outward. Pushing his heel harder into the marble, the fractures grew, snapping up the walls and pillars. He pulled down the chandeliers with a twist of his wrist, each snuffing out under a wave of cyan power.

The throne still blazed as Jarrod cornered his wolf-self on the platform. "You're losing."

The wolf stumbled backward into the royal seat, wide eyes on the proxiet. "You can't kill me."

"I don't need to." Jarrod drew his hand up and chains erupted from the armrests of the throne, circling around the wolf's wrists. "But you won't control me anymore."

Chapter 39

JARROD GASPED, GRIPPING HIS TEMPLES with a growl.

Something cool and damp pressed to his forehead, and he flinched, snatching the wrist.

Opening his eyes, they adjusted quickly to the darkness and fell on Corin's face.

What the hells?

He shoved Corin's wrist away and propped himself up, retreating until his back hit the stone wall behind him. "What are you doing?" He looked up, realizing he wasn't in the ballroom. "Where am I?"

Corin watched him for a moment before he turned towards a small table, lifting a wooden cup and offering it to him. "Our room. Drink this. Damien said you'd probably have a headache." He held out the drink until Jarrod took it.

The proxiet cringed and looked at the cup's contents. "This smells awful. Where is Damien? Did he get out of the ballroom?" Worry knotted his insides, and he drank the foul-smelling water.

"Ballroom?" Corin scooted closer and pressed the cloth to Jarrod's forehead. "Damien's probably asleep. He looked awful when he came out of that trance."

Jarrod looked down at himself. "Why am I not in the arena?"

Corin touched Jarrod's jaw. "You don't need to be in there anymore. How are you feeling?"

"You're not safe."

"Aren't I? *How* are you feeling?"

Pausing, the proxiet examined his own headspace. No threat surfaced from the wolf and he looked at Corin's neck, listening to the captain's heartbeat. While he could hear it clearly, it fueled no bloodlust and his vision remained clear of the hallucinations. "I don't know." He looked around the room, grateful to find it empty. He swallowed, rubbing the ache in his temples. "Where's Neco?"

"Hunting. Damien said you can still communicate with him."

Jarrod stiffened, hesitant to try.

"There's no need to rush. You should take your time."

"We beat him." Jarrod touched Corin's wrist, lowering it. "The bond is fixed. Is that what you're saying?"

His husband smiled and reached into his pocket. Withdrawing the gold wedding band, he lifted Jarrod's right hand and slid it onto his middle finger. "Damien said it should be. Only you will know if it's true. Any violent thoughts I should worry about?"

Jarrod shook his head. "No violent thoughts." He looked down at the ring on his finger, emotion tightening his throat. "Gods, how long has it even been now? I hardly remember anything."

Corin entwined his hand with Jarrod's, their bands clicking together. "We've been here almost three seasons. It's mid-autumn. Don't worry, I've been handling all the paperwork."

Jarrod gaped. "I will make this up to you."

Corin smiled, and it made Jarrod's body warm. "There's nothing to make up, my love. I knew what I was getting into when I asked you to marry me. And I'm good at paperwork, remember?"

"You knew I'd turn into a rabid beast?" Jarrod tilted his head. "And try to kill you on more than one occasion? Gods, the day you dropped into the arena I almost strangled you. And Rae... Nymaera. Neco tried to kill her..."

"But we're all fine. You're fine."

Jarrod tugged Corin into a hug, turning his face to breathe his scent near his hair. "Gods, I missed you."

Corin's arms wrapped around him, returning the firm embrace. He turned to kiss the side of Jarrod's head, then just held him. "It's over now."

Chapter 40

"DAMIEN SAID HE WANTS ANOTHER bowl." Rae set the serving tray down on a table. "And then he went back to sleep."

No idea how he's eating so much.

Corin looked up from where he crouched beside the fire pit, stirring the savory smelling contents of a cast iron pan set over the stones at the edge. He frowned at the empty bowl Rae extended to him. "Seriously? I'll have to go back to town for more supplies, unless you feel like gathering more from the garden?"

Rae shrugged. "There are still lots of carrots, but the potatoes are almost gone. Everything else is going to seed for the coming winter."

"It'd be so much easier if he'd eat meat." Corin wiggled the pan, tossing the contents. "I guess I'll get more beans soaking, too... Gods know he'll eat everything on his own and not leave any for the rest of us."

"We can roast something... Send Neco to hunt. He's been extra willing lately. How's Jarrod?"

She hadn't seen the proxiet since his bond had been repaired, tending to Damien's exceptional appetite and letting Corin monopolize her friend's time.

Corin's shoulders relaxed, and he smiled. "Good. He's good. Sleeping a lot, too, but he's... him." The captain shoveled the freshly cooked peppers and potato into Damien's bowl, plopping the remaining end of a loaf of bread on top. "That's the last of the bread. How about Damien? Is he doing anything other than sleep and eat yet?"

"Nope." Rae put the steaming bowl onto the serving tray, but sat at the table instead of hurrying it back to him.

He's asleep, anyway.

She touched the small round scars on her arm from where Neco had attacked her and she sighed. "I can't believe it's over, you know? It feels too good to be true. Like he'll deteriorate again and slip back into a chaotic mind..."

"Is that why you haven't come to see him?"

Rae swallowed. "I was just giving you two time together..."

Corin stood from the fire and joined her at the table they'd so rarely taken meals together at. "You don't need to do that. He'd like to see you. Especially before we get back to Helgath and everything pulls him away from us again. He misses you, too."

Taking a deep breath, Rae rolled her lips together. "How much has Damien told you about Kin? The Shade he's tending to? I don't think we can accompany you back to Helgath as quickly as Jarrod will need to go."

Corin straightened, furrowing his brow. He looked like Damien whenever he did it, and it almost made Rae smile. "What's the Shade have to do with any of it? I thought Damien said he started getting better."

Rae nodded and filled him in on what they'd learned from the tomes in the sanctum. "Before he passed out again, Damien said he figured out that Amarie doesn't have the Berylian Key, and that she *is* the key."

Corin whistled. "World would be a lot simpler without all this Art stuff. But you just said the book, recipe, thing, called for the Berylian Key *divided*. How is that possible if it's a person?"

Rae leaned forward. "Damien thinks he can sever her from the power, and from what Kin says, it sounds like she'd be grateful to be rid of it. We need to come up with a better plan once Damien's rested, but I'm afraid this will keep his attention for some time. Once Kin is better, he might have to come with us to Lazuli to help us find Amarie."

"Because this Uriel thing is bigger than Helgath's pending civil war?" Corin scowled. "Can't it wait?"

"I think it can, but only once Kin's out of the danger of his withdrawals. Then, technically, we have all the time in the world."

"Assuming nothing happens with Amarie. Or this Uriel thing." Corin sighed, rubbing his face. "When did our lives get so complicated?"

"I think it happened around the time I met Damien, but I can't be sure." Rae smiled.

Corin laughed. "My damn brother, always mucking everything up."

A Rebel's Crucible concludes with...

RISE OF THE RENEGADES

www.Pantracia.com

WICKED KINGS MUST FALL.

As Jarrod and Corin tackle the daunting task of swaying the politics in favor of House Martox, they endure a gruesome assassination attempt. The death of one of their own fuels Jarrod's rage, testing the wolven bond. But the Rahn'ka is nowhere near if something goes wrong.

Drawn into researching Uriel and the Shade who landed at his feet, Damien struggles to find balance. Feeling like he's failing fate, he makes a drastic decision when the Shade's condition unexpectedly worsens.

With war looming, every decision could make the difference between defeating House Iedrus or letting the tyrannical king destroy Helgath through uncontested rule. While they drift apart, a stark truth prevails.

Only together will they rise.

Rise of the Renegades is Part 4 of *A Rebel's Crucible* and Book 7 in the *Pantracia Chronicles*.

Made in the USA
Monee, IL
12 March 2024